Molly Lefebure started her writing career as a newspaper reporter in East London during the Blitz. She then worked for many years as the private secretary to renowned forensic pathologist Dr Keith Simpson, head of the Department of Forensic Medicine at Guy's Hospital. She is the author of several children's books and a memoir of her time working with Dr Simpson, *Murder on the Home Front*, which has been adapted for television. She was a Coleridge scholar and wrote two acclaimed books on the poet, and she was also elected a Fellow of the Royal Society of Literature in 2010. Her two novels for adults, *Blitz!* and *Thunder in the Sky*, are sweeping historical sagas and they are closely based on her own experiences during the Second World War. Molly sadly passed away in 2013 but her memory lives on through her writing.

Also by Molly Lefebure

FICTION
Blitz!

NON-FICTION
Murder on the Home Front

THUNDER IN
THE SKY

Molly Lefebure

SPHERE

First published in Great Britain in 1991 by Victor Gollancz Ltd
This paperback edition published in 2014 by Sphere

A CIP catalogue record for this book
is available from the British Library.

ISBN 978-0-7515-5272-0

Typeset in Garamond by M Rules
Printed and bound in Great Britain by
Clays Lt, St Ives plc

Papers used by Sphere are from well-managed forests
and other responsible sources.

MIX
Paper from
responsible sources
FSC® C104740

Sphere
An imprint of
Little, Brown Book Group
100 Victoria Embankment
London EC4Y 0DY

An Hachette UK Company
www.hachette.co.uk

www.littlebrown.co.uk

Dedicated to the great young men of the
Mighty Eighth

and to JG with many thanks
for all his help – never forgetting the
breakfast snacks

PRINCIPAL CHARACTERS

LORNA WASHBOURNE
BUNTY MCEWEN
VIOLETTA STACKS
MEGAN THOMAS *four friends from pre-war days*

GENERAL WASHBOURNE *Lorna's father*
MRS CUTHMAN *housekeeper to the Washbournes*
RUTH CUTHMAN *her granddaughter*
JEFFREY BOSCO *local vet*
MRS FRISKE *his assistant*
DAPHNE AND DICKY STACKS *Violetta's parents*
SIR HUMPHREY AND LADY BASTABLE *Bunty's parents*
SENIOR COMMANDER CHIPPERFIELD, ATS *Violetta's CO*

THE REVEREND SEPTIMUS BARKER *vicar of Fursey-Winwold*
MISS OCTAVIA BARKER *his sister*
MISS GLAISTER *local Red Cross*
TITUS SWANN *sexton*
MISS CUSK *village post-mistress*
DETECTIVE SERGEANT PLOMMER *CID*

MRS WELLS *landlady of Kenilworth Lodge*
THEODOR KAUFMANN
MR AND MRS PARSONS

DR AND MRS SCHWARTZ *all Kenilworth Lodge tenants*

GUS HARRIS *London Transport bus driver*
MR BARNES *training instructor for London Transport*
EDIE MOXTON *a bus conductress*

CAPTAIN 'BUZZ' CABRINI *American Red Cross*
ANGIE ROCKWELL *American Red Cross*
AMY MAY LOCKETT *American Red Cross*
COLONEL HERBIE BLENMIRE *CO Fursey Down USAAF Bomber Station*
ARMAMENT-SERGEANT MATLAK *USAAF Fursey Down*
VIC WENDELL *ball-turret gunner*
LANCE VOGEL *waist-gunner*
CAPTAIN WALDO STEIN *US Army*

Part One

THE YANKS
ARE COMING

I

The big open sky was cloudless and blue, empty of everything except sunshine and larksong. The weather was remarkably warm for May. Lorna, taking her dogs for an afternoon walk up the Beacon, was thankful that she was wearing a sleeveless dress. She pitied her sealyhams; they couldn't change into something cooler when summer arrived.

She reached the Beacon summit and propped herself against a five-bar gate to contemplate the scene spread before her. Winwold Beacon, a spur of high ground (or what passed as high ground in East Anglia) was celebrated for its uninterrupted views over the surrounding countryside. Historically, too, it was notable; here, in early times over a thousand years ago, fires had been lit to warn the local populace that Viking raiders were pillaging the land, ravaging and burning the little homesteads of the Anglo-Saxon farmers.

Time heals all things. Over the centuries Fursey Down had turned into a place far removed from warfare and violence, becoming a peaceful turfy common studded with the furze bushes from which it drew its name. Here and there cattle grazed. Beyond the common were fields of arable land dotted with those clumps of elms which were such an endearing feature of this part of the countryside, where Essex sleepily became Suffolk. Sheltered by one large clump was an old sprawling farmhouse, red-roofed and drowsy – Weldon Court, home of Lorna's family since her grandfather's day. Here Lorna Washbourne had been born twenty years ago.

The landscape of Lorna's birthplace was so deeply imprinted upon her mind's eye that she could have drawn every detail of it with her eyes shut. Timeless and unchanging, she knew that what she looked at now was almost exactly what her grandfather had seen when he had retired from the Indian Army and had returned to England to find a place which could be 'home' for himself and his wife during the final quarter of their lives. The Washbournes had originated in East Anglia, but having been a soldiering race since time immemorial had never been much good at putting down lasting roots. Nevertheless, Grandfather Washbourne had felt himself drawn to this corner of England from which his ancestors had come. His progeny had felt the same way about it and Weldon Court had been home to them ever since, whenever they happened to be in England.

Perhaps, thought Lorna, it was because they only lived at Weldon Court in, as it were, blissful snatches that they had all nursed such a strong love for the place. Familiarity is said to breed contempt; to have lived year in, year out, for ever and ever at Weldon might possibly have made it less precious. But this said, deep in her own heart she couldn't believe this was true. She herself had spent quite long periods of time away from Weldon and whenever she had left it she had felt desolately torn. She was convinced that if she were given the chance to spend her whole life there, never leaving it, the place would in no way lose its charm for her; she would simply love it more with each year that passed.

Indeed as a young schoolgirl, at boarding school in England because her parents were in India, she had made up her mind that whatever other members of the family did she would never leave Weldon (where she spent all her school holidays) once she had reached the age when she could decide what to do with her own life.

'Decide what to do with her own life!' Propped against the gate, absorbedly thinking about Weldon, she had sunk into a sort of trance, but this phrase, 'Decide what to do with her own life', brought her back with a jerk to hideous reality. Surely the past three war-torn years had taught her, taught all her generation, that there could never be any such thing as anyone being able to decide what to do with their own life? This was the one thing above all that nobody could decide: Fate made that decision.

Lorna, on the outbreak of war, had been eager to get into uniform like her two brothers, both Regular soldiers. She had been prevented from joining up by the objections of her father who, a retired general of the old school, believed that women should leave uniforms (apart from those of the nursing services) to be worn by men. After much persuasion, he had eventually agreed that Lorna might join the FANY, the First Aid Nursing Yeomanry Corps, and she had been on the point of signing up when her father, who had been flogging himself unsparingly on the regional committee for Civil Defence, had suffered a stroke which had left him semi-paralysed. Lorna had postponed joining the FANY and had stayed at home, helping her mother to nurse him. His recovery had been severely set back by the death of his eldest son, Tom, at Dunkirk. This had taken some getting over. Almost exactly a year later the younger boy, Tony, had died of wounds at Tobruk. Lorna's mother had had a fatal heart attack after hearing this news.

Surely enough for one family to suffer! But Fate had held yet another searing blow in store for Lorna.

After eighteen months of standing alone against Hitler, Britain found herself with strong new allies: first Russia; then the United States in the wake of Pearl Harbor. Fursey Down, requisitioned by the Government on behalf of the new ally, like many another hitherto remote backwater of south-east England, was earmarked as an airfield for the United States Eighth Army Air Force Bomber Command. Weldon Court, situated right in the centre of the projected airfield, must go.

So 'Look thy last on all things lovely,' Lorna now told herself, as she stood on the Beacon staring at the beloved scene spread out before her. She would never see it again. Any day now men and machines would set to work, and with clanging din and clouds of dust they would level her beloved Weldon Court to the ground; tear up the orchard, the elms; tear up the golden furze; destroy the entire place to build runways and hangars for American bombers.

Lorna realized, of course, that she should be thankful that her country no longer stood alone. But, that said, she knew, in the depths of her being, that she would never forgive the Yanks for taking Weldon Court from her. Even if they turned out to be the most splendid allies known to all history, she'd never forgive them.

She had already sworn a private vow that, once the work of destruction had begun, she would avoid Fursey Down like the plague for the rest of her days. She would preserve inviolate her mind's-eye vision of Fursey Down and Weldon Court as they had been, would always be, for her. Airfield and Americans for her simply would not exist. Here was one decision which, come hell or high water, she had every intention of keeping!

So she had looked her last on Fursey Down and Weldon Court, this Friday, 12 June 1942, the blackest day of her life.

Blinded by tears Lorna turned from the gate and plodded away. The two little dogs, seeming to understand, trotted dismally along behind her, close to her heels.

II

The miserable trio headed back for The Warren, Lorna's new so-called home; a large dark house of late Victorian vintage, on the edge of Fursey-Winwold village; the only house in the neighbourhood which she and her father had been able to find at such short notice. They both hated it. Indeed Lorna had thought that they should move right away from Fursey-Winwold. Her father, however, had disagreed. 'When war's on and you're in a tight spot, stick with your friends and neighbours. Keep together. Don't get strung out.' And that was true, reflected Lorna. If they moved away they'd have to start all over again making local friends.

Nevertheless, this said, Lorna would still have given anything to escape from the village, to get as far away as possible from Fursey Down and memories of Weldon Court. And, yes (be honest, Lorna, she told herself), she had to confess that she would also have given a great deal to have escaped from her father; not because she didn't love him, but because she now felt in bondage to him since devotion to him was no longer a matter of free will but an inescapable duty. She was tied to him, bound hand and foot to him.

At one point, earlier that year, when the conscription of women at long last had been introduced, she had believed that an escape route was opening ahead of her. She'd allow herself to be directed into anything, just to get away! She'd even go in a dreaded munitions factory!

But the Government had not demanded that she must desert her father. Not for her the excuse 'I'm obliged by conscription to leave him'. There was something called Household Release, which exempted women with children or invalids or aged parents to care for. Her father was an invalid *and* aged. Well, growing old anyway; older than his actual years. It was true that they had Mrs Cuthman, their cook-housekeeper, but she was now sixty-two and could hardly be asked to make the General her full responsibility in addition to her other duties in the household; furthermore, though she had been with the Washbournes for almost three decades, that was still different from being family. Lorna had to face it; she was all that her father had left, and he dreaded losing her.

She well remembered the morning when she had told him that she had received her call-up papers.

'Have you now? I thought they were due. But don't worry; nobody's going to press-gang the one and only member of my family left to me. Now I've lost your mother I must keep my daughter. That's essential!'

She had endeavoured to hide her desperation as she had replied: 'Isn't it rather necessary that I should go into some kind of service? The country is acutely short of manpower and needs women to fill the gaps. And this *is* a call-up! I mean, if it had been either Tom or Tony left as the one and only member of your family, they'd still have had to answer their country's call.'

'Totally different situation. Not the same at all. You're my daughter, not a son,' he had retorted emphatically. Then he had reached out and patted her hand, supposing that he was comforting her. 'Don't worry. You won't find yourself carted off.'

Nor had she been. No escape for her from Fursey-Winwold! She was imprisoned there.

This sense of imprisonment, however, had one thing to be said in its favour; it increased her sense of empathy with her soldier boyfriend, Ivo Bastable, in prison-of-war camp in Germany. She told herself that, if Ivo was spending his war shut up in a prison camp, she was spending her war shut up in Fursey-Winwold with Father. One fate was as inexorable as the other. They shared the experience of being victims in captivity.

On arrival indoors, after her walk up to the Beacon, Lorna hurried upstairs to finish preparing the guest room for her friend Bunty Bastable, Ivo's sister, who was coming for a brief stay. This friendship with Bunty dated back to their days together at St Hildegard's Secretarial College, where they had been students just before the war.

St Hildegard's! Lorna, as she made up Bunty's bed, found herself back there, among the typewriters and the notebooks full of

8

Pitman's shorthand. Dots. Dashes. Abbreviations. Shun hooks. 'Ready for dictation, girls? We are trying for forty-five words a minute this morning, remember! Starting now: "Gentlemen, I am happy to present our annual report which, thanks to the healthy upturn in the demand for steel . . ."' Those ghastly annual reports, taken from the *Financial Times*.

Miss Trott for shorthand, Mrs Plessey for typing, Miss Knott for book-keeping. Madame Bonnard-Krutz for French. Miss Binkle as head of all.

St Hildegard's Secretarial College, conveniently close to Regent's Park on the one hand (they ate their lunches there in fine weather) and Baker Street Tube station on the other, was an exclusive and expensive establishment which prided itself both on the class of girl it attracted and on the high standards it achieved in turning out excellently trained and qualified secretaries of impeccable efficiency, grooming and poise. 'Show me a top-drawer secretary unobtrusively but decisively at the helm, and the chances are that, nine times out of ten, you are showing me a St Hildegard's gal,' was the favourite maxim of Miss Binkle, the college principal, when interviewing the parent, or parents, of an intending entrant. 'Even if your daughter ultimately pursues a career other than secretarial, or simply settles down into marriage, her time at St Hildegard's will *never* be wasted. Everything that she learns here will serve her in good stead *whatever* path she may follow in future life.'

Shorthand, typing, book-keeping, filing and indexing, duplicating, office organization and etiquette, commercial English, foreign languages (choice of French, German, Spanish); how to use the telephone with poised efficiency, how to become a polished receptionist – all these were on the curriculum. Students were guaranteed to emerge with a typing speed of forty to sixty words a minute and a shorthand speed of eighty words a minute minimum – Miss Binkle was dissatisfied with students who could not reach at least one hundred and twenty words a minute shorthand. These attainments necessitated gruelling hard work.

To achieve a fluently effortless speed with the typewriter the girls typed to music. Mozart's 'Turkish March' was a great favourite with Mrs Plessey in pursuit of fluency with the typewriter. Lorna, who played this on the piano, thanks to Mrs Plessey had reached the stage where she shuddered at the mere sound of the opening bars of what formerly had been one of her favourite pieces.

Lorna's greatest friend at St Hildegard's had been her companion since childhood, Violetta, daughter of novelists Daphne and Dicky Stacks who lived at Winwold Manor, which made them neighbours of the Washbournes and had resulted in Lorna and Violetta being, from an early age, friends so close that they had been akin to sisters. They had gone to the same boarding school, where they had been inseparable, and from school to St Hildegard's, where their time-honoured twosome had developed into a trio when they had met Bunty Bastable.

Bunty (real name Stella, but she was never called anything but Bunty) aspired to fame behind the footlights. She had reached a compromise with her parents that she should go to the Royal Academy of Dramatic Art (RADA as she always called it) providing that she first went to St Hildegard's and acquired secretarial skills which would, as her father put it, 'keep her afloat should she fail to make the grade as Sarah Bernhardt'.

'Of course,' said Bunty buoyantly, 'Mother and Daddy *would* see me in terms of Bernhardt; they're both such impossible highbrows!' It didn't surprise either Lorna or Violetta to hear this; Bunty's father was the judge Sir Humphrey Bastable, who specialized in classical *bons mots* in court, while her mother concerned herself with the Arts, very much with a capital A. Bunty, on the other hand, saw herself as a second Gertie Lawrence and, when she remembered to do so, she cultivated a Gertie Lawrence manner and voice, but really 'She isn't one bit like Gertie Lawrence; she's herself and she should cultivate *that*,' said Lorna. Bunty, though not a beauty, was blessed with really lovely eyes, hazel with amber flecks in them, set very wide apart, and she also had, as all the St Hildegard girls had enviously agreed, 'simply fabulous legs'. She wore her heavy tawny hair in a long page-boy bob and used a dashing coral-pink Guerlain lipstick which all the others had considered the height of sophistication. She painted her nails to match. Miss Binkle had warned her about her appearance: 'You seem on the flighty side.'

Memories of Bunty Bastable as a 'St Hildegard's gal'! Lorna, putting embroidered cases over Bunty's pillows, smiled at these recollections, and then went on to smile at thoughts of Bunty at RADA, where she had spent the first two years of the war: Bunty 'dropping her voice' half an octave to give it the right husky sound and developing a throaty gurgle to match; adopting theatrical mannerisms and gestures which varied from week to week, according to which star she was worshipping at the moment; experimenting with make-up, plucking out her own eyebrows and drawing in Marlene Dietrich ones, and extending her cheek rouge up to her hairline ('You look like Mephistopheles,' Lorna had commented unkindly).

Finally Bunty had landed her first professional engagement, in a chorus-line of HP sauce bottles featured in an ENSA show. For several weeks she had pranced around, entertaining the troops as an HP sauce bottle, and then out of the blue, in the late autumn of 1941, had announced to her friends that she had become Mrs David McEwen; a wartime marriage, made without any fuss or preliminary notice. Her husband was twenty-three, an RAF Bomber Command pilot. He was dark haired, nice, and rather reserved in manner; Lorna and Violetta agreed that he was a much quieter type than they would have expected Bunty to have married. However, Bunty obviously adored him.

She had confided to Lorna that he was anxious that they should have a child – 'So that he can leave something of himself behind if he gets killed,' added Bunty, with a smile that was not really a smile at all.

'And are you pregnant?'

'No, I'm not. Efforts must be redoubled on his next leave!'

This conversation, thought Lorna now, as she smoothed out the bedspread, had occurred a mere seven weeks ago. David had been lost three weeks later, shot down during a heavy raid over Germany. Poor Bunty, struggling hard to get over her loss, had written to Lorna asking if she might come to stay a few days; being with Lorna would be such a help.

Lorna wished that they could have had Violetta with them, too. She was always so vivacious and amusing; much more so than Lorna felt that she could ever be. But Violetta, when the conscription of women had threatened to see her directed into a munitions factory, had forestalled her call-up papers by going of her own volition into the Auxiliary Territorial Service where she was now sweating out her first weeks as a squaddie.

Bunty's bed completed, Lorna gave a last glance round the room. All that was needed now was the final finishing touch of a vase of roses on the dressing table; Bunty shared Lorna's passion for roses. Passing through the kitchen on her way into the garden, in order to check that all was being done that needed doing, Lorna discovered Mrs Cuthman's granddaughter, sixteen-year-old Ruth Cuthman, who had now come to work at The Warren, standing at the sink carefully washing the china from the shelves of the kitchen dresser: china of a decorative rather than a utilitarian sort, including part of an old Wedgwood dinner service, with a splendid soup tureen as centrepiece. The kitchen was by far the sunniest, pleasantest room at The Warren; Lorna felt that it deserved a dresser of attractive china. Mrs Cuthman agreed: 'I always had a nice bit of china in my kitchen, even when I hadn't much else.'

Mrs Cuthman's husband had been a gamekeeper. 'He was a good husband, but violent in drink; I used to be black and blue all over.' He had died unexpectedly while still quite a young man. Mrs Cuthman had gone back into service (before marriage she had been a kitchen maid); she had become cook at Weldon Court in order to support herself and her child, Florrie, who had spent much of her time being cared for by her maternal grandmother, 'who never kept a proper eye on her'; with the result that, at the age of fifteen, Florrie had produced Ruth who, wholly unwanted by her young mother, had been brought up by Mrs Cuthman, with, as the child grew older, occasional periods of lodging in Ipswich with Florrie, who seemed to grow fond of her daughter without feeling any great responsibility for her.

For the past two years Ruth had been in Ipswich, working as a bottle-washer for a dairy. Mrs Cuthman, determined to get Ruth into a better class of work, had brought her back to Fursey-Winwold, where the girl had become trainee house-cum-parlour maid to the Washbournes, under whose roof, in any case, she had largely grown up. The move had been nothing dramatic for her, she was back among old friends. However, she did let drop to Lorna that she found Fursey-Winwold a bit quiet after Ipswich, and that, in any case, she was only waiting for her eighteenth birthday when she would join the Women's Land Army.

Lorna had been a ten-year-old schoolgirl when she had arrived home from the summer holidays to discover Ruth, barely five, installed at Weldon Court, under Mrs Cuthman's care. Lorna herself, in those holiday times, had been largely under Mrs Cuthman's maternal supervision and little Ruth had soon fallen into the role of being Lorna's plaything-cum-baby sister. Lorna and Violetta had played with Ruth as if she had been a kind of living doll; indeed there had always been something doll-like about Ruth, small, endlessly smiling; with round rosy cheeks, floppy light brown hair, and long, thick, straight eyelashes dropping down like a pair of little sun blinds over her round blue eyes every time she lowered her lids. Exactly, thought Lorna, like one of those china dolls which, when you tilted them back, lowered their lids and said, 'Ma-ma!' only instead of 'Ma-ma' Ruth said 'Lar-na!' As she grew older Mrs Cuthman had insisted upon Ruth saying 'Miss Lorna'; but the relationship between the two girls had essentially remained that of two playmates, one considerably older than the other.

The sixteen-year-old Ruth who had returned from two years of bottle-washing at Ipswich had been surprisingly unchanged from the Ruth of former days. She was still small and doll-like, with round rosy cheeks; the ingenuous blue eyes were the eyes of the guileless little Ruth whom Lorna had played with and had petted. The girl herself was as innocently fond of unsophisticated pranks and jokes, chatter and laughter, as she had ever been and, quickly over an initial shyness at finding herself installed back at The Warren with a recognized job as house-cum-parlour maid, fell into her old habits of happy prattle and confiding ways.

Ruth had her friends among the village girls, and at weekends would occasionally return to her 'mates' (as she called them) at Ipswich: it seemed that, as yet, she had no boyfriends; she confided to Lorna that boys were a 'silly nuisance'. Some of her friends already had 'steadies', but Ruth had her sights set on the Land Army and a career of dedication to agriculture. 'I wouldn't mind marriage to a farmer maybe, some fine day, but I'm in no hurry,' she said, smiling into the copper pan she was polishing as she chatted. 'And with a war on you no sooner meet a boy and grow friendly than he's called up, so what's the use? For the next few years, Miss Lorna, once I'm in the Land Army I reckon it's pigs I'll get the most out of.'

'You could do a lot worse than that,' commented Lorna, laughing. 'Plenty of time yet for you to start worrying about boys, Ruth.'

'I reckon so,' responded Ruth, vigorously polishing the burnished pan.

Now she remarked, as she carefully rinsed the Wedgwood soup tureen, 'This is a lovely thing, this tureen. I remember when I was little looking at it and thinking it's real beautiful.'

'I remember thinking the same thing when I was little,' replied Lorna, pausing on the doorstep before hurrying into the garden. She added, 'I still do think it's an absolutely beautiful piece.'

'Yes, Miss Lorna. Worth washing as careful as if it's a babby.' And Ruth positively crooned as she took up a tea towel to dry the tureen.

A crisp white cloth and tea things had been set out on a table in a shady corner of the lawn, in readiness for Bunty's arrival. Bunty, poor love, would be dying for a cup of tea after her journey from London.

And so it proved. Bunty arrived hot, sticky, smutty and weary, after having stood in the corridor throughout the journey, in a train packed tight with troops. 'Travelling's no joke these days!' were her first words of greeting, as she and Lorna embraced.

Lorna made sympathetic sounds: 'Let me show you to your room, and then we'll have a cup of tea.'

'Sounds bliss!' said Bunty.

She had noticeably lost weight, and in her wan face her eyes looked bigger than ever. Her vivid lipstick made a brave bid for high spirits which all too clearly, and understandably, had deserted her.

'What wizard roses, Lorna! Sweet of you.' Bunty bent to sniff the roses appreciatively. 'I'll unpack after tea, shall I?'

'Absolutely. Bags we go down right away. I'm dying for a cup of tea, so I'm sure you must be, too, after that gruesome journey.'

They fell spontaneously into the old schoolgirl idioms of their days at St Hildegard's.

They went down to the garden. 'Father's had his tea and is taking things quietly indoors,' said Lorna as they seated themselves beside the tea table. 'He finds this hot weather pretty exhausting.'

'How is he keeping?'

'Much the same. He has his ups and downs. He just about manages to walk with the help of two sticks, and he's always very tired by the end of the day. What he calls a dot-and-carry existence.'

They sipped their tea and ate a slice each of Mrs Cuthman's sponge cake. 'Any news of Violetta?' enquired Bunty.

'Yes, I had a letter from her, at long last, yesterday morning. I'll show it to you afterwards. All about her ATS training centre. You heard from her yet?'

'Only that first postcard, saying she'd write when she was allowed a spare moment to write in.'

'She says it's just like being back in boarding school.' Lorna cut them each another slice of cake. 'Still, I'm sure she did the right thing; the powers that be wouldn't have let her carry on doing secretarial work for her parents. No hope of that being called helping the war effort!'

'And, speaking of letters,' said Bunty, 'we've heard from Ivo; saying, thank God, he's well, and we're not to worry about him. He's asked me to tell you that he's written to you in reply to yours; poor boy, he's afraid that we mightn't get his letters, in the same way that he believes he doesn't receive all of ours. He says he feels so cut off.'

Just three years Bunty's senior, and a Cambridge undergraduate when Bunty and Lorna had been at St Hildegard's, Ivo had joined up immediately war broke out and had been captured by the enemy at the time of Dunkirk. He and Lorna, introduced to one another by Bunty, had become, in Bunty's terminology, 'more than somewhat smitten' by each other; Ivo had invited Lorna to Cambridge in May Week, in that last carefree summer before the war, and during the months of 'phoney war' had dated her every time he could get away from the Officer Cadet Training Unit. Though they had never actually become engaged, there had been an implicit understanding that Lorna would be waiting when he returned from France, where he had been sent just before the 'phoney war' had exploded into hideous reality.

Lorna said: 'That must be the worst thing – feeling cut off. I write to him regularly, even though I hardly ever hear from him. I agree with Ivo; I suspect that most of the letters we exchange never arrive. But I keep on writing in the hope that some will reach him; even the occasional letter must be for him better than none at all.'

'Same here. I write to him every week. So does Ma.' Bunty added: 'He's been a prisoner now for – let's see – two years. Grim.'

'And no sign of the war coming anywhere near to an end yet,' sighed Lorna dismally. Then she remembered her duties as hostess and pulled herself together. 'More tea?'

It had never been any surprise to Bunty that Ivo should have fallen for Lorna. She was pretty enough to expect to attract plenty of young men. Slight and elegant in figure, with delicate features, a real English rose complexion, and interesting eyes of a light aquamarine blue which contrasted with her sandy-gold hair, she had seemed, at St Hildegard's, to be all set for a future of capturing hearts galore. She herself was given to joking that her nose was slightly crooked, and when you came to look at her closely so it was; but not enough to mar her appearance – perhaps, indeed, it even added character to her face.

The Lorna of St Hildegard days had been made further appealing by a most engaging, open and spontaneous smile, often followed by a happy and unrestrained laugh. But this smile and the happy laugh had gradually become extinguished during the war years, under the succession of blows rained upon her. The Lorna Washbourne contemplated by Bunty now across the tea table was not really the same Lorna of the old days of St Hildegard's, any more than the Bunty at whom Lorna gave reflective looks was the old Bunty who had practised gurgling like Gertie Lawrence.

Their tea over, the girls lit cigarettes and sat listening to a blackbird who had suddenly started to sing in a pear tree. 'Gosh,' broke out Bunty after a few moments. 'How marvellously peaceful it is here! You'd never know there was a war on.'

'I don't know about that,' rejoined Lorna wryly, 'but I suppose it is a bit different from London.'

'It all seems pretty out of this world to me,' said Bunty, gazing round her at the garden, and at the fields beyond in their midsummer glory of buttercups.

Lorna replied slowly, gazing round her, too: 'It's been a simply beautiful spring and summer this year. I don't think I've ever seen things look more marvellous. Somehow, though, I can't bear to look at it much, because the contrast between all the countryside being so beautiful and the circumstances of our own wartime lives is just too terrible and sad.'

She broke off, wondering how she could be so tactless as to voice these thoughts aloud, since they must only be horribly painful to Bunty. For a moment or two Bunty said nothing, and Lorna felt increasingly miserable and embarrassed by her own thoughtlessness. Then Bunty said: 'I knew it couldn't last, you know – our marriage. David knew it, too. I mean, nobody can be lucky thirty times running! To survive his tour, he would have had to be lucky thirty times running.' She paused for a moment, and then went on: 'I promised him I wouldn't mope if the time came when he didn't come back. He said – and I agree, though it's not easy to keep it up – that the show must go on. That's what I'm trying to do. But you know about that as well as I do, Lorna. You've been through it, too.'

'Brothers are a bit different from a husband, Bunty. You've lost your husband.'

'Maybe in some ways you losing your brothers was worse than my losing a husband. You'd known your brothers all your life; they'd been part of your life ever since you could remember. David and I hadn't known each other any time at all really. I mean, we were terribly in love, but it seemed to be over before it had really begun. And we never even started that baby!' She added sadly: 'Perhaps we weren't in the right frame of mind for starting a baby. I reckon there's more to a baby than you think.'

Lorna, not knowing what to reply, reached out across the tea table and took Bunty's hand in a sympathetic squeeze.

'Well,' said Bunty rather chokily, after a few seconds of clinging to Lorna's hand in wordless acknowledgement of the feeling between them, 'I'd say it's time for me to go upstairs and unpack.'

As they walked across the lawn back to the house, a passer-by in the nearby lane waved a cheery greeting to Lorna over the hedge.

'Who's that?' asked Bunty.

'Our neighbour, Jeffrey Bosco, the vet,' replied Lorna. 'Fearfully hearty type. Old rugger blue, and all that. As broad as he's tall and as thick as he's broad. Has the loudest voice in the world and an even louder laugh.' She added wistfully: 'That was the lovely thing about Weldon Court – you didn't have neighbours right on top of you.'

'I don't see any neighbours right on top of you,' said Bunty, gazing round at the trees and open fields. 'Where does he live?'

'Who? Jeffrey? Up the lane about a hundred yards. The Firs. And on the other side we have Titus.'

'Titus?'

'Titus Swann, the village sexton. Never stops talking. Holds you with his glittering eye, like the Ancient Mariner, and teaches you his tale. He mows the grass for us and does the vegetable-gardening, and as no one here encourages him in his gossiping I don't think he carries too much tittle-tattle away from The Warren; nor do we show the slightest interest in getting tittle-tattle out of him.'

'What about the threatened Yanks? Have they arrived yet?'

'No, but they'll be here any time now.' Lorna shuddered as she spoke. She added with vehemence: 'When they do turn up, I, for one, intend having nothing to do with them.'

III

While Bunty was unpacking, Lorna read her Violetta's letter. It was written in violet ink, which she always affected, to match her name:

Dearest Lorna,
                News at last from the Front Line!
   I'm in a Victorian barracks (mustn't say where! TOP
SECRET!) taken over as an ATS training centre. Far from
comfortable – intended for rude soldiery. About seven
hundred young things come in here at a time, all bright-
eyed and bursting with enthusiasm, and emerge three weeks
later pretty well *crawling* on hands and knees! We drill and
march, much in the style of the chaps, and have lessons in a
classroom on a variety of subjects about which I won't bore
you; and, what with the uniforms and the sleeping in dorms
and the discipline and being among swarms of fellow
females all the time, it's so much like being back at boarding
school I'm starting to feel like fifteen all over again.

I've notched back into it all quite easily – except that I thought joining the ATS would be a forward emancipated step, and actually it's several steps back into the past. However, there it is; I've done it now: signed away my freedom for the duration, and that's that.

We've learned who to salute and how to salute, and all the bugle calls from Reveille to the Last Post. On Sundays we have church parades. Actually I find these rather moving; quite thrilling when we all march in – though I know it will surprise you to hear *me* say that! Shades of the poor old Flopper! Wonder if she has joined the ATS yet. She'd *love* church parades!

I don't look too awful in the uniform; I'd look even better if it fitted properly. You should see the knickers we're issued with! They would have been approved of by Miss Binkle. *Not* on the flighty side! Khaki, of course; we call them 'passion-killers'.

All for now. Let me hear from you some time. More riveting news in my next instalment!

        Luv
        Violetta

Bunty said: 'Hm. Bit difficult visualizing Violetta in that set-up. It'd drive me up the wall, to find myself a squaddie. Let alone the knickers.'

Lorna, too, found it impossible to visualize Violetta as a squaddie. She had no terms of reference which she could apply to Violetta in uniform, marching and drilling with a mass of similarly khaki-clad figures; yellowy-green, heavily stockinged legs, clumpy laced-up shoes; hideous little peaked caps; hair rolled up high above ill-fitting collars; chins up; arms swinging in unison: it was impossible for the mind's eye to conceive such an image of the beautiful, poised and slightly sardonic Violetta. Yet in her letter she almost sounded as if she were enjoying the ATS, and 'I don't look too awful in the uniform'. Well, that was probably true. Violetta would never look awful, whatever she wore.

Violetta was the truly beautiful one. She enjoyed a striking combination of dark hair and deep blue eyes; enormous eyes with thick black lashes, beneath strong, finely marked arched eyebrows. Her nose was straight, her cheekbones high, and her mouth was full and provocative. Her figure was what the cinema-industry magazines called 'curvaceous'. These brilliant looks had caused ripples of resentment amongst the less fortunate at St Hildegard's. Acrid voices would point out that Violetta's legs were too short and distinctly on the thick side. 'Haven't you noticed that she wears her skirts too long? It's to hide her legs.'

At last Megan Thomas had said firmly: 'No one is perfect. I think Violetta can be allowed to shade off at the legs; the rest of her certainly makes up for them.'

Megan Thomas, plain as a pikestaff, was the least attractive-looking girl at St Hildegard's, to put it mildly. Small, slight, pale and wispy, wearing her colourless greasy hair in a short bob with a straggly fringe, her pale blue eyes timid and blinking behind schoolgirl specs, she never wore make-up, never was seen to powder her shiny little nose. As painfully shy as she was plain, she had been ignored by all the other girls until the naturally kind-hearted Bunty had taken pity on her and had made encouraging sounds of friendship in her direction. Megan had responded, though timidly, and somehow before they had known how it had happened she had tacked herself on to Bunty, Lorna and Violetta. They couldn't get themselves to tell her that they weren't exactly crazy on her company, so they had resignedly put up with her.

Gradually the girls had learned a little about her. She had never known her father, who had been killed at the end of the First

World War. Her mother worked as a secretary in a shipping company; she and Megan lived in a small flat in the Cromwell Road, in genteel poverty. All their spare money had gone into Megan's schooling, and then into fees for St Hildegard's.

The other girls had pitied Megan immensely, thanking their stars that they weren't in her shoes.

Megan had made no attempt to conceal that she and her mother were intensely churchified. Lorna had been brought up to go to church and attend church parades, in a way that both Bunty and Violetta thought a little on the old-fashioned side, but even Lorna didn't spend her time seeking out special church services like Megan did; as if they were special cinema programmes you simply didn't want to miss, as Violetta had commented. This habit of excessive church-going, as the others had seen it, had resulted in Megan being given the nickname (behind her back) of 'The Flopper', after the Dickens character who was always dropping on her knees to pray: 'There she goes, flopping agin!'

Now Lorna asked Bunty: 'Has the old Flopper gone in the ATS, d'you know?'

'No idea,' responded Bunty. 'I haven't heard from her for quite a while. At that time she was still in that secretarial job she had in the City. She sounded as though it was taking her a long time to get over losing her mother. You know she was killed in the Blitz.'

'Yes, you told me. Poor Megan.' Lorna felt deep sympathy for anyone who lost their mother.

When Bunty had finished unpacking the girls returned downstairs and Lorna introduced the guest to the General. Everyone liked Bunty, and he proved no exception. She chattered away to him over dinner, keeping him amused. Lorna found herself really admiring Bunty. 'The show must go on.' Well, Bunty was trying hard to do her best.

Dinner over, Lorna and Bunty drank their coffee on the lawn;

the General remained indoors, listening to the wireless. For a little while the two girls sat with their coffee and cigarettes in amiable silence; then Lorna said, 'What are your plans for the future, Bunts?'

'I suppose, now I'm to all intents and purposes a . . . single bod again' – Bunty's voice trembled slightly, but she kept on bravely – 'I shall be back to being liable for call-up. As a married woman I was exempt, but I don't suppose that will apply to me now. The stage is out for anyone in my age group; so is secretarial work, unless it's connected with the services or a government department or something of that sort. So I'm planning to venture into something entirely new. I've decided to be a clippie.'

'A what?'

'A bus conductress. I've always wanted to be one, ever since I was little. Now's my chance.'

'A bus conductress!' Lorna sounded utterly aghast. 'But, Bunty, you can't do that!'

'Yes, I can, now there's a war on. Women were bus conductresses in the last war; between the wars they couldn't be, but now they can again. And I'm going to be one.' She added: 'I love London buses.'

'I can't think of being anything worse than a conductress on a London bus,' gasped Lorna. 'All that filthy noisy traffic; all those crowds of people. London in the rush hour! Spare me! You must be mad.'

'But, Lorna, I've just said that I love buses. And I love London; though it's marvellous to have a break from it at the present moment, I'd never live anywhere else except London. I belong to London; I was born and brought up there. I stayed there all through the Blitz. I didn't run away when the bombs began to drop.' Bunty's tone became defiant. 'I was going to RADA, in Gower Street, every day, right through the Blitz. And my parents stuck it out, too. It's true we dodged off into Sussex every now and again for a weekend' – Bunty's parents had a country house in Ashdown Forest – 'but we never evacuated ourselves there; the flat in Wigmore Street remained our HQ. Even when we had most of the windows blown out! I'm a *real* Londoner.'

'Absolutely,' agreed Lorna.

'And, though London's been blitzed,' continued Bunty, 'the theatres are open again, the concert halls, cinemas, everything. They're even having Promenade Concerts again. In fact, London's livelier than it ever was, what with all the servicemen on leave and everything.'

'Will being a clippie make you exempt from call-up?'

'Fortunately, yes. You see, by becoming a clippie I'm releasing a man to go in the services. It's a sensible thing for me to do really; quite apart from the fact that I know I'll enjoy it.'

'Where will you live in London? With your parents?'

'At the start I shall. I still feel I need familiar people around me to sort of prop me up. That's why coming to stay with you is so marvellous; a combination of blissful peace and you here as my little prop.'

Lorna thought to herself that she wasn't much of a prop for anyone these days; she often felt the need to be propped up herself. However, she mustn't disillusion dear old Bunts ...

Bunty was continuing: 'When I've got over this stage, feeling I need people, then I'll try to find a place of my own. Set up as a single girl again.' Her voice choked.

Lorna decided to change the subject. 'How d'you become a clippie? They don't let you on a bus without some kind of training surely?'

Bunty blew her nose and struggled to pull herself together again. 'First, you have a preliminary interview. I've had that and, though I haven't heard yet, I imagine I did all right. Next I have to have a medical. If I pass that, I go to the London Transport

Board's training centre in Chiswick. And after that you're given practical training on an actual bus. Then comes a three-month probationary period, and if you sail through that OK – hey presto! You're a full-blown clippie.' She added: 'And I wonder what Miss Binkle would have to say to that?'

'Show me a gal unobtrusively but decisively in charge of a bus . . . ' With these words Lorna burst out laughing; Bunty joined in shakily.

'Oh dear,' Bunty said, dabbing at her eyes with her hankie, 'you don't know how good you are for me, Lorna love.'

'Ah, well, all pull together, you know,' rejoined Lorna. To herself she thought that she should be good, by now, at this sort of thing; she'd had enough practice at bearing up under bereavement.

'Actually,' said Bunty, continuing with their former conversation, 'clippies aren't to be sniffed at. They have equal pay with the men; they fought that battle in the last war, and won it. There aren't many jobs carrying equal pay; even now, when there's a war on and women are being conscripted same as the men. We get called up, but we still don't rate equal treatment. Bloody unfair, when you think about it.'

'Absolutely. Couldn't agree more.'

They sat for a while longer, then Lorna suggested that they should take a stroll round the village.

Calling the dogs, they set off. Lorna pointed out The Firs, Jeffrey Bosco's place of residence; a nice late-Georgian house which, with a little attention, could have been so elegant, but which at present looked exactly what it was; the abode of a bachelor who was too busy to notice even where he lived.

'His senior partner's gone in the Army,' explained Lorna. 'So Jeffrey's left to carry on alone. He damaged his back or something playing rugger; otherwise he'd be in the Army himself. I suppose we should all count ourselves lucky that he isn't; he's the only vet left for miles around. And that', she added, changing the subject and pointing to a little red-roofed cottage peeping from the trees beyond The Warren, 'is where Titus Swann lives.'

'Everything pretty as a picture,' said Bunty.

Lorna led Bunty into the village and up the one and only real street that the place boasted. Lorna pointed out the post office, and Miss Cusk the postmistress watering roses in her tiny front garden. Bunty was shown the smithy; the Queen's Head public house across the road, where, Lorna assured Bunty, at this hour the blacksmith would be found propping up the bar, probably with Jeffrey Bosco as company, fortifying themselves for a Home Guard night exercise; the little police station with its front patch of cabbages, runner beans winding up sticks, and tomato plants; the village school and, nearby, the schoolhouse where, said Lorna, lived Miss Daisy Ewles, the schoolmistress. School and schoolhouse overlooked a village green complete with duck pond and white ducks, a row of almshouses dating to Tudor times, and an oak said to have been planted in 1588 to commemorate the defeat of the Spanish Armada, with another oak, a mere small sapling, standing not far from it, planted to commemorate the Battle of Britain.

'Gosh,' said Bunty, 'it's hard to believe this place is true; the war just hasn't touched it.'

Lorna said to Bunty: 'Let me show you this.' So saying she turned up a leafy lane running behind the almshouses to wind away from the village between orchards and allotments and at last to lose itself in glades of uncultivated bosky. Here was hidden an ancient barn which looked as if it had stood there for ever. Lorna pointed to its timeless hand-hewn oak door to which was nailed a piece of today's plywood, on which were painted the words FURSEY-WINWOLD INVASION COMMITTEE HEADQUARTERS.

Here, when France had fallen and Britain stood alone with only the Channel between Hitler and England's shores, and the country steeled itself for the worst, the remaining men of Fursey-Winwold (the majority between eighteen and forty having gone away into the armed services) had planned secret schemes to waylay and attack the German invaders should they arrive. The Invasion Committee formed the spearhead of the village defence, but the committee members knew that they had every villager solidly behind them. In every house and cottage firearms of all descriptions were kept meticulously cleaned and loaded, and where firearms were lacking knives had been grimly and horribly sharpened, by both sexes, during those never-to-be-forgotten days when the invasion threat had been at its height. Even Lorna, in secret, had had a carving knife prepared and ready. 'You can,' as Churchill had told the nation, 'always take one with you.' Which was what everyone intended to do.

As there was nobody in Britain who was not quietly aware of this moment of national resolve, when the unspeakable had become the highly probable, Bunty did not need to have the import of the barn and its notice explained to her. She looked at the barn, and she looked at the notice. In some ways enough to make one smile, in another way it made the blood curdle. 'Well, it didn't happen,' she said at last. 'And probably it never will now; Hitler's almost certainly missed the boat for that one. Now we have the Yanks on our side, and he's got his hands full with the Russians into the bargain, I reckon the day of us being invaded is over.'

The girls turned away from the barn and returned to the village to inspect the church, of Anglo-Saxon origin, and the Georgian vicarage next door to it. 'We'll go home this way,' said Lorna, turning into a pretty lane branching off opposite the church. 'It takes us past Winwold Manor, and I thought we might pop in to see Violetta's parents. Daphne Stacks told me she'd love to see you while you were here. You have met her, haven't you?'

'Not since before the war.'

The gardens and grounds of the Manor, a rambling house of early-Victorian vintage, bore a neglected appearance. 'The poor things have lost their gardener,' Lorna explained, 'and of course they haven't time to do it all themselves; especially as Daphne's now the commandant of our local branch of the Red Cross, and is so taken up with that job that she has to all intents and purposes abandoned writing, which means poor Dicky is shouldering their literary output single-handed. Now Violetta's gone, I've been doing some typing for him.'

The girls walked up a gravel drive that badly needed weeding. From behind a clump of rhododendrons screening the lawn came the sound of laughter and voices in social animation. 'Oh dear,' said Lorna, 'I hope we're not gatecrashing some kind of a party!'

'Perhaps we'd better go home; come back some other time,' suggested Bunty. However, it was too late; Daphne Stacks, coming out of the house carrying a large glass pitcher containing some kind of drink and much clinking ice, had spotted them and advanced with a cry of apparent delight. 'Lorna! You've kept your promise and brought Bunty to see us. How lovely!'

Daphne, neatly garbed in Red Cross uniform, was a tall pretty blonde in her early forties, still remarkably youthful in appearance and manner. She showed great enthusiasm at renewing acquaintance with one of Violetta's friends (but Bunty guessed that Daphne was always enthusiastic, whatever the occasion) and declared that Lorna and Bunty couldn't have shown up at a more opportune moment. 'I've three American officers here, on an advance recce for Fursey Down; I've invited a few senior local worthies along to meet them, and to have two young belles into the bargain will, I'm sure, make their day!'

Lorna found herself in a most awkward predicament. She had vowed that she would never speak to the Americans when they arrived, would never even condescend to notice their presence. Now here was Daphne Stacks, in the role of her hostess, about to introduce her to three of them under circumstances she couldn't possibly duck out of.

Lorna, heaving a heavy sigh of resignation, followed Daphne on to the lawn, Bunty behind her. Within seconds Lorna found herself, willy-nilly, being introduced in turn to Colonel Weiss, Major Ryan and Captain Cabrini of the Eighth United States Army Air Force. Smart and immaculate, with shoes polished to an eye-arresting gloss, the winged Eight insignia gleaming proudly on their caps which they raised politely in greeting, the three smiled, bowed, shook hands with the two girls. Bunty managed to smile in return; Lorna remained stiff and cool.

The senior local worthies, as Daphne called them, comprised Dr Murray, Fursey-Winwold's general practitioner, and his wife; the vicar, the Reverend Septimus Barker, and his sister Miss Octavia Barker, both well into their seventies but still full of zest for life; Mrs Hedley-Cowper, a formidable and wealthy widow, the pillar of various voluntary bodies and societies, including (her particular interest) the Soldiers', Sailors' and Airmen's Families' Association, known to its supporters as SSAFA; and, last but not least, Miss Glaister, Daphne's Red Cross second-in-command, immensely stout, very jolly, and looking exactly what Daphne always called her behind her back: 'a real good egg' – for which reason Lorna and Violetta invariably referred to her as 'Good Egg Glaister'.

Dicky Stacks brought the girls a glass each of what he said was cider cup from the glass pitcher. A skinny middle-aged man in a navy blue blazer and grey flannels, he darted around the company in a frenetic attempt to be the life and soul of the party. His pebble-thick spectacles gleamed as he turned his head this way and that; trying to keep an eye on everybody and everything, and simultaneously to join in conversation. He was now in his element with three airmen as guests; he nursed a lifelong obsession for aeroplanes and flying, frustrated by his appallingly bad eyesight which had prevented him from taking to the air himself. He had had to content himself with becoming what he termed 'an amateur aircraft buff'; he knew everything, or at least gave the impression of knowing everything, that there was to know about 'kites', as he always called them. He peppered his conversation with RAF slang, and had annoyed Daphne and embarrassed Violetta by attempting to grow a handlebar moustache, which, being wispy, made him look, Violetta complained, like something out of the Small Mammal House at the London Zoo.

Daphne, all animation, explained to Bunty and Lorna that Colonel Weiss was airfield administration, Major Ryan was organizing medical units, and Captain Cabrini represented the American Red Cross and was particularly interested in looking into possible problems of social welfare likely to affect American personnel at Fursey Down.

'Not that we're expecting trouble,' said the Colonel, smiling to show an impressive set of brilliant-white teeth. 'With all you good people so anxious to help, everything should go very smoothly.'

'We shall have our own full-time Red Cross staff,' said Captain Cabrini, also flashing a smile full of amazing teeth, 'but we shall need help from outside; all we can get – at least, at first. Service personnel will be arriving before the aircrews, so that should keep us real busy.'

'Aircrews comprise approximately one-fifth of personnel. It takes a lot of guys to get just one airman up into the sky,' intervened Major Ryan. 'Always surprises civilians, how much support is needed for just one airman.'

'And all these guys together are sure going to need a lot of taking care of when they come off duty,' said the Colonel. 'Which is where Captain Cabrini and his Red Cross buddies come in. With, we hope, the help of you ladies. We promise to find you plenty to do.'

Captain Cabrini said, laughing genially: 'No more taking this war easy now Uncle Sam's arrived.'

Lorna flung the visitors a glance of unconcealed hostility. You crass idiots, she thought. Hasn't anybody told you anything?' She wondered what the trio would say if they were shown the Invasion Committee Headquarters, with all its grimly horrifying undertones, and then she was obliged to tell herself that, as they so obviously knew nothing about what war was really like for those truly involved in it, showing them that headquarters would be a pointless exercise.

As for finding the ladies plenty to do . . . ! Running their homes under impossible conditions, queueing for hours at the shops for rations, trying to make sustaining meals out of nothing, caring for their own and evacuee children, mending and altering old clothes which couldn't be replaced because there were not enough clothing coupons for more than one or two items of new wear each year; and, on top of all this, knitting comforts for the troops; collecting books and magazines for merchant seamen bored below decks; collecting rose hips for syrup for babies deprived of vitamins and orange juice; blackberries for jelly; foxglove seeds for digitalis for heart cases; making camouflage nets; jam for the Women's Institutes; sorting second-hand garments for Rest Centres; lending a hand on the land potato-picking or harvesting; doing odd jobs round the house that the absent husband would normally have done – all this, and often a daily voluntary stint into the bargain for the WVS, SSAFA, the Red Cross, the St John Ambulance Brigade, Civil Defence, door-to-door collecting for National Savings. There was never any end to the way in which British women were flogging themselves. Not to mention the thousands who had gone into the women's services, or into the factories to make munitions. And now women over eighteen were being conscripted; the first time in history that this had happened: really taking their place alongside the men. And here came these unspeakable Yanks, eager to fill the empty lives of British women by finding them something to do!

Lorna sensed that she wasn't the only woman present who was finding the visitors a little hard to take. A taut silence had fallen during which the ladies were eyeing the transatlantic gentlemen fairly coolly.

'You don't have NAAFI?' enquired Miss Barker at last. Captain Cabrini looked baffled for an instant; Daphne intervened, as if translating: 'Our Navy, Army and Air Force Institutes, Captain. Canteens for our off-duty servicemen.' She turned to Miss Barker. 'Their system is quite different from ours, Miss Barker.' Then, turning once again to Captain Cabrini: 'We rely on numerous voluntary bodies to see to the welfare of our boys: NAAFI, YMCA, Church Army, Salvation Army . . .'

'SSAFA!' boomed Mrs Hedley-Cowper. 'WVS. *All voluntary bodies.* With us a matter for pride.' And she gave a meaningful roll of her eyes.

Miss Barker nodded vehemently. '*All* voluntary,' she echoed. 'All giving our services to serve our servicemen.' This tongue-twister rattled off in her customary distinct high-pitched voice.

'*And* their families!' intoned Mrs Hedley-Cowper.

Captain Cabrini stared gravely at them. 'Well,' he drawled, 'I guess our system in the States is somewhat different: we don't have all those separate voluntary bodies for a start. Everything's covered by our Red Cross, which is mostly financed by the Government. Our Red Cross staff are paid staff. We like it better that way. When Americans receive service they think it right to pay for it.'

'I suppose we can't expect to see eye to eye on everything,' conceded Miss Barker.

'It probably works quite well,' said Mrs Hedley-Cowper graciously.

'Works very well indeed, ma'am,' said Colonel Weiss. 'But the fact is we're bringing so many troops over into ETO—'

'Over into what?' interrupted Miss Glaister.

'ETO,' said the Colonel. 'European Theatre of Operations.'

'But you aren't in Europe yet!' said Dr Murray.

'Not in Europe? Where's this, then?' exclaimed Major Ryan.

A firm chorus of voices responded as one: 'This is England!'

The three guests looked puzzled once more, then exchanged smiles. 'Well, forgive us,' said Colonel Weiss. 'I guess we'll learn. But as far as the US is concerned this is the European Theatre of Operations and we're Eighth US Army Air Force shortly becoming operational in this neck of the woods.'

Major Ryan, his eyes shining with anticipation, said: 'This little island of yours is going to become one great crowded mass of airdromes. History will never have seen anything like it.'

A distinct chill of atmosphere could be felt as the British learned this glad news. At length Dicky enquired rather tautly: 'When do you expect Fursey Down to become operational, Colonel Weiss?'

'As of now, we're reckoning our Forts should touch down here some time in the fall maybe. Some of our airfields will be operational well before that; but fall is our schedule for Fursey.'

'So Fursey Down is to have Flying Fortresses, is it?' said Dicky.

'Yes, sir, the B-17. Greatest heavy bomber ever built,' said Major Ryan fervently.

'I seem to have heard that the RAF prefers your Liberators,' demurred Dicky.

'Yeah, but your aerial-bombardment strategy is wholly different from ours,' said the colonel. 'Yours is a night-bombardment strategy; our bombers fly by day. *And* they're self-defending. Need no escort.'

'The Fort's invincible!' declared Major Ryan. 'Bring this war to an end sooner than you ever dreamed. Yes, sir, the Flying Fort is gonna win this war in record time!'

Dr Murray murmured: 'But can a daylight bomber ever be invincible? The Germans supposed their bombers invincible at the start of the Battle of Britain. How wrong they were! *And* they had fighter escort!'

'That was a totally different set-up!' responded Colonel Weiss. 'The whole point about the Forts is they don't need fighter escort. Repeat, they're self-defending. And, what's more, they fly so high they're beyond the reach of enemy fighters.'

'No enemy fighter pilot in his right mind would engage a Fort,' said Major Ryan. 'Boy, those heavy babies bristle with guns; just bristle!'

'That's why they're called Flying Forts!' interjected Captain Cabrini. 'The Battleship of the Air!'

'Has a bomb-sight that can land a bomb in a pickle barrel from an altitude of twenty thousand feet,' said Major Ryan. 'There's precision bombing for you!'

'How does the crew breathe at that altitude?' enquired Miss Glaister doubtfully.

'Equipped with oxygen, ma'am,' said the Major. 'Liquid oxygen.'

'Everything on board except a swimming pool!' chortled Captain Cabrini. 'The Fort's a supercraft, flown by supercrews. Boy, the day those Forts fly over Germany will be Day One of the beginning of the end! Wow! When once those Forts fly, you guys, Germany will be defeated in a matter of weeks! Just wait for it!' He grinned, nodded, took out a cheroot, stuck it in his mouth, lit it and nodded at the company once again with an air of total finality.

'That's true,' said Colonel Weiss, nodding in his turn. 'Once the Forts are flying in strength they'll achieve in three months – maybe, like Cabrini says, even less – what your Bomber Command hasn't been able to pull off in three years.'

'Sure thing,' said Major Ryan.

'Look forward to it,' said Dicky.

At this point Daphne served sandwiches and coffee. There was much gallant offering of things to the ladies. Captain Cabrini settled himself alongside Lorna. Without preamble he began: 'And are you girls as eager as those old dames' – nodding towards Mrs Hedley-Cowper and Miss Barker – 'to give your bodies voluntarily to the service of the servicemen, huh?'

Lorna, astounded and startled in equal measure, stared at him speechlessly for a moment, then managed to say: 'I . . . I think you have misunderstood!'

'Sounded straightforward enough to me!' responded the Captain breezily. 'Kinda promising, too,' he added.

'Captain Cabrini' – Lorna was at her stiffest – 'I think you'll find you have a lot to learn in England!'

'OK by me, babe! When do we start?'

At this point Bunty said, glancing at her wrist-watch: 'Lorna love, I hate having to remind you, but I think perhaps we should be getting back to your father. We've left him on his own for rather a long time.'

'Yes, Bunty; you're right, duty calls! You'll excuse us if we fly, Daphne, won't you?' And without further ado Lorna grabbed Bunty's arm and together they made good their escape.

'Whew!' said Bunty, when they'd put fifty yards or so between themselves and the party. 'I've never met such a . . . !'

'Nor I!' gasped Lorna.

'Supercraft with supercrews! All over in three weeks!' Bunty's voice shook with indignation. 'D'you know what that unspeakable

Major said to me? Actually *said* to me? He said the US Air Force had come to show us how to win the war!'

'Oh, Bunty!' Lorna was appalled. 'I suppose he had no idea that you ...' she added.

'Have just lost my husband? I didn't mention that. Didn't say anything in fact. Looked across at you, saw you were obviously suffering with Cabrini, and decided that the time had come for us to call it a day.'

'I hope Daphne won't think we're both abominably rude!'

'Too bad if she does! I couldn't take any more of that!'

'Nor me, either! Captain Cabrini and the meaning of voluntary bodies!' And Lorna gave Bunty a vivid account of her conversation with the captain.

Bunty burst into fits of wild giggles. 'Poor Miss Barker! Voluntarily offering her body ... When you look at it that way, I suppose you can see how such a misunderstanding might arise!'

'I suppose so. Yes, I confess that there is a funny side to it! He'd certainly got hold of the wrong end of the stick; *if* he'd got hold of the wrong end of the stick! I must say he struck me as a total lout! Trying it on with a vengeance!'

'Imagine what Fursey will be like when that lot ...!'

Lorna's shudder could be heard. 'I dread the thought of it!'

IV

Next morning Lorna, anxious that Bunty should have a good rest during her stay, took breakfast up to her on a tray. Lorna then carried her own breakfast coffee and toast into the garden, together with the mail which had just that moment arrived. One letter was from Violetta. Lorna, as she sipped her coffee, started to read.

Well, ducky,

I'm through with training centre and have been posted; a huge camp, more up-to-date than those bloody barracks, but still far removed from what one normally thinks of as creature comforts. We sleep in huts; ten of us to each hut, not an inch of privacy anywhere at any time. The ablutions aren't calculated to promote cleanliness, but rather more to give you frostbite in unexpected places. Of course, it was all intended for the use of rude male troops, but the high-up ATS, all of them of the Old School, suffragettes every one of 'em with a vengeance, won't countenance that the intimate requirements of young women in any way differ from those of the male. Equal, we stand or fall – all along the lines from the latrines to the parade ground. It produces some hilarious situations, I can tell you. And some choice bad language; at least we girls are all learning to swear like troopers. You would, too, given this kind of treatment!

I've been put into clerical work – well, I would be, wouldn't I? Let it be known that you can type, and the typewriter automatically becomes your FATE. So there it is; I'm a typist in khaki.

I must confess that the shine is quickly wearing off this adventure. At first it seemed quite fun, but that amused feeling has departed, and I'm beginning to feel decidedly trapped. I'm stuck in this bleeding outfit for the duration – which probably means eternity.

However, let's be philosophical. We've lost our freedom, haven't we? We're told we're in this war in the cause of freedom, but when you lose all your freedom fighting for it where are you? Finding ourselves pushed around, having to put up with things we'd once never have dreamed of putting up with, finding ourselves in situations the very thought of which, pre-war days, would have made our blood run cold . . .

At this highly appropriate point Lorna's attention was caught by a distant thumping at regular intervals, accompanied by a steady rattling and clanking. For a moment she listened, puzzled; then she realized what it must be: the demolition workers starting to batter down Weldon Court.

She could hear every blow being inflicted on the place! She felt like some unfortunate being, huddled, hands to ears, while in another room a member of the family was being bludgeoned to death. She could think of only one thing to do: attempt to blot out the sound by making a din of her own. Abandoning her breakfast, she rushed to the drawing room, flung open the lid of the piano, seated herself at the keyboard and began thumping out Mozart's 'Turkish March' as hard as she could thump, with the relentless rhythm which Mrs Plessey had demanded in the old days of typing drill at St Hildegard's.

Presently Bunty came downstairs. 'Thanks for the Mrs Plessey,' she said, smiling.

Lorna cut her short with accents of woe: 'It was to blot out the sound of the sledgehammers knocking down Weldon Court. Can't you hear them?' Her eyes shone with tears.

Bunty cocked an ear. 'I can hear a lot of noise going on in the kitchen,' she said. 'Mrs Cuthman seems to be having something of a field day there.'

The daughter of a ploughman famed for his skill with his team of horses, Mrs Cuthman peppered her speech with expressions and exclamations picked up in childhood from her sire. 'Whoa!' she would say to the vacuum cleaner, or 'Giddup!' to a saucepan slow to come to the boil.

Now she was in the back kitchen among the weightier cooking utensils. 'Giddower!' She shoved a heavy fish kettle out of her way and sent its lid flying with a clamour. Not like Mrs Cuthman's usual well-controlled self at all. 'One thing you learn from horses,' she was fond of saying, 'you can speak to them sharply, but you get nowhere losing your temper.' This morning, from the sound of things, Mrs Cuthman had lost her temper. Or perhaps, like Lorna, she simply wanted to make a noise loud enough to drown the bludgeonings echoing from Fursey Down. With twenty-eight years of living at Weldon Court behind her, Mrs Cuthman's attachment to the place was understandable.

Ruth, engaged in her morning routine of dusting and polishing, said, 'Those thick old walls will take some knocking down, Miss Lorna. I reckon they're putting up a fight.'

'Please, Ruth! Just don't talk about it.' Lorna's eyes, brimming with tears, met Ruth's; the two exchanged a long and piteous look. Ruth said with a gulp, 'It's awful war means things like this happen, isn't it?'

'Yes, Ruth, it is. But so many people have lost their homes in this war' – Lorna gave a gulp of her own, but managed to continue, in an attempt to emulate her father's stiff upper lip – 'that we're in no position to belly-ache just because we find ourselves in the same boat.'

This was strong Washbourne stuff, but it only resulted in Ruth sniffing worse than ever and wiping her eyes with the duster. 'Will they knock down the orchard too, Miss Lorna?' Ruth had happy memories of that orchard; its daffodils in spring, its apples at summer's end.

'The whole lot, Ruth. Everything flattened for the aerodrome.' Lorna's voice was harsh with pain. Ruth's sniffs turned into sobs; it was understandable, Weldon Court had been her childhood home just as much as it had been Lorna's.

'Oh, come on, Ruthie.' Lorna put an arm round the girl's shoulders and gave them an encouraging squeeze. 'We've a good roof over our heads here, and no one can live in the same house for ever, you know.' But even as she uttered these reassuring words the query 'Why not?' stabbed into Lorna's mind, making a mockery of her assumed courage in the face of disaster.

'I s'pose not,' sobbed Ruth. 'Only Weldon was so . . .' She left it unfinished and, trying to be brave as Lorna wanted, blew her nose loudly and dismally in the duster.

'Yes it *was*, Ruth. And now fetch another duster, there's a dear, and get on with your work, else the morning will be gone before you're even started.'

Titus Swann, burly and red-faced, with huge scarlet ears and brindled stubble on his chin, turned up to mow the grass. 'That's they begun work on that airfield,' he said unnecessarily. 'Knocking down an old place because it gets in the way; makes you wonder what else may be gone by the end of the war because it was in their way.' He started up his mower with a din which for once Lorna welcomed; it quite drowned out the sounds from Fursey Down.

During the morning Daphne Stacks unexpectedly called. Lorna offered her coffee and apologized for the way in which she and Bunty had so hastily departed from the Manor the previous evening. 'I simply had to get back to Father.' Daphne politely murmured, 'Of course. Everyone quite understood.' Then she changed the subject. 'You do belong to the Red Cross, don't you, Lorna?'

'Yes, I do. I enrolled in the local branch when war began; my mother already belonged.'

'Of course! She was one of our most active members until your poor father . . .'

'It's because of Father I've done so little for the Red Cross myself.'

'We haven't seen much of you, that's to be sure. Which is why

I couldn't be certain whether you were a member or not. However, you'll have more time for it now that you've moved to the Warren. Weldon Court was a bit remote, I always thought. Rather out on a limb.' Daphne saw Lorna flinch, but continued firmly, 'I think you'll find that now you're closer to the village you won't feel so cut off.' Lorna opened her mouth to say that she had never felt cut off, but Daphne rattled on: 'There are masses of ways in which you can pull your weight, you know, even if you don't join up. And one thing I do know, and that is we are all going to have our hands full once the Americans arrive on Fursey Down. They're counting on our Red Cross to assist with canteens and so forth for their boys. So we shall all find ourselves roped in.'

Lorna drew a deep breath. 'I'm afraid you will have to count me out, Mrs Stacks.' The formality of the 'Mrs Stacks' was ominous.

'Count you out, Lorna dear? How do you mean "count you out"?' asked Daphne, puzzled.

'Just count me out, that's all. I'll do anything else you ask me to do, except help with the Americans.'

'But, my dear child, they're our allies!' exclaimed Daphne.

'It's because of Weldon Court, isn't it, Lorna?' said Bunty, suddenly glimpsing daylight.

Lorna made no reply; she felt as though she were choking.

'But, my dear Lorna, you can't blame the Americans for what has happened to Weldon Court!' burst out Daphne. Bunty said: 'I can understand how Lorna feels, though. It's rotten for her.'

'It's all part of what war means, I'm afraid,' said Daphne. 'Losing Weldon Court is . . . well, sort of part of the war effort.'

'How would you like to have Winwold Manor flattened and turned into a runway?' asked Lorna, her tone icy.

'I'd hate it!' rejoined Daphne heartily. 'But I'd do my best to put a cheerful face on it, and not nurse grudges. Besides, how will you avoid the Americans once they are here? Quite a number of them are to be billeted in this village, for a start.'

Lorna made no reply, but simply sat with a stubborn expression on her face.

'I shall expect you, Lorna, to pull your weight in the Red Cross like everyone else, once the Yanks are here,' said Daphne firmly, smiling a smile that, though sunny-seeming, had a distinct edge to it.

'Mrs Stacks, my – I think understandable – disliking for Americans apart, it would be quite impossible for me to undertake any regular canteen duties or anything like that when Father takes up almost all my time,' replied Lorna categorically.

'Don't you think,' said Daphne crisply, 'that you may be using your father's ill health as an excuse for not pulling your weight in this war?'

Lorna's face turned a bright pink, and her eyes flashed; Bunty, recognizing these as signals that Lorna was furious, began wishing heartily that Daphne Stacks had not paid this social call. Lorna, when she lost her temper and came out fighting, could be fierce. But she was too well brought up to quarrel with her guest; all that she did now was to reply, in a tone of icy calm: 'I think the employment exchange is the quarter to decide whether I am a shirker or not, Mrs Stacks.'

Daphne, too, knew her manners, and changed the subject to rapturizing over what a wonderful year it was for the lilac.

When she had gone Lorna said loudly and clearly to nobody in particular: 'Daphne Stacks, or no Daphne Stacks, I still intend having nothing to do with the Yanks!' After which no further reference was made, by either Bunty or Lorna, to Daphne's visit.

V

By the end of June, Bunty was back in London and learning to be a clippie at the London Transport Board's training school in Chiswick, travelling there by bus each morning from her parents' flat in Wigmore Street. She had passed her medical without any trouble and had been provided with a uniform of slacks, dust coat (worn instead of a tunic, over the slacks) and cap. This was summer uniform; in the winter the conductress had an overcoat to wear over the dust coat and slacks. Bunty's uniform was training-school issue; if she failed to 'graduate', she had to hand the uniform back.

The girls at training school with her came from all walks of life and backgrounds, but all shared Bunty's aim to stand in the place of a man on the platform of a London bus. Their training instructors were male and addressed them with a condescension which made Bunty, for one, wryly aware that London Transport was seen as fundamentally a male preserve and that women, a sub-species, were being taken on very much in the spirit of 'making the best of things'. There was particular condescension towards those members of the class who had hitherto been housewives. 'Quite a number of ladies who were running a home when war came are now running a bus and making a good job of it,' observed one instructor encouragingly to a young matron whom he was about to show how to punch tickets. 'Blimey, anyone who can run a home can run a bus standing on their head!' she retorted. The instructor pretended not to have heard this one, nor her *sotto voce* follow-up comment, 'The blooming sauce of the man!'

The classroom period of training lasted a week. They studied the topography of London Transport's area; poring over maps, and charts of routes. They learned all about the ticket system and how to make up a way-bill of the day's takings. They were given talks about how to deal with passengers; tact, discretion, courtesy at all times. 'Take special care of the old people, invalids, the blind, and cripples, and, it goes without saying, the kiddies.'

At training school Bunty struck up a friendship with a nineteen-year-old girl named Edie Moxton; always full of fun and bounce, with an india-rubber face with which she pulled non-stop grimaces as a form of wry self-comment upon what she was saying. She proved an entertaining companion. She informed Bunty that she and her widowed mother lived in Camden Town, that her father had died early on, of chronic bronchitis, and her mother, 'Always the breadwinner because of Dad being ill, just carried on, going out mangling and cleaning and that, after he'd died; just like when he was with us. She still works.'

Bunty divulged as little about herself as possible; simply saying that she had formerly been a secretary but, having recently lost her husband, a bomber pilot, she felt she wanted to do something different that would get her out amongst people and, by releasing a man from a civilian job, would help the war effort.

As might be expected, there was much eager anticipation among the girls as to actual 'postings'. When these were announced Bunty learned that she was to start on route 24 running between the Hampstead Heath depot at South End Green and Lupus Street, Pimlico. It was a route that took her across central London. 'I can't complain about a run including Charing Cross Road, Trafalgar Square, Whitehall and Victoria Station, can I?' she exclaimed jubilantly to Edie. 'Now I'll have to find myself a place in Hampstead; somewhere nice and convenient for my depot!'

'You shouldn't have too much trouble finding digs,' replied Edie. 'My mum works regular in Hampstead. I'll ask her to ask around for you. Mind you,' she added, 'it's an expensive district; you'd be better off in Camden Town.'

'I wouldn't have the Heath to wander over, would I, though?' countered Bunty. She had a sentimental urge to live in Hampstead;

David, who had lived there as a schoolboy, had been fond of taking Bunty for wanders over the Heath and telling her nostalgic tales of how he had once played highwaymen there. Hampstead would create an illusion for her of being close to David.

'All right, then, I'll have a word with Mum,' said Edie.

Their week of class instruction over and their respective routes well studied on the map, the girls commenced ten days or so of practical experience on the road under service conditions. Each recruit was accompanied by a male conductor with a long service record behind him; his role was to act as an instructor cum guide.

Bunty found herself under the wing of a grey-head old enough to be her father, perhaps almost her grandfather, who, upon introduction, eyed her doubtfully. For the occasion she had had her hair freshly permed and had bought a new lipstick; with the addition of a little blue-black mascara and a light dab or two of tawny face powder Bunty judged herself ready to play the role of a central London bus conductress. She was slightly disappointed by the disparaging look which Mr Barnes, her instructing conductor, bestowed upon her, and even more disconcerted when she heard him say, in an aside to their driver, Gus Harris, a small dry man somewhere in his late forties: ''ere, see what we've landed!'

That first morning four passengers got on the bus as it left the depot; Bunty clipped their tickets and smiled at them brightly. Mr Barnes breathed hard over her shoulder: 'Get the ticket right into the punch, at the right angle; that's the trick!' They swung along Southampton Road and turned left into Maiden Road; Bunty swayed perilously. 'Try to keep your balance; you don't want to spend your time hugging the passengers. It's all a matter of practice; you'll find your sea legs in a day or two.'

More passengers, more tickets. Mr Barnes stuck closely to her side, watching every movement and advising whenever he thought necessary. Bunty found this nerve-racking; the confidence with which she had started off began to ebb. She fumbled with her punch and tickets, and on one or two occasions forgot to ring the bell; he rang it for her, giving her a withering look. She was too busy, and rather too fraught, to have time to enjoy the route.

Trafalgar Square, Whitehall, Parliament Square. Bunty was by this time bathed in perspiration. 'Don't forget there's a top deck!' warned Mr Barnes. 'Fares to collect up there, remember!' Bunty pounded up the stairs; the bus swayed; she staggered between the seats, madly punching tickets, surveyed by the ever cool and commanding Barnes. 'Victoria Station. Remember you got to tell 'em where they are; they can't see half the time with the winders covered with this bleeding – beg pardon – stuff,' he said.

The windows, apart from a small round peep-hole in the centre of each, were covered with a kind of coarse sticky netting, to prevent splintered glass in the event of enemy action. Bunty, on the platform, could see where she was; the passengers travelled in a state of apprehensive uncertainty, never sure whether they had reached, or passed, their destination.

At last, Pimlico! Round St George's Square; past St Saviour's Church; Lupus Street hove into view. Finally the bus drew to a halt at the end of the run. Bunty fell, rather than stepped, from the platform. 'Cuppa char?' said Mr Barnes. 'Bet you can do with one.' Bunty felt that indeed she could.

'First run is always a nightmare,' said Mr Barnes over the cup of tea, showing Bunty a more human side of his personality. 'I can still remember my first run as a conductor. But worse still is the first time you're out on your own. At least, for now, you've got me.' Bunty tried not to look as though she privately considered this a mixed blessing.

By the end of the day she was exhausted. She had never felt so tired in her life. Yet she still had to finish making up her way-bill; the last straw, she felt, for the camel's back. Mr Barnes once more led her into the depot canteen and provided her with a cup of tea. He got one for himself, too, and settled himself at a table with her, offered her a cigarette, lit one for himself, and said: 'Now, pretend I'm not here to help you.' He then proceeded to read the evening paper which he had just bought, while Bunty sipped her tea, smoked her cigarette and stared glumly at the incomplete way-bill. A few minutes passed in this manner; then Mr Barnes flung down his paper in violent disgust, exclaiming: 'Strewth! Talk about a mess!'

Bunty rolled her eyes at him in despair. She knew she had made a bit of a hash of her way-bill, but she had been hoping he would make allowances for her.

Mr Barnes grabbed up his newspaper again and shook it violently. 'With Alexandria about to fall any moment, us still with no decent tanks after three years of bleeding war, and with the blooming Germans taking everything they set their sights on to take, and us letting 'em, we *are* in a nice way!'

A tide of relief rolled over Bunty; he was talking about the war, not her way-bill.

At last she had completed it. 'I've done my way-bill, Mr Barnes.'

'Give it here. Can't be a bigger botch than our Desert Army.'

Bunty handed him her way-bill for inspection; he stared intently at it, then he gave it back to her. 'All right. Hand it in, then home you go. I'll see you in the morning.' Bunty thought he sounded less than enthusiastic. Tempted to quit buses for ever and try her luck with munitions, she returned to her parents' flat. They were both out; she ate a dismal supper alone and went to bed early, feeling a total wreck.

Although Edie and Bunty had been posted to the same Hampstead depot, they rarely met one another there, as their schedules didn't coincide. Edie was on the 168 route, running between Hampstead Heath and Waterloo. However, occasionally

48

they bumped into one another and were able to have a cup of coffee and a chinwag, as Edie liked to call it. They swapped stories about their experiences on the buses; particularly about their respective instructors. Edie, unfortunately, was landed with a chap who kept stroking her bottom; however, 'He's easing off with it. Every time he gives me a stroke I tread hard as I can on his toe; so he's not so free and intimate as he was at the start, by a long chalk!'

'The one-six-eight route sounds spicy!' said Bunty, laughing. 'Still, I suppose you can chalk it all up as experience.'

'All part of what makes the world go round,' agreed Edie. Then, changing the subject, she said: 'I asked Mum to keep an eye open for somewhere for you to live in Hampstead, like I said I would, and she says, if you're interested, she can give you the address of a very select house she works at that's let out in service flatlets; nice roomy ones, well furnished. Run by a very nice woman, a real lady; widowed, a Mrs Wells. She only takes highly respectable quiet people. Very particular who she has in her house. It's a lovely part of Hampstead; near the top of Christchurch Hill. Handy for the depot, too; you only got to walk down the hill. Mum says if you're interested she'll tell Mrs Wells.'

'It's very kind of your mother,' said Bunty. 'Yes, I'm certainly interested.'

'I'll tell her, then. I reckon you'll find it ideal.'

VI

The select establishment so warmly recommended by Mrs Moxton was a large Victorian house named Kenilworth Lodge. Bunty was fortunate; a flatlet had just fallen vacant. She made an appointment by telephone to view the flatlet one evening after her day's work.

The evening arrived. Bunty walked up the hill from the bus depot in South End Green, thinking how pretty the Heath, the gardens, the old houses looked in the evening sunshine. It was not a district in which a girl could hope to rent a flatlet on clippie's pay. Bunty had thought she should manage, because she also had her widow's pension; but, as her father had pointed out, by the time she had paid her tax and benefit contributions she would certainly not have enough left to support a 'lifestyle' resembling that which she had grown up to expect. Bunty had declared herself ready to find digs somewhere cheaper than the best part of Hampstead; but Sir Humphrey had interjected firmly: 'Girls of your age are getting a raw deal in this war; you've lost the years of carefree enjoying yourself, wearing pretty clothes, having fun, that every young thing has a right to expect. And, into the bargain, you've lost your husband. So permit me to give you a hand with your rent; it's the least I can do, and it'll mean just a little extra cash in your pocket to spend on what scant fun there's left in this grim world inflicted upon us by Hitler.'

Kenilworth Lodge had a privet-hedged front garden of little round rockeries and flowerbeds, gravel paths and a weeping ash. The front gate gave a loud ferruginous sigh as Bunty pushed it open, and another sigh as she closed it behind her. The brass door-knocker was brightly polished, and so was the brass surround and flap of the letter-box.

The door was opened by a plump comfortable-looking little woman, neatly, almost sprucely dressed, and with an air of one who has learned to be no longer surprised by anything.

'Mrs McEwen? I'm Mrs Moxton.'

They shook hands. Bunty said: 'I've heard a lot about you from Edie.'

'Edie never lets up with the talk,' responded Mrs Moxton drily. 'Mrs Wells is this way, in her basement flat,' she added. She walked down the black and white tiled hallway, opened wide another door which stood ajar and called: 'The young lady is here, madam.'

Steps ascended from the basement; Mrs Wells appeared. She was a tall commanding woman somewhere in her middle to late fifties; with a clear rosy-cheeked complexion, a shrewd eye, a bright socialite smile and a brisk no-nonsense manner. She wore ruby-red-framed spectacles, a floral-patterned smock over a black skirt, and her mass of snow-white hair was arranged very carefully in an intricate coiffure of Marcel waves and ringlets. She smiled to show admirable teeth and said, in a loud, rather fruity voice: 'Mrs McEwen? How d'ye do. I'm Mrs Wells.'

More handshaking.

'Lovely evening,' said Mrs Wells, eyeing Bunty attentively from head to toe, and missing not a detail of her clippie's uniform.

'Beautiful evening,' responded Bunty.

'You have been very highly recommended to me,' said Mrs Wells graciously.

'Nice to know,' replied Bunty, wondering if Mrs Wells had been informed in advance that she was a clippie.

'I am very particular, I need hardly say, as to whom I take as my guests.'

'Naturally.' Bunty paused, then said: 'I suppose you know that I work as a clippie?'

'I don't mind what you work as, m'dear, as long as it's respectable and you pay your rent regular. Besides I can see that you are a lady.' Another gracious smile; then, in a brisker tone: 'Let me show you the flatlet I am offering.'

Mrs Wells proceeded to mount a flight of stairs covered in good-quality carpet in a mottled pattern of browns and greys; the kind of carpet that doesn't show stains. The walls were covered with embossed oatmeal-hued paper and ornamented with etchings of old London. The paintwork was cream. It was all highly tasteful.

On the window-sill of the first-floor landing was a large earthen-ware pitcher containing dried Cape gooseberries and grasses.

Mrs Wells produced a bunch of keys and unlocked the door of one of the back rooms on this landing. 'Number Three,' said Mrs Wells. 'My best single.' She showed Bunty in. It was a much larger room than she had anticipated; arranged as a bed-sitter, and well furnished in the same respectable colour scheme of brown, grey and oatmeal, but with bright chintzy scatter cushions on the divan, which had a brown fitted cover. The cushions teamed up with the curtains at the window, the panes of which, being criss-crossed with the usual wartime strips of brown sticky paper (a precaution against flying glass), afforded only glimpses, in little bits and pieces, of the back garden. 'Faces south,' murmured Mrs Wells. 'One of my nicest rooms.'

She stood still, in the centre of the room, for a moment, to give Bunty time to assimilate a general impression. There was a green tiled fireplace with a gas fire; over the fireplace hung a mirror. 'Slot gas meter; takes shillings,' murmured Mrs Wells, indicating the meter, out of view behind an easy chair. She then crossed the room and flung open a set of panelled doors, revealing a kind of large cupboard containing a fitted hand basin with a mirror above it; on one side was a cupboard for clothes, on the other a fitted chest of drawers with shelves about it. 'Washing facilities and dressing room,' said Mrs Wells, standing back to admire the *ensemble* in apparent rapture. She added: 'Each landing has its own bathroom, of course, and a convenience.' She closed the panelled doors and crossed the room to fling open more panelled doors on the other side, to reveal another cupboard arranged as a species of minute kitchen; gleaming and neat. 'Sink; ring cooker, with grill under; china cupboard, plate rack, cooking utensils, cutlery drawer, waste-disposal bin in cupboard under sink. Every facility. You won't find anything approaching this anywhere else in Hampstead,' said Mrs

Wells, showing off each item as she mentioned it and looking immensely pleased and self-satisfied with everything. 'Meat safe,' she concluded, with a splendid gesture, adding: 'In hot weather, such as we are having at present, I allow guests to use a refrigerator in the basement. One doesn't want one's meat ration to go off, does one?'

'One does not,' agreed Bunty wholeheartedly.

Mrs Wells continued: 'A cleaning service is provided daily. Mrs Moxton, who handles all that side of things, is, as I need hardly tell you, utterly reliable; a jewel. This said, guests are, of course, expected to keep their flatlets tidy and nice, as they would expect to keep their own home. Ash on the carpets, dirty fingerprints on the paintwork – that sort of thing, out! However,' added Mrs Wells, with an encouraging smile, 'I know I need not say any of this to *you*. Clean laundry each week; normally, in peacetime, it's clean towels twice weekly, but with a war on I am afraid we can only manage once a week, because of collection and delivery problems.'

'Of course,' said Bunty. 'It must be difficult to keep up your obviously high standards in wartime.' She hoped she sounded as she thought her mother would sound in a similar situation.

'I do my best,' smiled Mrs Wells. 'You will not find flatlets like these, I repeat, elsewhere in Hampstead; I venture to say elsewhere in North London. They are quite the best West End standard of thing; quite! The kitchenette alone!' She waved a hand at the kitchenette.

'Very, very nice indeed,' said Bunty.

'Five guineas a week,' said Mrs Wells, closing the doors of the cupboard-kitchenette. 'Including cleaning service, and you may sit in the garden when weather permits. Laundry charge, five shillings weekly. I have to charge that; the laundry has put its prices up so. On account of the war, they say, but *I don't see it.*' Her tone became awesome; she contracted her brows and looked severely at Bunty, who was suddenly reminded of the Queen of Hearts in *Alice in Wonderland*.

'I . . . I think it is all very nice,' said Bunty. 'Very nice indeed. I would like very much to come here if I might.'

'You may, Mrs McEwen,' responded Mrs Wells in her best gracious tone. 'I think we shall suit each other.'

'I should like to move in this weekend if I might.'

'By all means. Terms are weekly, but I ask for a fortnight's rent in advance when you move in, and a fortnight's notice if and when you wish to relinquish,' said Mrs Wells. 'Which is only reasonable.'

'Perfectly,' agreed Bunty.

'Would you care to come downstairs and join me in a cup of herb tea?' Said with another of her flourishes. 'Most refreshing after a day's work.'

'Thank you,' said Bunty bravely.

She followed Mrs Wells out of the flatlet; Mrs Wells locked the door behind them. She then crossed the landing and exhibited the bathroom and what she called the convenience: all, of course, in impeccable order. Bunty had not yet decided what to think of Mrs Wells, but the accommodation itself could not be better.

Mrs Wells now conducted Bunty downstairs into the basement, which had been converted into a roomy self-contained flat, decorated in the usual unobtrusive browns, greys, cream and oatmeal, but with rather livelier curtains than those provided for the tenants in their flatlets.

Mrs Wells said affably: 'Do please sit down, and make yourself at home while I prepare the tea.'

Bunty seated herself on the sofa. Facing her were french windows giving direct access to the back garden. The windows were wide open, affording a view of a neatly mown lawn and flowerbeds gay with colour.

The front door slammed as someone came in. Muted footsteps crossed the hall; a flatlet door was unlocked, opened, closed. Bunty began wondering what her fellow tenants would be like.

Mrs Wells emerged from her kitchen carrying a tea tray with a silver teapot on it and two fine porcelain cups and saucers. She placed the tray on the table and poured out the tea into the cups. The tea was scalding hot and could only be taken in small cautious sips. Mrs Wells, seated in a large chair flanked by a bamboo and chintz screen, said with a sigh, between sips: 'I'm a great tea drinker in the normal way of things. I find our present ration of two ounces a week quite derisory! I realize the Government can't give us more; there isn't more to be given. So I thank my stars herb tea isn't rationed. Not at all bad, d'you think?'

Bunty made a bright face, pretending to enjoy the brew.

'So you are a bus conductress,' said Mrs Wells, after a pause. 'I rode a motor-bike in the last war,' she continued. 'Considered rather fast. Me I mean, not the bike.' She gave a throaty laugh. 'I wasn't in the Army, of course. I delivered messages and parcels for my father's firm. He didn't pay me a salary, but he increased my dress allowance, which I suppose came to much the same thing. Wouldn't be much good today, though, with clothes rationing like they've imposed on us.'

'We get equal pay on the buses. I work a forty-eight-hour week at eighty-one shillings a week. That's the basic rate. If the war lasts long enough, I may move up the scale to five pounds a week; perhaps a bit more. Of course, while I am living here my father will pay the rent, though I confess that makes me feel as though I'm cheating. I really should try to live on my pay.'

'Be comfortable while you have the chance,' said Mrs Wells sagely. 'You never know, in this world, when things are going to change. I grew up very comfortable, very comfortable indeed, but I lived to discover what hard times taste like. Few have it roses all the way.' She paused, sipped her tea, sighed and changed the subject.

'You may be wondering about an air-raid shelter.' Her tone had become brisk and matter-of-fact again. 'There's one in the cellar; carpeted, with camp beds. I started off the Blitz with deckchairs, but a deckchair every night for six solid months is beyond a joke. So I said, 'Nothing too good for *my* guests,' and installed camp beds. Now, of course, the air raids have stopped. And I don't want them back again, either; camp beds or no camp beds.'

'Best to be prepared for all eventualities,' said Bunty.

'Under the present unfortunate circumstances an air-raid shelter is a must,' responded Mrs Wells. 'I don't trust that man not to have another go at us. But by and large my aim is to ignore the war. I took that line from the first. I refuse to kowtow to Hitler. Kenilworth Lodge will come out of this war with the same high standards that it boasted of before the war started. Indeed, I have been running Kenilworth Lodge since before Hitler was as much as even spoken of. Kenilworth Lodge will remain Kenilworth Lodge, DV' – she rolled her eyes to the ceiling, held them for a moment upraised to the Deity, then dropped them again – 'and be run in the same style long after Hitler has been forgotten. At least, it will if *I* have any say in the matter.' She paused and tucked her chin in, rather in the manner of a large snowy-headed bird preening itself.

Then she changed her tone. 'You get down to the cellar, by the way, down a flight of steps you'll find just beyond the side entrance into the garden, next to my front door. I have my own front door. I like to be totally self-contained down here; the captain in his cabin. I can go up into the rest of the house from this flat direct, if I choose, the way I brought you down just now, but if guests wish to speak to me they have to call on me formally and knock on my flat's front door. I have always made that a rule. This is flatlets; not a boarding house.' She made a boarding house sound low.

'Of course,' she resumed, 'one reason this house has remained select is because I take great care to only accept suitable tenants. Noisy people, common people, objectionable foreigners, persons of that sort are *not* acceptable at Kenilworth Lodge. This has been my golden rule from the first.' She paused to take another genteel sip of tea. 'It is true I now have one or two Jewish refugees in the house; but they have to have *somewhere* to go and, as I see it, we're all in the same boat as far as Hitler's concerned – sink or swim together. I like to see Kenilworth Lodge as a refuge from the storm. That said, I assure you I have vetted them all very carefully before letting them in.'

Bunty had a vision of Mrs Wells in the role of Mrs Noah, standing at the entrance to the ark, vetting the animals as they came up two by two.

'We should never forget,' said Mrs Wells, leaning towards Bunty confidentially, 'that we could be Jewish ourselves. All a matter of luck of the draw. It's a wonderful stroke of good fortune, Mrs McEwen, to be born British.'

'Absolutely.'

'This blessed plot. This happy breed. Not that we're all that happy at the moment, but you can see what the Bard was getting at, can't you?'

'You can.'

'The day will dawn, no doubt.'

'No doubt,' agreed Bunty, thinking to herself that conversation with Mrs Wells would surely compensate for any shortcomings Kenilworth Lodge might subsequently reveal.

When the time came for Bunty to leave, Mrs Wells showed her out by the front door of the basement flat. This meant that Bunty had to walk through the front garden of Kenilworth Lodge to gain the gate into the street. Mrs Moxton, in hat and coat, was leaving the house by the main front door at the same moment; probably, thought Bunty, not entirely by chance. 'Finished for the day, I am,' said Mrs Moxton. 'Off home now.' She joined Bunty on the pavement. 'Well, does it suit?'

'Yes, Mrs Moxton, thank you. I think it will suit me perfectly.'

VII

Bunty moved into Kenilworth Lodge at the end of the week, on Saturday afternoon. She arrived with her luggage and a big bunch of flowers with which to enliven the room, and spent the next few hours unpacking and getting herself settled in. Apart from clothes and the usual necessities of life, Bunty had brought next to nothing with her in the way of personal bric-à-brac such as family photographs or favourite small ornaments to enliven the room. She had one large studio portrait of David in uniform, taken just before their marriage, but this Bunty resolutely placed in a bureau drawer; she had felt that she wanted to have it with her, but she still could not bear to have it displayed in her room, watching her.

Having unpacked and put her things where she wanted them, she set about cooking her supper in the kitchenette. As it was her first night in the flatlet – indeed, the first time that she had had a real place of her own – she had splashed out recklessly and had bought herself a chop, choosing the largest and most succulent one she had been able to see in the butcher's shop: this had taken her entire meat ration for the week, but she had wanted to celebrate.

Bunty rounded off her supper of chop, boiled potato and carrots with a cup of coffee, sipped while leaning against the frame of her window, which she had opened wide to let in the evening air; the heatwave that had started in May was still with them. Bunty drank her coffee relaxedly, breathing the scent of the honeysuckle and jasmine from the garden below.

On the lawn were seated, side by side in deckchairs, a man and a woman, obviously a married couple, possibly in their early sixties. They sat without speaking; each locked in impassive silence. Bunty thought this odd behaviour, even in people who had been married for a long time and perhaps had nothing much left to say to one another. You'd think they'd find something to say, just every now and again. She wondered, rather sadly, if she and David would ever have grown like that.

Presently a youngish man appeared, dressed for tennis, carrying a racket and a small net bag of tennis balls. His large-featured face was embellished with a heavy moustache, and his dark hair stood upright, worn *en brosse*; his shorts revealed muscular hairy legs. His gold-framed spectacles glittered in the sunlight. He bowed politely to the couple in the deckchair and then, speaking German, began giving them what was obviously an animated account of the match he had just played, demonstrating ace shots with his racket and punctuating his performance with loud bursts of triumphant laughter or the occasional shrug of exaggerated despair. With his every movement the spectacle frames flashed and gleamed. Finally he raised his racket in an ecstatic gesture of victory. The couple in the deckchairs listened and watched in near silence, wearing dubious expressions; their fragmentary conversation with him was in German, and it was obvious that here were three of Mrs Wells's Jewish refugees. The couple seemed less than enchanted with the tennis player. After a while he bowed to them again, excused himself and retired indoors. Bunty heard him come up the stairs and let himself into the flatlet across the landing from hers, also overlooking the back garden.

Immediately he had gone into the house the couple on the lawn began to laugh. Clearly they regarded him as ridiculous. Bunty felt an upsurge of annoyance with them for this. True, there had been something rather ridiculous about the over-animatedly mimed game of tennis, the eccentricities of manner, the zesty verve with which it had all been done; but, thought Bunty, that was no reason to make fun of the man behind his back.

Mrs Wells now came into the garden and began a conversation in English with the couple. Their voices were low, and Bunty couldn't hear what they said, though plainly it was all mere polite chit-chat. Snatches of Mrs Wells's talk and laughter, however, wafted upwards; reminding Bunty of brightly coloured handkerchiefs tossed into the air and carried away on a breeze. 'Almost too hot ... not really England ... dear little Menton ... You never ... you must have ... Ah, Nice! ... My Albertine ... my pride and joy ... too rampant ... D'you think so?'

The window of the tennis player's flatlet was flung open with a thud, and a tremendously loud voice with a heavy mid-European accent bellowed down into the garden: 'Mrs Wells, Mrs Wells, I cannot find my little cushion. Where have you put him, please?'

Mrs Wells, who was leaning forward among her roses, sniffing them in rapture, spun round and stared upward in mingled horror and indignation. She shrilled: 'Whatever is the matter, Mr Kaufmann?'

'The little cushion from my easy chair. Since I have been out, playing tennis, he has gone. All over my room I have looked, I have turned the place absolutely downside up, but I cannot find him. Where have you put him?'

Mrs Wells shrieked back, at full pitch of her lungs: 'Will you have the kindness to come downstairs and speak to me quietly, instead of shouting your head off at me like a boor, disturbing the entire neighbourhood?'

'Where has that little cushion gone, is all I ask, from my easy chair? Without him, my chair is not easy.'

Mrs Wells tossed off a high-pitched laugh. 'Nonsense, Mr Kaufmann. That chair is extremely comfortable, whether it has an extra cushion or not. My easy chairs don't rely on odd cushions for comfort.' She moved across the lawn, to stand immediately below Mr Kaufmann's window, tilting back her head sharply in order to see him and speak to him without having to scream. 'In any case,' she said, staring upward and moving her lips with extreme distinctness, 'I must insist you come down here if you wish to speak to me.'

'And I insist I have my cushion returned.'

'I have decided to use it myself; it is exactly the right size and shape for my back.'

'For my back also, the right size and shape. I insist to have him. Besides, he is mine.'

'On the contrary, Mr Kaufmann, that cushion is mine.'

'Permit me to remind you, I rent him.'

'That, Mr Kaufmann, does not make him, does not make that cushion, yours.'

'For while I rent him, I regard him as mine. Mine also the chair he reposes on. The chair, without that cushion, is not complete. Do I expect to pay five guineas a week to sit on a chair hard as a hermit?' His voice rose to a crescendo. Mrs Wells said, as if suddenly weary: 'I will see that you are given another. The cushion from Miss Amhurst's armchair is much the same. I'll ask the housekeeper to fetch it to your room tomorrow.' And with this Mrs Wells stepped through her French windows into the house.

Mr Kaufmann addressed nobody in particular, his voice as loud as ever. 'My hat! Never have I known such outlandish goings-on! Mrs Moxton, who may call herself housekipper, but when it comes down to brass hooks in no more than a common char, plays musical cushions all round the house, encouraged by the chatelaine herself! In normal times, every guest would have left long since!'

Mrs Wells popped back out of her French window. 'In normal times, Mr Kaufmann, some people who are here now wouldn't be living here at all. Before the war I was *very* exclusive about my guests, I can tell you.'

'I am delighted, though I must confess surprised, to hear it, Mrs Wells.'

Mrs Wells made a sound indicating she could stand no more and flounced back into the house. The couple in the deckchairs exchanged furtive amused smiles. Bunty lit a cigarette and seated herself in a chair by the window. This was turning out to be really entertaining.

Somehow she had sensed that Mrs Wells and Mr Kaufmann had been enjoying themselves, and, moreover, had similar little squabbles not infrequently, purely for the fun of it.

From Mr Kaufmann's window crashed the opening bars of Tchaikovsky's First Piano Concerto. The people on the lawn glanced up; the music was certainly very loud. Before long they rose and went indoors. Bunty, who adored the concerto, lit another cigarette and gave herself to listening. Every now and again the music stopped for several moments; clearly Mr Kaufmann was playing it on a gramophone and had to change the records and rewind the instrument.

The evening light waned; when the piano concerto had ended Mr Kaufmann regaled himself, the night air and the neighbours with a selection of Paul Robeson recordings. Bunty continued to sit by her window, smoking and listening. Blackout hour arrived; instead of closing her shutters and drawing the heavily lined curtains Bunty turned out her lights and sat in the gathering darkness. Then the singing stopped; she heard Mr Kaufmann close his window.

She sat for a while longer, in silence now apart from occasional sounds of distant traffic and the voices of two people conversing in a nearby garden. She was savouring the sensation of being on her own; not entirely cut off from the rest of the world, not stranded in an alien place without family or close friends, but sufficiently distanced from these intimates, and sufficiently amongst strangers, to give herself a sense of distinct self. If she could not have David in her life, then this was how, at least for the present time, she wanted it. She had passed through that stage of mourning, which she had described to Lorna, when she required propping; now she had to emerge as a single girl again.

Because she was out all day on the buses, including weekend shifts, it was some time before Bunty made any direct acquaintance with her fellow tenants. Occasionally she glimpsed one or other of them in the hall or on the stairs. There was a small elderly woman in a knitted hat who went into the back garden early each morning; Bunty, while she drank her morning tea, watched the little woman shake crumbs for the birds from a small brass tray (it had become illegal, in wartime, to feed birds actual bread). The birds hopped round her on the grass at her feet. The little woman talked to them.

Mrs Wells made it a strict rule that she never gossiped about her guests (as she always called her tenants), but Mrs Moxton had no such inhibitions, and from her Bunty learned a considerable amount about the other people in the house.

'Who's the elderly little woman in the knitted hat who shakes crumbs out every morning for the birds, Mrs Moxton?'

'That's Miss Amhurst, Number Five. A dentist's receptionist and has been for years. She's a friend of the Parsons, Mr and Mrs; recommended them to come here when they got bombed out in Muswell Hill. He's something in the City. They're in Number Two, across the hallway from the Schwartzes. The four of them play bridge together in the evenings.'

The Schwartzes were the couple who sat in the garden without speaking. Jewish refugees from Berlin, said Mrs Moxton. Ground floor, Number One. 'Wealthy, or were. They left Germany just before the war; they were to be joined here by their daughter and her two little kiddies and her husband, but they left it too late getting out of Germany, so they're still in Berlin. Nothing's been heard of them of course; can't keep in touch with a war on! Mrs Schwartz says she hopes they'll all start a new life together in America, after the war's finished. Her son's in business over there.'

Mrs Moxton paused for a moment and then continued: 'Mr Kaufmann's another one, like the Schwartzes, who hasn't heard any news of his family since war broke out. He has an old mother in Budapest. Still, you can't really call him a proper refugee; he came over here before the war to learn English and study business methods in this country, and of course he got stuck here, couldn't get back. I think they interned him for a bit, but let him out as harmless. Now he's found himself a good job and considers himself quite the Englishman. Lives in Number Four across the landing from you; I've no doubt you've met him by now.'

'No,' said Bunty. 'I've only heard him playing music in the evenings. And having a wordy doodah with Mrs Wells.'

'Those two enjoy their little doodahs,' said Mrs Moxton drily.

One evening, when Bunty was seated by her window waiting for Mr Kaufmann to start his record recital and wondering why he was delaying doing so (she was sure that he was in, and alone) there came a knock on her door and, when she opened it, there stood Mr Kaufmann.

'Excuse me,' – his voice was a loud whisper – 'may I come in for a moment?'

'Certainly.'

He stepped into the room without further ado. Bunty surveyed him with interest. Viewed close to, he looked older than when seen bouncing about at a distance. His black hair was slightly tinged with grey, as were also his moustache and bushy eyebrows. His dark eyes had tired little lines round them, as if he puckered them, wearied by troublesome thoughts. Bunty was surprised to discover grey hairs and tell-tale lines in one so apparently buoyant and high-spirited by nature. A tragic love affair, perhaps? Maybe a character for the pen of a Charlotte Brontë? One of those bespectacled heroes who so interestingly broke the usual romantic pattern?

Mr Kaufmann's glance fell on her chair by the open window. She said, with a little laugh: 'You see, waiting for the concert to begin.'

'It is that which I have come to speak to you about.' He cleared his throat importantly. 'Mrs McEwen, if I have been annoying you, I apologize.'

'Annoying me?' said Bunty, puzzled. 'Annoying me how?'

'Mrs Wells says I am an annoyance with noise. I call it music; she calls it noise. She cannot tell the difference!' He rolled up his eyes, shrugged, and spread out his hands; the very epitome of despair over the abysmal hopelessness of Mrs Wells.

'But I love the music!' exclaimed Bunty. 'In fact I was thinking of coming to thank you for it.'

'Others have complained. Neighbours, if Mrs Wells is to be believed, have complained.' He shook his head.

'People are rum,' said Bunty. 'Imagine complaining about beautiful music!'

'Alas, Mrs McEwen, there will be no more beautiful music to listen to at your open window. From now on I must play music with my window closed.'

'A case of all good things coming to an end,' sighed Bunty.

'I shall be delighted if you join me in my flat to listen to a record or two.' He gave one of his polite little bows.

'But that would be lovely!' She hesitated. 'Do you mean this evening?'

'Whenever you wish. This evening, yes, if you would care to come and listen.'

Mr Kaufmann's flatlet was like hers, only he had filled his with personal clutter. Above his mantelshelf hung an amateur water-colour of Lake Geneva with the famous profile of the Dents du Midi in the background. A little steamer was travelling up the lake, and in the foreground was a small horse-drawn carriage. On the mantelshelf itself stood a row of framed photographs: one, in the centre, was of a plump, happy-looking, white-haired woman, smiling.

Bunty, looking at the white-headed smiling woman, exclaimed: 'What a lovely face!'

'My mother,' said Mr Kaufmann briefly.

To the left of this portrait of his mother was one of Mr Kaufmann himself, as a very young man, tremendously spruce in evening dress and obviously fancying himself. Bunty stared at it with carefully concealed amusement for a moment or so.

'Tea, coffee, Mrs McEwen, while you are waiting for the concert to begin?' enquired her host. 'I, too, have herbal tea, like Mrs Wells, but mine is much preferable to hers; I buy it at Fortnum's.'

Bunty, her heart sinking, said politely: 'I'd love to try it.'

Mr Kaufmann busied himself in the kitchenette putting an elec-tric kettle on to boil, measuring tea from an ornate tea caddy, producing tall glasses in silver holders. Then he began sharpening fibre needles for the gramophone. 'Naturally, for the expensive col-lection of records I have, I use only fibre needles. I pride myself upon being a connoisseur in all things, Mrs McEwen.'

'So I observe,' replied Bunty courteously. Then, because she could never resist other people's photographs: 'Do you mind if I look at these other portraits, Mr Kaufmann? Is this little boy here in the sailor hat you?'

'Yes. At the age of six.'

Already fancying himself, smiling smugly at the camera, he stood very upright; dressed in a velvet suit, bronze kid buttoned boots, very white high socks, and a round straw sailor hat with a wide brim and long streamers. His hair beneath the hat fell in glossy ringlets. He was wearing white gloves and held a small walking-stick.

'All dressed up for the camera,' said Bunty, smiling.

'No, no; my mother always dressed me like that whenever I went out with her. She liked me to look pretty. I am waiting there for the carriage to come to take me for a drive with Mamma round the edge of the lake.'

Bunty glanced up at the watercolour. The lake, the carriage. 'Yes,' said Mr Kaufmann, following her glance. 'A sketch I made (as you see, I am talented with my brush) showing the lake, the carriage, the steamer which I was sometimes taken on for treats. Each summer we went to Switzerland and stayed there by the lake with my Uncle Leon; that was where he lived. He was my mother's brother, and I looked on him as a father; my own father, who was considerably senior to my mother, died when I was two. You will see a photo of Uncle Leon on the wall in the corner; in his rowing boat with Mamma and myself. The boat was called *Emmy*, you will notice. After my mother.'

Bunty inspected Uncle Leon, a slight dapper little man with a goatee beard and a straw boater tilted rather over his nose; he was seated holding the oars. Mr Kaufmann, garbed in the velvet suit and the sailor hat, was seated next to his mother, who was wearing a large ornate hat and held a parasol. At the other end of the rowing boat was a servant with a picnic hamper.

'My happiest days,' said Mr Kaufmann with a long sigh. 'The

days of blissful childhood. Not that there was not also much pleasure in the years after the war when I was a young man: friends, tennis, university life, charming girls, dancing. I was extremely good-looking in evening dress, as you can see in that portrait of me there. Now I never seem to have occasion to wear evening dress. I have it packed away in a trunk . . . ' Suddenly, with these words, he seemed to freeze, his expression becoming one of horror. 'Moth! Moth!' he exclaimed. He dropped on his knees before his divan and began wrestling with a large flat suitcase which lay concealed under it. As he struggled to pull out the case he muttered to himself in staccato jerks: 'Packed and forgotten for months . . . and I a man who prides himself on taking good care of his clothes!' He tugged the case clear of the divan and flung open the lid, muttering to himself meanwhile: 'If the moths have been at it, then I am done for – sink, line and hooker. Fifty pounds won't buy me new evening clothes today; not of that cloth, that cut.'

As he spoke he removed sheet after sheet of tissue paper from the case and then, from between deeper layers of paper, he produced an evening jacket, braided trousers, a white waistcoat. These he spread out on the divan before examining them, each in minutest detail. He had quite forgotten Bunty. After this examination was completed he laid them back on the divan and stood for a while contemplating them, lost in thought, absentmindedly picking his nose.

At last, with rather tired movements, very different from his earlier frenzy, he began folding the clothes back in the layers of paper; then, allowing his gaze to roam round the room as if seeking inspiration, he whispered softly to himself: 'Balls, balls.' Bunty wondered if she should creep away. At this point the electric kettle, which had been boiling its head off unnoticed, began to smell ominous and to make cracking noises. Mr Kaufmann sprang to switch it off; then unthinkingly removed the lid and, grasping the kettle with a cloth and holding it at arm's length from him, he poured cold water into it from the tap. There was a fearsome hissing, and a jet of steam instantly shot out of the kettle, narrowly missing his face.

'Do take care!' begged Bunty.

'Try again,' said Mr Kaufmann, cautiously pouring further water into the kettle and putting it on to boil once more. 'What was I saying before all this happened?' He raised his eyebrows and opened his eyes wide simultaneously, making himself look remarkably like an owl. 'Ah,' he answered himself, 'moth balls! Moth balls,' he repeated, his gaze once more roving round the room. 'They might be anywhere. However, one thing is certain: they will not be with the biscuits!' This apparently was a humorous remark, and he accompanied it with a chuckle. 'They'll turn up, no doubt,' he said. 'I'll repack my suit later. For the present, our tea!'

Mr Kaufmann served the tea poured into the tall glasses; he placed a small round table at Bunty's elbow, placed a little round lace table-mat on that and the glass on the table mat. 'Now, which music shall we have? Since I have spoken to you about my Uncle Leon, a Chopin nocturne, I suggest. One he played often. He was a brilliant pianist. That he never performed before the public was a deprivation for the concert platform. Yet nothing would persuade him. He played for himself, in solitude, and for the few of his friends he knew could appreciate him. And, of course, for my mother and myself.' And Mr Kaufmann heaved another long sigh, gave the gramophone a final wind, carefully placed the record in position, having first wiped it caressingly with a small velvet pad, then, with meticulous care, set the record slowly revolving and applied the fibre needle to the record.

The music, the photographs and the watercolours, the tall glasses of tea combined to evoke an atmosphere of profound nostalgia. The room ached with a sense of exile. Mr Kaufmann played

69

records, sharpened needles ('The point of the needle is the crux of the quality of the music'), rewound the gramophone, insisted on serving Bunty a second glass of the herb tea which she found no pleasanter than that given her by Mrs Wells, and altogether proved the attentive host. At last it was time to call the session to a close; Bunty explained that she had to start early the next morning. She thanked him for the lovely evening. 'Not at all, Mrs McEwen; it is for me to thank you for your company. Another evening soon, I hope.' He added: 'Though I have made myself greatly at home in this country, and have become quite the John Bull, I still find myself lonely. I have many friends, tennis, bridge parties – oh, you would say, "What is he complaining about?" Compared with many I am very fortunate.' He spread out his hands. 'But, that said, war carries all away. This is now a lonely world to live in, thinking of what it once was. A little company, a little music, a glass of tea brings back feelings that not everything has been lost for ever.'

'We must hope for better times,' said Bunty, attempting an optimistic smile.

'Yes, yes, we must.' They said good-night, and Bunty returned to her own flatlet. Suddenly, without quite knowing why, she felt that perhaps she should put a photograph or two on her own mantelshelf. Lorna, Violetta and herself at St Hildegard's maybe. Certainly the portrait of David. It had lain in her drawer too long; she must fetch it out, to remind herself of what he had truly looked like. She was astounded how quickly you could forget what somebody, so intimately loved, had truly looked like. No doubt that was why Mr Kaufmann had all those photographs round his room; he didn't want to forget the absolute exact details. 'If you don't remind yourself, I suppose it *can* get lost for ever,' thought Bunty.

So David's portrait was now taken from the drawer and placed on Bunty's mantelshelf, to watch her as she moved about the room.

She found herself able to look at him without tears; to think about him without an utter sense of desolation. She had moments when she was shocked to think that she might be recovering from losing him; she didn't wish to be fully recovered yet; there was a kind of comfort, almost a satisfaction, in mourning which she was not yet prepared to relinquish. Once she stopped mourning for him, then she would have lost him completely. She said to the portrait: 'Don't leave me stranded *all* on my own. Just be a little bit around for me ... somewhere.'

VIII

The summer wore on. Bunty's three months as a probationer clippie were up, and to her immense relief and satisfaction she learned that she had made the grade. Her driver, still the original Gus Harris, congratulated her and stood her a lunch of vegetable pie and chips, dish of the day on the canteen menu. As they attacked their plates of food, he remarked: 'Mr Barnes said you'd prove to be a natural, and he was right.'

Bunty said, astounded: 'I thought he didn't think much of me.'

'Oh, no. He spotted good material in you from the start.'

Bunty was elated. Coming from Mr Barnes, this was praise indeed!

'Mind you,' continued Gus, 'your job's not going to be an easy one, now the place is filling up with all these Americans. Don't know how many more of 'em are expected to arrive but, if you ask me, they're going to turn out to be a real nuisance.'

It seemed that overnight London was full of Yanks. As far as the natives could discern, they had all come to England to have a good time, and top of their list of priorities for having a good time was a sightseeing trip to London and making the girls. Slung with expensive-looking cameras, they roamed, like tourists rather than soldiers, in groups round central London, rubber-necking, and importuning anything and everything they saw in skirts.

Bunty found her bus besieged by Yanks (as they were all called, irrespective of whether they came from above or below the Mason–Dixon line) all clamouring to know where the bus was going and if it would take them to Madame Two Swords Wax Museum, West Minister Abbey, Bucking Ham Palace, Saint Paul's, Traffel-gar Square, 'any places that had been bomb damaged' and, of course, Piccadilly, where they hoped to meet the notorious 'Piccadilly girls' it seemed they had all heard about.

In addition to these non-stop questions regarding destinations, Bunty had to fend off a further flow of pressing enquiries. 'Say, peaches, you gonna get off this bus with me when it stops? You can't? That sure is a pity. Where'll you meet me, then, when you've finished the run?'

'Lady, you're beautiful. Don't bother with punching that ticket; just look at me with those great big bedroom eyes of yours and say you're gonna love me.'

They crowded round her, blocking the other passengers, refusing to pay attention to her requests that they should pass down inside the bus, find seats on the top deck, get off at the next stop, or simply get lost.

'Honey, I doan wanna ticket, I doan wanna seat, I doan want nutt'n in the whole blame wide world except your phone number.'

They didn't even have to be on the bus. From the pavement would come an exuberant yell: 'Say, you guys, see that cute thing on that bus platform? Thirty-eight, twenny-four, thirty-six! Gee, I'd like to have her in my hotel room tonight!'

Bunty did her best to remain coolly polite, briskly no-nonsense and businesslike as her mentor, Mr Barnes, had counselled her to be if she had passengers aboard who tried to turn fresh. 'Don't let 'em get away with the hanky-panky,' Mr Barnes had warned. 'Straight away, give 'em a taste of the frozen mitt. You're a representative of London Transport, and London Transport expects respect for members of its staff. Tell 'em if they can't behave, then get off the bus.'

With the happy holiday-mood Americans seething round her, Bunty, suitably poker-faced and icy-voiced, handed out tastes of the frozen mitt, intent on preserving the dignified image of London Transport. But this seemed only to stimulate them to further excesses of importuning, or made them downright cross. 'OK, sourpuss, have it your way!' shouted one thwarted GI who had pestered her for a date all the way from Cambridge Circus to Parliament Square, and had finally driven her to tell him to get off the bus or else. 'I ain't staying on this funeral car anyways!' And he leaped from the moving bus on to the pavement, narrowly missing a lamp-post and making poor Bunty shudder. 'Don't ask me to fight your war for you!' he shouted, as his final shot.

'I've never known anything like it,' said Bunty to Edie. 'D'you think they behave like that back where they come from?'

'Don't suppose so,' said Edie. 'It's because they're away from home. Shaking a loose leg.'

'Pity they ever left home!'

'They've come over here to win the war for us. Been told that by several of them,' responded Edie dourly.

Edie, too, had successfully come through as what she termed 'a full-blown clippie'. The two girls were having supper together at the Coventry Street Corner House, jointly celebrating. When they had eaten they went to see the revue at the Hippodrome.

Afterwards, walking across Leicester Square, they were accosted by two GIs wanting to know if they were Piccadilly girls. Edie's response was a ferociously indignant snort. Bunty, wondering if they truly realized they were in fact asking if she and Edie were common prostitutes, replied: 'No, we're theatregoers.'

One GI looked blank; the other said: 'Where do we find the Piccadilly girls?'

'You might try Piccadilly for a start. This is Leicester Square,' snapped Edie. 'And you might try to learn the difference between respectable girls and tarts; it'd save you trouble.'

'Save *us* a lot of trouble, too,' muttered Bunty, as she and Edie marched off briskly, having dealt this rebuke.

'Blooming sauce of them!' said Edie.

'It's not that I'm particularly narrow-minded,' Bunty wrote to Lorna, 'and in the normal way of things I don't mind chaps paying me a spot of attention, but who in hell do these Americans think they are? And, even more so, who do they think *we* are? It's beyond a joke when a girl can't be in central London without having to run the gauntlet of a swarm of young louts who seem to think they've crossed the Atlantic purely to lay the female half of London's population.'

One afternoon in Trafalgar Square a slim and trim little girl in American Red Cross uniform boarded Bunty's bus. Honey-coloured ringlets showed from under her cap; she wore madly smart emerald-green-framed spectacles, and her mouth was generously lipsticked lollipop pink. Without being really pretty she was takingly eye-catching. Bunty thought to herself that only the Americans knew how to make smart spectacle frames, and only American girls nowadays could obtain a marvellous shade of lipstick like that. In England you were lucky to find any lipstick at all.

'Bunty!' cried the little American Red Cross girl.

'Megan!' A Megan so transformed that Bunty hadn't recognized her until she heard her voice.

Bunty (caught in a swarm of GIs all clamouring at once for tickets and her phone number and wouldn't she give them a date and which depot would they find her at and would she put this one down by Ly-cester Square and this one in Char-ring Cross Road and would she tell this one when he had reached the Piccadilly end of Shafts Berry Avenue, and 'Say, peaches, are they your own teeth?') managed somehow to find time to pull a mad face at Megan indicating surprise and delight at seeing her and indicating that she herself was being generally driven round the bend by the unruly swarm of Yanks. Then: 'This bus doesn't go up Shaftesbury Avenue and we've passed Leicester Square. Sorry, you've missed the stop; you'll have to get off next stop and walk back. Sorry, but I don't give my phone number to strangers.' She ignored the question about her teeth and icily ignored the questioner, too; he had bought his ticket before becoming apparently beguiled by her teeth, so she had no need to look his way again. But he refused to give up. 'Say, kid, those teeth of yours genu-ine?'

Megan moved up the bus towards Bunty. The tooth-enraptured GI, noticing her in her American Red Cross uniform, rose courteously and offered Megan his seat. Accepting it, she beamed sweetly upon him and his noisy companions. 'You boys having a good time here in London?' she asked them affectionately.

'Yeah, ma'am, we sure are,' they chorused back politely.

'Been to any theatres yet?'

'Taking in the Hippodrome this evening,' said one voice. 'Got tickets for the Victoria Palace,' said another. 'The Windmill!' cried someone else. From the back of the throng came a loud wolf-whistle. Everyone burst out laughing; Megan joined in.

Bunty stood gaping at her in astonishment, quite forgetting her own role as a clippie.

'Tried Rainbow Corner yet?' enquired Megan.

'Yeah, ma'am. It's sure a nice place to go.'

'D'you work there, ma'am? Think I saw you there.'

'Just started there, part-time,' said Megan.

'I guess it's what's needed in a place like London,' said the boy who admired teeth. He made London sound rather disappointing and provincial. Bunty wondered where he came from. Smilingly, Megan asked him.

'Kansas City,' he said proudly. 'Been there, lady?'

'I've never been to the US,' said Megan. 'I hope to some day.'

'Don't miss Kansas City,' he said.

'And don't miss Philly,' sang out another voice.

'New York!' cried out a third. 'New York makes this dud burg look like a one-horse town.'

'I'll take the good old Smoke any time,' responded Megan buoyantly.

'Like a Camel?' said the New Yorker, whipping out a packet.

'Smoking on the top deck only!' intoned Bunty, remembering her duty to London Transport.

'The Smoke. That's what we Londoners call London,' explained Megan.

'Well, I guess everyone prefers the place they stem from,' came the rejoinder, with the gallant afterthought: 'London's pretty nice, too, if it produces girls like you.'

Megan sweetly smiled her thanks.

As she prepared to dismount from the bus Megan said to Bunty: 'Can we meet somewhere this evening for a chinwag? About eight o'clockish, say, at the Café Royal? I'd love to buy you a drink.'

'Great,' agreed Bunty. 'Love to.' She added in a hasty gabble as the bus drew up at the stop: 'You certainly know how to handle these Yanks. They drive me up the wall!'

'All they want is mothering,' replied Megan as she skipped off the bus.

'Mothering!' echoed Bunty dumbfounded. It was the last thing she supposed the GIs wanted.

When the girls met in the bar of the Café Royal just after eight

Bunty greeted Megan with the words 'I've booked a table upstairs for us after our drinks. Supper on me. I hope you'll have the time to spare. I think we should celebrate two St Hildegard's girls one of whom has graduated as a clippie and the other as a full-blown Yank.'

'Sounds dandy to me, sister,' rejoined Megan, laughing.

The place was packed; it was popular with the Free French, and there were a lot of them present that evening. Megan ordered champagne cocktails. 'I've never had a chance to toast a clippie before,' she said. 'It calls for a touch of style.' Adding with a beaming smile, obviously meaning every word: 'And it is *so* lovely to see you again, Bunty! I'd almost resigned myself to losing you for ever.'

Bunty felt a heel. Ever since arriving back in London she had been telling herself that she must get in touch with Megan; but the thought of the girl had been less than stimulating, and Bunty had put off and put off trying to contact her. The poor mousy Flopper. And now here she was, a stunning little blonde! 'Show me your hairstyle,' said Bunty.

Megan, blushing slightly, pulled off her cap, revealing a smart crop of small blonde ringlets. 'Bubble cut,' she said. 'All the craze right now. Bubble cut and perm.'

'Looks wizard on you, just perfect. It suits you, Flopper, it really does.'

'I'd forgotten you used to call me that,' said Megan.

Bunty said: 'I'm sorry. It just slipped out. I won't call you it again, not ever.'

'But I'd like you to. It reminds me of the old times; St Hildegard's. It was such good fun at St Hildegard's, wasn't it?'

Before they could start reminiscing about St Hildegard's the champagne cocktails arrived.

'Here's to the clippie!'

'Here's to the Yankee girl!'

'Tell me all about how you became a clippie, Bunts. It's the last thing I'd ever thought you'd be.'

'First, you tell me how you got yourself into a Yank uniform, Flopper. It's the very last thing I ever thought you'd do. Plus blonde bubble cut and all.'

'Well, when at my call-up interview I said I'd like to be a Wren I was told "No dice"; the Wrens are over-recruited, and the choice was simply between going into the ATS as a cook, spud-bashing, at fourteen shillings a week, or work as a secretary for the American Red Cross at five pounds a week.'

'So not unnaturally you chose the American Red Cross.'

'Who wouldn't have done? Though, I confess, I was more than a bit apprehensive about it. I wasn't certain I'd measure up. I don't mean as a secretary; I'm a darn good secretary, though I say it myself. But I was afraid I was too mousy. You know how you expect American girls all to be like Ginger Rogers and Greer Garson.'

'So you threw caution to the winds and invested in a blonde bubble cut.'

'My interview was in Grosvenor Square; that's where the ARC have their offices. Grosvenor Square – and the past three years I've been working in Fenchurch Street! Bit of a difference.' And Megan gave a rueful smile. 'I honestly don't think I could have summoned the nerve to go for the interview if I hadn't had my hair done.'

'Nothing like a new hairdo to stiffen the backbone,' said Bunty.

'Dutch courage, but better than none,' said Megan. 'And of course when I got there it was the standard of my work as a secretary they were interested in, and of course that more than measured up. Miss Binkle was right about St Hildegard girls; she certainly put us through our paces, but at least we emerged with something to show for all the pains that were taken over us.'

'Bet they wish more of Miss Binkle's little nuggets would come along,' said Bunty.

'Mind you, they were surprisingly strict about my family background and all that; Uncle Sam doesn't employ non-Americans without taking a pretty close look at them first, specially not as Red Cross.'

'Can't have their boys exposed to the wrong types,' murmured Bunty drily.

'Anyway, I landed the job,' Megan concluded triumphantly.

'What d'you actually do in the American Red Cross? What's this mothering lark?' asked Bunty.

'In the office I'm engaged purely on the secretarial side of admin work. But now that the new big social club for the GIs has been opened at Rainbow Corner in Shaftesbury Avenue they need staff to match the size of the club, and so I've been roped in to do part-time work as a hostess. Officialdom is keen on the GIs having opportunities to become acquainted with the British.'

'Whew! You're a glutton for punishment!' exclaimed Bunty.

'I enjoy it,' said Megan. 'And I like the GIs.'

'You obviously get on well with them; mastered the art of coping with them to a T,' sighed Bunty. 'Personally I find them an utter pestering bind. Besides, the way they swagger, as if they owned the place! And expect every female in the metropolis to go into gibbering drooling raptures over them. Who the hell do they think they are?'

'Brash as they seem at first glance,' rejoined Megan, 'they're many of them overawed by London. For a start, most of them have never seen a city anywhere near this size before. How could they? London absolutely knocks them for six; though naturally they do their best to be blasé about it. Actually,' she continued, 'London's a very dangerous place for inexperienced young chaps like so many of them are. Innocents, pretending to be worldly wise. What my

79

friend Katie from California calls a lethal combination. That's why the ARC has opened all these clubs for them, so they can feel they have some kind of a home base.'

'You sound like Wendy with the Lost Boys.'

'I feel a bit like that sometimes.'

'Don't trust Captain Hook, don't eat plum cake and, above all, beware of the crocodile!'

'They come from a land of Puritans, Prohibition, protective mums and everyone nice as pie.'

'I'm sure you're right; but let's face it, Megan, they certainly give the impression that the sooner they lose their pristine virtue and get swallowed by the crocodile the happier they'll be. All heading for the "Piccadilly girls" as fast as good old London Transport can get 'em there.' She glanced at her watch. 'Time to eat when we've finished these drinks. That table won't be held for us indefinitely.'

They dined upstairs on the balcony; the place buzzed with voices and tingled with the frenetic excitement peculiar to wartime London at night. Uniforms everywhere; everyone living for the moment. The waiters, most of them distinctly long in the tooth, all the younger men having been called up, moved between the tables mechanically, in the clutches of a physical exhaustion only overcome by sheer professionalism. The girls ate *pâté maison*, chicken Kiev and, for dessert, charlotte russe; anything and everything Russian being the rage. The food all tasted of wartime's monotonous nothing-on-earthness, but none the less seemed pleasantly palatable to Bunty who had been supping at home for the last three nights on a casserole dish concocted from half a pound of tripe and half a cow heel presented to her by Mrs Moxton; a generous gift made possible because, as Mrs Moxton put it, 'One of the ladies I do for has an under-the-counter association with her butcher'.

Megan, eating *pâté maison*, asked Bunty: 'And how are Lorna and Violetta? You haven't mentioned either of them yet.'

'I haven't seen either of them for ages; Lorna's still at home taking care of her father, and typing for Dicky Stacks in her spare time. She writes fairly often. Violetta writes to me only now and again; she's a squaddie in the ATS and does typing all the time and sounds rather browned off with it all at present. She says she's hoping for a commission in the New Year, when she's going on an officers' training course.'

'It would be super if we could all get together again some time.'

'Wizard,' agreed Bunty. She paused, then added sadly: 'That's the worst thing of all about the war, how it splits everything up; tears people apart, friendships, families, marriages, everything. It's like being turned overnight into a sort of shipwrecked sailor, stranded alone, and trying to keep in touch by sending messages in bottles.'

'St Hildegard's seems like another life.'

'Yes. One that's gone for ever.'

Their talk, over the rest of dinner, dwelt upon the dear old days at St Hildegard's, which, treadmill as it had seemed at the time, in retrospect appeared carefree in the extreme. 'All we had to worry about was shun hooks!'

The time came to say good-night. They parted with assurances they'd see one another soon. Then they exchanged the brightly lit, warm interior of the Café Royal for the blacked-out streets and a raw night beating with rain. Bunty made for the Underground, Megan for the bus which would take her to Cromwell Road. An American voice greeted her from the gloom: 'Say, are you one of those Piccadilly girls we've been hearing about?'

'No, I'm not, and if I were I'd have more sense than to be out on a night like this, and I'm surprised you haven't,' retorted Megan, and ran for the bus she saw looming, just perceptibly lit, out of the wet and the dark.

Megan's flat, when she reached it, was icy cold: as she only lit the gas fires in her bedroom and sitting room when she was at home, the place in the winter never had a hope of being warm. She scuttled into her bedroom to light the fire; then undressed and put on pyjamas and a once cosy dressing gown now grown painfully thin. She put out her daytime clothes ready for the morning. Then she filled a rubber hot-water bottle and placed it in her bed and with the remaining hot water in the kettle made herself a ready-mix chocolate drink from the American PX. The door into the living room was open: from the mantelpiece her parents watched her; a framed photograph, faded now, of them on their wedding day, he in uniform. He had been killed a few weeks later, in some futile attack. The father she had never known, but had been able to believe in because there was this photograph to show that he had been real.

Megan returned to her bedroom and slowly sipped her chocolate drink, huddling on the rug before the fire. Once more her thoughts travelled back to Bunty, and how good it was to be in touch with her again and, through her, in touch with what Megan always thought of as the St Hildegard's gang. Happy days! And in the evening she used to return home to this same old flat, and sit in this same bedroom by this same gas fire and work on her Pitman's shorthand shun hooks and grammalogues, while her mother cooked the supper. Happy days that would never come again.

Then: 'Time for bed, or I'll never get up in the morning!' She wound up and set her alarm clock for a quarter to seven, turned off the gas fire, kneeled beside her bed to say her prayers, stood up and, still wearing her dressing gown over her pyjamas (the only way to ensure remaining warm during the night), she jumped into bed, switched out the bedside light and curled herself into a ball with the covers drawn up over her head, and fell asleep.

IX

Christmas drew near. Megan telephoned Bunty. 'What are you doing on Christmas Eve?'

'On the buses until six. After which I shall find myself rather at a loose end, because my parents are going away for Christmas, to be with my grandmother; which, after all, is only fair to her. What will you be doing?'

'I shall be on duty at Rainbow Corner. We're expecting record crowds, and it's a case of all hands on deck. If you'd like it, I think I can wangle permission for you to come along. We shall need some nice young English lasses for the GIs to cut a rug with. Dancing, carols, and I've no doubt a spot of supper can be managed for you. I know you don't much care for Yanks, but it'll be better than spending the evening alone, won't it?'

'It's most awfully sweet of you to think of it, Megan,' said Bunty gratefully. In spite of her choice of independent lifestyle, she had been rather dreading the thought of Christmas Eve without her family. The old Flopper, though not family, was at least a face from the past, and a cheerful face at that.

'I'll be on duty there at seven; you'll find me at the information desk. Wear something reasonably glam if you've got it.'

'Last thing I'll wear is my clippie uniform. Don't want to be asked the way to Madam Two Swords and West Minister Abbey all evening!'

There were several clubs for the GIs in London, of which the two most popular had hitherto been the Eagle Club in Charing Cross Road and the Milestone Club in Kensington, but Rainbow Corner, which in December 1942 was still in its experimental stage, having only just opened, had already become the favourite GI rendezvous. Londoners knew it as the old Café Monico, which had been destroyed in the Blitz. The building had been restored, its new decor

83

of Stars and Stripes red, white and blue giving it, both outside and in, a lively appearance (except at night, when the blackout camouflaged it as effectively as any other London night spot, so that finding it for the first time was only helped by the numbers of Americans you suddenly started colliding with in the dark).

Its aim was to provide a café-style social club with lounges, games room, writing-room, library, an International Room accommodating three hundred couples for dancing, programmes of daily entertainments, doughnut and coffee counters, even a 'home-town' barber shop. Cheery hostesses, impeccably sisterly in their approach, added to the 'just like home' atmosphere, a microcosm of what the boys had left behind, created for them in the very heart of London.

Above the information desk was a huge and arresting arrow pointing west with the accompanying sign: 'New York – 3271 miles.' Megan usually did her stints at the information desk from six in the evening till ten, after which she would have a coffee and a snack and gossip about this and that with some of the other Red Cross girls before returning home.

'But what do you *do*, exactly? I mean, d'you just stand there joshing them and chatting them up?' enquired Bunty who, having fought her way through a swarm of GIs into the club, had discovered Megan at the information desk in animated banter with a group of young, very young, chaps who were obviously having the time of their lives. They had now drifted away, and Bunty had seized the lull to make her presence known to Megan.

'Well, chatting them up is part of the job,' said Megan, 'making them feel at home directly they come in. But I fix them up with every kind of information and help, from a bed for the night to an organized taxi tour of the sights of London with a guaranteed cockney cabbie. Or, if they want it, they can have an introduction to a British family, or I can fix them tickets for a show, or guided walks round Richmond Park or Kew or Kensington Gardens, or any place they fancy. And they receive advice reminding them that London has its seamy side and is full of pickpockets and con men just waiting for the Yanks. You can't complain there's no variety in this job.'

A GI, looking slightly furtive, came nervously up to the desk and leaning towards Megan asked her something in a low voice. She replied in the same discreet tone, obviously directing him somewhere. He went off. Bunty said: 'What did he want?'

'Should be confidential but, seeing that you're genuinely interested in what we're doing here, he said a friend had told him there's a comfort station here and he wanted to know if that were so and, if so, where to find it.'

'A comfort station being the same as a restroom, I suppose. Why can't they call things by their real names?'

'No, no,' said Megan, in her usual matter-of-fact manner, 'a comfort station is another name for a Blue Cross, or prophylactic, station. We have one of them on the premises, too. "Cater for every need and eventuality", that's the motto here.'

'Just as well, seeing this place is on the very doorstep of Piccadilly,' said Bunty. 'Your Lost Boys, I reckon, are going to need more Blue Cross than Red Cross before they're through.'

At this point a tall beaming blonde in ARC uniform appeared. 'Here's my friend Katie McCann,' said Megan. 'She's going to show you round the place and fix you up with a dancing partner.'

Bunty and Katie were introduced. 'Hi,' said Katie, with a polite little duck of the head, cocked on one side. 'Hi,' said Bunty.

'See you later, girls,' said Megan. 'Have yourselves a good time.'

'Sure thing, kid,' responded Katie; then, turning to Bunty: 'Like to see round this joint before we fix you a beau?'

'Love to,' replied Bunty. And off she went with Katie, while Megan dealt with a GI who was trying to trace two buddies.

Katie and Bunty inspected the library (almost empty this night), the games room, and lounges where the GIs and girls sat chatting.

'These all hostesses?' asked Bunty.

'Oh, no, honey,' responded Katie firmly, 'in our ARC clubs there's no sitting down with a GI if you're a hostess; intimacy of that sort just isn't allowed. We're very strict that there must be total respect for the hostesses. Only time a hostess can sit with a GI,' she added with a twinkle, 'is if she's helping him with a letter. You'd be amazed, or perhaps you wouldn't, how many boys suddenly need help when it comes to spelling.'

The place glowed with light, warmth, Christmas decorations, and vibrated with voices and laughter. From somewhere in the basement came the sound of a big swinging band; an inimitable American sound.

'We'll have a coffee and then go get you a partner,' said Katie. 'D'you jive?'

'Not really. I've never had a decent chance. It's banned in most of our dance halls, and certainly in all the dinner-dance places.'

'It's not banned here,' laughed Katie. 'You'll soon learn,' she added.

They drank coffee and dunked a doughnut each. Bunty said: 'You certainly organize a good time for them here.'

'That's what they're in London for, a good time. It's the greatest place to spend a leave. The boys can enjoy a real good fling in London.' Katie gazed round happily, the gratified maternal look in her eye that Bunty had seen in Megan's.

'A bit like the ball before the battle of Waterloo?' ventured Bunty.

Katie looked puzzled. 'Come again?'

'Never mind,' rejoined Bunty. 'They're having a good time, full stop.'

'Having the time of their lives. Like they say, a last real good fling before they go back home and settle down.'

Bunty dunked the remaining piece of her doughnut. Too soggy, it sank, disintegrating, to the bottom of her cup.

'Let's go get you a jiving lesson,' said Katie, jumping up. They went downstairs together to the International Room, already thronged with couples jiving to the big-band sound. 'There's a nice boy for you,' said Katie, making for a sandy-headed youth who was standing alone watching the jivers with a slightly lost look on his face. Katie dived at him. 'Hi, soldier, what's your name?'

'Chuck,' he said, a shade apprehensively.

'Hi, Chuck. Meet Bunty. She wants to learn to jive. Teach her?'

Chuck's eyes gave Bunty a quick going-over. He brightened. 'Sure thing,' he said.

'See you later,' smiled Katie and vanished, leaving Bunty to be led on to the dance floor.

A naturally good dancer with an instinctive response to rhythm, Bunty was soon swaying, twirling, stomping and generally abandoning herself to the admonishments and urgings of Chuck. 'Attababy!' 'Give, babe, give!' 'Come again, girlie!' 'Hoddog!' He chewed gum throughout, for which she could not but admire him; it took some skill. When they stopped at last, because the music had stopped, she asked him: 'How'm I doing?'

'Swell,' he said proudly. 'Just swell.' He took out a packet of gum. 'Try some?'

'I'm afraid I'd swallow it the wrong way and choke, jiving like that.'

'Come *on*, kid.' He drawled out the word 'on' in an encouraging tone. 'If it goes the wrong way, I'll turn you upside down and shake you.'

'OK. In for a penny, in for a pound, I guess.' Bunty popped the piece of gum (stuff which in point of fact she loathed) into her mouth and began to chew.

'You're a sport, kid,' he said. 'C'mon, let's go.' The band's sound blasted the air again; they resumed their jiving.

Presently the music changed; Artie Shaw's 'Stardust'. Chuck wrapped Bunty in his arms, drawing her close to him and pressing his cheek against hers. They revolved, shuffling their feet, glued to the same spot; their chewing jaws moving up and down in amiable harmony. 'Dancing on a dime,' said Chuck, giving her a squeeze of immense approval. 'Sure is nice.' He sighed and closed his eyes. Bunty, noticing that almost all the other couples had their eyes shut, too, closed hers. She wondered what David would say to all this, and then told herself dismally that it really didn't matter a damn what he would have said because he simply wasn't around any more to say anything. When 'Stardust' ended they jived again, and then again.

At last, in a lull, Chuck said: 'How's about a Coke?'

'Lovely,' said Bunty.

Leading her by the hand, he took her to a soft-drinks counter and bought them each a Coke, which they drank straight from the bottle. 'Let's go sit on those stairs and cool off,' suggested Chuck. 'This may be a cold country but, boy, it's plenty hot in there!'

They sat on the stairs, and he put his arm round her shoulders and gave her another appreciative squeeze. 'Gee, you're the nicest thing that's happened to me for a long, long time. Where'd'ja come from?'

'Hampstead. Where d'you come from?'

'Rexburg, Idaho. Been there?'

''fraid not. I've never been to the States.'

'No kidding?' He sounded surprised. 'Well, there's always a first time. Tell you what, I'll take you back there with me. How's about that?' He squeezed her again.

'Now you're turning desperate,' said Bunty, laughing.

He burst out laughing too. 'That's nice,' he said with real appreciation. 'I like that. I like a dame who's a wisecracker. Say, d'you live far from here? Live alone?'

Bunty had been wondering for some time how an evening like this ended. Chewing the eternal gum, he looked at her with blue, ingenuously hopeful eyes; his healthy freckled face touchingly fresh and boyish. 'I live in a flat in North London,' said Bunty.

'You have a flat?' Optimism shone from his every feature. 'Where's the address?'

At this juncture they were abruptly joined by two more GIs, gum-chewing like Chuck, and of about the same age. 'Hi, bud,' said one with curly dark hair and a wicked eye, 'let's meet the dame.'

'She don't want to meet you,' said Chuck. 'She's happy with me. Ain'tcha, babe?' giving Bunty another squeeze.

'Aw, c'mon, fella, you can't keep everything that's good,' said the other GI, who was on the stout side, with an agreeably languid, easy manner. 'Introdooce us.'

Bunty leaned forward with one of her great smiles. 'I'm Bunty.'

'Bunty, hey? Pleased to meet you. I'm Greg.' He extended a large fleshy hand. Bunty shook it firmly.

'Woody,' said the other GI, offering his hand promptly, not to be outdone. 'Glad to know you, Woody,' said Bunty.

These introductions over, Greg and Woody seated themselves on the stairs, too. Chuck said: 'Hey, you leave me and Bunty alone, see? She's just telling me about her flat. She don't want nobody else to know about her flat, ain't that so, Bunty?'

'Flat?' Woody's eyes lit up. 'Say, here's a dame with a flat! What's say you forget this dumbo here' (giving Chuck a friendly push aside) 'and take me back to your flat, eh?'

'She don't want you in her flat,' drawled Greg. 'Don't want you mussing her or her place up. I can see she's particular. Thass why she's giving me those great big gooey looks; she knows I have a way with dames you boys just can't match.'

Bunty started laughing. She had felt, the moment they had joined Chuck and herself on the stairs, that they should be encouraged; there was safety in numbers. Chuck, for his part, however, was clearly none too delighted by this development, and in a way she felt sympathy for him.

He had been convinced he was doing fine until these interlopers came along.

'C'mon, honey, let's get back on that floor,' said Chuck.

Bunty said: 'I think I shall have to be getting back to Kenilworth Lodge. I've a busy weekend ahead of me.'

'Kenny who?' asked Woody.

'That your boyfriend?' From Greg.

'You have a boyfriend waiting for you back home?' asked Chuck mournfully.

'You heard her,' said Woody, much amused at Chuck's obvious disappointment. 'Kenny Lodge, she said.'

'Kenny Lodge,' repeated Bunty, nodding her head up and down.

'Wearing a ring,' observed Greg, eyeing Bunty's wedding ring.

'Yeah,' said Woody reflectively. 'She's married. Kenny Lodge your husband, huh? You Mrs Lodge?'

'I'm not married,' said Bunty. 'Not any more.'

'Divorced? Thaddit?' Woody was intrigued.

'Who's this Kenny Lodge, then?' asked Chuck, beginning to look a little baffled.

Bunty now scented the way ahead. Assuming her best Gertie Lawrence manner (not practised by her for some time, but still at her fingertips when she needed it), she gurgled: 'Expect me to tell?'

'Wow,' said Greg admiringly. 'This dame's hot.'

'Sure is,' said Woody, impressed.

'So you got Kenny with you tonight, huh?' pursued Greg.

Bunty nodded, giving an arch drive-you-mad smile.

'How's about tomorrow night?' enquired Chuck. He was obviously the dogged type.

'I said I'd got a busy weekend,' responded Bunty sweetly.

'Kenny staying for Christmas?' ventured Woody.

'Can't tell. Won't tell,' teased Bunty.

Greg gave a low long whistle under his breath. 'Tell ya, guys, this dame's sump'n.'

'Not Kenny?' Woody's eyes glistened. 'Some other guy?'

'I really can't possibly tell you boys things like that!' cooed Bunty.

'Who's the night after?' asked Chuck, half in despair and half fascinated.

'You mean Boxing Day?'

'Have him there with you all day, too?' breathed Woody.

'This is a different guy,' said Greg.

'I said I have a very busy weekend,' murmured Bunty.

'Ma'am,' said Woody in accents of the profoundest respect, 'I guess you're real experienced.'

Bunty shrugged lightly. 'Yes, you might say that.'

'Gee,' said Chuck. 'And I been dancing with you all evening!' His face glowed with pride.

'What you doin' here at Rainbow Corner, then?' enquired Greg courteously.

'I was invited along to dance with you boys, and was lucky enough to be introduced to Chuck,' replied Bunty, rising to her feet. They rose, too. Bunty, knowing she held them in the palm of her hand, smiled on them with gracious condescension. 'It's been so lovely meeting you all, it really has.' She turned to Chuck. She felt sorry for him; he really was a sweetie, she thought, a nice nice boy. She leaned towards him, smiling into his eyes. 'Chuck, it's been one of the nicest evenings ever, it really has. You dance on a dime like a dream.'

'You'll be here again, ma'am?' he managed to stammer, gazing at her.

'Who knows? Watch out for me, won't you?'

'Sure,' gasped Chuck.

Greg said: 'Sure thing!'

'Walk you home?' said Woody. 'Just to take care of you for Kenny?'

'I'm afraid I'll need to have a taxi,' said Bunty. 'It's late. I really mustn't keep Kenny waiting.'

'A dame with real class,' sighed Greg.

'Sure puts on the style,' agreed Woody.

'Tell us your phone number?' pleaded Chuck.

'You'll find me under the name of Sanders,' said Bunty. 'Now, if you boys could put me into a taxi ...'

'Sure thing. Right away.' They all rushed upstairs, each determined to be the one who put her into the taxi. Bunty floated up after them. Megan, at the information desk, surrounded by GIs, managed to call to her: 'Going home?'

'Think I'd better, m'dear. I have a very busy weekend.' Bunty maintained her Gertie Lawrence voice. 'I've had a wonderful time,' she added. 'I'll give you a ring. Have a merry Christmas.' She was going to say more, but at that instant Chuck, Woody and Greg burst upon her. 'Taxi's waiting, ma'am! You're on your way!' Megan stared in frank amazement as the three bore Bunty like royalty out of the Rainbow Club. A taxi was drawn up outside; Woody opened the door and held it wide for her. 'Hampstead,' she told the driver. 'High Street, and then I'll direct you again.'

She paused before she finally got in and turned to her escort. 'Good-night, boys, and thank you again for the lovely lovely time.'

'Pleasure, ma'am,' chorused Woody and Greg.

Chuck gave her a kind of nervous pat on the arm that turned accidentally into a stroke on the bottom as she climbed inside the cab. 'Watch out for you, babe,' he said wistfully.

'You do that thing, dear Chuck. And have a happy happy Christmas and the best of New Years!'

The cab drew away. Bunty fell back in her seat. 'Whew!'

The cabbie said: 'That used to be the old Monico, didn't it?'

'Yes,' said Bunty. 'It's for the GIs now. Real Christmas celebrations there tonight.'

'They're a long way from home.'

'They are.'

'Had four of them in my cab the other day. Said London beats Denver, Colorado. Said they'd never known anything like this before. Different from what they're used to.'

'I bet it is,' said Bunty.

Megan watched the three GIs who had escorted Bunty to her taxi now re-enter the club, deep in conversation. As they passed her desk Megan heard the podgy one of the group say: 'Listen, fellas, forget her. She'd cost too much. She's high class.'

'Wonder how much a dame like her . . .' said the little dark one.

'Aw, shucks, how'd I know? This is London, England, an' she's top bracket. Back home in Wilmington they just don't come like that. You don't even *see* them, buster. They ain't there to see.'

'She sure was sump'n,' sighed the sandy-headed boy.

'Sure was!' agreed his pals in unison.

Heavens, said Megan to herself, as they drifted from view. Whatever did dear old Bunty . . . ?

The crowds in the entrance hall were thinning out; it was getting on for midnight, and everyone who could squeeze into the dance hall below had squeezed themselves into it. Soon the dancing would stop and the carols begin. Rainbow Corner always remained open all night; no GI need ever feel himself a waif or stray in London. Megan had offered to stay on duty till midnight on this occasion, giving the girl who should have been at the desk a chance to jive. As she listened to the distant sound of the band swinging its way through the last number a very young and slightly drunk GI approached her desk and asked plaintively: 'Where's the trees and lights?'

'There's a tree over there, look,' replied Megan, pointing to a gaily lit tree in a corner of the entrance hall. 'And there are more downstairs where any minute now they'll start singing carols. Like to go down and join in?'

He repeated in his same disconsolate tone: 'Where's the trees and lights? Crummy, this burg is, real crummy! Back home where I come from, we light the whole goddam town up at Christmas; trees with lights all the way down the main street, and candles in all the windows. That's what I call Christmas!'

'We can't do that here, in wartime, with the blackout. Light up London, and we'd have a load of bombs on us in no time! You're in the front line here; the ETO, remember? Why not go downstairs and join in the carols? Just about to start.'

'I don't want no limey carols. I don't want no crummy limey Christmas!'

At this juncture the carols began; the strains of 'Silent Night' sung by many voices, at first softly, then growing in volume, rising from the gathering below. Megan felt her heart turn over. As for the young GI, he crumpled against the information desk, buried his head in his arms and burst out crying like a child, gasping between his sobs: 'I don't want no crummy limey Christmas! I wanna be back home!'

Megan, overcome by sudden compassion and forgetting all the rules about hostesses never becoming familiar with the soldiers, flung her arms round him and hugged him wordlessly, tears running down her own cheeks. Meantime a late flurry of fresh GIs poured in from the street, eager to get to the carol service. They hurried past Megan's desk, smiling genially in her direction without really taking her in, chorusing their greetings: 'Merry Christmas, girlie! Merry Christmas, babe! Merry Christmas!'

Part Two

UNEXPLORED
TERRITORIES

X

Darling Violetta,

You can't imagine what these Yanks are like! They're beyond belief! They're loud-mouthed, bumptious, hideously rude, think they own the world and, to cap it all, sex mad. In short, they're bloody awful.

Your mother does her best to keep reminding us females, when we complain, that they're our allies. Some allies, I say! They've requisitioned my home, bulldozed it to the ground, and now expect me to spend my evenings in a wretched canteen serving them buns and coffee, and into the bargain pester me to give them a free roll in the bushes afterwards!

No use telling these pestering louts that you're not that sort of girl, either. All they say is 'Aw! Don't act the starchy limey. Let your hair down, babe!' Actually, I wouldn't call our generation a starchy one, would you? We've grown up to think of our parents as starchy, but not us; educated on D. H. Lawrence and Freud, and reading Hemingway and Aldington, not to mention good old Lady Chatterley (in French, of course, because of being banned in England, though freely available in Paris. Remember you smuggled her in concealed in a magazine devoted to knitting patterns?).

And if there'd been no war, and Ivo hadn't vanished into the clutches of the Germans, the betting is that I wouldn't have kept my girlish virginity intact for so long! But this doesn't mean that the prize is going to go to any random gum-chewing Yank.

Titus Swann says it's because they're young chaps who have escaped from home and Mom to the other side of the Atlantic, and are determined to make the most of it. (They're always talking about Mom; Mom seems to be a power in the land in the US.) Jeffrey Bosco says armies of occupation always behave like this and we women should have expected it. But who ever expected the Americans to see themselves, over here, as an army of occupation? However, to judge by their behaviour, that's how they see it.

Bunty says it's just as bad in London; she's been driven round the bend by them. Or was, till she got the hang of them. She says once you get to know them you discover they're green as hell; just trying to show off. Though she does add that, green as they may be when they arrive, they're all keen to make up for lost time. Well, one thing I do know: they're not going to make up their lost time with me!

I suppose that in the ATS, whatever else you have to put up with, you're not bothered by Yanks! *And* you're spared having to pull your weight (as your good mother calls it) in a blooming canteen and social club serving coffee to our so-called American cousins!

Which is where I have to trundle off to now.

All luv

Lorna

PS. Sorry to have been rather rude about your mother in this letter. I've had a bit much of the wretched canteen lately, and it's cheesed me off.

The airfield and camp on Fursey Down had been built and, though the Flying Fortresses and their crews had not yet arrived, the place was already bursting at the seams with what the Americans called 'filler personnel': a service squadron with headquarters, ordnance and quartermaster companies; specialist detachments of all kinds such as were demanded by a self-sufficient airfield and heavy bomber station. Some of the men were housed at the camp in Quonset huts, the American equivalent of British Nissen huts. The rest were billeted all over the surrounding countryside as well as in Fursey-Winwold village.

The Red Cross ladies, led by Daphne Stacks, had done as they had promised and had organized a canteen and social club, in the village hall, on behalf of the Americans. However, it had quickly become clear that this was not the kind of off-duty activity the young men really wanted.

Daphne found herself interminably discussing the problem with the agitated members of her Red Cross committee. 'We *must* see if we can find more to occupy their free time when they're off duty.'

'If that's the way they behave when they come off duty, it would be better if they never came off duty!' rasped Miss Barker. 'They're all healthy young men; they shouldn't need all that time off duty.'

'That's why they behave as they do, because they're all healthy young men,' replied Daphne wearily.

'Of course,' said Miss Glaister, ever anxious to pour oil on troubled waters, 'we mustn't make wholesale generalizations about them. Many of the ones turning out couldn't be nicer. That nice Steve billeted with old Mrs Lamb helps her with all her heavy household chores, and Daisy Ewles has that wonderfully helpful Sergeant Dawson, and the Rollinsons can't speak too highly of their—'

'Yes,' cut in Miss Barker, 'we know all that, but far too many of them are anything but house-trained. Just live to be out on the tiles.'

'We mustn't forget they're men,' said Miss Cusk.

'That sums it up,' said Miss Barker.

'We mustn't lose sight of the fact that they're our allies and have arrived here in our great hour of need, and the last thing we want is to sound carping and ungrateful,' said Daphne.

'Oh, I think we all agree to that,' rejoined Miss Glaister. 'But, that said, I do think a word in the ear of one of the officers in charge at the camp . . .'

'Hear, hear,' said Miss Barker. 'I think this committee must ask you to do that, Daphne.'

'Very well,' sighed Daphne. 'When the right opportunity occurs, I will.'

Lorna genuinely detested her stints in the village canteen and had fought hard not to participate in this service for the Yanks she hated so profoundly, but Daphne had overridden her. So Lorna, making no attempt to conceal either her resentment or her dislike of Americans, took her place, twice a week, behind the canteen counter.

Walking home afterwards through the village, in the dark, always found the Red Cross ladies on the alert for importuning Yanks. 'In the blackout they can't tell your age, so years are no protection,' as Miss Barker commented. Lorna, the one genuinely youthful member of the Red Cross team, had the company of Miss Cusk and Good Egg Glaister for part of the way, but the last lap of her route had to be made on her own. She marched along with a brisk and aggressive stride, chin up, arms swinging: she liked to think that, though, in the dark, it was impossible for any predatory Yank to *see* her virago's silhouette, he would at least *sense* it. 'Get the message I'm not what he's looking for!'

But the message didn't always get across. One evening, as she was striding up the lane leading to The Warren, she was appalled to hear heavy masculine footsteps crunching along behind her. She quickened her pace; the heavy tread, too, quickened. She was undoubtedly being followed. His stride was longer than hers; he must soon overtake her. Remembering her father's military maxim, 'Attack is the best means of defence', she rallied her courage and, turning upon her shadowy pursuer, asked in a loud and intimidating tone: 'Young man, do you behave like this at home?'

A bellow of familiar laughter informed her that she had made a hideous mistake. 'Yes, young lady, I do,' boomed the Bosco baritone. 'Prowl up and down here every night, I do, waiting for nice little things like you to fall upon.'

'Oh, all right, Jeffrey; very funny and all that,' retorted Lorna testily, thankful that the darkness was hiding her blushes of chagrin. This would be all round the village in no time. Too good a joke for Jeffrey not to repeat; how she'd mistaken him for a rapacious Yank!

'Actually,' said Lorna icily, as he, still laughing, caught her up and fell into step, 'though it may strike you as very funny that the women of this village are pestered out of their lives every time they put a nose out of doors, we women ourselves are fed up to the back teeth with it. It's an affront to us all, and we greatly resent it.'

'I can understand that.' Jeffrey, anxious now to mollify her, changed his tone. 'The village resounds with shock-horror stories which, even if only half of 'em are true, reflect pretty badly on the sons of Uncle Sam. But, that said,' he added, 'I don't know why all you ladies are so surprised by what is going on. Surely you must realize that these sort of things are bound to happen when hundreds of young men are dumped in a rural area in the back of beyond, with no thought whatever given to providing an outlet for . . . er . . . their natural high spirits and inclinations.'

'So you condone their behaviour, do you?'

'I'm not condoning anything; simply saying that I fail to see why you're all so amazed by it. Since time immemorial armies of occupation have behaved in the way these chaps are behaving – and far worse. If this country had been occupied by foreign soldiery more often, instead of not having had a taste of it since William the

Conqueror, the women would have known better what to expect, and you wouldn't all be inviting trouble by walking around by yourselves as though it was peacetime.'

'But, Jeffrey!' Lorna's indignation was mounting to explosion point. 'The Americans aren't supposed to be an army of occupation! They've come here as our allies.'

'You're absolutely right. But they're young chaps, separated from their wives and sweethearts, herded in camps in a foreign country, in what they call a theatre of war: they see it in a way very different from how you see it, I assure you. Foreign women are foreign women, even if they're on the Allied side; and the way a young chap posted overseas behaves with a girl on foreign soil is quite different from how he behaves with a girl of his own nationality on home ground.'

Lorna drew a long weary sigh. 'I understand what you're saying, Jeffrey. But that doesn't alter the fact that it's pretty poor behaviour on their part; there are supposed to be close links between their country and ours.'

'Growing closer every minute, too, from all one hears!' burst out Jeffrey, laughing again.

Lorna gave an impatient snort. 'You can't be serious about anything for long, can you?' she exclaimed.

'Perfectly serious, I assure you. It's a very real problem, for all the parties concerned.'

She tried to peer up into his face to see how genuinely serious he looked, but it was too dark for her to see his features properly.

They had reached the gateway to his drive; he stopped by it, so did she. 'But look here, when all is said and done, Lorna' – and he truly did sound serious now – 'if you take my advice you'll avoid walking about by yourself at night. I'm sure most of them are perfectly decent young chaps, making allowances for the circumstances they find themselves in, but there's bound to be a few bad hats among them, can't expect otherwise. I always exercise the dog this hour of night, and it'll be no trouble at all to meet you when you come out of that canteen of yours and see you home.'

'That's awfully kind of you, Jeffrey.' Lorna was caught between two stools; she welcomed the offer of a male escort on canteen nights, but she wasn't certain she wanted the regular company of Jeffrey.

'No trouble, I assure you,' he responded heartily. 'As I say, I always take the dog out at this hour, so collecting you into the bargain and walking you home with the dog will be nothing to me. In fact the dog's probably more trouble than you are; I don't suppose you keep bunking off after random smells.'

'Hardly, Jeffrey.' She thought to herself, not for the first time, that his attempts at humour, though they probably went down well with local farmers and the blacksmith, were distinctly lacking in the finesse preferred by less earthy society.

'Well, let me know which nights you're on duty with the coffee urn, and I'll be there to pick you up afterwards.'

Thereafter Miss Cusk, Miss Glaister and Lorna, when they emerged into the night, following their stints in the canteen, found themselves being met by Jeffrey and his dog. 'I must say it's a comfort,' observed Miss Cusk. 'And must be especially so for you, Lorna dear, on that last lonely part of your walk. Men are so useful in some ways, and such a nuisance in others!'

However, the American presence was far from being disapproved of by every female in Fursey-Winwold; many of the village girls, deprived of British male company by the war, positively fell upon the Americans. Here was manna in the desert! The less inhibited lasses found themselves having the time of their lives.

Lorna thought it advisable to warn Ruth Cuthman about the perils of going out with the Yanks. It was true that Ruth was not, so far at least, interested in the opposite sex and had confided that she thought boys a silly nuisance, but Yanks might well strike her as a more glamorous and attractive species than the local lads.

'The Americans may seem fun to go out with, Ruth, but the truth is many of them haven't the first idea of how to behave decently with girls and young women, and you put yourself at great risk if you start mixing with them.' Lorna added, remembering that the girl was barely sixteen, 'You do know what I mean, don't you?'

'Oh, yes, Miss Lorna, you hear all sorts of tales of what goes on.'

'There you are, then. You don't want to find yourself mixed up in anything like that. Dreadful things can happen to a girl once she starts to run wild. So give those American boys a wide berth. If they ask you out, say no. It may seem you're missing good times, but take it from me, it's better to be safe than sorry.'

Ruth, solemn-faced, nodded her head.

'And it's not just a matter of going out with them; you should be on your guard when you're walking by yourself. If you can, always have the dogs with you.'

Ruth once more nodded earnestly. 'You'll not forget what I've told you, will you, Ruth?' said Lorna, anxious to drive home her good advice.

'Oh, no, Miss Lorna,' replied Ruth, lowering her eyelashes and raising them again in emphasis. 'I'm sure you're right; I'll keep well away from them. And I'll not go walking alone, I promise that.'

Lorna repeated, 'You can always take the dogs, you know; they are always ready for a walk.'

Most of the male inhabitants of Fursey-Winwold also entertained strong reservations about the Americans. Dicky Stacks was among these, and he didn't hesitate to voice his annoyance when, on strolling into the dining room for lunch one day, he found the table laid for three.

'Hello. Someone coming for lunch?'

'Yes, Captain Cabrini. Remember him?' Daphne replied in her

brightest tone. She guessed only too well what Dicky would have to say to this one. And, sure enough, he said it without hesitation.

'Cabrini coming to lunch? Whatever for? I thought we'd seen the last of him!'

'No, he's back on Fursey Down. Getting the American Red Cross aeroclub there off the ground. And as our Red Cross is going to be involved in it, too, I'm afraid Fursey-Winwold will be seeing quite a lot of Cabrini.'

'How d'you get an aeroclub off the ground when you can't even put your planes up?' grinned Dicky. Adding, as he lit his pipe: 'What is an aeroclub anyway?'

'Well, as you've probably already gathered, the ARC is very hot on clubs for the boys. They grade them in star categories. Some, the largest, like the big clubs they've opened in London, are designed to cater for men on leave. They're in the three-star category. In the two-star category are about a hundred or so "aeroclubs" catering for the larger of their airfields, one of which is Fursey Down; so, Fursey Down is getting an aeroclub.'

'And what does that mean in terms of human misery?'

'Games room, library, lounge, snack bar . . . It's all on a pretty lavish, sizeable scale, as you'd expect with the Yanks. It's to be run by a director – that's Cabrini of course – and two full-time American Red Cross girls, who haven't shown up yet, with British help. Which of course means us; me, the Good Egg, Miss Cusk, Miss Barker, poor Lorna and the rest.'

'Shan't be seeing much of you, then. Even less than I do already.'

'There's a war on.' Daphne sounded cheerful about it; she was enjoying being head of the local British Red Cross.

Wheels crunched in the drive; a jeep drew up at the front door. Daphne, glancing out of the window, said: 'Speak of angels. Here he is.'

'Damn the fellow.'

Captain Cabrini smelt strongly of Vapex, which he kept sniffing lugubriously from a large white handkerchief. He obviously had a shocking cold in the head. He shook hands glumly, saying unconvincingly: 'Sure good to be back.'

Daphne installed him by the fire while Dicky went to find one of his few remaining bottles of cognac. Daphne, seeing him returning with it, had a brief exchange with him in the hall. 'We're not giving Cabrini that?'

'Have to.'

'Why? Isn't there any of my home-made apple beer left?'

'I need a restorative and, by the looks of him, Cabrini needs one, too.'

'At this hour of the day, Dicky?'

'Call it a *digestif* like the French do. You're entitled to a *digestif* any hour of the day. *Digestif*, Cabrini? Loosen up that catarrh of yours. Knock those little germs on the head, eh?'

'Sounds a mighty good idea,' said Captain Cabrini. 'I've plenty of 'em to knock.'

'You'll have one, Daphne? Prevent you picking up anything from Cabrini.'

'Super,' said Daphne.

Dicky poured the cognacs. Daphne, raising her glass, said brightly: 'Here's to the Fursey Down aeroclub!'

They each took a mouthful of cognac. Cabrini said: 'We'll be lucky to get a Doughnut Dugout, the rate we're going.'

'What on earth's a Doughnut Dugout?' enquired Dicky.

'Kinda tacky little fox-hole joints we fix for the GIs in way-out areas. Requisitioned garbage cans, old shoeboxes, disused cabin trunks, derelict freight crates. That kinda thing. Most anything goes, as long as you can squeeze a carton of doughnuts, a hostess, a flask of hot coffee and a coupla GIs into it.'

'I'm glad about the hostess,' said Dicky. 'What is known as the gracious touch.'

'Watch it, buster,' said Cabrini. 'Our ARC hostesses ain't there to be touched, nohow.'

'Bit difficult not to touch her, under those circumstances, surely,' said Dicky.

'There's touching and touching, mister. You gotta learn the difference,' said Cabrini. 'It's an art.'

'D'you have many of these Dugout Doughnuts?' asked Daphne brightly.

'Doughnut Dugouts, lady. A dugout doughnut's different. Has a hole in the middle,' responded the Captain. He added: 'Cabrini's a smart guy. He notices things.'

'More cognac, Captain? You can feel that catarrh loosening up?'

'Can begin to feel like the cement's giving way a mite,' said Cabrini. 'Mind you, not without a struggle. It kinda fancies itself settled in for the winter.'

'Many Doughnut Dugouts round here?' asked Dicky as he replenished the glasses. 'As my wife was trying to ask.'

'Nope. It's too civilized here. Tell you where we put them, out in places like that terrible fen country. Real God-forsaken. Mind you, we have Clubmobiles, too. They're those Green Line coaches of yours. Tell me you requisitioned them in the Blitz as emergency ambulances. Now they've been made over to us. Tour the more remote camps that don't have canteens of their own.'

'They have hostesses?'

'They have three. Coming up for the Ritz class, the Clubmobile. Three hostesses, clubroom complete with newspapers; and they're none of your English newspapers, neither, they're good American newspapers with strip cartoons, and you'd be hard put to find anything boring as news in them. Nothing's too good for the American GI. Plus he gets coffee and sinkers. What more's a guy want?'

'Plus three untouchable hostesses,' said Daphne.

'That's right. All the works.'

'What's a sinker?' asked Dicky.

'Doughnut,' said Daphne promptly. 'Even I know that by now.'

'See, she's learning,' said Captain Cabrini.

'Beats me how you squeeze all that into a Green Line bus,' said Dicky.

'And there's bunks for the hostesses,' said Cabrini. 'Three bunks. One apiece.'

'Three no-touch bunks,' said Dicky.

'Anybody trying to infringe the Hays morality code in one of those bunks would be caught *in flagrante delicto*, wedged in position,' said the Captain. 'But that kinda rabbit hutch thing isn't for Fursey Down. For Fursey Down it's the real McCoy; one of the best aeroclubs ever. Which is why I'm calling on you good folks this morning. Have to talk turkey with Mrs Stacks about manning the canteen when we open up.'

'Any idea when that will be?' enquired Daphne.

'Things are going pretty slowly. I've gotten kinda sceptical about dates. I reckon Fursey won't be operational now before March, but we want the aeroclub ready as soon as possible; there's no aircrews yet, but there's plenty of other guys there at the airbase who sure could use a social club right on hand instead of having to shift all the way to this village when they want to relax.'

The cognac had had a mellowing effect by this time, resultantly lunch turned out to be quite an enjoyable little social occasion; starting with soup and followed by something Daphne called a risotto, and concluding with a dessert of stewed apples and junket. They discussed plans for the aeroclub, which of course led to the problems of dealing with such large numbers of young men dumped down in the remote English countryside without the restraints of family or home town. 'They're bound to kick over the traces a bit,' said Dicky. 'In a place where nobody knows him, a young chap feels free to behave in a way he'd never dream of behaving at home.'

'That's so,' said Captain Cabrini.

'It may be understandable,' said Daphne, 'but we women are becoming pretty fed up with being pestered the way some of your chaps pester us, I must confess. I know it's said that troops always go on the rampage a bit when they get away from home, but' (here was her chance to register the complaint her committee members had asked to have made) 'there's supposed to be a cousinly relationship between the States and us, and one honestly doesn't expect to have one's cousins in full cry after one . . . er . . .'

'Trying to yank one's knickers off,' said Dicky, adding: 'Sorry about the pun. Unintended.'

He avoided Daphne's eyes.

'Trouble is,' said the Captain, 'official policy is that all our guys should be encouraged to fraternize with the British; bring the two sides closer together, you know? That's nice. But there's fraternization and fraternization, closeness and closeness, and nobody ever figured that the close close clinch would catch on so fast.' He fiddled about with his junket. 'Fact is, between ourselves, what's going on is becoming a kind of embarrassment to us.'

'But you must have anticipated something of this sort,' said Dicky. 'It's always a major problem with troops stationed overseas.'

'You British with your experience recognize that. But we've not shipped large numbers of troops overseas like this before. We did in the last war, but that was under rather different circumstances; they had a lotta fighting to do when they reached France. Here, there isn't any combat, not yet anyways. It's a new situation for Uncle Sam to handle.'

'Uncle Sam, if you'll forgive me saying so, was a bit of a chump not to see this one coming up,' said Dicky.

'What do people at home think about it?' asked Daphne. 'American mothers can't be too happy about the kind of reputations their sons are getting themselves over here.'

'The folks back home?' Captain Cabrini sounded genuinely astonished. 'Doggonnit, they don't know a thing of what's going on and nor will they. The mothers and sisters back home will be the last to hear about it; their sons and sweethearts won't write home about it, that's for sure, and nobody else is going to tell them, that's for sure, too. It's not the picture the American public wants of its boys. We American's didn't want none of this war in the first place, but now we're in it, no fault of our own, and these boys have come over to fight this war on the side of democracy and that is what they're seen as; not a lotta young guys making the most of a break from clean living and all that tedious Sunday-school stuff they were raised on, but crusaders for democracy. That is what the GI is in the eyes of the folk back home, a clean-living crusader for democracy. You won't shake that one.'

'Well,' said Daphne. 'There's nothing to say, then, is there?'

'They're not all that bad, Mrs Stacks,' said Cabrini.

'No, of course they're not. There are some absolute ducks among them,' said Daphne courteously.

'And, if you'll forgive me mentioning it, ma'am, it does take two. And Uncle Sam hasn't provided the girls.'

'Sometimes one rather thinks he should've done,' said Daphne. 'Not so many doughnuts, perhaps, and rather more . . .'

'Dugouts,' said Dicky. 'Sorry,' he said quickly.

Daphne, casting him a cold look, turned to Captain Cabrini. 'I hope I haven't offended you, Captain Cabrini, by raising this matter of the behaviour of some of your boys. But it's causing a good deal of concern in the village; have to keep an eye on our daughters, you know. And I suppose, in a way, it is a concern, too, of the Red Cross.'

'It will promote things that will be very much the concern of the Red Cross, I guess.' He had risen to leave. Lunch was finished.

'One way and another the Red Cross is going to be kept pretty busy,' said Daphne. 'Your Red Cross and ours.'

'I guess,' repeated Captain Cabrini.

'As long as we work together, Captain Cabrini.'

He smiled and held out his hand. 'My name's Buzz.'

'Call me Daphne.'

As he drove away in the jeep Daphne and Dicky waved from their porch. 'A decent chap when once you get to know him,' said Dicky.

'They mostly are, I guess,' rejoined Daphne.

She reported to her Red Cross committee that she had registered, on their behalf, a complaint about certain aspects of American behaviour. She also informed her ladies that the village canteen and social club would be closing and they would henceforth be expected to assist, as voluntary staff, at the Fursey Down aeroclub.

Lorna had decided that, Daphne or no Daphne, she would draw the line at this one. 'Mrs Stacks' – Lorna always addressed Daphne in this formal style when crossing swords with her – 'I cannot go to Fursey Down. I'm adamant about that.'

Daphne assumed a cold expression. 'And why can't you go to Fursey Down?'

'I'm surprised you have to ask me.' Lorna sounded reproachful. 'It's my old home, remember?'

'Oh, Lorna, you're not still nursing grievances?' Daphne assumed a light manner, as she often did when approaching a heavy subject. 'Let's try to forget the past, and concentrate on the present, shall we?'

'Mrs Stacks, I know all that. But I intend never setting eye or foot on Fursey Down again, as long as I live. That's my vow, and

I'm sticking to it. Wild horses will not drag me to Fursey Down,' concluded Lorna with dramatic intensity. 'I mean that, Mrs Stacks.'

Daphne shrugged. 'How schoolgirlish!'

Lorna, sensing that further conversation would lead nowhere, murmured, 'Goodbye, Mrs Stacks,' and hurried off home.

A long buff envelope marked 'On His Majesty's Service' and 'Ministry of Labour' was awaiting Lorna when she arrived indoors. With a sudden stab of apprehension she opened the envelope; it contained a printed official notification that her exemption from directed labour, within the category of Household Release, was to come under review, and she must report to her local labour exchange. In other words, the powers that be were going to have another try at conscripting her.

She told nobody about the forthcoming interview. When the day arrived she took the local bus into the market town where the employment exchange was located, and duly presented herself in the reception room. The official who interviewed her was a bespectacled little woman with a surprisingly sympathetic manner. Lorna explained her domestic predicament. 'My father really needs me. It would be frightfully difficult for us both if I were called up and sent away from home.'

Last time it had been accepted that she had legitimate household ties. This time the ties weren't sufficiently cogent to save her from conscription; her country's need was greater than her father's.

None the less her interviewer showed consideration for Lorna's position: Lorna, asked to describe her duties in caring for her father, had given a full account of how she spent her time, and in order to show that she was not a slacker or work-shy she had also mentioned that in her spare time, having once trained as a secretary, she typed and did secretarial work for Dicky Stacks. Her interviewer observed that, rather than that Lorna should go into the ATS as a cook, or into a munitions factory (the two main choices open to her), she should opt for the remaining choice, which was to be a secretarial worker in the American Red Cross. 'It would really be a happy decision for you personally, Miss Washbourne, as it would enable you to continue living at home, since the request for a woman of your age group to fill this post comes from the airbase at Fursey Down, which probably you will have heard of. Under all the circumstances, I think you should be directed into this job.' She gave a smile which said: 'You see, even in wartime officialdom can show it has a human face.' Aloud she said: 'I hope you will find this a happy decision for you.'

She rose; the interview was over. Lorna, more than half-stunned, found herself in the street, standing in the rain, staring at the passers-by without seeing them, and saying to herself: Dear God, I've been conscripted into a job working for the Yanks on Fursey Down.

Wild horses wouldn't drag her to Fursey Down? What a splendid phrase that had been! But wild horses weren't needed; a mild little woman in specs, with a sympathetic manner, had done the trick.

XI

Darling Bunts,

Well, here I am. I've been conscripted at last, and guess where? To Fursey Down; to work with the bloody Yanks – American Red Cross, secretarial. The same choice as the Flopper had – munitions, spud-bashing in the ATS, or secretary in the ARC. The choice facing all our age group at the present time, it seems.

Some would say thank God for St Hildegard's; it's saved us from the work bench and/or the potato bucket. In my case, I'm inclined to think *anything* would have been preferable to this! In fact I was on the point of opting for munitions (in spite of all the fearsome warnings given me by Violetta), when the labour exchange official who interviewed me gave me my marching orders for Fursey Down, under the impression, obviously, that she was giving me the Ritz treatment. So here I am. No fate could have been worse, as far as I'm concerned. I *cannot think* of anything I would have wished for *less*.

In order to work here (not, mind you, that I wanted to, as I think I need hardly say), they checked into my family background, past history, education, religion, politics, etc., etc., as if I were being chosen as a possible bride for a future king of England. No unsuitable types are allowed within the conclaves of Uncle Sam. Mustn't besmirch the morals of their men by letting them within arm's length of possibly undesirable females (Ha ha! Pause for sardonic laughter). Don't want to imperil young American males – hope you're hysterical with laughter by now! Anyway, I passed the Hays morality code inspection and here I am: wearing an ARC uniform which (I hate to say it, but I have to) is well cut and fits, unlike British uniforms for Other Ranks, and stockings which are quite the nicest I've worn for three years. Ditto underwear.

I may now go to a PX store and buy all the things that poor old you can't get for love or money, because you're only a crummy Britisher and therefore a second-class citizen on the world scene.

And I can eat all their FOOD – eat and eat and eat, till it's coming out of my ears. No rationing for the Yanks! What they eat at home they eat right here, and to hell with there being a war on. Hamburgers, Boston cream pie, beans, tinned peaches (can you remember when you last *saw* tinned peaches?), oranges (remember those things called oranges, Bunts?), proper sausages (not those things stuffed with sawdust that the British are reduced to eating); chicken Maryland, pies, lasagne, steaks; fudge cake, strawberry shortcake, cherry pie; cookies, muffins; peanut butter, maple syrup, doughnuts; I could continue for pages more. All they really lack is fresh eggs; which, of course, they can't fetch over from the States like they do the rest of the stuff.

The remarkable thing is they've no moral compunction about guzzling their heads off while the rest of us over here are pretty near starvation. Their excuse is that they tried feeding the American personnel, on first arrival, with the same food as their British counterparts ate, but it quickly undermined American morale and efficiency.

They simply won't understand that the need for stringent food rationing in Britain is because we're an island and everything has to come to us by sea, and we're short of shipping room in a merchant fleet which is under constant attack from hordes of U-boats. The convoys can't bring more than they can bring; and lots of other things besides goodies to eat are needed over here to fight this war. That's why we exist on such lean rations; and do it, moreover, without grumbling. I tried to explain to an ARC girl that complaining about wartime food was considered contemptible, and think of all the merchant seamen who lose their lives bringing us what food we have got! But what's the use of talking to that lot? So precious shipping space is devoted to bringing to Americans in Britain the food to which they are accustomed, without which, they say, poor creatures, they couldn't function. Meanwhile *our* rations are further cut.

Luckily few British, except those of us working with the Yanks, have any notion of how they're feeding while the rest of us tighten our belts till we're blue in the face. If more people did know, I reckon there would be a riot! And if you could see the food that's wasted! I reckon enough is thrown away in one week, here on Fursey Down, to provide the equivalent of a month's rations for the entire Fursey-Winwold village.

Well, no use beefing. That's how it is. I try to eat as little as possible of their food when I'm down here, as a point of honour. If the vast majority of my fellow countrymen can't guzzle like this, why should I?

Captain Cabrini (remember him?) is director of the aeroclub and has two American Red Cross girls as assistants. Daphne Stacks's lot provide voluntary helpers; they take turns coming in the evenings. Daphne was frightfully put out when I came to work here secretarial full-time; she seemed to see it as unpatriotic. However, she hadn't a leg to stand on, because I'd been directed into it as part of the war effort! She complained I'd left her short of voluntary canteen help; so now I stay on in the evening twice a week and give a hand in the aeroclub canteen.

Actually I'm the only girl in the Red Cross section of the admin office, and I'm not so much a secretary as a shorthand typist. Fortunately Miss Binkle turned us all out hot stuff at shorthand; and I've always enjoyed it. So that part of it is all right. But the fact is that things here are pretty poorly run, and general morale low; chiefly because the CO is so useless – doesn't like the British, doesn't like the country, doesn't like the climate, doesn't like me. Fortunately I don't have a great deal to do with him. Perhaps I needn't say that our feelings of dislike are mutual.

Perhaps things will improve when the Fortresses arrive. Understandably, everyone is horribly frustrated because there are no bombers here and nothing is happening. They genuinely believe that when these B-17s (proper way of referring to the Forts) get on the job the war will be over in no time. They even say that there won't be any need for ground forces to invade Europe at all; a few weeks, or at the most months, of bombing from the Forts, and the Germans will crumble.

Well, as my old father is fond of saying, 'Never underestimate the Germans.'

I can't recognize Fursey Down. Hardstands, hangers, runways, buildings, Quonsets, and surrounding it all acres upon acres of mud; reminding you of pictures of the Western Front in the last war. The aeroclub is built right on the spot where our house used to be. No further comment necessary.

Darling Bunts, all for now – you'll say it's enough! Write soon.

> All love
> Lorna

PS. In all fairness I have to say that everyone at Fursey Down is much nicer to me than I'd expected. But, that said, they're a rum lot. They think the same about us, of course.

XII

The Flying Fortresses flew in to Fursey Down one drizzly late afternoon towards the end of March; hidden by cloud until the moments of final descent. Their thunder announced them; at first a distant yet solid bank of sound, gradually but steadily growing closer and increasing in volume until it filled the universe with a deep-throated, heavily thudding roar that at last was right overhead, threatening to split heaven and earth.

An immense rumbling shook the air as everyone raced out towards the hardstands, raising their eyes to the vibrating sky as they ran, but seeing only the low ceiling of cloud which met the mist creeping over the twilit downland. Then the runway lights were switched on and through the cloud came the bombers; four squadrons, twelve aircraft to each squadron. The planes put their lights on, and one by one they peeled off, turned in and touched down, to taxi on to the hardstands; monster craft, with guns jutting out from every part of their long bodies.

As the first crews emerged from the leading planes, ten men to each crew, the solid crowd of onlookers fragmented into individual figures running, cheering, waving their welcome. There was backslapping and a din of shouts and noisy laughter; the crews, clumsily lumpy in their layers of flight clothing and burdened with gear, moved slowly through the enthusiastic throngs towards the airfield buildings.

When, later, the crews appeared in the aeroclub they seemed very young. Good Egg Glaister, who was on duty, remarked upon their youth to Buzz Cabrini, who said: 'Average age nineteen; same as your boys in the RAF.'

The Good Egg sighed heavily. 'It's shockingly young, though, when you come to think about it.'

'It's the prime age for aircrews,' replied Cabrini. 'Old enough to know machines and how to fly them and get the best from them; young enough to have trigger-quick reactions, and not to appreciate the full implications of what you're ordered to do.'

'It's dreadfully young to be ordered to die,' said Miss Cusk, who had lost a brother of that age in the last war, the baby of her family.

'At nineteen you're never gonna die,' responded Cabrini.

Miss Cusk thought of her brother Eddie. Eddie had never been going to die.

The newcomers were noticeably conscious that they were aircrew, fighting men; strutting and swaggering round in their leather flight jackets and talking incessantly of their Forts – 'the big-assed birds' as they called them. The women serving in the canteen were obliged to be captive audiences to the preening young males, who never tired of telling the ladies of the British Red Cross that the Forts and their crews had come to win the war, something that the British hadn't been able to pull off even after three years.

Serving the coffee and Cokes, the American muffins, the doughnuts and peanut butter sandwiches and candy bars, the Red Cross contingent from Fursey-Winwold were regaled with accounts not only of the Fort's now famed ability to bomb and hit a pickle barrel from twenty thousand feet, but also of the barrage of overlapping fire which came from its bristling heavy machine guns. The standard combat box formation of eighteen Flying Forts produced a mass of interlocking fire from a hundred and sixty-two guns all told. How's about that? Forts had proved in battle, over the past months, that they could fight their way to a target and fight their way back, unescorted and irrespective of how much damage they might receive in the process. 'Boy, those heavy babies sure can take it!' And did they shoot down the Kraut fighters? They surely did.

Dicky Stacks, to whom Daphne recounted these glowing details of Fort invincibility, grinned derisively. 'Your little lot have certainly been reading their own newspapers! The American public,

I fear, has been fed a rather inflated picture of Eighth Air Force successes.'

'Our little lot are still so green I doubt if any of them have yet met a real live German fighter,' said Daphne.

The newly arrived aircrews were indeed very green, but there was no way in which they could be anything else; they had come straight from their training schools in the United States. They had come over anticipating that they would get stuck in straight away, bombing German targets and shooting down Luftwaffe fighters. Visions of heroics could be read in their ingenuous eyes. They had, as Dicky Stacks said, been reading their own newspapers. The truth was that few German targets had as yet been bombed by the Forts, and the air battles were yet to come.

There was barely any flying for the new arrivals, let alone heroics. The weather of what was an exceptionally cold, wet spring kept their planes grounded, day after day.

'Not that they'd've been flying over Germany; they wouldn't,' said Buzz Cabrini, as he sat with Lorna and the two American Red Cross girls, Amy May and Angie, behind the counter of the aeroclub coffee bar, with a riot of young chaps horsing around, creating a non-stop din.

Angie Rockwell, strawberry blonde and slightly the senior of the two girls, came from Long Island. Amy May Lockett, a pretty, wide-eyed brunette, hailed from Baton Rouge. She spoke in a Southern drawl, delightful to the English ear. They made a strong contrast to one another, though Lorna couldn't have put her finger on exactly how the contrast revealed itself. But one thing the pair were in agreement about, and that was behaviour of the aircrews.

Terrifyingly high spirits were the hallmark of these new crews; they appeared on the point of bursting with energy and the urge for action. Buzz, in his thirties and, comparatively speaking, an old man, eyed them with resignation. Like everyone else on the staff, he was finding them exhausting.

'At this stage,' resumed Buzz, 'they should still be training on milk runs; short missions over targets near the French coast, that kinda thing. And the Luftwaffe fighters don't waste their time patrolling over those soft targets; no, sir, they're waiting way back, waiting for the real ball game to start.'

'Soon be summer now,' said Angie hopefully. 'Then the boys can fly every day.'

'No guarantee it won't rain even though it's summer,' said Lorna.

'Oh, no!' wailed Angie. 'D'you mean summer weather will be no finer than this, Lorna? Cold and raining every day in summer?'

'Probably,' said Lorna. 'Usually is, most of the time.'

'But, gee,' gasped Amy May, 'what are you saying? When *are* the boys gonna be able to fly? Right now they're grounded day after day; if so happens they are able to become airborne, all set to fly on a mission, they're called back to base because of worsening visibility, and the mission's cancelled. They're becoming kinda badly frustrated, not to mention over-vibrative, with all this nervous tension of starting out and then aborting. That's why they all act so noisy and hyperactive.' Amy May, before joining the ARC, had done a course in behavioural psychology and was still strongly under its influence.

'If they don't get their milk runs, they're gonna find the going tough when they're sent on rugged missions they're not ready for,' said Buzz contemplatively. 'Horsing around like this may take some of the sass out of 'em, not to mention their night performances, but horsing by day and chasing chicks at night ain't gonna prepare them for those bomb runs, and that's the truth.' He helped himself to another doughnut and dunked it, then slooshed it into his mouth. Lorna wished he wouldn't; but there it was.

'They reckon they've had their combat training,' said Angie. 'Next, they say, it's the real thing.'

'Since when have they had combat training?' asked Buzz contemptuously. 'They've played combat games. When they begin to meet the Luftwaffe and the gunners open their guns on live Krauts, that'll be combat training.'

'Well, let us hope those skies up there clear,' said Amy May. 'Else those B-17s will just have flown over here to sit on those hard-stands.'

'Who am I to talk about combat training anyways?' said Buzz, moving away from the counter. 'I'm just a sinkers-and-sociability expert myself; guy who fiddles while Rome burns. See you girls later.' And he moved off to quench a tornado of high spirits raising the roof in the library, a so-called 'silent room'.

'Any time now,' said Angie, glancing at her watch, 'we'll be having a quiet spell. Those boys will be getting on their bikes and setting off for town.'

'And heaven help those little girls they find there,' said Amy May.

'Amen to that,' said Lorna, meaning it.

Angie had been right about a spell of quiet; pretty soon the would-be terrors of the skies were, in spite of banks of drizzling rain, whizzing away into the dusk, a bevy of reckless cyclists. The sound of their laughter and bicycle bells faded into the distance. The nightly ritual of chick-chasing was on.

Fursey Down was strictly a man's world, and the Red Cross girls had become used to the feeling of being there very much in a secondary role: dispensers of coffee, sinkers and sympathy. The new arrivals, having made the customary attempt to lay the Red Cross girls (that, after all, was what girls were primarily intended for, wasn't it?) and having met with no success, turned to local talent, leaving the Red Cross girls to become part of the aeroclub fixtures and fittings; in other words, the girls weren't there, and masculine talk flowed merrily on, irrespective of the female listeners. Lorna, in this way, learned some remarkable things which greatly advanced her education. One nugget of enlightenment was the reason why the packs of young predators spinning off on their bikes always took with them their raincoats, fair weather or foul. It transpired, from man's talk in the coffee bar, that British girls had a habit of copulating standing up, fully clothed, which meant that if the man wore a raincoat it acted as a kind of camouflage for what was going on.

This preference for the upright clothed performance was largely due to the fact that most quick clandestine sex was an outdoor activity and, the British climate being what it was, the ground was usually too muddy to lie on, while the low temperature of the air did not encourage reckless exposure of bare flesh. Also, British girls preferred 'wall jobs' because they believed they couldn't get pregnant that way.

'Well, best face it: war and sex always have gone together,' said Buzz philosophically. 'Some folk even now don't believe that; still clinging to the notion like it's sinkers the boys want, not sex. Right here, we're testing that one pretty thoroughly, and I reckon we're entitled to say, with confidence, that sex rates way ahead of sinkers with the all-American boy every time.'

Lorna, serving coffees and sinkers in the evenings and listening to the talk of the crews, was obliged to think to herself that sex seemed way ahead with the all-British girl as well.

'There's this chick keeps saying *no* all the time, so I say, "What about *yes* for a change, huh?" and she says, "Yes, what?" so I say, "Yes, please," and she says, "OK if you'd said 'please' in the first place you'da got it much sooner."'

'I made her on what I thought was a kinda window-sill. Can you imagine when a train went underneath us and I found it was the parapet of a doggone railway bridge? But the chick, she knew it all the time; said: "I think the trains add that extra kick." Jeez, I nearly kicked it myself when that train went under!'

'The English countryside, setting of bards and backwaters,

surely reels under the impact of Uncle Sam,' said Buzz, when Lorna repeated this anecdote to him.

'If you ask me, the reeling isn't all one-sided,' retorted Lorna.

'I guess we'll grow used to one another in the end. Only needs the war to go on long enough,' said Buzz; adding gloomily: 'And, if this darn weather doesn't let up to give us a chance to get our missions flown, it looks as if the Hundred Years War of the history books is gonna seem short in comparison with this one!'

Morning after morning found Fursey Down enshrouded in banks of cloud (Lorna much amused the Americans by calling it 'Scotch mist'). Whatever it was called, it ensured that the Forts would be grounded for yet another day. They stood on the hardstands, guns thrusting; huge frustrated birds of prey, seemingly peering impatiently into the mist which inhibited their flight. Designed specifically for killing, and imbued with the cruel dignity of professional killers, they were each incongruously bedizened with a jaunty nude, executed in bright pink paint, flaunting her charms in a wanton sprawl across the bomber's fuselage.

It was the prerogative of the pilot to name his bomber; the nudes made explicit the name of the aircraft. You could, sighed Lorna, see only too well the direction in which the minds of these young men forever seemed to turn. *Dyna Might, Daisy May, Blonde Bomb Shirl, Piccadilly Warrior, Pregnant Pearl, Nice 'n' Teazy, Sight Seein' Suzy, Risin' High, Available Vee, Big Doll, Target for Tonight, Flak Floosie, It's All Yours, Star Stripper, Hell's Belle, Shoot-up,* each name accompanied by a gorgeous girl, generally stark naked, though not always so: *Nice 'n' Teazy* sported a set of minute frilly briefs and bra, and *Hell's Belle's* otherwise nude charms appeared to be bursting from out of a graduation-ball gown. *Star Stripper* was removing a flimsy bra which, when gone, would leave her totally bare.

The girls were nothing if not explicit. *Dyna Might* didn't leave much doubt that she would; *Daisy May* had such grossly over-inflated breasts that she looked like some kind of pink rubber dinghy with double spinnakers. *Pregnant Pearl* had a balloon coming from her mouth saying RIGHT ON TARGET! and a stick of five bombs showering from her, so to speak, undercarriage. *Target for Tonight*, like *Available Vee*, left little, if anything, to the imagination. *Sight Seein' Suzy* had her sights most visibly on display. So had *Miss Cami Nix*. Indeed, *Miss Cami Nix* struck Lorna as so extraordinarily wanton that she stood staring at her for several minutes, wondering whatever the Germans would make of an enemy who painted his bombers in such an astonishing fashion. Then, averting her almost hypnotized gaze from *Miss Cami Nix*, Lorna hastened towards the aeroclub.

Buzz Cabrini greeted her with: 'You've made Armament-Sergeant Matlak a happy man, Miss Washbourne. Seeing you stood out there admiring his works of art. *Miss Cami Nix* is his latest masterpiece and boy, is he proud of her! He devotes all his spare time to surpassing himself painting those dames.'

'A pity he hasn't something better to do with his spare time!' retorted Lorna acidly.

'Jeez! Heaven protect me from you starchy English broads!' rejoined Buzz.

Lorna thought to herself that learning to get on with the Yanks was a case of one step forward and two steps back.

In addition to the nudes on the fuselages, some crews had the ladies painted on the backs of their leather flight jackets into the bargain. The effect achieved was nothing short of extraordinary; particularly in the case of the crews of a craft whose pilot favoured excessive mamillary endowment in the female form. It really seemed that the more the crews became disgruntled by the wretched weather, the lack of opportunities to fly, the aborted missions, and the general atmosphere of frustration which increasingly gripped

Fursey Down, the more grotesquely adorned with billowing pink flesh did the flight jackets become.

'I suppose,' wrote Lorna to Violetta, 'in the RAF they must have the same urges – for girls, I mean – but, thank God, our lot don't go round daubed with paint like Indians on the warpath. The way the crews swagger about, with naked females plastered all over them, is utterly grotesque. I've asked Amy May, our behavioural psychologist (amateur, but keen), why they do it, and she says: "All young men need to play peacock. It's a form of courtship display!" Well, if that's courting, I'll opt to remain single!'

Violetta wrote back: 'The British male is bad enough (have you ever been barked at full in the face by a drill sergeant half-insane with his inflated ego?) without having to pile on the agony by studying the habits of the Yanks. I avoid Yanks like the plague, as a matter of principle. Still, if the proper study of womankind *is* Man, you'll be able to major, as they say, in the all-American male.'

One Saturday evening Lorna was quietly at home, about to drink after-dinner coffee with her father. Mrs Cuthman had popped round to the parish church to polish the brass, and Ruth had gone to the cinema with a girlfriend. Lorna was just on the point of pouring the coffee when there came a knock on the door. Wondering who it might be, she went to open the door; she could discern two dimly outlined figures on the doorstep. A Yank youth's voice asked: 'Say, are you the girl we've been told about at the camp?'

'The girl you've been told about at the camp?' repeated Lorna. 'Which girl would that be?'

'A girl the fellas told us about,' said the voice of the second youth.

'I'm Lorna Washbourne and I'm American Red Cross at Fursey Down camp, which is where I suppose you come from,' responded Lorna briskly. 'But as for a girl you've been told about at the camp . . . ' She was genuinely puzzled. 'Who would have told you about me, and why?'

Indications of embarrassment came from the doorstep. The first youth said: 'Just a girl they told us about at the camp. I guess we've got the wrong address.'

The second voice added: 'Sorry to have troubled you, Miss Washbourne.'

'You don't know the girl's name?'

'No. We just heard about her, and thought we'd call.' The first young man, trying to make it sound casual.

'Just thought we'd call in for a coffee, or sump'n,' said the second.

Lorna, thinking of dispelling the starchy image, said: 'Why not come in and have a cup of coffee with me? My father and I were just about to have one. Do join us. He'd like to meet you. He's always pleased to meet young chaps in the services.' To herself she thought wryly: 'Well, if they're that keen on paying calls, now they can pay a call on us.'

Lorna sensed that the pair weren't crazy on the idea of accepting her invitation, but didn't know how to refuse it. She led them into the big panelled living room. Looking at them, now they were in the lighted house, she recognized their faces, though she didn't know their names. They were both sergeants. The smaller of the two, who seemed to be the spokesman, was a study in quick lively movements. Curly dark hair protruded in a mop from under his cap, which he wore cocked at a jaunty angle; he had an engagingly ugly face, with a flattened nose and one eye slightly higher than the other, suggesting that at one time he had had a bad accident of some sort. When he grinned, which he did frequently, he revealed a gap in his upper row of teeth.

The second, who was better-looking and probably, back home, considerably less naturally raffish than his companion, affected a sardonic jaded manner, as if he had been several times round prior to his present sojourn on this weary planet, and knew it all backwards. They were neither of them far into their twenties.

They followed Lorna into the room, looking round them with frank curiosity. Lorna said to them: 'I know your faces well, but I don't know your names.'

'Vic Wendell,' said the smaller one.

'Lance Vogel,' said the other.

Lorna, smiling her best hostess smile, announced: 'Daddy, here are two boys from the camp on Fursey Down who have come to call on us. Isn't that nice?' She introduced the visitors, respectively, saying to them: 'This is my father, General Washbourne.'

They both looked more than startled.

The General said: 'Forgive me not getting up. Chair-ridden, you see.' He shook hands with them, looking at them with eyes that had not lost their keen power of penetration.

The visitors, of perfectly normal appearance as they made a frontal approach, quickly revealed, as they rather awkwardly accepted chairs and sat down, that on their backs, in the neighbourhood of their shoulder blades, they both sported an enormous pair of painted female breasts with startling vermilion nipples. Above the breasts simpered a rather squashed-looking face (there had not been much room left by the artist for a face) surrounded by a profusion of yellow hair. Below the breasts there was an indication of legs.

It had always taken a great deal to shake General Washbourne throughout the course of his long and active life, and even now, when well past his best, he remained admirably imperturbable in the face of all surprises. 'Well, well,' he said, 'and now what do you two young chaps do? Tell me about yourselves.'

Lorna, for her part, had recognized the double spinnaker bosoms sported by each sergeant as unmistakably the hallmarks of *Daisy May*.

Over their coffee and some of Mrs Cuthman's home-baked fat-less ginger biscuits which Lorna found for them, that they might have something to dunk, Vic and Lance talked, first rather restrainedly and then perfectly freely, about themselves and *Daisy May*. It was unfortunate that *Daisy May* had not yet enjoyed much of an action-packed life, but the two boys managed to create a pretty good idea of what she might have done had she been given the chance; and themselves, too. Lance, one of *Daisy May*'s waist-gunners, and Vic, her ball-turret gunner, didn't conceal their disgruntlement that, so far, they hadn't been able to bring the war to the rapid conclusion that they confidently anticipated once they and their group truly went into action.

'It's the weather that's against us,' said Vic. 'You limeys must be great survivors, to live with all this rain.'

'In the past,' said the General, 'we've always rather thought the climate was on our side.'

'Not on ours,' said Lance.

'If you're a gunner,' said Vic, 'you want to use those guns; not see them getting rusted up.'

'Apart from being frustrated gunners – and there can't be a much worse fate than that – are you enjoying being over here?'

'No, sir, not much,' replied Vic, dunking a ginger biscuit and shaking his head glumly. 'Country's too small; you feel fenced in. And there's too much mud and too many people stuck in it: I reckon that's your trouble over here, too many people stuck in the goddam mud.'

'No room to spread yourselves,' said Lance. 'No room to loosen up.'

'You need more space,' said Vic. 'Back in the States we've got space. That's why we've got a lift on you all. More space.'

'Well,' said the General, concealing his amusement, 'we've been here a long time now, and I think it's rather like when you've lived a long time in one house; you cease noticing the disadvantages and settle in, and there you are – nothing would induce you to leave the place.'

'Unless you're booted out,' rejoined Lorna bitterly.

'Well then, of course, you have to move on,' said her father. 'That's life.'

'This is a nice place you've got here,' said Vic. 'Been here long?'

'Not very,' said General Washbourne. 'No time at all in fact.'

'It's good to move around,' said Lance. 'Keeps you flexed up.'

'Never grow too attached to a billet,' said the General. 'Always be prepared to move on if you have to.'

Lorna wished that she had his philosophical disposition. She knew that he hated The Warren and missed Weldon Court almost as much as she did, if not equally so. It was simply that he had lived longer, she thought, and had learned to be more resigned about things than she could ever manage to be; and to have more forgivingness in his nature.

The guests decided that they must go. 'Have to get back to camp.'

Lorna said: 'I'm sorry you never found that girl you were looking for, but maybe when you get back to camp you'll find someone who can give you the right address.'

'I guess,' said Vic. 'But it's been a pleasure, even if it's been the wrong girl.'

'Swell evening,' said Lance. 'Swell talking to real British.'

'You must have met others of the species,' said the General.

'Yeah, that's so; we have. But not the kind you talk to much when you're with them,' rejoined Vic with a grin.

The pair then shook hands courteously, said their thanks over again, and departed, presenting, as they walked to the door, the extended charms of *Daisy May*.

When they had gone the General said: 'If they parachute down and land on their faces in enemy territory, the good old Hun is going to be a bit flummoxed as to what sex the Yanks are using for bomber crews.'

Lorna said, laughing: 'They're crew members of *Daisy May*. That was *Daisy May* painted on them.'

'*Dead Cert Daisy* would be a better name,' said her father. 'Still, they seemed pleasant enough young chaps; and it was nice of them to call. Friends of yours?'

'Not specially.'

'I couldn't imagine they were quite your type. Still, friendly enough young fellows. Nice meeting them. Nice to meet one's allies occasionally.'

'Americans are very friendly people,' said Lorna, wondering which girl in the village they had really intended to visit.

XIII

In early April, Lorna heard from Violetta that she was shortly getting a weekend pass and proposed spending it in London. Violetta now had her commission and was a 2nd Subaltern. Since passing out of Officer Cadet Training Unit her letters had become few and far between; she made the excuse that she was frantically busy. 'Oh, for the good old days of being in the ranks! Compared with the life I live today, there was nothing to do.' But now she was to have a whole weekend at liberty. 'I've been in touch with Bunty, and she says she will be happy to put you up for two or three nights, so do try to do that thing, Lorna love! It would be wizard if we could have an evening together, you, Bunty and me. I could make the Friday evening. The rest of the weekend would be out as far as I'm concerned. I'll be tied up with a *heavy date* (DON'T TELL MA!), but I'm sure you'll have a lot of fun the rest of the weekend with Bunty; you can ride on her bus!'

Bunty soon backed this up with a letter of her own. 'Do try to make it, Lorna. It really would be too super for words.'

Lorna was shortly due for some leave. She enquired rather nervously whether she might take it at this juncture and was told that she might, so far as the office was concerned; Colonel Hatton would be away at a conference. It was with Buzz that the decision lay.

Buzz, when asked, said: 'Sure thing. Take a weekend away. It's just a matter of fixing a stand-in for Saturday night with one of the other girls.' He referred to all the canteen helpers as 'girls', even Miss Barker. 'All hell's gonna break loose here when the new CO comes; at least, it should. There's a lotta things need putting right. So take time off while we're still on Easy Street.'

'Are we getting a new CO?' exclaimed Lorna, unable to conceal her delight at the news. She was finding her sessions with the present man increasingly trying; his dour dislike of her and of all things British tested her patience to the limits. 'All that you people over here are serious about is tea and muffins.' If she had to hear that many times more she'd scream in his face.

'Should be here any time now,' replied Buzz. 'Don't know who he will be as yet – Security plays things tight to its chest these days – but one thing I do know and that's like I just said: he'll be a busy guy when he does arrive, trying to get this joint and these crews right.'

Lorna pedalled home with a light heart that evening. A few days in London with the St Hildegard's lot was a prospect guaranteed to raise her spirits.

She found Ruth at the big kitchen table cutting out a summer frock from some red and green cotton material. 'That's pretty stuff you have there, Ruth.'

'Yes, Miss Lorna, isn't it? It used to be curtains. I was telling Miss

Cusk I was going to Ipswich to look for material for a summer frock, and she said, 'Oh, you don't want to spend coupons when you don't need to; I've what might be the very thing,' and she fetched me out these curtains. She wouldn't take anything for them, either.' Ruth's slow Suffolk voice drew out the words with quiet satisfaction.

'That was very kind of her.'

'A kind body is Miss Cusk; no doubt of that.'

Lorna watched Ruth carefully cut round the paper pattern pieces pinned on the material. The girl's normally rosy cheeks were suffused even redder by bending so intently over the table.

'What I'm looking for,' resumed Ruth conversationally, this tricky piece of cutting accomplished, 'is a red handbag to match. I need a new bag ever so, and I've been saving up for one, and now thanks to Miss Cusk I don't have to spend money on stuff for a dress, so I can afford a really nice bag. But I've been all over the place looking, and I can't find a red one anywhere, not even in the Ipswich shops.'

'I'll keep an eye open for one when I go up to London,' promised Lorna.

'Oh, Miss Lorna, if you would!'

Lorna began making nightcaps with a big packet of drinking chocolate Angie had given her. 'Here you are, Ruth, a special treat tonight, by courtesy of the Yanks,' she said, handing Ruth a mug of chocolate. 'Coo!' exclaimed Ruth, receiving the mug eagerly. 'What did you do to earn that?' she added, with one of her merry, teasing smiles.

'Do?' Lorna's eyebrows rose slightly. 'Why, what should I do for it? One of my friends at the aeroclub gave it to me, out of pure kindness of heart.'

Ruth sipped the chocolate. Then, 'Well,' she said, laughing, 'whatever you did, it was worth it.'

Lorna always found Ruth's laughter infectious, so she broke out laughing herself; yet at the same time she couldn't repress the slightly uneasy thought that her dear innocent little Ruth was sounding just a mite disconcertingly worldly wise. Lorna's laughter gave way to an anxious, 'I do hope, Ruth, that you haven't forgotten what I said about American boys . . .'

'Oh, don't fret about me!' retorted Ruth, still merry. 'I never have anything to do with 'em.'

'They're probably perfectly decent young fellows back home with their own families, but once they're over here, and chick-chasing as they call it, they throw decent behaviour to the winds.'

It was Ruth's turn to assume the tone and manner of an experienced senior gently addressing an ingenue. 'Don't you fret, Miss Lorna,' she repeated, with solicitude. 'I know all about how those Yanks behave; heard all about it. Shocking tales you get told by those that know them. But take my word, me and my friends steer well clear of them.' Then she changed the subject and began scanning the instructions for the dress pattern she was cutting. 'It's a good thing Miss Cusk gave me such nice wide curtains; this skirt looks like it's cut on the bias.'

'She thinks I'm a fussy old hen,' Lorna thought, wryly. 'I should remember she's growing up and can take care of herself.' Yes, little Ruth, when the chick-chasers arrived on the scene, was the sort who could be relied upon wisely to make herself scarce.

Lorna poured three more mugs of chocolate and carried them into the study where her father and Jeffrey Bosco were deep in discussion of whether or not the Western Allies should open an immediate second front to relieve the hard-pressed Russians. Jeffrey, now that Lorna no longer needed escorting home of an evening from the village canteen, had developed the habit of dropping in of an evening, two or three nights a week, to chat with General Washbourne; Lorna was obliged to admit that these neighbourly visits had a markedly cheering effect on her father. Jeffrey had a reputation for an astonishing repertoire of funny stories; he was also prepared to listen, apparently with genuine interest, to the General's lengthy discourses on how the war was being bungled by Top Brass.

The two men broke off their conversation when Lorna entered with the mugs of chocolate. 'My word,' said Jeffrey, 'that smells delicious.'

'This,' said Lorna, handing round the chocolate as if bestowing some priceless substance, 'is a perk from Fursey Down.'

'Very good too,' said the General appreciatively.

'I'm always in two minds about accepting things that the rest of the population can't get for love or money,' sighed Lorna. 'Still, it is so very nice, and makes such a lovely change from Mrs Cuthman's rose-hip tea.'

'Anything'd be ambrosia after that!' Then Jeffrey remembered his manners and pulled himself together. 'Well, it's awfully good of you to spare me some of your rose-hip tea when I drop in . . .'

The General said, kindly relieving the guest of his embarrassment, 'Shocking stuff, that rose-hip muck. One of the things I shall eternally hold against Hitler.'

Jeffrey, happily restored to his customary buoyancy, exclaimed, 'It's plain daft, Lorna, to be squeamish about accepting things the Yanks offer you. However much you make your disapproval obvious, they're not going to tighten up their eating habits in line with the rest of us because you turn down a packet of drinking chocolate.' Lorna stared at him over the brim of her mug; as so often when she contemplated Jeffrey, her expression was dubious. He continued, 'I tell you, we've now reached a stage in this war when it's just plain dumb not to take the chance to eat any extra grub that's going.' Lorna closed her eyes for a second and gave a slight shudder. 'Take me, for example.' Jeffrey became increasingly expansive. 'It's no secret that these old farmers, tucked away in the back of beyond, don't pay too strict an attention to rationing: eggs, bacon, sausages galore, the odd chicken, even the odd leg of mutton. Sheep falls down dead, or a pig, for no good reason; well, you'd be bonkers not to eat it, wouldn't you? So, between you and me, I feed pretty well; don't mind being paid in a couple of pounds of home-made sausages with a dozen eggs thrown in and a pig's trotter or two. Not to mention being asked to take pot luck in the kitchen pretty regularly, after I've been called to drench a cow or stitch up a prolapse or some such. I save my meat ration most weeks and pass it on to the old girl.' This was Jeffrey's way of referring to his Labrador and at one time had set up an unfortunate rumour that he was married.

'I suppose it does make sense,' murmured Lorna faintly.

'Of course it makes sense. You lay hands on everything you can get and stop being a muggins.'

Lorna thought to herself that if she were going to adopt this attitude she could scarcely resent the Americans for eating everything they could get. She should beam upon them in approval when they asked for peanut butter and jelly sandwiches spread thick, or took a fistful of sugar lumps for their coffee.

However, Lorna was obliged to concede that there was more than a grain of sense in what Jeffrey said. After all, if his Labrador got his meat ration because Jeffrey fed on illicit bacon and sausages, why shouldn't The Warren occasionally enjoy a small luxury from Fursey Down? Jeffrey, as if reading her thoughts, concluded, 'Why cut off your nose, Lorna, to spite your face?'

'You're right. I guess I'm just being foolish,' agreed Lorna reluctantly.

'At this stage of things, yes, you are. When people are reduced to siege conditions, which it's no exaggeration to say we British civilians are, pride has to go out of the window. That's a pretty dress you're wearing,' he added, casting his eye over it.

'The pre-war guest bedroom curtains,' replied Lorna, with a small smile.

'Look better on you than on a curtain rail,' responded Jeffrey gallantly. Lorna murmured her thanks and poured more hot chocolate.

Conversation now turned to Titus Swann's recent demand that his former charge of half a crown an hour for his gardening and handyman services should be raised to three shillings, to keep pace with what he called 'wartime inflation'. Lorna said, 'I don't mind being generous to people when I think they've earned it, but the trouble with Titus is that he spends half his time talking, and I don't see why one should pay him extra for that.'

'Well, I'm not there for him to talk to,' said Jeffrey. 'He just cuts my grass and goes. Mind you, now that Frisky has arrived on the scene he's not adverse to a good chinwag with her when he gets the chance.'

'No doubt,' replied Lorna drily. Frisky, otherwise Mrs Friske, was a young woman vet whom Jeffrey, overworked beyond endurance, had recently engaged as a locum for the duration. Her husband was in the Army overseas. Mrs Friske had taken up residence in the bungalow formerly occupied by the departed head gardener of Winwold Manor. Fursey-Winwold, being the gossipy place it was, speculated freely upon Mrs Friske's personal relationship with Jeffrey.

Titus, of course, had been foremost among the gossips and speculators. 'A lady vet,' he had grinned to Lorna, when Mrs Friske had first appeared. 'I've heard of some funny names for lady partners in my time, but never one who was labelled a vet. Jeffrey Bosco's pulled off a new one there.'

Lorna had snapped, 'Women *are* becoming vets nowadays, so I think we must not be too amazed when one turns up at Fursey-Winwold.'

'No amazing me these days by what turns up at Fursey-Winwold,' Titus grunted in reply. 'Nor what goes on in Fursey-Winwold, neither.'

Lorna, looking aloof, pointedly made no reply to this one. It was, she told herself, Jeffrey's own business entirely whether his relationship with Mrs Friske was exclusively professional or otherwise. Mrs Friske, it must be said, was rather attractive in a poodlish sort of way, with bright eyes and a mop of curly hair. If she could wag her tail, thought Lorna, she would certainly do so. Titus had obviously taken a fancy to her and if she turned up at The Firs while he was gardening the sound of his voice assumed a relentless key, flowing steadily without pause and reminding Lorna of the ditty, 'Old Father Thames keeps rolling along.'

'So, Jeffrey, are you intending to give Titus this extra sixpence an hour he's asking for?' now enquired the General.

'As I don't intend cutting my own grass, I don't see what the alternative is to paying up and looking pleasant,' responded Jeffrey. 'If I tried keeping that so-called lawn down in addition to everything else it would certainly be a case of the grass that broke the camel's back.'

'Out of the question for me to mow a lawn,' said the General. 'And Lorna certainly hasn't the time nowadays, even if she could handle it. It isn't a job for women; that mower of mine is a heavy thing. Well, I suppose he'll have to get that extra sixpence and we'll all have to keep out of the way when he's here, so that he has no one to talk to.'

Lorna decided to retire upstairs and put all this in a letter to Ivo. Village life. Most of her letters to him now were about village life; it was an innocuous subject, and reasonably entertaining; a bit like a second-rate Beverley Nichols she was becoming, she thought to herself with a wry smile.

She never wrote to him about the Yanks: he mightn't like to

think of her getting involved with the Yanks. But mowing machines and Titus Swann, Ruth and Miss Cusk's curtains, even Jeffrey Bosco and the enigmatic Frisky, all this was perfectly suitable stuff with which to beguile a prisoner's boredom. She took out her pen and her writing pad. 'Darling Ivo . . .'

The following weekend she was in London, sitting with Bunty in the bar at Oddenino's, with Piccadilly Circus vibrating a mere hundred yards or so distant. The two girls had a dry Martini each while waiting for Violetta and Megan to arrive.

'Well,' said Bunty, beaming happily at Lorna, 'and how's life with the Yanks on Fursey Down?'

'Oh, I'm making out, I guess. How's life with the Yanks on the buses?'

'I'm gradually mastering the art of handling 'em; learning to josh them along and all that. And in return, I must confess, being showered with Yank largesse. It pays to be a smiling London clippie with Uncle Sam around.' Bunty glanced towards the door. 'Here comes Violetta. My, doesn't she look svelte!'

Violetta, as a junior officer, certainly looked trim, cool and poised. Her hair, under her ATS cap, was styled in a thick glossy roll just clear of her collar; her discreet make-up – shell-pink lipstick, Vaseline-brushed eyelashes, the barest touch of colour on her cheeks – was in keeping with the rest of her appearance, from well-cut tunic and skirt and spick-and-span gloves to her highly polished shoes. An equally smart leather handbag was slung over her shoulder.

The girls greeted one another with little squeals of pleasure. A few moments later Megan arrived to complete the quartette. It was like the old days.

'Drinks on me,' said Violetta. 'What will you dear old things have?'

The drinks came; they toasted one another. 'All together again at last! Just like being back at St Hildegard's.'

They looked at each other, smiling happily. Violetta, Megan and Lorna in their respective uniforms; Bunty in a floral dress with a black edge-to-edge coat and a smart little black toque with a veil which reached just below her eyes. Hats were unrationed; it was just a matter of being able to afford them. Bunty had been saving up for this one. To accentuate her eyes behind the veil she had heavily mascara'd her lashes. Altogether she was feeling rather pleased with her appearance; a nice change from being, and looking like, a clippie.

'Now tell us what you're doing this weekend, Violetta,' she exclaimed, taking out her cigarette case. And, before Violetta could say a word: 'Any of you girls care for a Lucky Strike?'

Lorna refused with a shudder, Megan with a laugh. Violetta in mock horror said: 'Wherever d'you get those dreadful things?'

'My loot,' responded Bunty cheerfully. 'We clippies all get bags of loot from the Yanks; they shower us with candy, chocolate and gum, and whole packs of cigarettes – two hundred to the pack. That's generosity for you!'

'If you want two hundred of their frightful cigarettes,' said Violetta. 'I smoke Players Number Two myself.' She took out her own cigarette case. 'Anyone?'

Lorna accepted one. Violetta lit first Lorna's, then her own.

'Snobs,' said Bunty, laughing. Then she added, adopting her best Gertie Lawrence manner and voice: 'I genuinely enjoy a Lucky Strike, so there!' And with a throaty laugh and theatrical flick of her cigarette lighter she lit the cigarette she had popped in her mouth, quite forgetting her veil which instantly ignited, producing a flare of flame, a piercing scream from Bunty, and a mingling of cries and horrified shrieks from the other girls.

The veil flared up and then, providentially, fizzled out like an indoor firework. Bunty, now without eyelashes and made interesting with a singed fringe of hair, removed what was left of her toque and stared at it disgustedly. 'Damn. That bloody headpiece cost me a fortune, and now look at it!'

Her companions, in their relief that the accident had not been more serious, subsided into near-hysterics, clutching one another and choking in their laughter.

'That's right. Let's all make a spectacle of ourselves, shall we?' said Bunty, peeved by the smiles and amusement aroused in the people around her.

'Sure you don't need the fire brigade, lady?' asked an American voice behind her.

Bunty ignored the speaker and, attempting sangfroid, said: 'I wonder, Violetta, if I might ask you for a gasper after all? That wasn't a particularly lucky strike for me, I feel.'

'I think you were *jolly* lucky,' said Lorna, able to speak again at last. 'Your whole head might have gone up in flames.'

'Your face has gone quite pink,' said Megan, leaning across the table to peer at Bunty. 'I shouldn't be surprised if you have blisters on your nose tomorrow.'

'She's really going to need to wear a veil for a day or two,' said Lorna, beginning to giggle again.

'One doesn't receive the sympathy one expects from one's friends,' said Bunty. 'At least not from you lot.'

'It's only the veil that has been burned,' remarked Megan, examining the toque. 'If you take it back to the shop where you bought it, I'm sure they can quickly make it as good as new again.'

'Your mascara has run, too,' said Violetta. 'And I bet if you try washing it off the skin of your nose will come off with it. What's more, you've lost your eyelashes, and they'll take ages to grow again.'

Bunty hastily took a mirror from her bag and peered in it anxiously. 'Oh *gawd*,' she groaned.

'Lucky you're not out to make a good impression on anyone this evening,' said Megan.

'She was trying to impress us,' said Violetta, 'with her Lucky Strikes and her tricky little hat. That's what comes of showing off.'

'Well, at least I've given you something to talk about!'

'Good old Bunts,' said Lorna fondly. 'Never a dull moment when you're around, is there? And now' – she turned to Violetta, assuming a carefully casual tone of voice – 'let's have the answer to that question Bunty asked you just before she set fire to herself. What are you doing in London this weekend, Violetta? Anything special?'

'Apart from seeing us,' added Bunty.

While waiting for Violetta and Megan to arrive, Lorna and Bunty had agreed that they must find out from Violetta more about that heavy date which had to be kept dark from her mother.

Violetta smiled an enigmatic smile. 'Just planning to have a good time, that's all,' she said, flicking ash from the tip of her cigarette.

'But who's the guy who's the heavy date your poor old mother mustn't know about?' pressed Bunty.

Violetta took a deep breath of cigarette smoke and, tilting back her head, blew it slowly down her nostrils. 'Really, dears, a bit inquisitive, aren't you?' She added: 'Nobody you know.'

'Then, surely you can tell us who he is?' said Lorna. 'The name will mean nothing to us.'

'If it means nothing to you, why d'you want to know?'

'Tell us about what you do in the ATS now you're a commissioned officer,' said Megan, sensing that Bunty and Lorna would get nothing out of Violetta and also rather feeling that Violetta was entitled to keep her private affairs to herself.

'What am I doing now in the ATS?' repeated Violetta. 'I've just been appointed a welfare officer.'

'That's interesting,' exclaimed Megan, meaning it.

'Promises to be,' said Violetta.

'What sort of thing does a welfare officer have to do?' enquired Lorna.

'Problems of the rank and file,' said Violetta. 'Arranging compassionate leaves; advice of all kinds. Lining them up at regular intervals to see whose tummy is bulging. Telling them what VD is and what they should do about it if they think they've got it. Trying to see that they persevere in their moral values now they've escaped from home.'

'How d'you find out when they're not persevering in their moral values?' asked Bunty.

'Actually,' said Violetta, 'you learn a lot from what you read in the latrines.'

'Read in the latrines? How d'you mean?'

'Actually it's quite extraordinary the extent to which they're addicted to scrawling on lavatory walls and doors. They all seem to carry pencils in there with them and write pretty well everything you can think of.'

'Give us some samples,' said Bunty.

'Well, sometimes it's innocuous information like where they come from: "I'm a lassie from Lancashire", so somebody else scribbles next to that, "You can't beat Pontefract" and then another scribbles, 'Good old Stoke Newington!" and the next one writes, "Try to beat Cardiff!' and then some joker rounds it off by scrawling, "Let me have a leak and I will." That sort of thing.'

'Don't see much lack of moral tone in that,' said Bunty.

'I said that's the innocuous stuff. Other times you get something like "Corporal Jones has a ten-inch thing but he's not much cop with it", so the next girl writes, "That don't stop him waving it around", and the next girl writes, "I've quietened him down; given him the clap." That, of course, provides me with something to pass on to the MO.'

'I do hope not!' exclaimed Bunty, bursting into laughter.

'Well, you know what I mean,' rejoined Violetta, laughing, too.

'Whatever would Miss Binkle say?' gasped Lorna, choking with the giggles into her handkerchief.

'She would say, "Show me a gal who shows initiative and a practical approach to her work," and I will reply, "It is almost certain that you are looking at a gal from St Hildegard's,"' intoned Violetta.

'She always said, when she spoke of the possibility of war, that she hoped all her gals would not stint their effort but give of their best,' gurgled Megan.

'There you are, Violetta, a thought for your weekend,' said Bunty naughtily.

'Dear me!' exclaimed Lorna to herself, 'we *have* changed. More than I would ever have supposed possible.'

When Violetta had exhausted her stock of anecdotes Megan talked about the excitements of Rainbow Corner, and Bunty followed this with an exuberant account of life on the buses. Then it was Lorna's turn; she was obliged to admit that doing secretarial work at Fursey Down was pretty routine stuff most of the time, but having discovered that her companions were prepared to be amused by things which once they would only have talked about with raised eyebrows, Lorna diverted them for a while by describing Sergeant Matlak's bevy of beauties, and the extraordinary visual effects of giant female bosoms displayed on the backs of young chaps.

'Heavens, Lorna, I didn't realize you were exposed to things like that!' exclaimed Bunty merrily.

'Exposure seems to be the *mot juste*,' said Violetta.

'What would Miss Binkle have said!' It was Megan's turn to voice the ritual question.

'"Show me a gal on the back of a flight jacket . . ."' began Bunty. Once again they all went off into gales of laughter.

After the evening was over and Lorna and Bunty were travelling home together on the Tube to Hampstead, Lorna said: 'Well, we didn't get far with finding out about Violetta's heavy date, did we?'

'She was determined not to divulge.'

'I wonder what she means exactly by a *heavy* date?'

'Judging by her general knowledgeable prattle about light reading in the latrines and what not, I'd suppose that her idea of a heavy date means the whole hog, wouldn't you?'

'I'd imagine so, yes.'

'So much for the girl who perseveres in her moral values when she's escaped from home,' said Bunty, laughing.

The following morning, while Bunty was on duty, Lorna went up to the West End to fulfil her promise to Ruth of searching for a red handbag. Finally she ran one to ground at Dickins & Jones. It was a nice bag; quite expensive, more than Ruth would have paid for a handbag. Lorna decided to give it to the girl as a present. 'She's a dear little soul and turning out to be a real good worker. She deserves something in the way of a small bonus, to show she's appreciated.'

Lorna also bought an elegant red pigskin wallet to go with the bag. In the wallet she tucked a ten-shilling note as what she called 'a starter'. Ruth would really appreciate that!

In the evening Bunty and Lorna went to the theatre to see Michael Redgrave and Valerie Taylor in *A Month in the Country*. Next day, Sunday, Bunty had free; the girls were invited to morning coffee with Mrs Wells. 'I always like to meet the friends of my guests; it adds to the interest of things,' she had explained to Bunty. Now, eyeing Lorna with a curiosity she barely concealed, and smiling smiles which, by their scintillation and frequency indicated strong approval of the obviously well-bred Lorna, Mrs Wells served coffee and made sprightly conversation.

'D'you know our happy Hampstead at all, Miss Washbourne?'

'This is my first visit to Hampstead actually, Mrs Wells.'

'You are here when the trees are bare; but take my word for it, Miss Washbourne, Hampstead is above all else a *leafy* spot. Where little Keats heard the nightingale, y'know. London's most beautiful borough; not merely the jewel in the crown, but the Koh-i-noor.' Mrs Wells, coffee pot in her hand, made an expansive gesture. Then, turning to Bunty: 'After your coffee you must take Miss Washbourne on a tour of the village, or even, with young legs like yours, on a tramp to Ken Wood. Ah' – with a gusty sigh – 'to have young legs again!'

Bunty, behind Mrs Wells's back, gave Lorna a broad wink.

'But this is not, of course, your first visit to London, Miss Washbourne?'

'Far from it,' replied Lorna. 'I lived in London myself when I was at secretarial college before the war, with Bunty.'

'London is the centre of the universe,' continued Mrs Wells, now fully into her stride. 'Some say Paris, some say Rome; but Julius Caesar, wise man, wasn't content till he reached London and stood in the shadow of St Paul's.'

Another wink, even broader than the first, from Bunty.

'Hitler knows it, too,' continued Mrs Wells. 'Why else, d'you suppose, has he bombed us with such a vengeance? And,' she added, dropping her voice dramatically to a gloomier key, 'will no doubt do his best to flatten us again before he's done for. However' – scooping herself back up half an octave – 'let's forget that beastly little man for the time being. More coffee, Miss Washbourne?'

Afterwards, as they returned upstairs, Lorna murmured to Bunty: 'She's certainly value for money!'

'Every time! I don't begrudge a penny of the rent. She alone is worth it, and then there is—' But here Bunty broke off abruptly; Theodor Kaufmann was standing on the landing, rapping on Bunty's flatlet door.

'Ah, there you are, my dear Miss Clippie!' He had taken to calling her this, an affectionate pet name of his own invention. 'I am knocking you up with a big proposition. Why do not you, together with your charming friend, to whom I cannot wait to be introduced' – he gave Lorna one of his bows – 'do me the honour of permitting me to escort you to my favourite hostelry in the village, the Holly Bush, for a shandy and a luncheon sandwich, with perhaps afterwards a stroll on the Heath?'

'Sounds a simply ripping idea, Theodor,' rejoined Bunty. 'Terribly sweet of you.' He always stimulated her to superlatives, he so infectiously abounded in them himself. She then introduced Theodor to Lorna; he bowed again, smirked, shook hands heartily, smirked some more. 'How pleasurable! Can spring be far behind?'

'We'll put on our outdoor things and be ready in a jiffy,' said Bunty.

'Be well shod; we may meet mud,' warned Theodor.

Once in Bunty's flatlet the two girls gave way to fits of giggles. 'You see what I mean . . . !'

'Oh, Bunts, I do! The whole household is completely priceless.'

'Well, if not all of it, much of it. And Theodor certainly takes the cake. Mind you,' added Bunty, as she laced up her walking shoes, 'he's really rather a sweetie once you get to know him.'

Theodor, in his best winter overcoat and armed with an umbrella ('Insurance that it will not rain'), marched them up steep and narrow streets flanked by agreeable old houses and cottages to the Holly Bush, a little pub perched overlooking Heath Street. 'My favourite hostelry,' he explained. He ushered them into a bar-parlour with a coal fire and ordered three shandies ('The perfect English quaff') and cheese and pickle sandwiches. He chattered and laughed, all vivacity and glittering specs, as usual showing off his self-acclaimed easy familiarity with English.

'So you have met our Mrs Wells, Lorna? You will permit me to call you Lorna? This chummy pub atmosphere encourages informality; moreover Lorna is such a charming name and, also, how much its association with your literature! "Thy life or mine, Carver Doone!"' He placed his hand lightly on Lorna's arm. 'The true ring of the English novel, pressed upon me when small by my uncle, to whom my gratitude is consequently eternally grateful. What bereavement to live without Macaulay and Meredith, not to mention the Lost Mohicans!'

Lorna had always realized that, of the St Hildegard quartet, Bunty would be the least likely to stick to an orthodox choice of friends, but she had never expected a Theodor Kaufmann to appear on the scene. She watched him and listened to him in fascination, watched Bunty listening to him and laughing, and then thought of David McEwen's portrait standing faithfully and mournfully on Bunty's mantelshelf. Bunty, in her need for living company and comfort in this arid wartime landscape, might well find a comic Kaufmann exactly what she needed.

'You must visualize for yourselves highwaymen roistering here; Dick Turpin and his Brown Bass, for example, ready at any moment to gallop north pursued by Fleet Street Runners.'

Bunty said, straight-faced: 'How marvellously evocative you make it sound, Theo.'

'I have been reading local history: a small booklet – unpublished, alas – by our Miss Amhurst. It covers everything connected with Hampstead from legs of mutton to Anna Pavlova. I previously had no idea of the scope of this one little district. The Heights of Parliament right the way down to the oak gospels. Extraordinary!'

'What precisely were the oak gospels?' enquired Lorna.

Bunty said cheerfully: 'Whatever they were, I reckon by now they'd be collector's items.'

After the pub lunch they walked across the Heath to Ken Wood and then back to Kenilworth Lodge. The afternoon was, like the

Heath itself, dun-coloured and muddy; the oppressive grey sky seeped in smoky melancholy upon a horizon of distant rooftops punctuated by church spires. If spring were merely just around the corner, as the waxing buds on trees and shrubs proclaimed was the case, then it was holding back as if painfully loath to put in an appearance.

Theodor never stopped talking, gesticulating and generally making himself the life and soul of the party. As they retraced their steps to Kenilworth Lodge it started to drizzle. Theodor unfurled his umbrella, taking a girl on either arm and drawing the two close to him to share the umbrella's protection; holding the umbrella with his left hand and having Lorna on his left arm, Bunty on his right. 'My umbrella insurance has not come up trumps. None the less, how very nice this is! It reminds me of my student days; so many girls, one regretted that one wasn't blessed, like some Hindu deity, with umpteen arms to place round umpteen waists simultaneously. For me this is quite a recapturement of lost youth.'

As they climbed up the hill, they met the Schwartzes walking down it: arm in arm and, as usual, in silence. As the two parties passed each other the Schwartzes bowed affably, but still without speaking. Theodor and Bunty bowed in like manner to them.

'Who are they?' enquired Lorna, when she felt she was out of earshot of the Schwartzes.

'Mr and Mrs Schwartz, Flatlet One,' replied Bunty. 'They come from Berlin.'

'They look nice people,' said Lorna, 'but rather sad.'

'It would be understandable,' said Theodor. 'They have left their daughter and her family in Berlin.'

Lorna sighed. 'Yes, I can see that would be a worrying thing. What will have happened to them, I wonder.'

Bunty wished the question had been left unasked. Theodor said: 'Who knows? ... *Nacht und Nebel.* Night and fog.' His voice sank in despair.

The drizzle turned to a positive rain, falling coldly in the waning light. Bunty, firmly changing the subject, and as usual determined to try to look on the bright side of things, said: 'Hard as it is to believe at this moment, in a few weeks' time summer will be on the way and everything green and lovely.'

'When it is summer,' answered Theodor, his subdued voice and manner very different from his usual flamboyant vein, 'you cannot believe it will ever be winter. And when it is winter, then it seems equally impossible to believe in summer. So, in peacetime, it is out of the question to accept the idea of war. Then, suddenly, war becomes an appalling reality, and peace is now some fantastical dream. "Peace?" we ask. "You speak of peace – some mythical time when men weren't killing and persecuting? Pull me another, and wait for the bells!"'

He drew a long painful sigh and gathered the girls closer against him. With his free hand he felt for Bunty's; the real man below the joke surface seeking some kind of unspoken reassurance. 'Pull me another, and wait for the bells.' Bunty let him take her hand and squeeze it. Rain dripped from the umbrella in sad drops.

They regained Kenilworth Lodge, thanked Theodor for the delightful time he had given them, and retired into Bunty's flat to brew tea and have a last gossipy *tête-à-tête* before Lorna left to catch her train back to Fursey-Winwold.

Lorna, installed in a carriage, decided to write to Ivo to while away the journey. He would be amused to hear about the St Hildegard's reunion; he had always found St Hildegard's an entertaining, if comical, subject – unreal, ridiculous, delightfully naive, like an Angela Brazil girls'-school story. 'What's the latest about St Hildegard's?' he would ask Lorna, with a slight grin breaking on his face at the very mention of the name – a name itself idiotic when you thought about it. St Hildegard's.

Lorna took out her fountain pen and pad and began thinking of exactly what she should say.

'I've been in London this weekend staying with Bunty in her Hampstead flatlet. We had a wizard St Hildegard's get-together: Bunty, me, Violetta Stacks – I'm sure you'll remember her; not a girl to forget! – and little Megan Thomas. It was fascinating, all exchanging news about what each of us is doing now . . . ' But here Lorna came to a stop. Bunty with her buses full of Yanks; the Flopper at Rainbow Corner; Lorna herself describing gorgeous nudes on the Flying Forts and the backs of flight jackets: Yanks, Yanks and nothing but Yanks. As for Violetta and her hieroglyphics in the latrines! Lorna couldn't even begin to imagine herself putting any of that in a letter to Ivo.

So in the end she wrote nothing. Instead she sat thinking, asking herself if you could really go on imagining yourself to be in love with a young man whom you hadn't seen for years, from whom you hadn't even received a letter for over a year – who might in fact be dead. It was rather as if Bunty continued to write letters to David. But Bunty knew that David was no longer there to write to. There was still a chance that Ivo was alive somewhere, and waiting for Lorna's letters, and believing that she would still be waiting for him when he arrived home, if he ever did arrive home. On the other hand, romantic as this notion was, would any young chap who had been in prison camp all these years really feel like this? Truly want that girl, who had become no more than a wan memory boosted by occasional letters, to be a waiting reality when he got back? Such a prospect might fill him with horror, only he'd be too decent to say so. The whole thing could develop into a fearful mistake. Lorna suddenly found herself nursing the suspicion that she wouldn't be writing to Ivo again. Not that she had fallen in love with anybody else. She hadn't. But it wasn't right to go on playing charades with Ivo.

When she arrived home it was late. Ruth was still up, busy at the sewing machine, making her red and green dress. She greeted

Lorna with the broadest of smiles; it was nice to come home to such a happy face, thought Lorna. 'Had a good time?' beamed Ruth.

'Wizard, thanks, Ruthie. How's it been with you?'

'Oh, nothing out of the usual. Getting on with this dress, in my spare time, and that. I went to Ipswich Saturday and saw my favourite film, *Dangerous Moonlight*. Fourth time I've seen it now and every time it makes me cry worse'n the time before. Did you manage to see anything nice?'

'Bunty and I saw a play, but whether it was anything you'd have enjoyed I don't know. Oh, and I went shopping.'

Ruth obviously had been waiting for this moment; her eyes began to sparkle in anticipation. She ventured hesitantly, 'Were you able ... did you find ...?' At the same time her naturally optimistic nature kept her smiling at the thought of what she hoped, indeed *knew*, was about to be produced by Lorna from the canvas hold-all bag she was now delving into.

'Tell me if you think this will do.' Lorna tried to sound casual as she handed Ruth a tissue-paper-wrapped parcel. Ruth took the parcel with an excited giggle and pulled away the paper. Then, as she revealed the red handbag, 'Coo! It's exactly right! Just the very sort of thing what I wanted.'

She examined the bag inside and out, giving little exclamations of delight. 'All real leather. And a purse and a mirror. *And* a matching wallet. Coo, it's really swanky!' She looked up at Lorna, big eyes bigger than ever, and just a little apprehensive. 'How much do I owe you for this?'

Lorna said, happily. 'Forget it, Ruth. It's a present.'

'A present? D'you really mean it? I wasn't expecting it to be a present.'

'I know you weren't, Ruth. But you've been working hard and one way and another I think you deserve a good present.' Lorna looked as happy about giving Ruth the bag as Ruth did at receiving it.

'And a good one it is, too!' Ruth, quite overcome, leapt up, flung her arms round Lorna and gave her a great hug. 'Oh, you're a real dear, honest you are!' She sank into a chair, patting and stroking the bag, crooning over it. 'I'll never part with it!' She raised her eyes to Lorna's, then once more bent over the bag, re-examining its interior. This time she opened the wallet, to give it a full inspection. She discovered the money. 'A ten-bob note.' She stared across at Lorna. 'Did you . . . ?'

'Just to start you off.' Lorna's smile was almost as broad as Ruth's.

'Crumbs, talk about a present and a half!' Ruth shook her head, words almost beyond her. She jumped up and gave Lorna another hug. Then she resumed stroking and patting the bag. 'It's just what I've always dreamt of having, a red handbag like this. I never thought I'd get it, though.'

'In life you do occasionally have a dream come true,' replied Lorna, smiling at the girl's naive pleasure, and thinking wistfully of herself at that age, before the war, when she had had so many dreams, and had believed in them all.

XIV

Next morning, when Lorna arrived at Fursey Down, Angie and Amy May announced: 'The new CO is here!'

'Colonel Blenmire,' said Angie. 'He seems a real nice guy. Been in combat in North Africa, too.'

'He fetched in last night,' said Amy May. 'Maybe he'll bring a change in the weather.'

Later in the morning Lorna was told that Colonel Blenmire would like to see her. She went to his office. When she knocked, a curt voice called to her to come in. The new CO was sitting at his desk, watching her advance across the room. Unlike Colonel Hatton, who had been a heavy-jowled man with arms and legs which had stuck out of his person at all angles, and who had appeared to be perpetually surprised to find himself called upon to make decisions, Colonel Blenmire was, by contrast, tall, rangy and decisive; in his early to middle thirties, and much handsomer than Lorna had imagined he would be, with large blue eyes that had an intimidatingly hard glint in them as he stared at Lorna in undisguised appraisal. Then he stood up and gave her an impersonal handshake in formal greeting. 'Good morning, Miss Washbourne. You are Miss Washbourne, I take it?'

'Yes. Lorna Washbourne.'

'Sit down, Miss Washbourne.' He indicated a chair; Lorna seated herself on it. He reseated himself behind his desk, facing Lorna. His voice and manner suggested complete confidence in himself and his power of authority.

Lorna sat motionless on her chair waiting for him to speak. He said nothing for a moment or two, but stared at a typed sheet of paper before him on his desk. Then he looked up from the paper, at Lorna, his eyes still cold and watchful, and said: 'See here, Miss Washbourne, I'm afraid I've been left a bad report on you.' His tone, brisk and military, reminded Lorna a little of her father in his earlier years.

Lorna found herself rather at a loss for words. She had been well aware that the departed CO hadn't liked her, and had been fond of finding fault with her, but she hadn't anticipated that he would go to the lengths of blighting her reputation in this manner. At last she asked, keeping her voice cool and dispassionate: 'Of what does he complain, precisely, sir?'

'Precisely, he complains of your slipshod standards of work, your inaccurate shorthand and careless, poorly presented typing; unpunctuality; lack of interest in your work; inability to do your job properly; insubordination of manner . . .'

Lorna, in her usual way when made exceedingly angry, betrayed nothing of her feelings except by first turning very pale and then becoming equally flushed. Her eyes took on an icy shine and became highly attentive. She fixed them on the reading Blenmire; he raised his own eyes in a disparaging glance at her. For a long moment they exchanged a hostile glare. Then he resumed reading the report. 'The Colonel says he wondered why you came to work here, and furthermore why you thought you were any possible use as a secretary in the first place. He suggests you be advised to seek employment elsewhere.'

'Given the sack?'

'In effect, yes.'

Lorna said, in her most frigid manner: 'No prospect would please me more.'

'He thinks it was a mistake, your wanting to work here.'

Lorna, thinking to herself that, as she was going to be sacked anyway, it didn't matter if she spoke her mind, said: 'There seems to have been a total failure to understand that I came here as a conscript. We conscript the women in this country now, you know. I was directed to come and work here because I am a trained secretary, and this camp had applied to the labour exchange for a young woman to do secretarial work. I was given no choice. Let me assure you that, had I been a free agent, Fursey Down would have been the last place I would have chosen. Sir.'

This crisply delivered broadside, every syllable of which fell tinkling from Lorna's lips like ice cubes, brought no response from Colonel Blenmire, who merely fiddled a little with a gold propelling pencil with which he had been underlining observations in the report.

Lorna continued: 'I was trained at what was probably the best secretarial college in the country. I left it as a top-grade product. Since then I have worked for a well-known novelist, who provided me with a reference when I was sent here. One of the late CO's troubles was that he simply didn't know how to make use of a highly qualified secretary like myself.'

'He didn't think you were a highly qualified secretary. Anything but. As you must surely realize by what I've read you of this report.'

'If you wish to get rid of me, sir, then of course you are entitled to do so. I am sure I shall be of greater service to my own country in some other job.' Lorna paused, then resumed: 'But I think it would only be fair if, before you get rid of me, I might be given a chance to work here for one more week, so that you may ascertain for yourself whether I am so abysmally incompetent at my job as that report suggests.'

He'll get shot of me without further ado, thought Lorna, and then it will be munitions for me, no doubt; but nothing could be more demeaning than working here for the Yanks.

Colonel Blenmire said impassively: 'That seems reasonable. But if you aren't up to standard, the standard of this force, Miss Washbourne, then you must surely go.'

'Of course. I understand perfectly. Sir.'

The interview was over. Once outside Colonel Blenmire's office Lorna began to quiver all over with pent-up anger. Since she was forever being reproached for her nation's alleged habit of constantly stopping for 'tea and muffins', she decided to live up to that reputation for once and get herself a coffee in the aeroclub canteen. She badly needed one.

In the aeroclub she bumped into Buzz Cabrini. He glanced at her face, took a hasty double-take and then asked nervously: 'How's things this morning, kid?'

'I've just had an interview with Colonel Blenmire,' replied

Lorna, her manner still icy. 'It seems that our late unlamented CO left an appallingly bad report on me.'

'Join the club,' answered Buzz laconically.

'He didn't leave a bad report on you, too, Buzz?' exclaimed Lorna, astonished. Buzz was the last person, she would have thought, to have prompted an uncomplimentary report.

'He surely did. On all of us. On everybody.'

'Have you been threatened with the sack?'

'Replacement? Sure. We mostly all have. Threatened clean sweep all round.'

'Has he said that *everyone* is hopeless at their job? Colonel Blenmire must smell a rat; cotton on that his predecessor wasn't that good at his own job.'

'Colonel Blenmire has been sent here as a replacement for that very reason,' drawled Buzz, lighting one of his beloved cheroots. 'Guess someone must have reported bad on the reporter,' he concluded, and disappeared into his office, closing the door behind him. Lorna went to get her coffee.

Over the next few days Lorna stumbled over rankling pride in all directions; biting strictures had been left behind on pretty well everyone, and resentment ran high. Tommy Taylor, the second-in-command, who had never disguised his impatience with his old CO, found himself described as 'impossible to work with and a very real impediment to progress'.

'Well, well,' said Buzz. 'Takes a lot for a guy to become an impediment. You should be proud, Tommy.'

'That useless bum,' said Tommy. 'The only progress he knew about was by his own weight through the seat of his chair. Well, if Blenmire swallows all that crap . . .' He left his sentence unfinished. 'I'll show him,' added Tommy grimly.

Lorna, who should not have overheard this conversation, realized that she was not alone in being determined that Colonel

Blenmire would be shown, beyond dispute, that his predecessor's verdicts were without real foundation. In every direction people began putting on spit-and-polish performances which quickly made Fursey Down a challenging place in which to be working. Little joshing and laughter was heard; taut-faced people moved briskly about their jobs, showing the new boss of the outfit why he just shouldn't believe a single breath of condemnation breathed by the departed chief.

Lorna played this game as hard as anybody; she took dictation, pounded away at her typewriter, silently placed impeccable letters and memoranda on Colonel Blenmire's desk for him to sign, noted telephone calls and messages with faultless precision, adhered with clockwork punctuality to her daily schedule. It had to be said, of course, that in her case she was certainly not deviating from her previous mode of conduct; as one of Miss Binkle's gals she had always been a model of secretarial excellence. But now she was surpassing herself.

Colonel Blenmire, for his part, settled without delay into a regime of long hours, dispatch in all things, and an impassivity of manner bordering on the taciturn. He spent most of the day with the crews, still kept grounded by the weather; in the afternoons the Colonel would appear in his office and turn his attention to administrative matters. He remained late at his desk each night. He didn't seem to know much about relaxing. If the personnel of Fursey Down was set to show *him*, equally he appeared determined to show *them*. Angie voiced general opinion when she said: 'When he first arrived I thought he was a real nice guy, but the way he's turning out, six flags over Jesus, is kinda unnerving.'

Occasionally Lorna and he exchanged a few words of conversation, but it was always of a formal nature: Lorna had made up her mind that she certainly was not going to initiate any thaw between them. On one occasion he remarked, 'I suppose this rain has to give up some time,' and Lorna replied: 'One would like to think so, but experience prompts one to caution.' Another time he remarked, 'Not so many letters for me to sign tonight,' and Lorna came back with: 'Well, one doesn't complain of that when one is the typist, sir.'

At the end of the week's trial which Colonel Blenmire had conceded to Lorna, he gave no indication of whether she should quit or had proved herself good enough to stay on. Finally, one evening when she was on the point of leaving to go home, she nerved herself to take the bull by the horns and ask point-blank what the CO had decided.

'Excuse me, sir, but I am wondering if you have decided whether I am to stay on here or not.'

He continued signing letters without replying. Lorna thought that he could not have heard the question and was about to repeat it when he suddenly said: 'Why do you ask that?'

Lorna felt a surge of resentment. Why shouldn't she ask him? She had a right to know what was going to happen to her. She said stiffly: 'I must, I think, be forgiven for asking a direct question on this occasion. One realizes that once one has become a mere manpower pawn, as it were, that one basically loses control over one's destiny, but even so one does expect just a little respect as an individual.'

The Colonel put down his pen. 'Don't think me rude,' he said, 'but would you please say that again?'

Supposing that he must be slightly deaf, Lorna, raising her voice, intoned with even more than her usual bell-like clarity of speech: 'One realizes that once one has become a mere manpower pawn, that one basically loses control over one's destiny, but even so one does expect just a little respect as an individual.'

'Thank you,' he said. 'It was that last bit I wanted.'

'Oh?' Lorna wasn't sure what he meant.

'It's the ones,' he explained. 'They just slay me. Don't get me wrong,' he added quickly. 'I'm not poking fun; I genuinely think those ones of yours are just the greatest things out. I love 'em.'

'Ones?' Lorna both sounded, and felt, perplexed. Then it dawned on her what he meant. 'Oh, I see. You mean, the way in which one speaks.'

'Yeah. Go on. Give me more.'

'Oh.' Lorna began to wish she had not embarked upon this conversation. 'Well, one cannot do it at the drop of a hat,' she said, a little tartly. Then, remembering that, after all, he was her CO for as long as she remained at Fursey Down, she resumed: 'When one is accustomed to that form of speech I am afraid that one does not attach so much importance to it, or even notice it, as much as one would if one had been brought up never to hear it.'

'Hey,' he said, 'that's hot stuff. That's the real McCoy.'

'Thank you,' said Lorna. 'Don't you ever use ones in the United States?'

'Mrs Roosevelt does,' he replied thoughtfully. 'But she's about the only one who does. And she was sent to school in England, I believe. And she gets laughed at for it, too.'

'For using ones? Or for going to school in England?'

'For using ones. She speaks real English English.'

'Well, so one jolly well should,' retorted Lorna warmly. 'If one is going to speak English, then one should see that it's proper English and not something slipshod.'

'This is a real feast,' he said. 'I thank you.'

Lorna wondered if she might now go home, and was about to ask his permission to leave when he said: 'About that question you asked me just now, I supposed that you realized you would be staying on; took it for granted that you would be, as nobody had requested you should be replaced.'

'I never take anything for granted,' retorted Lorna grimly. 'Specially not in wartime.'

'Very wise. I've taught myself not to.'

'So that means I shall be continuing in this job?'

'It does.'

'I'm glad you think I'm good enough,' said Lorna, with a just discernible touch of irony.

'You are. Perfectly satisfactory. More than satisfactory in fact; your work is of a very high standard indeed.'

'Thank you, sir.' She paused; then asked: 'Would it be all right if I were to go home now?'

'Surely. Though I was hoping you would join me in a drink before you left. Just to celebrate that you'll be sticking around here for a while.'

Lorna, who had had a hard day's typing, and was thinking how nice it would be to return home and relax by taking her dogs for a stroll, tried her best to look as if she would enjoy lingering a while to have a drink with Colonel Blenmire. 'Thank you very much, sir,' she said politely.

The Colonel went to a cupboard and took out a bottle and two glasses. 'I hope you drink Bourbon,' he said. 'I much prefer Scotch, but that's gotten so it's like crying for the moon.'

'I've never tried Bourbon.'

'Well, try a little now.'

'Only a very little,' said Lorna nervously. 'I have to ride my bike home.'

'Oh, you'll just coast along after this.'

He poured two drinks, handed her one and said: 'Well, here's to you, working for me, and Fursey Down.'

'You, me, and Fursey Down,' echoed Lorna, thinking that the office in which this little ceremony was taking place was situated more or less where her family's dining room had once been.

'Gee, let's sit down and relax,' said Colonel Blenmire. They had been standing up, as though at a cocktail party. They seated themselves on two not very comfortable chairs; he said: 'Tell me about yourself. I always like to know something about my staff. Where do you live? I imagine not far from here.' His manner, previously always so cold, had now become pleasantly friendly.

'I live in Fursey-Winwold village with my father. He's Regular Army; well, he's retired now, but he was Regular. We're an army family.'

'Is that so? Mine, too.'

'And now you've taken to the air.'

'Yes. But don't forget our air force doesn't have autonomy like yours. We were an army air corps that didn't become an air force until two years ago; an army air force. We guys may fly, but we're still Army.'

'So you haven't really broken with family tradition.'

'No. D'you have brothers?'

'To carry on our tradition? I had two . . .' And Lorna began telling him about her family, encouraged by his manner which was genuinely interested and sympathetic.

To her amazement she even heard herself telling him about Fursey Down and the loss of Weldon Court.

'You poor kid; that's awful to hear! You must feel it.' He looked at her with compassion. 'No wonder you say Fursey Down is the last place you'd ever have chosen as a place to work.'

'I try not to think of it now that I have to come here,' said Lorna. She added: 'But it's hard not to.'

Without any difficulty they had slipped into real conversation, as opposed to the usual trivial chit-chat of persons having an office drink together.

'I think you're a real sport to take it the way you do,' he said. 'To work here in a building that stands on the very spot . . .'

'I always swore I wouldn't. Although my mother and I joined the Red Cross when war broke out, I never expected to find myself working like this for the American Red Cross. Everything always seems to work out so differently from what one expects. Before the war I was at a secretarial college, as I told you. My parents thought it a good thing for a girl to have secretarial training; always something to fall back on. Actually I loved every minute of it; I think all the girls did.'

And she found herself telling him about St Hildegard's, and Miss Binkle's 'Show me a top-drawer secretary unobtrusively but decisively at the helm ...', and Miss Plessey's typing exercises in time to Mozart. Lorna, when in a relaxed and happy frame of mind, could be highly entertaining, and he certainly seemed to find her so, laughing his head off at her anecdotes about Miss Binkle.

'And in the end none of you became secretaries after all, that it?'

'Oh, no. The Flopper – that's Megan – she became a first-class secretary somewhere in the City and now she's a secretary with the American Red Cross in Grosvenor Square. And Violetta joined the ATS and until she got her commission was in a sort of typing pool. Only Bunty has really made a clean break with the typewriter; she's become a clippie – you know, a London bus conductress. She spends her time among swarms of GIs, all wanting to ride on her bus. You can't begin to imagine the questions they ask her!'

'Tell me. This I must not miss.'

They had another Bourbon each, and she told him about Bunty's adventures on the buses; and how she had burned her veil with a Lucky Strike – part of her 'loot'. He laughed a lot more. 'Gee,' he said, 'talking with you like this is making me get back to feeling human. This, and the Bourbon.'

'It's really rather good – the Bourbon, I mean. My father always likes a whisky, or a brandy maybe, at night; but, as you say, it's like asking for the moon. Sometimes, just very occasionally, one strikes lucky with something under the counter.'

'It's pleasant to have a drink at the end of the day when things have gotten tacky. I don't mean when I'm flying missions,' he added. 'Then I don't drink.'

'What d'you mean, tacky?'

'Well, like it's been taking over the command here. Having to feel your way, like you're crossing a minefield.'

Lorna thought it best to change the subject. She asked pleasantly: 'Which part of the States do you come from, Colonel Blenmire?'

'Maryland. Born and raised there, and still have my home there with my wife and two children. My mother lives with us. D'you know the States at all?'

Lorna shook her head. 'I've never been there, I'm afraid.'

'You must try it some time. It's certainly worth a visit.'

When Lorna rose to leave, saying that she must return home or her father would be wondering what had happened to her, she thanked the Colonel politely for the drinks: 'It really was awfully nice of you, sir.'

'Off duty,' he said, 'my friends call me Herbie.'

XV

Next evening, when Lorna took Colonel Blenmire the day's letters to sign, he said to her: 'Did Miss Binkle instruct you in how to set up and work a real good filing system?'

'Miss Binkle was hot stuff on filing systems.'

'Have you ever had experience of a filing system? In your work as a secretary, I mean, not simply when you were a student with Miss Binkle?'

'Oh, yes. The Stackses, the whodunnit authors I told you I've done secretarial work for, have a tremendous filing system, and one of the things I was doing for them was reorganizing that and making it much more comprehensive than the former one.'

'This airfield and camp form a pretty sizeable set-up, with well over two thousand personnel all told. Although I'm sure the office staff have done their best, their filing system is pathetic; it'll never work. I want a real good efficient filing system for Fursey Down. You're here, and you say you can do it. So how about giving it a try?'

Lorna, given carte blanche to organize a system to the best of her ability, threw herself into the work with zest. She was given a small office to herself; this she found a tremendous thrill. Fursey Down being a great place for early-morning starts (the Forts, when flying on a mission, woke everyone up at crack of dawn), Lorna eagerly arrived in her new office each morning at seven-thirty prompt, riding on her bike along lanes where the hedgerow banks were clotted thick with primroses, while overhead, in the pale April blue, the Forts, little silver specks glittering in a maze of contrails, steadily climbed high into the air, to assemble in their battle formations. For the weather had improved; gone were the days when missions were scrubbed because of poor visibility.

Uninterrupted, Lorna would work until late afternoon when Herbie Blenmire, back from flying on the mission and looking weary, would come into her office to see what she had achieved during the day. She would explain to him how her filing system was developing, to receive his encouraging 'You're doing noble, kid. Keep at it.'

The first time he flew on a mission with the Fursey Down crews, Herbie, having congratulated Lorna on her day's work, roamed round her office for several minutes, fiddling with things in a desultory manner which suggested to her that he had something on his mind that he was half inclined to speak to her about, and half not. He picked up a pencil sharpener and put it down, twiddled a door knob, sniffed a bunch of primroses in a jar. Finally, thinking to provide him with something to latch on to in the way of talk, if he wanted it, Lorna said conversationally: 'How did it go today? All the chaps who've been out seem very cheerful.' Adding, suddenly worried lest she had spoken out of place: 'But maybe I shouldn't ask you questions like that.'

'You can ask any questions you like. I don't have to answer them,' he said rather grimly.

Lorna, wishing that she had kept her mouth shut, began putting things away preparatory to closing down for the night.

'It went OK,' said Herbie. 'The group came back intact.'

'May they continue to do so,' said Lorna.

He seated himself in the desk chair, a revolving one, and gave it a moody spin, lifting his feet from the floor and gripping the abbreviated arms, meantime staring intently at nothing in particular. 'They're the cockiest bunch of Yankees that ever came down the road,' he said. 'They sure think they're hot stuff.'

Lorna made no comment to this; she thought it best to remain silent.

'They'll pretty soon learn different,' he continued glumly.

Lorna could think of no comment to this, either.

'Trouble is, during the three, four weeks they've been over here they should've been flying. Flying plenty, and learning. What you learn in flying school, what you learn in training in the States, isn't going to help you much when at last you're in action in the skies of the ETO. These kids, when they reached here, needed a good spell in kindergarten. Plenty of practice flights, milk-runs; but this they have not had.' He gave his chair a spin in the opposite direction. 'The crews that came in the summer – call them the first wave – they went through kindergarten when they arrived; they had their milk runs. But for this second wave of crews there's been no chance of any easing in; and this Fursey Down lot have been particularly unlucky – left to kick their heels when kicking their heels was the last thing they needed.'

'The time for milk runs is over?' hazarded Lorna, sensing he needed dialogue, but afraid to sound as if she were probing.

'Yeah, I guess,' he said with a deep sigh, sending the chair revolving again. 'Seems we're into rugged missions now.'

Lorna placed the cover over her typewriter. 'Well, I'd best be off home, Herbie.'

'Sure thing, kid. See you.'

She left him revolving on the chair.

Outside, on the hardstands, the Forts stood lined up, silhouetted against the evening sky, their guns jutting. Lorna, wheeling her bike, for the concrete was greasy and slippery, passed *Daisy May*, *Available Vee*, *Piccadilly Warrior*, *Flak Floosie*, *Star Stripper*, *Hell's Belle*. Sergeant Matlak, from whose inspired brush most of the lovely ladies of this line-up had come, was putting the finishing touch to a new venture in fuselage decor, a large rose.

'That makes a change!' observed Lorna.

Sergeant Matlak, solid and solemn, perched on the top of a ladder, replied: 'Yeah, kinda purty.'

'Any special sort of rose?' Lorna, anxious now to be friendly with everybody, tried to sound really interested.

'I guess a rose is a rose is a rose,' said the Sergeant. *'Rosie's Roosters*, this kite's gonna be called. When I done the rose, then comes the rooster. An' he won't be so darn easy – no, sirree – 'cos he has to be stood so he's layin' bombs. Geddit?'

'Laying bombs instead of eggs?' ventured Lorna.

'Yeah, you goddit. Cap'n Coster – he's the pilot – thinks that's kinda satirical, I guess. But when you're asked to paint a body layin' bombs, like it's *Pregnant Pearl*, you have to make good darn sure those bombs are coming outa the right spot, *and* you've left plenty nuff room for three, four rows maybe.'

'Complicated,' said Lorna.

'Lady, in this world nutt'n's easy.'

'Which of all these ... these gorgeous girls d'you think is your *chef d'œuvre*, Sergeant?'

'Come again?'

'Which of these girls d'you think is your best?'

'Wa-aa-aal' – he drawled the word contemplatively – 'I guess it's *Star Stripper*. She's real provocative and yet she's got class. That's no mean achievement.'

'D'you use anyone you know as a model?'

'Lady, if I did, I wouldn't tell! But, no, I don't. I guess you might say these dames just come to mind.'

'Well, good luck with the rooster. Good night!' And Lorna prepared to mount her bike and ride off. Sergeant Matlak called after her: 'He'll be ready by morning!'

Lorna suddenly drew up. A thought had crossed her mind. She returned to the sergeant. 'Who's Rosie?' she asked.

'Mrs Coster,' said the Sergeant. 'Cap'n Coster up an' married her just before he left the States, he tells me. They never learn.'

'Let's hope Rosie has good luck,' said Lorna.

'Like me to paint a good-luck message?'

'Won't that spoil the design?'

'Tucked among the petals,' said Sergeant Matlak. 'Who will know?'

He raised his brush, poised in inspiration. Lorna left him to paint in peace.

Next morning she was woken by the song-thrush in the lilac below her window, and was thinking, How lovely! when the preflight tumult of Fortress engines warming up drowned out every other sound in the world. Another mission would shortly be setting out from Fursey Down. A rugged one, if Herbie had spoken aright. Lorna, crossing her fingers for him, lay listening to the sound of the engines. Impossible to sleep again, once one had been awakened by that din! Soon she got up and had breakfast of tea and porridge. Shortly after six she took the dogs for a walk.

It was a bright morning. Take-off time had arrived and the air beat and vibrated with the tumult of the Forts leaving the runway and clambering up into the sky. At last, when Lorna was on her way to Fursey Down, the noise overhead changed into the full-throated, throbbing, pounding roar, the steady relentless thunder of the Fortresses flying in formation, so immensely high above that they looked like dots; this morning, craning her neck and straining her eyes, Lorna could discern a huge two-wing formation.

At the airfield everyone was in a tremendous state of excitement. 'It's the largest attacking force the Eighth has sent out to date!' Amy May told Lorna breathlessly. 'Well over one hundred B-17s, can you imagine? It makes you feel kinda sorry for the Germans.'

The day wore on. The mood on Fursey Down was one of exhil-aration mingled with high anticipation of the return of the group in triumph in the late afternoon. 'They'll sure flatten that goddam target.' 'If the Eighth can send out a force like that three times a week, say, what's the betting the war will be over in six weeks?'

At four in the afternoon Lorna was seated at the back of the can-teen sipping the cup of tea which she had persuaded everyone that she, as an English woman, must have every day, at the same time, on the dot, if she were not to fall apart. 'After all, if they can't fight this war unless they're fed on hamburgers and tinned peaches and ice cream and Coke and peanut butter, then I'm sure I'm entitled to insist on one cup of afternoon tea,' Lorna had told Bunty in a letter she sent her about the new job.

Angie and Amy May took advantage of Lorna's tea break to have a cup of coffee each and dunk doughnuts. The three girls this after-noon sat near an open window, listening, each hoping to be the first to hear the thunder of the returning Forts. At last, after one or two false alarms, they heard the distant sound of a group of B-17s flying in the direction of Fursey Down. The girls leaped up and ran outside, where a crowd was already assembling on the hardstands, staring at the sky.

A small formation appeared, flew over, heading for another base: part of the returning mission, but not the Fursey Down lot. Expectancy gave way to disappointment. Lorna, to take her mind off the waiting, and privately not only surprised but also annoyed with herself for being so caught up in the general mood of excited involvement, sought out Sergeant Matlak to enquire whether or not he had finished the rooster. 'Nope. Cap'n Coster had to take out Rosie without the rooster. I'll produce that bird when they get back. Reckon there'll be bombs for me to paint in, too.'

'Did you smuggle in the "good luck"?'

'Sure thing. Very nice. I'll show you by 'n' by.'

The heavy throb of engines; two, three Forts, limping back, flying as if with huge effort low over the Down. 'Ours!' As they turned in towards the runways two of the Forts dropped bright red flares, indicating that they had dead or wounded aboard. Then three more planes, thudding home with labouring gasps, coming in very slowly and shuddering with effort, and again they were dropping flares – falling, it seemed to the onlookers, like great gouts of blood.

Ambulances with surgeons sped up to the end of the runway, as more planes loomed in the distant sky. A pall of shock almost amounting to disbelief had fallen over the airfield. The reality of battle was being brought home in the literal sense; brought home to base at Fursey Down.

A seventh plane, seriously damaged, struggled in, touched down and immediately careered off the runway. The next, unable to get its wheels down, belly-landed in a shower of sparks. Fire engines sped. Meanwhile ambulances rushed off the field taking the wounded to hospital. All had become confusion.

More planes limped into view. Angie and Amy May, sobs in their throats, stood counting them in. The men who fell rather than clambered from the planes looked decades older than when they had embarked that morning.

Another plane and then another; *Piccadilly Warrior* shot to bits and still airborne only by a miracle, *Risin' High* lurching drunkenly. Then *Star Stripper* flew in, battered and dropping a flare. Lorna felt her heart pounding. The plane landed on the runway; an ambulance was ready waiting. Everyone was running towards the plane; she herself remained on the hardstand. Then she saw the crowds part and the ambulance driving off fast and Herbie Blenmire and his co-pilot, Captain Yeo, walking slowly along the runway with the remaining seven members of the crew. Lorna turned and went back to her office and began covering up her typewriter and putting her things away. Her knees were shaking. Amy May put her head round the door; she was crying. 'There's seven Forts still missing. Seven out of the twenty-four from Fursey Down. I can't believe it.'

Herbie didn't appear in the office that evening; Lorna hadn't supposed that he would. After finishing in the office she was on duty in the canteen; Good Egg Glaister and Miss Cusk were also there, being particularly cheerful in a brisk sort of way as counterpoise to the mood of black depression which otherwise enveloped the aeroclub. 'Ah, well,' Lorna heard the Good Egg saying to Angie, 'we mustn't let these things get us down, must we? "Carry on as usual" must be our motto.'

Presently some of the returned crew members appeared, to mingle with the other men already in the club. They all looked drained; and few, if any, made the attempt to maintain the stiff upper lip and flip throwaway humour which Lorna, the Good Egg and Miss Cusk considered the automatic response in the face of wartime calamity. Indeed, little attempt at conversation was made at all; people sat around in glum silence, with cans of Coke or dunking their interminable doughnuts, and if they spoke to each other it was in a muted manner which only heightened the general atmosphere of melancholy. Occasional stray snatches of talk reached Lorna's ears. 'His ship caught a bad burst, one o'clock high, right in the pilot's compartment. And that big bird simply turned over and went straight down with all four engines roaring.' 'Four jumped; the rest of us stayed in.' 'That ship didn't blow; it just melted apart.' 'I wouldn't've believed that flak if I hadn't been in it.' 'The big ones sure die hard.'

One boy, his face twitching every few seconds, gave her some idea of what had happened. 'Like they were waiting for us; knew we were coming. It's being said some Luftwaffe recce pilot spotted us early on and gave the alert. They waited till we had broken formation and were in trail for the bombing run; then, oh boy, did they let us have it. Swarms of 'em, all coming in head on. Head on! The flak was sump'n terrible, too, but the fighters stayed right there all through. You have to hand it out to those Kraut pilots. On that showing, they'll take some beating.'

By the end of the evening five bombers were still missing: *Dyna Might, Hell's Belle, Rosie's Roosters, Shoot-Up* and *Nice 'n' Teazy*. A crew of ten to each plane; that made fifty young airmen who hadn't returned. One boy, hearing this news as he sat dunking a doughnut and staring hard at nothing, suddenly burst into tears. Angie ran to him. 'Get him into the sickbay, quick!' rasped Buzz Cabrini. Lorna and he made for the boy, whom Angie was already hauling to his feet. The poor soul was removed with a despatch which, Lorna thought, was akin to brutal: Angie and Buzz between them had him hustled away before many people had realized what was going on. Lorna returned to the canteen. Amy May, shaking her head, said: 'An upset like that can spread so very quickly.'

The few missions that had been flown so far from Fursey Down had met with little opposition; no planes lost, no injuries among the crews, who returned cocky and pleased with themselves, on top of the world. Now their woebegone faces told of their discovery of the unspeakable.

Shortly after the removal of the weeping youth, Herbie Blenmire came into the aeroclub and began to circulate among the crews, chatting with them. He looked tired, but less disturbed by the experiences of the day than his unhappy subordinates. However, they seemed to revive a little in his company, and Lorna noticed that he even succeeded in raising a few wan smiles. Presently he came to the coffee bar and was soon seated talking and dunking doughnuts in a manner apparently completely relaxed. The atmosphere became generally brighter and less tense. Miss Glaister said to Lorna: 'I admire that man; he must be exhausted, for from all accounts he was right in the forefront of things, but you can see he's the sort who always gives that extra ounce of himself.'

Before he left, Herbie caught Lorna's eye. 'And how was the gal at the helm today?'

'Fine, thanks. Working away, Binkle-style,' responded Lorna. Close to him she could see how tired he was.

Next day low cloud had formed again, and no mission was flown. Herbie worked in his office. He inspected the progress of the files and discussed the extent to which there should be a system of cross-reference. Lorna said: 'One doesn't want it to become too complicated, yet on the other hand one needs something soundly comprehensive.'

'Precisely how I would have put it myself.'

'You agree?'

'Oh, absolutely.'

'I hope you're not laughing at me. I take my work very seriously.'

'As everyone should.'

Lorna paused, then said: 'I hope it's not impertinent of me to remark upon it, but you did a world of good coming into the club and talking to the chaps like that last night. They were all feeling pretty down in the mouth.'

'They'd finally made the discovery, poor little devils, of what war is really about. It's always tough when you realize for the first time.' He went to the window and looked out at the hardstands. 'Five planes sure leave a gap.'

There was a pause while he continued staring at the hardstands.

Lorna stared at her fingernails, varnished shell-pink with varnish Angie had given her and which had turned out to be much pinker than Lorna had expected and now seemed extraordinarily frivolous-looking and out of place.

'There are two or three things', said Herbie, turning slowly from the window, 'that can't be taught, however good the training. Things that can only be learned by doing them. And fighting in battle is one.'

He walked across to the swivel chair, seated himself in it and spun round.

'Trouble is, killing, which is mostly what battle turns out to be about, involves dying, and it's pretty hard the first time you meet that one.'

'Yes,' said Lorna, thinking of her brothers.

'Other trouble is, the more missions you fly the better your know-how; you start to get the hang of things, and you can only get the hang of things by flying missions, but what you can't bet on is that Dame Fortune, or whoever she is, will let you live to fly enough missions to start getting the hang of it all.'

'No,' said Lorna.

He asked her sharply: 'Am I boring you?'

'Oh, no, Herbie! I'm not saying much because I'm thinking,' explained Lorna hastily. 'What you've said is all very true and it's made me . . . think.' Her voice trailed away, and she said to herself that she sounded pretty lame.

'I needn't have said all that to you, I guess. With your family background you know all about it. But these young guys here, they're farm boys from Oklahoma and Montana and such places, many of them; raised in a world that believed itself apart. And they've been given planes to fly that they've been told are invincible. You don't get killed in a Flying Fort. They felt safe in 'em. Until yesterday. Then they were blasted. It hit home: nothing's safe in war.'

'No,' said Lorna, once more thinking that this office in which they were talking was pretty well on the spot which had been her family's dining room.

'One thing our boys have got to get into their heads,' said Herbie grimly, 'is that the Germans have cracked the myth of the invincible Flying Fort and its gun-power.'

'How've they done that?'

'In the past fighter planes have always attacked from the rear, so the assumption of the guys who armed the B-17s has been that fighters will always attack from the rear. Which, of course, the Germans are no longer doing; being the stuff they are, they've now taken to attacking head on.'

'Why have fighter planes always attacked from the rear?' asked Lorna, genuinely interested.

Herbie, flicking her a glance, replied: 'In order to shoot the bomber down with a burst of no-deflection fire.' He paused, then said: 'You know what that is?'

'I'm afraid I don't,' murmured Lorna humbly.

'Deflection is the angle that has to be added to the aim to allow for the forward impetus of a moving target. No-deflection shots at a moving target, true no-deflection shots, can only be fired from directly astern or directly frontal positions. And, as it's a golden rule in warfare always to surprise your enemy whenever possible, the Luftwaffe boys have switched to frontal attack. Suicidal, because of the closing rate: must take a helluva lot of nerve. Nobody our side ever supposed they'd try it. But there it is; they're doing just that thing. And Fort guns aren't positioned to deal with it.'

'My father says you should never underrate the Germans.'

'Your father's said a mouthful there.' Herbie rose from the swivel chair. 'Well, back to work, I guess.'

Angie and Amy May the previous evening had buoyed up their own spirits and had tried to buoy up the spirits of others by remarking at frequent intervals that the missing Forts mightn't have been able to make Fursey Down but had touched down instead at some other airfield. But no news of the Forts had come through from any other airfield, and this hope had by now dwindled into non-existence. There remained the chance that they might have come down in the sea and their crews been picked up by RAF Sea Rescue. But no good news of this nature was forthcoming, either, and soon the rising toll of lost planes and their crews created a tragic perspective in which *Dyna Might*, *Hell's Belle*, *Rosie's Roosters*, *Nice 'n' Teazy* and *Shoot-Up* were remembered chiefly because they had been the first names on Fursey Down's ever-growing list of casualties.

XVI

Lorna had always loved the spring: the countryside bursting into fresh green, flowers and birdsong; the cuckoo arriving to call all day; the Fursey Down larks pouring out their hearts in joy as they climbed into the sky. Days that began for Lorna with an early awakening, lying in bed watching the light grow at the window and listening to the dawn chorus swelling outside.

This year the Flying Fortresses obliterated spring. At the magic moment when the dawn chorus was sounding its first, tentative opening chords, the earliest small birds piping in the garden shrubs, to be answered by the thrush in the lilac below Lorna's window, with the newly arrived cuckoo chiming from the wood, there erupted a clamour of distant engines: that ceremonial deep-throated chanting of first light, the mighty Forts warming up. Another mission day had started, to move into what climax of fury and frenzy in some alien sky, culminating in battle-weary bombers limping and staggering back to the airfield, dropping blood-red flares as they agonizingly lowered themselves towards the ground where the apprehensive onlookers counted them in, knowing that not all who had flown out could hope to return.

Merely to know the mission day by its distant sounds and sights, as those local people not closely involved with the airfield knew it, was an experience of ever-present disturbance and brooding; thoughts of destruction and death inescapably taking precedence over the normal preoccupation with vegetable crops and cows. War, however physically distant, loomed and lived, round the clock, at the back of the mind: the glittering hosts of bombers thrusting in geometrical precision across the sky in early morning; the battered giants returning, by ones, twos and threes, heavy with the exhaustion of battle, as evening took over day. The entire countryside lived under the shadow of the Flying Forts; both literally and figuratively.

But for those like Lorna, who had become closely involved with the life of an airfield, the feeling of subjugation to the inexorable B-17s was overwhelming. She found herself sucked into an existence which seemed to sever her from Fursey-Winwold and life as she had hitherto known it. She would never have believed it, but it was now true that Fursey Down (which she had sworn she would never more set foot on, once it had ceased to be the traditional Fursey Down that she had known and loved) had become, in its transmutation as an airfield for the B-17s of the US Eighth Air Force Bomber Command, of infinitely greater significance for her in terms of emotional demand and energy than it had ever been before.

Twenty-five missions completed a tour for an American airman (for the British and Germans it was thirty). His tour completed, the airman returned to the States; but this return appeared increasingly hypothetical as the casualty rate among the aircraft and crews steadily rose. A succession of calamitous missions and harrowing experiences reduced the boisterous, bumptious youths, cockily eager for battle, into subdued shadows of themselves, unable to see any future beyond their next few missions; informed as they were by hard statistics that the average member of a Flying Fort crew would be dead before he finished his tour.

Previously these young men had been nothing more to Lorna than anonymous aircrews. She had not been interested in the respective roles of the ten men making up a crew, had barely known what these roles were. Now she could identify crew individuals not only by name, but also as pilot, co-pilot, bombardier, navigator; flight engineer, radio operator, waist-gunner, tail-gunner or ball-turret gunner (there were two waist-gunners to each crew). She could also say which crew flew in each of the bombers.

Much of this information she picked up from Angie and Amy May, who possessed a wealth of information about the 'boys', not only as aircrew, but in their private lives as well: which of them were married, which single, which divorced, which bedevilled by extra-marital involvement; which awaiting news of an expected baby at home; which a compulsive gambler, which a threatening deserter; which on the brink of 'going Section Eight' (breaking down psychologically); and so on.

Lorna, for her part, found herself infinitely more interested in what the boys had to tell her about their planes and their mission experiences. One of her liveliest informants was her old friend the ball-turret gunner Vic Wendell, who lived a charmed existence in his revolving sphere slung under the bomber's belly, where, curled up in a foetal position, with a gun to each side of his head, he spun and tilted under his own frenetic momentum, aiming and firing at the Messerschmitts and Focke-Wulfs.

Wendell felt strongly about guns. All the gunners felt strongly about their guns, but Wendell felt the strongest. As the Forts had not been designed to repulse frontal attacks by German fighters it was the bombardier and the navigator, in the nose of the Fort, who were now called upon to open fire on the Luftwaffe pilots, rather than the trained gunners in their positions further to the rear. Wendell was scathing about this state of affairs. 'There's us six enlisted men, six sure nuff trained gunners, reduced to taking pot shots at the Wolves flashing past after breaking away, fading targets, while those two-bit untrained jerks man the nose compartment where all the action is, and try to act like they know how to use a gun.'

'It does sound silly,' said Lorna, 'but from what one hears so many of the things that happen in wartime are silly.'

'You can say that again,' said Wendell.

The crews spoke of their battle experiences in short bursts; vignettes, vivid because completely unstudied.

'The first we knew the fighters were there was the flashes from the cannon of the FW190s flying abreast and meeting us head on.'

'There's nothing worse than seeing a sister ship in flames and going down in her death throes, dying hard.'

'Germany sure is a beautiful country, so peaceful-looking and green. Makes you wonder why they ever started a war.'

'The co-pilot had his head blown clean off by a cannon shell; blown clean off. It was like those pictures you see of John the Baptist. Half his head went into the bomb bay but the other half just blew to bits.'

'When our fighter escort reached their point of no return, they quit; they had to. Our Thunderbolts turned for home; the Wolves struck. It was that quick. Two of our bombers went down. It was the fastest attack you ever saw.'

Like fragments of a jigsaw puzzle, Lorna tried to piece them together, to form a picture of what went on when the Forts and their crews were in action during those hours between early-morning take-off and late-afternoon return.

But before a mission could be flown there had to be a moment of high ceremony when the bombs were given life. Until that moment they were mere metal pigs packed with high explosive which could not explode. When the bombs were taken from the dumps where they were stored, on the edge of the airfield, and fetched on carriers to be loaded on to the Forts waiting on the hardstands, they might be dropped on to concrete and nothing would happen. They were lifted and installed in the bomb bays of the aircraft, to hang, shackled, in their racks: black, and sinister with potential.

An armament sergeant took up station under the open bomb bay of each Fort. Above him, in the plane, perched on the catwalk spanning the bomb bay, the Fort's bombardier held a box of fuses, while the sergeant held a wrench. Working together turn and turn about, with infinite care, a fuse was first inserted and then tightened in the nose of a bomb, then another inserted and tightened in the tail. The two men worked in unviolated concentration until every bomb in the bomb bay was armed. Now the Fort carried a load of death.

Lorna, watching the Forts on the hardstands before they taxied on to the runway, thought of this ceremony taking place in each plane's bomb bay. A clumsy movement or some error of judgement or accident from slackened concentration could promote an explosion: it was the first moment of truth in a day which would doubtless hold many before it was over.

Who might return and who might not had become a deadly lottery; a daily game of Russian roulette played out in the sky. Death had been transformed from a distant idea, in which nobody had quite believed, into an ever-present reality, terrible in its depredations. Today could no longer reckon on tomorrow, or morning on seeing the evening.

Sometimes when Lorna sat typing letters which would be placed ready to be signed by Herbie when he returned from the mission, she would have a vision of the typed sheets of paper lying eternally on his desk, awaiting a signature which would never be written.

Occasionally the crews, in their snapshot glimpses of a day's events, would reveal their CO in action. 'Old Pappy' was the nickname they gave Herbie Blenmire, when speaking of him behind his back. 'Bogies were coming in from all directions. The intercom went mad with everyone trying to report all at once. "Fighters at nine o'clock high! Fighters at four o'clock low! Fighters at twelve o'clock! Fighters at six o'clock!" It was bedlam. Then, the first chance he got, Old Pappy came over the intercom, cussing us. He cussed us with the finest goddam cussing I ever heard; and from me that's sure sayin' sump'n, for I come from the best family of cussers I ever come across, until Old Pappy, and he beat all. And at top speed, too. He cussed us for breach of discipline; said we were the worst crew he'd ever come across; said we were a menace with our shouting and crazy behaviour; said discipline was essential in a Fortress, essential for not only our own survival but the survival of our sister ships and the success of the mission. Yes, sir, he certainly let off!'

'Old Pappy tore into us for wasting ammunition. Said: "You're using up that ammo like there's a store round the corner. Well, there *ain't*."'

To Lorna, Herbie growled at the end of the day: 'They seem to have been taught everything but discipline.'

The invincibility of unescorted Flying Fortresses had by now been thoroughly demolished as a concept; the problem was that a long-range fighter which could escort the Forts all the way to their targets in Germany, engage the Luftwaffe fighters in fuel-consuming combat on equal terms, and still have enough petrol to return to base, had not yet come into production. The Allied fighters available as escorts for the Forts (the 'Little Friends' as the Americans called them) always had to turn back long before the target area was reached, leaving the Forts to carry out the most vital part of their mission unprotected, with the result that the bombers suffered fearsome casualties.

Herbie's attitude towards the Forts was pragmatic. 'Basically there's nothing novel about the Fort; it's really no more than a version of the ancient Roman strategy of blocks of armoured massed infantry. All that we've done is to move an old idea up into the sky where, as with the Romans, it's simply a matter of holding formation while you fight your way in, and then fight your way out.'

'It doesn't seem to work awfully well with the Forts,' sighed Lorna, thinking of all the casualties.

'No, but it was a real nice idea. And some people still have faith in it,' said Herbie drily. 'And so happens they're the people who count.'

'The armchair theorists, not the aircrews.'

'That's always the way.'

Lorna thought of her father's army stories on much the same lines.

'Anyways,' said Herbie, 'I have my orders, and they are to bomb a series of given targets in accordance with our daylight bombing strategy, and to lick the crews under my command into an efficient fighting force. Far as I'm concerned, it's as straightforward as that.'

Then, rising to his feet and making for the door, the time allotted for relaxation over: 'Right now it's holding formation that counts. Holding formation!'

On days when they weren't flying missions the crews were sent up on exercises devised by their CO to further the process of licking them into shape. There was much grumbling about Old Pappy's severity as a taskmaster. 'Rugged missions plus rugged exercises. When does a guy get a break?' said Lance, in canteen converse with Lorna.

'He doesn't,' she replied. 'Supposed to be good for you, all this, you know.'

Daisy May's pink bosoms rose and fell on Lance's back as he heaved an immense and weary sigh. 'Good for what? I'm not likely to be around, way this war's going, to cash in on any benefits lined up for later.'

'Better you are at battle, better chance you'll have of finding yourself still around at the end of it all.'

'Oh, now you're talking *some*,' retorted Lance sarcastically.

'Well, as you've no alternative, you'll just have to grin and bear it, won't you? Colonel Blenmire won't change *his* behaviour, that's one thing for sure, however dim a view you may take of his way of carrying on.'

Lance said gloomily: 'That guy should be banned under the Geneva Convention.'

'You've told me often enough that the Forts are going to win this war in record time. Let's hope that's so. But one thing's for sure: there's no easy way to bring it about.'

Lance heaved another vast sigh. Then: 'I guess I'll go join a buddy, seein' I'll get no sympathy outa *you*,' he said. 'Hard as concrete, you are. Wouldn't feel for a fella, I reckon, even if you knew he was flying in Purple Heart Corner.'

The crews frequently spoke of their dread of finding themselves flying on a mission in what was known as 'Purple Heart Corner': the particularly vulnerable position on the bottom edge of a Fortress formation when viewed by the Luftwaffe assaulting head on; a position inviting attack, as the Germans always concentrated on the loosest element in a formation. The Purple Heart, the United States award given to men wounded in action, was especially associated with this unpopular place in a B-17 formation. Because of the understandable aversion to Purple Heart Corner a system of squadron rotation had been introduced. Strong sympathy was always expressed for a squadron when its turn came to occupy this hot spot.

One mission morning, when Lorna arrived at Fursey Down, Angie and Amy May greeted her with the news that *Daisy May* was flying in Purple Heart Corner that day. Lorna thought of her friends Lance and Vic, and crossed her fingers for them.

When evening came and the Forts returned four were found to be missing, among them *Daisy May*. Lorna, on duty in the canteen, was given this heavy news by Buzz. 'However, it's a mite premature to start tolling bells,' he said. 'They may have ditched in the drink, with a good chance of being rescued, or they may have limped back to some other airfield and we'll be getting a call to ask come pick them up.' His attempt at an encouraging smile was not altogether successful.

Soon the talk in the coffee bar among the returned crews was that the four missing planes were all from Purple Heart Corner. Moreover there were eye-witnesses to describe the drama in which these four had been involved. On the return flight two badly damaged bombers in Purple Heart Corner, *Flak Floosie* and *It's All Yours*, dropped out of formation, hoping to struggle home slowly on their own. Almost at once they had been set upon by 'jackals', as enemy fighters molesting damaged Fortresses were called. Two sister ships, *Daisy May* and *Available Vee*, had thereupon abandoned their places in the formation to join the wounded bombers and help them ward off the jackals: conduct absolutely forbidden under penalty of court martial; breaking formation voluntarily in the face of the enemy being seen as desertion.

The jackals had at once turned upon *Daisy May* and *Available Vee*; fresh enemy fighters had arrived to join the running attack upon the four bombers. The rest of the Fortress formation continued on its homeward flight, abandoning the four breakaways to their fate. 'That's battle procedure; we had no choice.'

'I don't envy those guys,' said a voice. 'Either they don't get back to base, which means they all went down to the jackals, or else they make it back to Fursey Down to find Old Pappy waiting for 'em. It spells murder either way.'

This was greeted by a burst of mirthless laughter.

Soon someone appeared with the news that Old Pappy had returned and had been seen stalking to his quarters, grim-faced. The mood in the aeroclub became tinged with apprehension.

Presently the rumour was circulating, and was then confirmed, that *Daisy May* and *Available Vee* had made emergency landings at an RAF airfield near the coast, being extensively shot up, and with seriously injured men aboard. *Flak Floosie* and *It's All Yours* had ended up as smoking piles of wreckage long before reaching the sea, destroyed by the jackals.

'Well,' said Buzz at the end of the evening to his Red Cross girls, when they were having their own coffees and sinkers alone in the bar before shutting up for the night, 'Herbie's taken a lot from this group, but if this isn't where he blows his top clean off and vows he'll take no more I'll be more than mighty surprised, I'll be darned flattened.'

What Herbie said to the crews subsequently, when the time arrived for him to voice his wrath, became part of legendary history, to be repeated in the years to come whenever veterans of the Group found themselves together. He said (in borrowed British vernacular) that they were the worst bloody bunch he had ever had under his command and he could not imagine what he had done to deserve them. He also paraphrased from the Duke of Wellington that he didn't know whether they could ever succeed in frightening the enemy, but the thought of having to fly into action with them frightened *him* good and plenty.

Yet, by some perverse alchemy, their CO's searing attack, which should have withered them to perdition, filled the crews with pride that they were deserving of such ironical insult, such blasting scorn; invective so scathing that (at least, it seemed to the recipients) it approached the laudatory. 'My, it was sump'n to hear him!' they could be heard exclaiming afterwards. 'Gee, did you hear what he said? The worst bloody bunch he's ever had! Can't imagine what he's done to deserve us!' 'Boy, that was the richest doggone speech I ever heard yet.' Their flattered delight knew no bounds. 'Well, I've heard him take off before, but that sure was an all-time high.' 'He made us eat crow, and how!'

'You have to have something to make a man like that insult you like that,' bragged Lance to Lorna. 'Have to have real potential.'

'We'll show him,' said Vic. 'We'll show him what his bloody worst can do.'

With their CO's lashing strictures ringing in their ears they elected to call themselves 'Herbie's Worst – the best darn bomb outfit in the ETO'.

'And you can reckon on us living up to that,' said Vic, swaggering out of the aeroclub with his breast-bedecked shoulders squared in determination.

XVII

The weather was hot; the midday rush hour frenetic with crowds of sightseeing Yanks, all in holiday mood. Bunty pointed out Nelson's Column to a GI who had asked to be shown it, and when he got off the bus at Parliament Square he handed Bunty a big pack of chocolate bars, 'For you, Bright Eyes', adding: 'You look like my kid sister.'

A US Army captain who had asked for Parliament Square remained on the bus. He had got on at Leicester Square, and had sat staring at Bunty all the way down Whitehall. She called to him: 'Parliament Square. Don't you want this stop?'

'No. I made a mistake.'

'Then, where is it you want to go to?'

'The finish of the final stage, I guess.'

'Lupus Street?'

'I guess so. If that's the final stage.'

Bunty took the extra fare from him and punched him another ticket. He had large dark eyes with long brown lashes, and throughout the rest of the journey he continued to contemplate Bunty pensively. By the time they reached Lupus Street terminus he was the only passenger left. Bunty collected her gear together, saying to him, politely but firmly: 'This is Lupus Street. The bus doesn't go any further.' He responded, equally politely: 'I hope you'll excuse me taking the liberty of asking, but I wonder if you would care to have dinner with me this evening?'

Bunty was used to receiving all manner of invitations from the GIs, but had not yet been propositioned by a passenger of the officer class. For a moment she was almost tempted – he was well mannered, nice looking and elegant – but then she decided it would never do for her to start being picked up by strangers who happened to ride on her bus, and so she replied: 'I am afraid that

I am already engaged for this evening.' She accompanied this refusal with a courteous little smile and hurried after Gus Harris into the depot.

They took their dinner-break. Gus Harris said: 'Met that friend of yours, Edie, on the way to the depot this morning.'

'Oh? How was she?'

'Didn't have time to say much, but' – Gus gave a leery wink – 'she had a loverly collection of lovebites round her throat.'

'Homer, I expect,' said Bunty. Homer was Edie's Yank boyfriend.

'Blooming Yanks.'

'She says Homer's different,' said Bunty.

'Reckon he will be, too. Blooming werewolf by the looks of it,' rejoined Gus, grinning. 'All tarred with the same brush, that lot,' he added.

'What? All werewolves?'

'All sex mad, the Yanks are,' said Gus piously. He was a much married man with five children. He was now wearing a virtuous expression which, Bunty thought, was not entirely convincing.

After their dinner break they returned to the bus. Two passengers were seated in it, waiting for it to start: a middle-aged woman in a headscarf tied like a turban and with the air of exhaustion Bunty now associated with married women who took on factory work in addition to their domestic burdens of husband, home and children; and the gallant American captain.

He asked for a ticket to Hampstead Heath. Bunty gave him one of her more severe looks. 'It's a long ride from here, you know.'

'I enjoy nothing better than riding on buses.'

He rode back and forth on the bus for the rest of the afternoon. At the end of each run he repeated his request to Bunty that she should have dinner with him. Bunty, on each occasion, replied: 'I'm afraid I can't. I've already said, my evenings are all taken up.

Wouldn't you like to ride on another bus for a change? You must be getting to know this route rather well.'

'I am. I just love it.'

'Is that young chap bothering you?' Gus asked Bunty.

'Not really. He's very polite. No trouble. Just says that he loves the route.'

'Well, let me know if he becomes troublesome,' said Gus.

At the end of the day, when Bunty left the South End Green depot and began walking uphill towards home, she observed that her day-long passenger had vanished. He had remained on her bus till the end; she had wondered if he would try to follow her home, but now he had disappeared.

The Heath was beautiful in the early-evening sunshine. A blackbird was singing; Bunty loitered, listening. Then she resumed walking, thinking about the potato flan she proposed to make for her supper. It should last her for two nights, perhaps three. She was wishing she had some nutmeg to go with it, but that was like crying for the moon. Then she heard footsteps following her. She glanced over her shoulder; the captain was coming up behind her, now carrying a bunch of pink roses. She realized that when he had disappeared it had been into a florist's shop.

She rounded upon him angrily. 'I don't like being followed. Please go away.'

'I'm not following you. Merely strolling behind you – by sheer coincidence in the same direction.'

'I don't like it. Go away.'

'Am I breaking any law?'

'You're pestering me. Making a nuisance of yourself. The first policeman I see, I'll have you arrested.'

'Rely on me, ma'am, to act the gentleman. First bobby we see, I'll hand myself over.'

'You're being a most frightful bore.'

'My misfortune. Some – undoubtedly not many, but some – take to me immediately.'

'A facetious bore!' And Bunty resumed marching up the hill. She was wondering how on earth to get rid of him.

They were nearing the gate of Kenilworth Lodge. She rounded on him once more, this time in pleading. 'Look, I'm asking you to please *please* go away! I've put up with you on my bus all day—'

'I was fully entitled to ride on your bus. I paid my fare. You issued me with tickets. Nothing irregular about that, I guess.'

'Don't you understand? I want you to go away!'

'Are you sure that is what you really want?'

'Most certainly.' She told herself firmly that it was, too.

'What a pity! At least let me present you with these roses before I go; a little thank-you for a most delightful day.'

He held out the roses to her. She shook her head.

'Hey, come on now,' he said. 'You took a load of candy bars from a GI; I saw you. What's wrong with a poor guy like me offering you a bouquet, lady? Am I dirt?'

Bunty, not knowing quite what to say to this, allowed him to put the roses in her hand.

'Well,' he said, 'I guess that's it.' He gave her a last lingering look, meantime heaving a huge sigh. At that moment, when Bunty was almost certain that she was at last on the point of being rid of him, her elbow was warmly gripped from behind and Thoedor Kaufmann's voice boomed genially in her ear: 'Congratulate me, congratulate me! A packet of biscuits!' He waved a packet of some kind of biscuits in her face, then held out the packet for her to read the label, with the exact gesture of a *sommelier* presenting for approval a bottle of choicest wine, his eyes fixed on her in smugly confident expectation of her delighted approval.

Bunty automatically responded by reading aloud: '"Jacobs Cream Crackers."'

'"Jacobs Cream Crackers"!' repeated Theodor, in ringing tones, ecstatically brandishing the packet. 'A gift', he continued, 'from a valued neighbour who shall remain nameless. But don't let me keep you on the pavement like this; I have in my flat the Schwartzes and a bottle of actual cider. All we need, dear Bunty, is for you to join us. And, of course, your companion, too.' Theodor turned, with a courteous slight bow, to the American who at once shot out his hand, saying: 'Waldo Stein, from Manhattan. Pleased to meet you!'

'Kaufmann. Theodor Kaufmann. Delighted to meet you!'

They shook hands warmly. Bunty hissed: 'Captain Stein, you really mustn't inflict yourself . . .'

'Infliction? Not the slightest!' Theodor swept Bunty and Waldo Stein through the gate and up the front garden path, propelling them forward with magnetic force of personality, intoning the while: 'Any friend of yours, dear Bunty, is a friend of mine. Just as I hope that any friend of mine must be . . . and so forth.' He changed his tone. 'The back door we must go in at. I left it ajar while I popped out for the biscuits; the truth is I have lost my front-door key and am trying to replace it without telling Mrs Wells . . .' This last in a whispered gabble as he bundled them down the narrow side passage, opened the back door and crammed them through it into the always murky little rear hallway, saying: 'Americans are fortunately informal people, or so one always gathers, my dear Stein.'

'Oh surely, surely,' agreed Waldo, at that instant stepping on something crouched eating out of a saucer. There was a yowl and a demented spitting. 'What in the world was that?' gasped Waldo.

'Only our landlady's cat. Not, I fear, of an amiable disposition,' replied Theodor. 'Especially when trodden on.'

'Who would be?' muttered Waldo.

Bunty gave way to a violent fit of muffled giggles.

'This way, this way,' urged Theodor, bundling them up the stairs.

'My, it's dark,' said Waldo, tripping on the bottom stair.

Theodor explained: 'Blackout precautions. The rear window here is painted black to economize on curtaining. You don't have it in New York?'

'We call them drapes.'

'Drapes?' Theodor was obviously baffled, but refused to admit to it. 'Ah, drapes.' He bundled Waldo ahead of him. 'Up the stairs. These are the back stairs. Formerly, I suppose, intended for the servants. Through this door. Now, here we are, on my landing.' Evening sunshine unexpectedly flooded over them from the landing window. Theodor flung open his flatlet door. 'Please enter! My castle, my den, my roost!'

He held the door wide open while Bunty, followed by Waldo Stein, stepped into the room. The Schwartzes, who were seated, rose to their feet, making polite little sounds upon seeing Bunty.

Introductions were made. There was much courteous bowing, handshaking and smiling, Waldo Stein being very proper and formal.

Bunty resigned herself to the situation. She had done her utmost to be rid of Captain Stein. Blast Theodor!

He was now playing the busy host. 'You know the British Isles, Waldo? You will permit me to call you Waldo?' He opened the bottle of cider as he spoke.

'By all means, Theodor. I'd be upset if you didn't. Know the British Isles? Hardly. I visited England several times before the war with my parents but never roamed far beyond central London. I have vague memories of Hampton Court. I look forward to getting to know it all a bit better, this time round, on furloughs; if I get any. I'd like to make Scotland, too.'

'Scotland. Ah, Scotland!' Theodor rolled his eyes in ecstasy. 'The

Highlands! Romantic! Wild! Walter Scott! Pitlochry. Oban. Aviemore. I have seen them all. But my goal, my aim, are those beautiful he brides, which Dr Johnson so loved and enjoyed.'

'Excuse me, whose brides?' enquired Waldo.

There was a pause during which the Schwartzes exchanged sly glances which said that here was their host making himself ridiculous as usual. Bunty, struggling to remain straight-faced, said nothing.

At last Waldo resumed, admirably deadpan: 'Sure you don't mean she brides, Theodor? I've never heard that Dr Johnson ...'

Theodor quivered suspiciously. 'I have mispronounced something?'

'Hebrides, Theodor, Hebrides,' murmured Bunty.

'Heb-ri-dees.' Theodor repeated it slowly, with an air of disbelief. 'There is no logic whatever to the English language. Heb-ri-dees. Well, well.' He shook his head.

'Very beautiful, I believe,' said Waldo. 'I kinda fancy going there, too, some day.'

Theodor poured the cider which, it transpired, had been won by him as first prize in an office raffle. 'It must be vintage cider,' said Bunty politely. Cider had vanished from the scene ages back. She took the glass in her hand and watched intently the bubbles rising in the amber liquid. 'How pretty it is,' she exclaimed. At the same time she thought to herself: What a pass we have reached when cider seems an exciting drink!

Theodor was now opening the packet of biscuits with the air of assumed modesty usually associated with a host serving caviare. The first biscuit he eased from the packet broke into several pieces; in addition, it did not look a healthy colour. At once all suspicion, Theodor popped a fragment in his mouth and masticated it slowly and thoughtfully, his facial expression one of the profoundest concentration. Then, 'Stale!' he pronounced.

Disgustedly he tossed the packet of biscuits on to the table.

'I don't see how they could be otherwise,' said Mrs Schwartz. 'All biscuits are sheer gold dust nowadays and Jacobs Cream Crackers haven't been on the open market for I cannot think how long. Whoever gave you that packet of biscuits must have had it in their cupboard a good two or three years.'

'I knew, from the colour alone, that they were wrong,' said Theodor.

'There's nothing *wrong* with them,' retorted Bunty. 'They're very stale, that's all. They wouldn't *poison* us.'

'Precisely,' said Dr Schwartz. 'Have you anything else to offer us? For if not, then *faute de mieux* . . .'

'I could possibly knock up one or two watercress sandwiches,' said Theo dispiritedly.

Waldo began laughing.

Dr Schwartz picked up the despised packet and took a biscuit for himself. It, too, fragmented upon removal from the packet. He ate the fragments ruminatively. 'Everything considered, these biscuits seem to me to have lasted rather well. Not at all bad in fact.'

'But they break immediately one touches them,' objected Theo.

'Yes, but if you study their fracture line . . .' Dr Schwartz, with a scientific air, took another biscuit which at once fell into fragments in its turn. He took a third; this, too, collapsed into bits. 'They all break in precisely the same way. The packet has been dropped.' He manoeuvred all the fragments into his mouth. 'So far as flavour is concerned, they aren't that bad, considering their age,' he concluded, when he was able to speak again. He proffered the packet to his wife. 'Try one.'

'Wait, wait, let me give you a plate,' exclaimed Theodor. He fetched a plate for Mrs Schwartz, who took a biscuit, watched it disintegrate and then nibbled the pieces, giving the slightest of giggles as she did so. 'Let me try one,' said Bunty. She, too, experimented with a biscuit. 'My stars,' she said, 'I'd forgotten what they taste like. Remember them with Stilton?'

'Don't!' groaned Theodor.

Waldo sat watching this scene and listening to them all with the beguiled expression of a child at a pantomime.

'Who gave you these biscuits, Theodor?' enquired Mrs Schwartz, after the packet had been handed round again.

'Well, to make no secret of it, our good Mrs Moxton gave them to me,' replied Theodor. 'In return for a small kindness on my part: a tip for removing mildew stains. She said: "Call in when you're passing. I may have a little something for you!"'

'Sounds a dangerous woman!' said Waldo, much amused.

Bunty suddenly remembered the pack of choc bars in her handbag. She took them out with much the same flourish with which Theodor had originally produced the Cream Crackers. 'Perhaps I might add these to the feast?'

'Holy smoke, where d'you get those?' gasped Theodor, goggling.

Dr Schwartz said: 'Have you been removing mildew stains, too? Mrs McEwen, I thought better of you.'

'Loot,' said Bunty. 'From a GI on my bus today. Because I reminded him of his sister.' She opened the pack and handed it round. 'A whole bar each?' asked Mrs Schwartz, hesitating.

'Of course,' said Bunty. 'I've no doubt I shall be given plenty more.' She handed over most of the candy the Americans gave her to Gus Harris, for his children.

'Where do they get it from?' said Theodor, taking a bar.

'It's their issue,' said Waldo. 'There's no shortage of candy.'

'How much do they issue you with?' enquired Theodor.

'I said, there's no shortage. Candy galore.'

The others, unwrapping their choc bars, looked at him with solemn eyes.

'Comes from the PX,' said Waldo. 'It costs, but only a fraction of what you'd pay for it back home. The same with cigarettes; the normal PX ration per man is up to four cartons of two hundred cigarettes a week, costing eight cents each packet of twenty, plus one tin of tobacco, usually Prince Albert, and four cigars. They cost two cents each, which is about a penny each, I guess.'

'What's a PX?' asked Theodor.

'It's a store for American service personnel. We can buy the kinda things there we can't get in the shops over here.'

Bunty was glad to see that he was turning rather red in the face.

'Well,' said Dr Schwartz, 'if Uncle Sam can get away with it, why not?' He shrugged, smiled round at the company in general and then started playing with the silver paper wrapping off the choc bar.

Waldo's discomfort was apparent. Theodor, anxious to make him less ill at ease, said encouragingly: 'Tell us about yourself, my dear fellow. What are you in? Tanks? Infantry? Army Pay Corps? Your uniforms are so different from what we normally see over here, they tell us nothing.'

'I'm in Intelligence. In an office. Real dull,' replied Waldo with one of his heavy sighs.

'And you live where, when at home?'

'Manhattan. New York.'

'Manhattan? Aha, among the skyscrapers?'

'Not quite. Riverside Drive; but it's not far from the skyscrapers. We can see them close enough.'

'You were born there?'

'No, I was born and grew up in Paris. I didn't go to the States till I was – let me see now – till I was fourteen. Then my parents shifted to the States. They had relatives there, and business interests.'

'Then you are a European, my dear fellow,' said Theo, much relieved.

'I fear not. I'm an American. My father was an American and my mother, too.'

'Whatever he is, or is not, he is a good Jewish boy,' said Dr Schwartz, smoothing out the piece of silver paper until it was wrinkle-free.

'My grandparents came to the States from Odessa,' said Waldo.

'From Odessa? Mine, too,' said Dr Schwartz. 'All the troublesome Jews come from Odessa. All the intellectuals and the modern Hebrew poets: Bialik and Tchernikovsky came from Odessa. Isaak Babel came from Odessa. The violinists, the great child prodigies, come from Odessa: Elman, Zimbalist, Gabrilowitsch, Heifetz. All from Odessa. Now comes Waldo Stein. What more can you ask of Odessa?'

'Do you play the violin, Waldo?' enquired Theo eagerly.

'Yes, but badly. I disappointed everyone.'

'There is a limit to the world's need for Jewish infant prodigies brandishing violins,' said Dr Schwartz. 'We should be relieved to have been spared yet another one.'

'So what did you do in life, before you were drafted?' pursued Theo.

'I went to Yale.'

'Oh? And did what?'

'Nothing. I had a great time.'

'This boy is encouraging,' said Dr Schwartz. 'He must fill his parents with hope.'

'You had no serious subjects? One generally has at least one serious subject,' said Theodor.

'I was serious about the war,' said Waldo. 'I prayed till I sweated for the US to enter the war. The night of the day of Pearl Harbor I drank champagne. And three days later when Hitler declared war on the States I threw a party. Boy! Was that some party! The happiest day of my life! And next day I signed on.'

'Without waiting to be drafted?'

'Why wait?'

'And now, after all that, they have put you in an office,' said Bunty.

'For the time being anyway,' said Waldo.

'Where else could he be so intelligent?' asked Dr Schwartz.

Theo shrugged. 'It seems rather pointless.' He paused, drained his cider and asked: 'And do you live in barracks?'

'In barracks?' Waldo sounded startled. 'No. I'm in a hotel in Knightsbridge.'

'That must be expensive.'

'I wouldn't know. It's been requisitioned for the people in our department.'

'Americans don't live in barracks,' said Mrs Schwartz. 'Not unless they are very unlucky.'

Theodor asked Waldo: 'D'you play tennis by any chance?'

'I do, but probably not up to your standard,' replied Waldo cautiously. 'It's like my violin – lets me down.'

'Bridge?' asked Dr Schwartz.

'Anytime.'

'Well, I don't know about the answer to your prayers, but that certainly sounds like an answer to ours,' said Mrs Schwartz. 'Theo, he plays bridge.'

'Splendid.'

Bunty watched the four of them settle down to bridge without ado. Completely forgotten, she took up her roses and her handbag and crept off to her own flat. She put the roses in a big glass jug of water, sat by the window and smoked a cigarette. She knew what bridge fiends were like; she had an uncle who was one. Anyway, the roses were nice.

XVIII

Waldo telephoned Bunty the following evening. He said without preamble: 'I'd like to take you to a Promenade Concert some evening with dinner afterwards maybe. How about it?'

'Won't you be playing bridge?' Her voice had an edge.

'I'm playing bridge next Tuesday. I reckon I can manage almost any other night, to suit you. I'd really like it if you would.'

Bunty was determined not to make it too easy for him. After all, who *was* Waldo Stein? 'I'm very much tied up at the moment. Ask me again on Tuesday evening, if you still feel like it. I may have a clearer view of things by then.'

She thought this might dampen his ardour a little, but Tuesday evening found him tapping on her door. Bunty was sitting by her window, knitting and listening to the wireless. She asked Waldo into her flat. 'Can I offer you a coffee now that you're here?'

'I guess not, much as I'd like one. The others are straining to start their play.'

'D'you play well enough for them?' She knew they all took bridge seriously, especially Theodor who refused to play with the Parsonses because they weren't good enough.

Waldo said: 'They're just about in my class if I condescend a little.'

'Well, false modesty is no virtue, that is true,' said Bunty, laughing.

They made a date to meet at the Albert Hall for a Promenade Concert, to which Bunty would be going anyway as she had a season ticket, and he would take her out to dinner afterwards.

As they chatted, making these arrangements, Bunty noticed that Waldo repeatedly stole glances at the portrait of David on the mantelshelf. Finally, as Waldo rose to go, his eyes once more resting on the portrait, Bunty said: 'That's my husband, David

McEwen; in the RAF, Bomber Command. He was shot down about a year ago.'

'Theodor told me. I'm sorry.'

'It happens all the time.'

'I guess so. But that doesn't make it any less tough.'

'You'd better get back to that bridge. They'll all be champing at the bit.'

The evening at the Prom wasn't a success. Bunty and Waldo had scarcely arrived on the Promenade floor than they were recognized by one of Waldo's brother officers, a Peter Sakowski, who took an instant fancy to Bunty and despite their efforts to shake him off stuck close to them throughout the concert. When it was over he invited them to have dinner with him at the Knightsbridge Grill. Waldo said: 'Nice as it is of you, Peter, I'm afraid not. I'm taking Bunty to the Savoy.'

'Then, let me take you both to the Savoy.'

'It's still very nice of you Peter, but I'm much afraid—'

The obstinate Peter cut Waldo short. 'It's my last night of leave. Don't make me spend my last night of leave alone.'

Bunty and Waldo exchanged a desperate glance. Peter said: 'Give me an evening to remember, both of you.'

Waldo said: 'It's up to Bunty.'

Bunty, thinking how horrid to have to spend your last evening of leave alone, even if you were a Peter Sakowski, said: 'Then, let's go to the Knightsbridge Grill. It's nice and near. And perhaps Waldo will take me to the Savoy another time.'

The Knightsbridge Grill was crowded, hot and noisy. It was a popular place. Peter became rather drunk. Waldo sulked. Bunty was wearing a pair of new shoes which pinched her feet. Most of the dishes printed on the menu were no longer on it.

When they emerged from the restaurant Peter and Waldo began arguing about which of them should see her home. Bunty, fed up and in agony from her feet, spotted a taxi cruising along on the look-out for Yank fares – British civilians no longer interested the cabbies, who received enormous tips from the Americans. Bunty flagged down the cab and jumped in. 'Hampstead, please.'

The cabbie eyed the Americans. 'Aren't they with you, miss?'

'No,' said Bunty, 'they're not. You'll have to take a poor limey this time. Lady in distress.'

She slammed shut the cab door at the instant Peter and Waldo spun round looking for her, both shouting 'Hey!' The taxi driver, amused, shouted back at them, derisively, 'Lorst her!' and drove off, with Bunty sighing in relief and pulling off her shoes. She couldn't get them on again and had a tortured hobble up the gravelled garden path to the front door of Kenilworth Lodge. 'So much for my evening out with Captain Stein,' she said conversationally to David's photograph.

The next night she went to the Albert Hall alone. She liked going to concerts by herself; you didn't need to talk to anyone. It was a Brahms concert, and when she arrived home she said to David's portrait: 'You would have enjoyed that one, darling.'

She was about to settle down to a cup of beef tea made with an Oxo cube which Megan had given her, rare as a nugget of gold and deriving from some Eldorado-like Yank source, when she was called to the phone. It was Waldo. 'Why did you leave without saying good-night yesterday evening?' he asked aggrievedly.

'I was afraid you might lose the argument about which of you should see me home, and I didn't want to find myself with that gruesome Peter What's-it,' replied Bunty.

'That lying creep. I thought you liked him?'

'Liked him? Certainly not. I was sorry for him, having to spend his last evening of leave alone, but I didn't *like* him.'

'The lying creep. That was no more his last evening of leave—'

'Why didn't you say so?'

'I wasn't sure enough to call him a lying creep to his face. Next day I found out he was lying for sure, but then it was too late. But I can say it now without fear of a bloody nose. That guy's a lying creep.'

'We're agreed on that one anyway.'

'You'd say, too, he was a lying creep?'

'Absolutely.'

'Great.'

There was a pause. Waldo said: 'What about tomorrow night?'

'I shall be going to the concert; it's the first performance of the new Vaughan Williams symphony. He's conducting it.'

'I'll meet you there. I'll stand by that fountain thing in the centre. Afterwards we'll eat some place, but we'll decide where when we meet. I said the Savoy because I wanted to squelch that goop, and I certainly will take you to the Savoy one evening, but I think it should be somewhere more intimate this time round. It'd be nice to get to know you.'

'A hamburger in a telephone kiosk?'

'What we call a booth. Yeah, maybe. I'll work on it.'

The weather had turned hot suddenly, and the Albert Hall the next night was stifling. Because of the Vaughan Williams symphony the place was crowded; the promenaders were packed together like pilchards. Bunty, a little later than she had intended being, couldn't get anywhere near the fountain. She was obliged to stay wedged where she was. Her printed programme carried the usual little notice: 'In the event of an Air Raid Warning the audience will be informed immediately, so that those who wish to take shelter, either in the building or in public shelters outside, may do so. The concert will then continue.' It made it sound such a fearfully bad show to wish to take shelter. And with the venerable Sir Henry Wood (this was his forty-ninth Promenade Concert season) continuing to conduct the orchestra regardless of the onslaught of the enemy how would any member of the audience dare to confess to a cowardly wish to play safe?

But this evening nobody would be faced with this dilemma of decision because the audience was so crushed together that individual movement was out of the question.

The concert began with Mendelssohn's overture, 'A Midsummer Night's Dream'. At the finish of the overture a large number of latecomers were allowed on to the promenade floor; Bunty found herself relentlessly pushed forward towards the centre. Between the people she could now glimpse Waldo's dark head as he stood by the fountain. Just before Vaughan Williams came on to the platform to conduct his new symphony Waldo turned his face in Bunty's direction and caught her eye. She flung him a look of wild despair. He responded with a grimace of his own; a contortion of the features which somehow conveyed delight at seeing her, horror at her predicament, sympathy, and personal suffering (like everyone else he was being relentlessly squeezed from every direction). Then Vaughan Williams came on to the platform, there was an outburst of enthusiastic applause, followed by intense expectant silence. The symphony began.

It was the Symphony in D, and of it Waldo subsequently remarked that it was the kind of thing which gradually grew on you; but at this first hearing Bunty was far from enthralled and had great difficulty in preventing her mind from wandering from the music. The airlessness and heat increased with every moment; the flowers banked before the orchestra wilted and swooned, while among the packed promenaders people began to drop, subsiding floorwards, but through lack of space usually were caught before they reached the ground and were held dangling like a smitten puppet until one of the ambulance corps could struggle to them and remove them outside or, more usually, until they revived of their own accord, to resume dazedly listening to the music and doubtless praying for the interval and escape. Indeed, the stoicism displayed by the afflicted promenaders was of the highest degree; if one were going to faint (thought Bunty) then one should at least do it in the style of these promenaders at the Albert Hall – refusing to succumb until the very last possible minute, standing pallid and swaying, barely conscious, until at last their legs gave way beneath them and deathly drops appeared on their livid faces.

At this point Bunty reminded herself that she had come to the Albert Hall to listen to the music and not to ruminate upon the fine art of fainting. So she began to concentrate fiercely on the scherzo and what the programme notes described as its theme of pentatonic character against which would presently be heard a phrase on solo flute and bassoon. The theme climbed steadily upward, higher and higher, then dropped suddenly. And just as suddenly the floor seemed to drop away from under Bunty's feet; a most peculiar sensation. She gave a gasp and stared quickly up at the great domed ceiling overhead, her reaction being that the Albert Hall had been struck by a bomb and was collapsing. 'In the event of an Air Raid Warning the audience will be informed immediately . . .' Well, someone had forgotten to inform them! But this could not be. She was imagining things. Concentrate. Watch out for the phrase on solo flute and bassoon. Or had she missed it?

The floor gave way under her feet again. She felt herself to be, quite literally, going through it. Sinking. It's a bomb after all, she thought. Too late now to take shelter, either in the building or in public shelters outside. I've had it. We've all had it.

The next she knew she was lying on the floor of a long dark tunnel with figures stooping over her. Something cold was being held against her forehead, and small gusts of air swished to and fro across her face. A misty haze made it difficult to see; there was a buzzing in her ears. The haze gradually lifted; a St John Ambulance nurse was stooping over her applying a cold compress to her brow, and Waldo was crouched on the other side of her agitatedly fanning her with his programme.

The tunnel became the passage which encircled the arena; Bunty could not for the life of her recall how she had got out there. 'Heavens!' she said. 'What happened? Let me sit up.'

She struggled to sit upright. The nurse and Waldo pushed her back.

'Lie down, you dumbo,' said Waldo.

'You just fainted, dear,' said the nurse. 'You'll be perfectly all right in a moment or two. Just lie still.'

Presently they helped Bunty to her feet. She clung rather shakily to Waldo. 'I'm sorry I was so silly,' she said. 'It was the heat. And that music.'

'Anything in D is always disturbing,' murmured Waldo soothingly.

'Get her to the fresh air,' advised the nurse.

Bunty was propelled to the exit and seated on a step while Waldo fetched a taxi. In this he and the nurse installed her, and Bunty found herself riding through the park. Waldo sat beside her holding her hand while she rested her aching head on his shoulder. 'I've never known it so airless,' she said. 'People were going down like flies. I'm amazed you didn't pass out yourself, Waldo.'

'Me? The boy from Odessa?'

The taxi emerged from the park and began moving down Oxford Street. Presently it turned off to the right, into Soho.

'Where are we going?' asked Bunty, raising her head. She had supposed herself on the way home.

'Ley-On's Chinese restaurant,' said Waldo. 'I'm told it's good.'

'Oh, Waldo, I couldn't eat a thing. I'd much rather go straight home.'

'Don't be ridiculous. The best possible remedy for *any* weakness is food.'

At Ley-On's they chose a table near the door where they had the benefit of draughts of air from the street. The restaurant was cool and quiet. Waldo took up the menu firmly.

'I shall choose you something light, but nourishing.' He scanned the menu. 'An omelette, I think, with a slight scattering of mushrooms.'

'Can't I have bean sprouts and cucumber? That's nice and cool.'

'Very well, bean sprouts and fried sliced chicken. Chicken is more nourishing for you in your enfeebled state than cucumber. And, oh, fried savoury rolls and crispy noodles with pork and onion, New York-style, and a chicken-liver chop suey, and when we've dealt with that we'll think again.'

'Waldo, I couldn't possibly eat all that.'

'You don't have to. I'll get it eaten all right.'

'Pork! Jewish, and you eat pork?'

'You sound just like my mother. Except that she doesn't even know I eat pork.'

'Waldo, you surprise me, eating pork. I don't know any other Jew who eats pork.'

'Don't sound so worried; the world isn't going to end. I belong to a new generation, and we've done a lot of thinking about this and have decided that prejudices beget prejudices, and if Jews want Gentiles to drop their prejudices against them, then Jews must be prepared to drop some of their prejudices, too, including the better-known ones like not eating pork. Make yourself different from the rest of the world, and the rest of the world is bound to resent you.'

'D'you want to be like the rest of the world?'

'Not madly. But I don't want to be a marked man, either. Or, if I am a marked man, I want it to be for something rather more distinguished than not eating pork. I don't mind people saying, "Stein is Jewish, and therefore he's cleverer than the rest of us," though even that's pretty dangerous, and I wouldn't mind hearing them say, "Stein is Jewish, and therefore he's braver than the rest of us," though that's unlikely, but I feel kinda pooped when I hear them say, "Stein is Jewish and so he doesn't eat pork".'

The waiter, smooth and smiling, like a little peeled almond, took the order and slid away. Bunty returned to their conversation.

'D'you find you cause a sensation, eating pork?'

'I'm not trying to cause a sensation. I'm trying to prove I'm ordinary, like other people, not a sensational pork-eating Jew. You're missing the point.'

'D'you like pork, now you eat it?'

'I think it's overrated. But you're still missing the point.'

Bunty stared thoughtfully at him. He said: 'There's more involved than pork.'

The food arrived; platters and mounds of it. Bunty said: 'We'll never eat all that.'

'Want a bet?'

The food began to disappear at a surprising rate.

'I wonder where they get all these things from, like bamboo shoots and bean sprouts and chicken livers and noodles. Ordinary people never see them,' said Bunty. 'It's a marvel to me this place can still be so good.'

'They're probably eating their way through their own emporium.'

'Let's hope it lasts out.' Bunty helped herself to more. She said: 'Where is your office, Waldo?'

'On the Eisenhowerplatz.'

'Where's that?'

'Grosvenor Square.'

Bunty sighed, wondering if London could ever be the same again after this invasion.

She helped herself to pork and noodles. 'I think I'll try my hand at Chinese cooking,' she said. 'It's all little bits of lots of different things, and I think it might make the rations stretch further.'

'I'll try taking you out to dinner every night.'

'Every night? You'd soon be bored.'

'Feed you up. You're undernourished. That's why you fainted.'

'Don't be silly. The British wartime diet is in fact a very healthy one. People aren't ill half as often as they were before the war. And that's official.'

'The war takes your mind off your ailments.'

'I haven't any ailments, thank you.'

It was Waldo's turn to sigh now. 'Peter said you'd be a difficult one.'

Bunty looked at him sharply. 'Difficult one? How d'you mean?'

Waldo fiddled with his noodles. 'Well, difficult to loosen up.'

'I like his cheek, the lousy little flea!' exploded Bunty.

'I doubt if a flea could be—'

'Oh, very funny, aren't you?' Bunty was scarlet in the face with anger. Then, remembering that Waldo was, as it were, her host for the evening, she got herself under control and changed the subject. 'You say you hope to see as much of Britain as you can while you're over here. Where do you most hope to go?'

'Failing the He Brides, I guess Cornwall; Tintagel, all those Arthurian places. Like to come with me?'

'I suppose you and Peter have had a bet about that one, too?'

Waldo immediately became furious in his turn. 'If that's your opinion of me . . .'

'Well, you shouldn't behave like such boring, stupid little boys, all you Yanks.'

'I hate you for those remarks.'

The hitherto amicable supper became tense and unpleasant. Waldo, very sulky, lit a revolting-smelling cheroot. When he had settled the bill he followed Bunty out into Wardour Street and slouched beside her, without speaking. They walked into Shaftesbury Avenue. Suddenly there were Yanks everywhere. A taxi drew up and disgorged five of them. Waldo, with instant reaction, hustled Bunty into it and jumped in after her. 'Hampstead,' he told the driver.

Bunty sat on the upholstered seat; Waldo pulled down one of the folding seats opposite, sat on it, put his feet up on the seat beside Bunty and commenced blowing cheroot smoke all over her.

'You can put me down at Tottenham Court Road,' said Bunty. 'I'm not prepared to tolerate your odious behaviour.'

Waldo ignored her, puffing away and throwing ash about.

'Can't you stop smoking that odious thing? It reeks.'

'I know. I buy them specially, to smoke when I'm in the company of people I loathe.'

'And take your feet off the seat. It's insulting to have a man lolling around and behaving the way you're behaving. You're like the worst kind of GI.'

'What you asked for, kid. Insult a Yank, and he'll insult you, plenty.'

Suddenly, at a traffic light, the taxi braked violently, shooting Bunty forward all in a heap on top of Waldo. Without a word he pushed her back on to her seat. A few moments later the taxi lurched forward again, this time to miss a pedestrian who was crossing the road, and again Bunty was shot forward on top of Waldo. In silence, as before, he pushed her back. The taxi turned up Chalk Farm Road, where the road had recently been repaired and was consequently in an exceptionally bad state; the poor old taxi lurched and bumped and then, once more, made an abrupt stop at the lights. Bunty, despite desperate efforts to keep her seat, shot forward again, this time giving herself a smart blow on the chin. Waldo clasped her warmly. 'Won't you stay, *amore mio*? It would be ungallant to repulse these repeated attempts at reconciliation.'

'Go to hell, I *hate* you.' And Bunty scrambled back to her seat.

Waldo threw his cheroot out of the window and swung his feet to the floor. Bunty ignored him.

They arrived at Kenilworth Lodge. Waldo got out of the taxi by one door, Bunty from the other. Waldo paid the fare. From the privet bush beside the Kenilworth Lodge front gate Mr Parsons's voice came softly but clearly: 'Don't linger round here. We are expecting the enemy to attack in precisely four and a half minutes.'

'What in hell?' said Waldo. The voice from the privet bush said: 'You have four and a half minutes in which to say good-night and for Bunty to get indoors. So get a move on, do.'

Bunty said to Waldo: 'It's a Home Guard exercise. They take themselves very seriously.'

'Four minutes,' said Mr Parsons. 'And I can't guarantee you won't be taken hostage.'

'You'd better go, Waldo ... But how will you get back to Knightsbridge? You'll just have missed the last bus, and the last Tube train left a good twenty minutes ago.'

'I'll walk,' said Waldo. 'It'll do me good, finding my way back in the dark.' Oddly, he sounded as if he meant it.

'Three minutes,' said Mr Parsons ominously.

'Follow the twenty-four bus route, Waldo. You should be able to remember it.'

'Two minutes.'

'Good-night,' said Bunty. 'And thank you for a lovely evening.'

'See you tomorrow night? By the fountain?'

'Yes. I'll try to be there early.'

'I advise you to get a move on,' said Mr Parsons in steely tones. 'You're blocking my line of fire.'

Bunty held out her hand. 'Good-night.' Waldo seized it between both his and gave it a violent squeeze. It was too dark by now to see each other's face.

'So long.'

'See you tomorrow.'

'Sure thing!'

Bunty turned and ran up the garden path and let herself into the house. Behind her a whistle blew and there came a salvo of blood-curdling shouts, followed by a loud bang and a Roman candle effect. Bunty wondered if Waldo had got away in time.

Next evening, when she arrived at the Albert Hall and hurried to the agreed rendezvous by the fountain, Waldo was not there, nor did he appear. He was not there the next night, nor the next. Bunty strained her eyes looking for him on each occasion, and was left disappointed and dejected. She began to wonder if he had been injured in the Home Guard exercise! She asked Mr Parsons, who was wearing dark glasses to conceal a black eye. He said: 'Your Yank escort? No, he went off pretty quick when the Germans attacked. Just as you might expect.'

At last a scrappy card arrived, postmarked Inverness. 'Sorry to have disappeared like this. C'est la guerre. Remember me to the lunatic in the bush. He was a stitch. Who was he? See you. W.'

After that, no more from Waldo Stein.

XIX

The clear blue skies of June gave way to a wet early July. With the change back to poor weather conditions the big rugged missions into Germany came to a temporary halt: Command despatched bombers on shallow penetrations, mostly to France. Things at Fursey Down became less fraught.

Herbie went away to a conference of senior officers. Buzz Cabrini said, 'No good will come outa that,' and shook his head ominously.

The camp band (which already prided itself on being a good one) had a new injection of impetus in the guise of a waist-gunner, a trumpeter who saw himself as a second Harry James. Dances were held at the aeroclub frequently, but now they seemed to be going on all the time. The band was keen to get in as much playing as possible while their trumpeter was free to swing his trumpet rather than his .50-calibre machine gun. Everyone in the camp wanted to hear the band play and (if there were any girls around) to dance; the Red Cross girls found themselves in great demand as partners.

Lorna, who was never happy on a dance floor except in a long dress executing the formal dance steps she had learned at finishing school, found herself being taught to jive by Vic Wendell, with Lance Vogel co-operating.

They encouraged Lorna to explore a new side of her personality. 'C'mon, babe, this ain't gonna bite ya,' said Vic. 'Let ya hair down and relax. Give yaself to it. C'mon, give!'

'Trouble with you is, you've always lived in corsets,' said Lance. 'You gotta take 'em off; loosen up. Let yourself go, kid, let yourself go.'

They started off in a purely light-hearted style; friendly, rather brotherly. But then they became really interested, and their manner became objective, professional. 'You got real possibilities,' said Vic, after he had been watching her jive with Lance. 'Nice statistics, real classy gams, good sensa rhythm once you get going; but there's not enough oomph innit.'

'Thass so,' said Lance, after he had watched Lorna performing with Vic. 'You're still handling it with tongs. Still all muffins and tea, 'steada hotdogs an' Coke. You gotta break out.'

Lorna said: 'It's nice of you boys to take so much trouble, but I'm honestly not sure I'm worth it.'

'Aw, c'mon! You're doing swell. Wouldn't trouble with you if you weren't a promisin' proposition.'

Buzz said: 'Wonder what Herbie will say when he comes back to find his cool English secretary he's so proud of is set to become a world-class rug-cutter.'

'It gives a girl sump'n to do,' said Amy May.

The music of the hour for the Americans was the music of their big swing bands: of Glenn Miller, Tommy and Jimmy Dorsey, Artie Shaw. It was not new up-to-the-minute music; its charm for its fans lay in nostalgia: it was the music the bands had played for the college kids of 1939 and 1940, who in 1942 and 1943 were in uniform serving in the ETO. The Miller hits ('Little Brown Jug', 'Moonlight Serenade', 'In the Mood', 'Blue Skies', 'Chattanooga Choo Choo', 'String of Pearls') not to mention Tommy Dorsey's 'Stardust' and 'I'm Getting Sentimental over You', stirred memories of evenings spent at popular locations. 'Meadowbank – on Route Twenny-Three; the Newark–Pompton Turnpike, in Cedar Grove, New Joisey,' the aeroclub patrons would chorus, recalling what the announcers had said in the old days, advertising the Glenn Miller, Tommy Dorsey, Artie Shaw engagements there. Or: 'The Glen Island Casino, overlooking Long Island Sound. Remember?' 'Gee, I do; indeed, I do.' Another voice said: 'I was at La Salle when Miller came there to play.' 'Oh?' said Angie, her eyes misty. 'He played for us at Middlebury, too.'

Lorna, listening to their talk, understood why the music was more to them than just the beat, the sound, the words when it had words to go with it. For her the beat and the sound became increasingly intoxicating the more she heard them. And as she stepped it out, twirled, spun and stomped with Vic and Lance she began to appreciate that there was something more to Americans than the annoying, dismaying or downright shocking things which went so obtrusively against the grain with the English. They had this marvellously alive whizz, bam and zoom about them; they *hit* it. She faced up to Vic, small and intense, like a spark; enmeshed with him in the rhythm of 'In the Mood'. 'Gee, kid, that's groovy!' he shouted approvingly, touching the tip of her finger and rotating her like a yo-yo held on an invisible cord. They twirled about and about, meticulously keeping their motions within the confines of the sound.

Lance took over for 'String of Pearls', winding her away from Vic and establishing a new, stylish, cool mode of jiving; not looking at her nor she at him, but making themselves very felt to each other, as the bars of the music mounted tensely, held a few bars with drumming underneath, descended, rose again like a succession of stepladders. Then 'I'm Getting Sentimental Over You'; dancing on a dime, rotating so slowly they were almost not moving, swaying gently as they rotated, Lance humming the melody in her ear as he chewed gum, his eyes fixed on nothing in particular, she watching the shapes and shadows enclosing them. Then back to Vic for 'Tuxedo Junction', winding it, and one another, up like a humming top gyrating.

'You found it, kid,' said Vic, when it was over. 'She's found it,' he said to Lance.

'Sure thing. Said she would,' responded Lance, lighting a cheroot.

'D'you think?' said Lorna hopefully.

'No kidding,' said Vic. 'That was the real McCoy.'

He took out a packet of gum and thrust a piece in his mouth. Then, recalling his manners, he turned to Lorna. 'Care for a chew?' She was so happy she accepted a piece, though actually she loathed the sensation of gum in her mouth. 'Let's go get ourselves a Coke,' said Vic. He offered Lorna his crooked arm. 'Grab a wing?' he asked. Lance stuck out his arm the other side. 'Likewise?' he said. Lorna, holding an arm of each, walked across to the aeroclub coffee bar. Behind them the band struck up the final number of the evening, 'Stardust'.

Herbie returned the next day. Nobody liked to ask him questions. Finally Lorna hazarded: 'How did it go?'

'OK,' he said briefly. 'All we want now is for the weathermen to give us a run of highs.'

On Friday, 23 July the RAF Met men reported that a series of lows which had hung over Europe was now giving way to a high. Herbie announced to the crews that this was what they'd all been waiting for ('Who says?' commented Lance to Lorna) and here at last was the chance for the Eighth truly to blitz Fortress Europe.

For six consecutive days the Eighth flew rugged missions against top targets. Then came a night of violent thunderstorm, and the weather broke well and truly. The Eighth, grounded again, sat back and took stock of the past week; now being called 'Blitz Week'. Gloomy news spread fast among the groups, and it was quickly common knowledge that something like a hundred Forts had been lost during that one week, or had been damaged too badly to fly again, and some nine hundred men were missing, wounded or killed. The Boeing production lines were now turning out B-17s in numbers which almost passed belief, but trained flying crews were another matter. The casualties during Blitz Week alone amounted to the equivalent of the flying complement of nine squadrons. This would take some making good.

'The truth is,' said Lance, 'though the high-ups won't admit it, the Eighth is now flying suicide missions.'

'You can say that again,' said Vic.

Lance continued: 'The guys who have never had to fly in combat themselves keep telling the crews that things can't go wrong if you hold good formation and fire those wonderful fifty-calibre guns that are so effective just as long as the enemy attacks from the right direction. Everyone who has flown on a real mission can tell those wise guys at the top their talk bears no resemblance to the truth. But wheresa use? Far as those big boys are concerned we're expendable. When there's no aircrews left they'll ask what went wrong. "What's happened?" they'll say. "Sakes, where've all those doggone crews vanished to?" They'll look around for more, and there won't be more. Then maybe they'll think again. But until that time comes we can just expect to be chewed up like we're in supply for ever.'

'It's imposing on us,' said Vic. 'Trying out their ideas on us, is what I call imposing.'

'It's fair enough within limits,' said Lance, 'you've gotta allow it seemed a good war-winning idea before it was put to the test: a self-defending daylight bomber the enemy couldn't destroy. And they had to put it to the test; they were entitled to do that. What they're not entitled to do is to go on and on pitching the same curve over and over once they know it's a sure all-time loser.'

'Herbie knows it's a loser,' said Vic. 'He flies missions with us; he sees what happens. He should tell 'em.'

'Colonel Blenmire,' retorted Lorna, with a certain bite to her tone (she was thinking to herself that a degree of discipline was necessary), '*Colonel Blenmire* is a regular soldier and as such knows perfectly well what he should do and what he shouldn't. He's been given his orders and he carries them out. I have no doubt he has reported very fully on the missions, but if he has orders to follow a strategy and make it work, then he will follow it and make it work.'

'And if everyone but the blamest idiot can see it *don't* work?' queried Vic derisively.

'I admired that man,' said Lance. 'But now I don't. He could stop all this if he wanted. He knows as well as we do what goes on and how the odds are stacked against us. He knows we're being asked to do the impossible. He should speak up.'

Lorna quietly passed all this on to Herbie during one of his chair-spinning sessions. He said: 'This kind of talk can be heard right now in all the groups. It's understandable; but it doesn't lead anywhere. All right, they're being asked to do the impossible. In war, there's nothing exceptional about being asked to do the impossible.'

He revolved away from her and, staring from the window at the Forts on the hardstands, asked bitterly: 'Do they suppose it's easy for me to send all those young fellows to die in the sky?'

Lorna still remained silent, overawed by this question.

'What is needed', said Herbie, spinning this way, then that, 'is a really big one. A put-up-or-shut-up job. Prove or disprove the daylight theory once and for all. The losses may be high, but if what we pull off is good enough, then the powers that be will say we can ride the losses. If, on the other hand, the losses outweigh the achievement . . . well, then, there'll have to be a rethink.'

'But aren't the losses high enough already? You say a really big one; but wasn't Blitz Week a really big one?'

'I doubt if the high-level planners would think so. They've some real ambitious schemes.'

'Well, it's time for me to go home,' said Lorna. She felt profoundly depressed.

Herbie said: 'Have a word with Buzz before you leave. He's working on a gala scheme.'

'A gala?'

'Yeah. You know. He feels we all need cheering up some.'

Buzz, it transpired, had decided that with all this talk of a 'big one' in the air the time had come to throw a 'real big dance'. 'There's too much gloomy talk around; we'll show what Fursey Down can do.' The date was set for Saturday evening three weeks ahead. A committee was formed, on which both Lorna and Daphne sat.

Buzz, who chaired the committee, said: 'This is going to be a real elegant occasion. Not one of your common hops, but sump'n everyone's gonna remember, look back on, for years to come. "Were you at the Fursey Down Gala Ball? No? Well, then, don't talk to me of gala balls." That kinda job, see? I've discussed it with Colonel Blenmire, and he's given the notion his full blessing. The dancing will be in one of the hangars; we'll have our own band, because that band as some of you may know is the best damn swing outfit this side of the Atlantic. We're having a decorations subcommittee to decorate the hangar and the aeroclub, and I'm already in touch with a Mayfair, London, contact with regard to some of the trimmings. We're having proper printed invitations, the sort you'll want to take and frame afterwards. I tell you. It won't be a tuxedo affair, but it'll be near enough. Our main trouble, I guess, will be collecting sufficient girls, and I expect you all to help with that one. We need lotsa girls; but, that said, I need not remind you that they must be reg'lar girls, meaning in English respectable girls. We'll fix collecting-stages, and send round transport for them; nobody will find themselves walking home in the dark unless they want to, and then it's up to them. There'll be a buffet supper *and* a cabaret show afterwards. Gonna be the real McCoy.'

After the committee meeting was over Buzz took Lorna aside. 'You do one thing for me, sugar? Tell the Colonel we don't want no mission flown before or on Saturday August fourteen that makes off with our trumpeter. Maybe he is the best waist-gunner in the group, but too bad; we ain't losin' him till after our gala.'

XX

Over the next three weeks Fursey Down's bombers participated in a deception scheme aimed at making the Germans think that invasion of the Pas de Calais was imminent; this ruse, it was hoped, would halt further German troop movements to Russia. The missions flown were uncomplicated and provided good kindergarten experience for the many replacement crews who had now been hurried on the scene.

Meantime organization of the Gala Ball (as it was grandly called on the invitation cards) went steadily ahead. The invitation cards themselves were no-expense-spared items (Buzz's description); engraved, with a tasteful decorative motif of the Stars and Stripes and the Union Jack entwined. Everyone was invited; everyone, that was to say, who passed the vetting of the Gala Committee. All the villagers of upright reputation, which meant pretty well everybody. All the British Red Cross ladies and their husbands. All the American Red Cross workers for miles around; females preferred.

Farmers with wives and daughters found themselves invited. A WAAF contingent stuck out in the sticks on a hush-hush job was invited. There was an all-out scouting round for girls in general, as long as they were 'reg'lar'; or at least passed for 'reg'lar' ('Heaven knows who is really reg'lar and who's not, these days,' as Buzz Cabrini murmured to Lorna). Trucks, jeeps and buggies were laid on by the camp to pick the guests up and take them home afterwards, almost everyone by now being deprived of petrol and with their cars put away for the duration.

Those not wearing uniform were asked to wear 'gala-style dress'. What exactly the American definition of 'gala-style dress' might be, the puzzled yet intrigued British were not certain. People began turfing through half-forgotten drawers and trunks on a voyage of discovery among old clothes, curtaining, odd items of fancy dress.

'Amazing what we used to wear,' said Miss Glaister. 'And not so very long ago, either.'

Miss Barker found a red satin number with handkerchief points which she had once worn to a diocesan soirée in honour of the then Bishop of Uganda. 'Did I really wear that? I recall that it had a matching stole with it. I wonder where that has hidden itself?'

'Does it still fit?' asked her brother.

'I would imagine so. I'm as thin as I ever was. Just ages older.'

'Try it on.'

'Not unless I can find the stole.'

The stole remained elusive, but she discovered a very nice black silk shawl that went rather well with the dress and a piece of black lace with jet beading which, worn as a cravat, helped to conceal the ravages of time.

Mrs Murray, who was clever with her sewing machine, converted a blue chenille dressing gown into an effective wrap-over dress and then, fired with her success, went on to transform some tangerine velvet curtains into an eye-catching ensemble for Daphne Stacks. 'You have the panache to carry it off, dear,' said Mrs Murray reassuringly.

Dicky Stacks, shown the finished product, said: 'Blimey, the Queen of Sheba in person! What shall I wear to partner that, I wonder?' He settled on a costume he had once worn at a party during a Caribbean cruise: Russian-style silk shirt over black evening trousers tucked in scarlet pirate boots, with a scarlet cummerbund as finishing touch.

Lorna had decided to invite Ruth to the Gala Ball. She was, perhaps, on the young side, but she would be one more girl to partner the many young men, and though she would be mixing with the very Yanks whom Lorna had hitherto always insisted should be given a wide berth by Ruth, that said, it was hard to imagine that Ruth could come to harm at a well-organized occasion in the aeroclub.

Mrs Cuthman had commented to Lorna, 'Don't you think it's maybe . . . ?' leaving her question to hang, as was her habit, openended on the air. Lorna had responded in like style, 'I think she'll have the time of her life, and as I'll be there to keep an eye on her . . . Besides, with so many from the village going, it'd be a pity for her to feel left out.' 'Yes, that's true,' Mrs Cuthman had agreed.

So Ruth had been invited, and had gone off to Ipswich to have her hair permed and styled specially for the occasion.

She had returned obviously very pleased with herself; her former simple bob had been transformed into a considerably more elaborate affair, with the side hair taken up above the temples and secured there, while the ends had been arranged in a cluster of curls on the top of her head. Her back hair hung down with the ends turned under.

'It's the Greta Garbo look,' Ruth had explained to Lorna. 'Anna What's-it . . . you know, when she ended up under the train.'

'Dear me, Ruth, not a very happy example!' Lorna had exclaimed, laughing.

'Well, it's that style, anyhow. D'you think it suits me?'

'Highly becoming, Ruthie. Suits you very well.' Lorna didn't think much of it really; like all cheap wartime perms it tended to be frizzy. But there it was; Ruth had reached the age when she wanted to look like Garbo.

'She always ends up in a bad way,' Ruth had continued with lugubrious satisfaction. 'That's because she always falls in love.'

'You make falling in love sound like a guaranteed recipe for disaster, Ruth!'

'Well, she's always unfortunate, you see. Either a queen, and can't marry; or falls for a man who already has a wife, or she catches TB, or gets betrayed. She's one of that sort never finds happiness, thinks she has, but it never can last.' Ruth heaved a long, heavy sigh, her eyes glistening sentimentally. 'And as Marie Wollooska she grew that thin, well, you could see Napoleon was all wrong for her. Another cup of tea?'

'Yes please, Ruth.' They had been sharing a pot of tea together in the garden.

Ruth, pouring more tea, had asked, 'You ever been in love?'

Lorna, thinking of Ivo, had replied hesitantly, 'I ... I'm not really sure. I once thought I was, but ...'

'If you're not sure, then I reckon you've never been. You see, it's not the number of men you know.' Ruth had waved the teapot in a sort of slow motion, to emphasize the point she was making. 'Take when Garbo was Camille, she knew all those men ... well, that was in Paris,' Ruth had added hastily, 'but all the same she knew all those tons of men and then along came one of them and he was the real thing. Nothing to do with good times, or letting her hair down, or money, nothing like that.' The teapot had once again been given a brandish. 'No, he just happened to be the man for her. The one meant for her. The others didn't count.'

'It was only a film, Ruth.'

'Yes, but films are based on real life, you know. Unless they're *King Kong*, or *Tarzan* or something.'

'Well, it just goes to show that if you insist on looking like Garbo you must prepare for a dismal end,' Lorna had replied, jokingly, and thinking of Bunty trying to make herself look like a variety of stage and screen stars. Why, at one point in growing up, did you always want to look like somebody you could never remotely be in a month of Sundays?

'Maybe I'll try Betty Grable next time,' had been Ruth's response. 'But I'll go to the Gala Ball like Garbo, now I've had it styled that way.' She had added happily, 'There's a lot of film stars to choose from to look like.'

At last the evening of the great occasion arrived. Tex, the waist-gunner double of Harry James, had mercifully survived his missions of the past three weeks ('I can't guarantee anything,' Herbie had told Lorna. 'You know as well as I do that a milk-run may end in disaster for a guy if he's unlucky'). The hangar was transformed with red, white and blue draperies, flags, paper lanterns and great clusters of coloured balloons; the British hadn't seen anything like it since 1939. The aeroclub, too, was lavishly decorated with red, white and blue hangings, more flags, and red, white and blue paper chains. A covered walkway connected the hangar with the aeroclub; it was less than dimly lit, because of blackout regulations, but at least it prevented the guests from wandering off across the airfield and getting lost in the dark. Buzz had hung one or two coloured lanterns in the walkway to make it less sepulchral, but these were removed by an outraged guest who turned out to be the village air-raid warden.

The evening started officially at eight; the Committee members arrived early. Guests, when they arrived, were first ushered into the aeroclub; here they left their wraps and raincoats (the August evening being on the damp and chilly side) and were given favours: the ladies roses, the gentlemen carnations. Next came a cocktail in the bar of the officers' mess; the cocktails, an invention of Buzz, were pineapple juice, orange juice, sarsaparilla and rum (there was a rumour that pineapple and meths made a good cocktail, but the Committee had rightly refused to countenance it). The Americans seemed able to obtain almost anything they wanted, apart from fresh eggs and alcohol: Buzz, however, had produced a mysterious supply of rum for this special occasion.

People stood around chatting, laughing, sipping their drinks and, in the case of the non-uniformed, eyeing one another's costume. Good Egg Glaister was resplendent in a lime green crêpe sleeveless dress with a gold lamé jacket. Miss Cusk wore a navy georgette skirt with a saxe blue sateen coatee trimmed with diamante buttons. Jeffrey Bosco, like Dicky Stacks, sported a vivid scarlet cummerbund. Mrs Friske was in shocking pink with a long string of pearls, and two little pink combs stuck in her hair, pushing her mop of curls into an upright tuft over each ear. Mrs Kirkpatrick, who farmed on her own at Long Bottom and had once been suspected of a romance with Jeffrey, wore an amazing full-length gown of black lace with large cape sleeves and a white tulle scarf tied like a turban, which made her resemble the Queen of the Night. A splendid diamond brooch, undoubtedly real, was pinned in the centre of the turban, scintillating with every movement of her head. Mrs Hedley-Cowper also wore diamonds, and black velvet, and looked remarkably handsome. Miss Luce, a dehydrated blonde of uncertain years, who ran an antiques shop out in the middle of nowhere and survived on her reputation for 'being good for wedding presents', sported a feathered headdress which, as everyone whispered to everyone else, 'came out of stock'. She carried a fan and was attired in an Erté-type twenties outfit. It was all quite fascinating.

Lorna had pondered long over what to wear. Since her mother's death she had rather gone out of her way to avoid being smartly dressed or intentionally attractive in her appearance, going in for muted colours and country-type clothes. She had a party dress she had bought and worn in Venice when she had holidayed there with her parents in the last summer before the war; it had a tight-fitting, pleasantly low-cut sleeveless black velvet bodice with a full skirt of deep flounces in shot silk taffeta, emerald green. She had black pumps trimmed with emerald green bows to match the skirt, and black silk stockings (which, when examined now, fortunately proved to be without serious flaw). Round her neck she had worn a black velvet ribbon with a big white and apricot tinted silk rose. She had made quite a sensation and had enjoyed herself tremendously while wearing it. Now she took dress, shoes, stockings, ribbon and rose out from the wardrobe where she had kept them carefully put away, like a memento of a time which would never come again. She dressed herself up and surveyed herself in the long mirror from her mother's old bedroom. She had forgotten that she could be such a pretty creature.

Feeling somewhat nervous, but confident that she undoubtedly looked delightful, she made her appearance at the Gala Ball, a little late because she had been with Buzz checking on last-minute details of the buffet. Buzz had simply looked at her and yelped 'Wow!'

She had said, twirling round: 'Will I do?'

'If I'd known you'd look like that, I wouldn't've asked anyone else tonight. I'd have kept the gala all to myself and you.'

She walked quietly into the aeroclub bar and immediately found herself face to face with Dicky Stacks. 'My,' he said, ogling her, 'this *is* a transformation!'

'The same might be said of you,' replied Lorna. 'Where did you find those magnificent boots?'

'Port of Spain. Like 'em?'

'Absolutely ripping. Pity you don't wear them more often.'

'Hardly wartime wear. I've been keeping them for the victory celebrations.'

Lorna spied Ruth Cuthman, who had just arrived in a truck along with a bevy of other young girls. Coiffured *à la Garbo*, she was wearing her newly completed red and green frock and proudly clutched Lorna's present to her; the red handbag. Lorna went over to her to tell her, smilingly, how nice she looked. Ruth smiled demurely in return; she seemed a little overwhelmed by the aeroclub and its festive appearance, the people, the costumes. 'I never knew it would be like this,' murmured Ruth, staring round her with her big blue eyes wider and rounder even than usual.

'I hope you're going to enjoy every minute of it, Ruth,' replied Lorna, encouragingly. She didn't want the evening to be spoiled for Ruth because she was feeling shy.

'Oh, I shall enjoy it all right. It just takes a minute or two of getting used to,' said Ruth, giving a long look at Mrs Kirkpatrick with her cape sleeves, white tulle turban and glittering diamonds. 'D'you think that diamond ornament's real?' added Ruth, in a whisper.

'Most certainly, Ruth; I'm sure it must be,' responded Lorna.

'It's not half a whopper!' And Ruth stared harder than ever.

Lorna, turning away, found Jeffrey staring at her. She walked over to him, smiling. 'Hello,' she said.

'Hello.'

Lorna, attempting to expand the conversation, said: 'I like the cummerbund but I'm sorry you've allowed Dicky to beat you with the boots.'

'Boots?' said Jeffrey with an effort, as if collecting his wits. 'Should I be wearing boots? I thought we were going to dance.' He glanced at his feet as he spoke; he had on evening pumps of considerable vintage, with faded piqué ribbon trimming. 'I was feeling rather proud of these,' he added plaintively.

'Where did you get them?'

'I didn't get them; I had them. They were my grandfather's.'

'Really?'

'He was a veterinary surgeon in the Indian Army. Colonel. Specialized in mules.'

'I see what you mean. In their own quiet way they *are* rather superior.'

'And there were you admiring those beastly vulgar things Dicky Stacks is hoofing about in.'

'I'm sorry, Jeffrey; I should have known better. I shan't admire them again.'

'You'd better not, or you will sink below redemption in my opinion.'

'Oh dear!'

Jeffrey took a gulp of cocktail. 'Actually,' he said, 'you're looking beautiful.'

'Oh, thank you! I bought this dress in Venice before the war.'

'It's not just the dress. I mean to say, it's a jolly nice dress, but you . . . well, I like the whole thing.'

'Oh, *thank* you, Jeffrey!' For some reason this compliment from him made her feel really good.

They stood chatting and watching the stream of guests flow in. Miss Barker and her brother, the Reverend Septimus Barker, appeared; she in her red satin dress with the handkerchief points, and silk shawl and shimmering lace cravat, he in sober black enlivened by an embroidered canary yellow quilted waistcoat. The pair approached Jeffrey and Lorna.

'Oh, Mr Barker, I do hope you don't mind me saying so, but I do admire your waistcoat!' exclaimed Lorna.

Mr Barker replied: 'It's made from one of my sister's old dressing gowns. It's rather warm for this time of the year, but Octavia thinks it gives me a needed dash.'

'I think you both look wonderful. Don't you think so, Jeffrey?'

'Absolutely. Fursey-Winwold should be proud.'

'It's a beautiful dress, Miss Barker.'

'Thank you, m'dear. I've been admiring yours, too.'

'Admiring the *tout ensemble*,' said the Reverend Barker gallantly.

Angie brought them a tray of drinks. As she departed Jeffrey said: 'She's a pretty girl. Does she work here?'

'Yes. Angie. One of the American Red Cross girls.'

Good Egg Glaister advanced, gleaming like a polished sun. There was such a distinct atmosphere of dressing up for the occasion, an element almost of fancy dress, that people felt no inhibitions about admiring one another openly. Moreover it was so intriguing to see what reserves of *recherché* costume everyone seemed to have been able to discover once they had started looking.

'This lamé jacket? Unbelievable, isn't it? I bought it at Selfridges; nineteen thirty-seven. To see the New Year in at the Troc.'

'Are we celebrating something special? Or is this just a party for the sake of one, as you might say?' enquired the Reverend Barker.

'I suppose it might be thought of as a kind of birthday party,' replied Lorna. 'The Eighth Air Force flew its first mission a year ago next Tuesday, I believe. But really I think the decision was taken to have a party because everyone thought it would be fun.'

'No better reason, either,' said Jeffrey.

Herbie appeared at this point. A mission had been flown that day, and he was awaiting its return; he looked tense as he always did at such a time. Lorna introduced him to the Barkers, Miss Glaister, Jeffrey. He said how nice it was for him to meet local people at last. 'You've all been so wonderful to the boys, with your general hospitality and kindness, but I never have time to get out to meet you.'

A move was made towards the hangar; dancing was about to begin. Everyone began to shuffle along the walkway, joking about Tunnels of Love and Ghost Trains; the cocktails had been stronger than they had seemed at the time. 'A pity there aren't a few corpses or skeletons scattered around,' said Dicky Stacks. Herbie, who was walking beside Lorna, took her arm. He said: 'Has anyone told you you're looking a million tonight?'

'Yes. Compliments galore.'

'I'm not surprised.'

They reached the hangar, passed through a baffling arrangement of blackout screens and found themselves in a flood of lights, red, white and blue hangings, flags, balloons. A platform had been arranged at the further end for the band. There was a bar serving soft drinks and beer, and set with vases of red and white carnations and blue paper streamers in silver holders. The whole effect was so unexpected after the murky tunnel, and so brilliant, that people literally gasped. Cries of astonishment and admiration filled the air. Herbie stared round him, as bowled over as anyone. 'Well, this beats all!'

The band entered and climbed on to the platform. The immaculate appearance of the entire American personnel had already brought approving comments from the British guests. 'They all look so smart.' The members of the band had so soaped, creamed, combed, groomed and polished themselves that they positively gleamed. Everyone eyed them expectantly, though the British, few of whom had heard an American swing band live, didn't know quite what they were expecting.

The bandsmen took up their instruments, looked at their leader, who was also the trombonist in Glenn Miller style, and waited for his signal. He gave it, almost imperceptibly; the drummer began to drum, Tex the trumpeter swung up his trumpet like he was swinging his fifty-calibre gun into an FW-190 and the sound burst into a riot and exploded over the company. But how to dance to it? The well-tried routines of foxtrots, quicksteps, two-steps seemed hopelessly inadequate. Yet obviously they hadn't all been invited there just to stand and listen. At this point Vic Wendell walked across the floor to Lorna, standing between Herbie and Miss Barker, grinned at her broadly, and said, with a polite duck of the head, 'Care to cut a rug, babe?' extending his crooked arm invitingly as he spoke.

Lorna, slightly embarrassed at finding herself apparently about to lead the first dance of the evening with the irrepressible Vic as partner, cast Herbie an anxious glance of enquiry. He nodded slightly and smiled, obviously amused. Lorna took Vic's arm; he led her proudly to the centre of the floor and, 'Let's go, kid!' he said.

For many of the audience the marvel of the thing was not so much the expertise of the dancers as that one of them was Lorna Washbourne. The onlookers' eyes followed her every movement in total fascination. Then Herbie turned to Miss Barker and said: 'Ma'm, how about it?'

'My dear Colonel, I couldn't possibly do that!'

'You don't have to. And neither could I do it, if it comes to that.

Let's try something a little more conservative.' Before she knew where she was, the Colonel, an expert dancer in his own way, was guiding her through the drummings and trumpet-blasts in a syncopated quickstep with short glides at the turns; something which she would never, in her wildest dreams, have supposed herself capable of managing.

The sight of Lorna and Miss Barker, hitherto regarded, each in her own way, as a rigid example of strict tradition, performing on the dance floor in a style intrinsically transatlantic had a galvanizing effect on the rest of the company. Everyone seized a partner and took to the floor. The Americans jived and jitterbugged. Some of the British tried to emulate them, with varying degrees of success; twiddling, stamping, wriggling and twitching as if seized with St Vitus' Dance; others stuck to the kind of dancing they knew, introducing slight variations in tempo.

Presently the music changed. 'Moonlight Serenade' had everyone circling slowly, 'dancing on a dime'. Herbie was obliged to hand Miss Barker over to Jimmy Yeo – the sound of a Fort, coming in from far off, had Herbie hastening out to the hardstands.

The bombers came in regularly and steadily, the roar of their engines at times threatening to blot out the band. The combination of music and bombers was a strangely potent one and gave the evening a flavour which none present ever forgot. '"There was a sound of revelry by night",' murmured Mr Barker to nobody in particular.

After dancing with Vic, and having a Coke with him, Lorna took the floor with Lance, who was also eager to show off her accomplishments in juxtaposition with his own; unfortunately the other dancers were by now all enjoying themselves too much to be interested in what other couples were achieving in the way of terpsichorean marvel. After Lance there came a succession of partners for Lorna, culminating in Jeffrey, who by now was really letting himself go. He was, as Violetta had once described him, a good dancer 'in a large kind of way'; he needed plenty of room, and he was vigorous. To the swung version of 'Little Brown Jug' he and Lorna danced a kind of Highland Fling, with the occasional whoop from Jeffrey, which the band interpreted as rebel yells and, entering into the spirit of the thing, replied with yells of their own.

It was now time to go in to supper. The buffet was arranged in the aeroclub canteen; the guests eyed in astonishment the long garlanded buffet table with, as centrepiece, an enormous cake with fudge and marshmallow topping and surmounted by small flags and stars, and flanking it on either hand a bewildering array of hamburgers, hotdogs, cold turkey breast, ham, salads, cheeses, canapés, tartlets, sandwiches, American muffins, stuffed pancakes, pies, cookies, strawberries and cream, cheesecake, ice cream. It was like something out of a dream. The guests displayed undisguised greed; but, interestingly, their stomachs had got out of the habit of such feasts, and most people suddenly found they could not eat as much as they had expected.

Supper was followed by the cabaret, which took place in the hangar. Chairs had been placed, but people at the back, unable to see properly between the heads in front of them, hit on the bright idea of climbing up to sit on the girders above. With the help of a ladder the more agile were soon perched aloft in rows like swallows. Lorna clambered up happily enough, then wished that she hadn't; she was not all that high off the ground, but it felt high. She was immensely relieved to discover that Herbie had climbed up after her; he perched beside her and put his arm round her. 'Can't have you falling off. I couldn't do without you, you know.'

'I don't know why I came up here. It looked a good idea from below.'

'Always the way. There's many an aircrew thinks just that same thing. I say it to myself, many a time.'

The cabaret began. There was a comedian who played the piano and wisecracked, followed by a conjuror, followed by an acrobatic dancer who also performed balancing tricks involving champagne bottles. They were all three good in their own way, but the acrobatic dancer, whose well-proportioned body was scantily clad in little scraps of silver gauze, could scarcely make a movement without raising storms of applause mingled with piercing wolf-whistles.

Apart from the spotlights on the acrobat the hangar was in darkness. Cigarette smoke curled up from the people below, drifting across the sloping beams of the spots and losing itself in the shadows among the girders. Herbie lit cigarettes for himself and Lorna, drawing her more closely to him during this hazardous business of fetching out the cigarettes and lighting them without disturbing his or Lorna's equilibrium on the girder. Having drawn her close to him, he kept her pressed close; she set up no resistance to his warm firm clasp, but put her arm round him, holding on to him and feeling ridiculously secure in what was quite a perilous position. Everyone on the girder was pressed together; when one person laughed or cheered a ripple ran along the whole row. Had one fallen, all would have gone.

The acrobat had now reached the grand finale of her performance: she had arranged the bottles in a circle and, standing on her hands, proceeded, to the strains of 'Moonlight Serenade', to 'walk' round the circle, clasping a small Stars and Stripes pennant between her elevated feet, while the spotlights played dizzy criss-cross patterns over her. It was a moment which seemed to go on for ever: breathless to watch, because at any instant disaster might overtake the acrobat and everything fall apart; yet at the same time one hoped for, and more than half anticipated, triumph, and counted every gleaming gold-necked bottle which she successfully put behind her, like glowing seconds in a rapt moment of time.

Lorna, perched aloft, clinging to and clasped by Herbie, the champagne bottles and the white and silver body of the acrobat flashing and shining in the gyrating mesh of lights, the music rising and falling in the background, felt that she had been carried back to one of those childhood visits to the circus; occasions which, even as she had revelled in their feast of excitement, colour and sound, she had known must end and turn out to be like fairy-tales: utterly real while in the telling but, when finished, quite untrue.

The show triumphantly concluded; everyone was applauding. Lorna, unable to clap because of clutching Herbie, swung her legs up and down, laughing. He said: 'My, you sure have a swell pair of gams there, babe.'

'Oh, Herbie, you sound just like a GI!'

'Do I? Well, if it's so, I take it as a compliment.'

'I suppose it's catching!'

'I guess so. All these young chaps around makes you young again – not you, me I mean. You *are* young.'

The ladder was fetched out and the perilous descent from the girder made. It had been a dusty seat; people brushed themselves and their partners down. There was a lot of laughter and joshing. The chairs were being carried from the hangar; the band returned to the platform, and dancing began again. Herbie said to Lorna: 'Care to cut a rug, kid?'

They danced together for the rest of the evening, stopping occasionally to drink a Coke or some of the fruit punch that had now appeared. Lorna felt happier than she could remember having felt for years.

People seemed definitely to have paired off in this final part of the evening. Jeffery was dancing with Angie, Daphne Stacks with Tommy Taylor, Dicky Stacks with Mrs Friske; Mrs Hedley-Cowper circled round sedately with the Reverend Barker while Miss Barker partnered Buzz Cabrini. Lorna noticed Vic Wendell jiving with Ruth Cuthman, her shyness long since gone.

The evening ended with 'Stardust'. It was the number the band always finished off with. Herbie locked Lorna close to him; they revolved slowly, cheek to cheek, staying on the one spot. All around them swayed and revolved other couples, wrapped in the same semi-mesmerized trance. The lights were dimmed; it was like dancing in another place, another time; almost as if it were in another life.

Then the lights came on; the national anthems were played. The Gala Ball was over. Herbie lined up with the Committee to say good-night to the guests as they passed between the screens into the walkway. Although most people would probably be seeing each other again within a matter of days, if indeed not on the morrow, everyone behaved as if parting were of serious import. Something – nobody quite knew what – was being said goodbye to in a way the Americans would have called 'for real'. And at the same time everyone knew that it had been an evening they would never forget.

Finally the last guest disappeared. The Committee members had a final nightcap each of the fruit cup laced with Bourbon. Daphne Stacks rather hurried away; she said she didn't want to keep Dicky waiting. Herbie said to Lorna: 'How are you getting home?'

'I came in my own car this evening.' She received a small petrol ration through the American Red Cross.

Arm in arm she and Herbie groped along the walkway. When they reached the aeroclub he fetched her wrap for her; it was a black velvet cloak with a lining that matched the flounces of her dress.

'You look like something out of a story-book,' he said.

'I feel rather like it.'

They left the club and went across the hardstands towards where she had left her car. It was a quietly moonlit night with enough light in the sky for the Forts to be silhouetted, their wings huge, their guns thrusting up from their bodies with an air of menace.

'I trust you'll be coming back,' he said. 'I feel rather as though all I'm going to be left with is your slipper.'

'I'm sure I shall be back, but the other me; one of Miss Binkle's gals.' She laughed nervously and wrapped her cloak more closely round her, shivering in the shadow of the Forts.

'D'you have to go?'

'But of course.' The circus was over; the fairy-tale ended.

'I don't want to lose you.'

Suddenly he took her in his arms and kissed her hard and seriously. For a moment she yielded, then burst into tears, pushed him away, ran to her car, jumped in and drove off.

XXI

After she had driven a short distance Lorna stopped the car, drew into the side of the road, rested her arms on the steering wheel and her head on her arms and had a hard cry. Quite why she was crying, or even behaving so, she wasn't certain, and didn't really ask herself. Then at last she sat up, blew her nose, dabbed her eyes and face dry with her hankie and, still giving an occasional sob, took out and lit a cigarette.

Now that she was able to sit back and look at the thing coolly she began to feel surprisingly angry with herself, and not only angry but also ashamed. Herbie was a nice nice chap; he was no brash chick-chasing youngster but a mature, thoroughly decent man. That he was married really had nothing to do with it: there was a war on; he was miles away from home; if he continued to fly missions he was unlikely to survive to return home. They had liked one another from the start, and their liking had increased the better they got to know one another. It was not surprising, under this assembly of circumstances, that sooner or later he would want to make love to her. War was not peacetime. And she was supposed to be a grown-up woman, was she not? Yet what had happened? He had kissed her, and she had burst out crying and fled like some silly little schoolgirl.

She must grow up, she told herself vehemently. Not that Herbie would be interested in her after this (another sob rose in her throat, while at the same time the thought crossed her mind how on earth would she face Herbie again, after she had behaved so stupidly?); but there were bound to be other occasions when she was kissed (well, she had been kissed before, but she meant properly kissed, like Herbie had kissed her this night, which felt quite different – even Ivo hadn't kissed her like that), and if she were going to burst out crying every time ... But at that point her self-reproachful ruminations were cut short by a vehicle coming along the lane from behind her. She had left room, she thought, for another car to pass, but it stopped level with her. She hoped she wasn't going to have trouble; nowadays you never knew who was driving around at night.

Blackout restrictions meant that headlamps were dimmed into non-existence and night driving had become a kind of blind man's buff. The other vehicle was no more than a dim black block; it looked a bit American, the sort of thing loosely designated as a buggy. The driver wound down the nearside window, and Lorna, deciding to be brave and risk being grabbed by the throat rather than huddling crouched over her wheel like a sitting duck, wound down her window halfway and got in a word first. 'Yes?' she said crisply in her best Miss Binkle manner. 'What is it?'

'Lorna,' said Herbie's voice. He sounded upset. 'Why aren't you home? Are you OK?'

'Perfectly, thank you. Just having a smoke.' She tried to make it sound the most natural thing in the world that she should be parked by the roadside, having a smoke, in the small hours.

'You had me worried. I called your home, and old Mrs – I can never remember her name – said you weren't back yet. It had me real concerned.'

'You telephoned at this hour and woke poor Mrs Cuthman?'

'I judged I'd timed it so that you'd just have arrived back in. I wanted to—'

'How fearfully inconsiderate! I'd told her to go to bed and not to worry if Ruth and I were rather late. She shouldn't have been disturbed.' Lorna sounded more like Miss Binkle than ever.

There was a slight pause; Herbie seemed rebuffed. Lorna could hear a small wind sadly blowing along the top of the hedge. Then Herbie said: 'I wanted to apologize.' He stopped, then continued: 'It was very wrong of me, to presume the way I did that you felt about me the way I feel about you.'

He seemed about to add more, but Lorna interrupted him. 'No, no,' she heard herself saying. 'It wasn't wrong of you; it wasn't at all.' Her words came in a rush. 'It was very stupid of me. Please forgive me . . . You see, I really like you very much.'

He drew a deep breath. 'No kidding?'

'I really do.' It sounded rather feeble, said like that, Lorna thought; but it brought a decisive response from Herbie.

'Stay right there,' he said loudly and clearly. 'Don't drive off.'

She heard him getting out of his vehicle; he came round to her car on the passenger side and got in.

'Oh, Herbie!'

They hugged each other; he kissed her as he had kissed her under the Forts, but this time she didn't burst into tears. He held her under the cape, feeling her body with his hands. They became all tangled up with the steering wheel.

'This doggone car's no more'n the size of a walnut,' said Herbie. 'Let's get into mine.'

Clinging to his hand, she allowed herself to be half-pulled, half-pushed into his buggy; it wasn't much better than her car as far as actual room was concerned. Everything was a muddle; they had too many clothes on, her bodice was too tight, and he couldn't undo the hooks; the full stiff taffeta flounces of her dress were incredibly in the way, their bodies became knotted together and then they slid off the seat; they bit each other, clutched, grabbed, heaved; Herbie, cursing, opened the door to give them more room; and they stopped caring what a muddle it was, and the moon, which had been behind a cloud making everything dark and chaotic, suddenly appeared at the right moment when everything had smoothed out and Lorna saw Herbie's face and smiled at him and he said: 'Gee, what a life.'

Presently they straightened out and took stock, as Herbie called it, and half-sat, half-reclined on the seat, smoking and watching the moon.

'Well, I don't know, Miss Washbourne,' said Herbie at last. 'Do I take you home, or what?'

'What would *what* be, Herbie?'

'Oh, I guess . . . I'd guess I'd put you in one of those big birds and fly you off some place where nobody could ever bother us again.'

'That'd be good.'

'You'll buy that one?'

'Yes, please.'

They heard a car coming towards them from some distance ahead.

'We're blocking the road,' said Lorna.

'We are, too . . . Who in hell has to be driving around at this godforsaken hour anyways?'

Herbie drove the buggy forward and made room for the approaching car to pass, which it did; then stopped when the driver found Lorna's car parked empty.

'It's not the police, is it?' murmured Lorna.

'Best means of defence is to attack,' said Herbie. 'Trouble is I've lost my darned shoes.'

'So've I,' said Lorna, stooping to rummage under the seat.

Herbie got out of the buggy and walked back along the road in his socks; Lorna heard a very English voice ask: 'Anything wrong here?'

'Nothing whatever,' replied Herbie's voice, ringing with assured confidence. 'All fine and under control.'

'This abandoned car . . .'

'Not abandoned. My friend's.' There was a pause. Herbie said cheerfully: 'We'll be driving our separate ways in a moment or two.'

'Just thought there might have been trouble. Good-night.'

'So long.'

A door slammed, and the car drove off. Herbie returned to Lorna. 'That was a gent.'

'The police?'

'No, no; some kind of military guy. I couldn't really see him in the dark. But having grasped the situation he didn't linger; did the decent and drove on.'

'I think I'd best get home, Herbie, before it grows light, so that I can let myself into the house without being caught red-handed by the milkman.'

'Sensibly said. The girl at the helm.' He stumbled over something on the grass verge. 'Hot dog! Found 'em.'

'Your shoes?'

'Yeah, in the grass. Beats me how they landed there.'

'I've found mine, too, under the seat.'

Hugging each other as they walked, they went to her car.

'I'll call you,' he said. 'About midday, how's that?'

'Make it just before one.'

She arrived home, parked the car in a lay-by near the front drive and stole indoors without disturbing anyone. She fell into bed, and after lying awake for a while, thinking about Herbie, suddenly fell sound asleep just as it was growing light.

She slept till nine-thirty; then bathed, dressed and presented herself in good order for breakfast. However, by this time she was beginning to feel extremely anxious and guilty about Ruth Cuthman. Lorna had promised Mrs Cuthman that it would be perfectly safe for Ruth to go to a dance at the American camp because she herself would keep an eye on her throughout and make particularly certain that Ruth travelled home securely in a truck with the other girls. This Lorna had not done.

True, she had kept an intermittent eye on Ruth for much of the evening, but as it had worn on Lorna had paid less and less attention to her and, when the time had come to go home, events had put Ruth right out of Lorna's mind. She hadn't given a thought to whether Ruth made it safely home or not. She hadn't given a thought to Ruth, full stop.

It was with immense relief that Lorna now discovered Ruth in the kitchen making the breakfast toast. The girl looked trim, serene and all in one piece, with no signs of wear and tear upon her.

Lorna said: 'Good morning, Ruth. You seemed, from what I saw of you, to have a really good time last night.'

'I had a smashing time!' Ruth's face shone like a small polished sun; her eyes danced and sparkled.

'And the truck dropped you off safely here in the village?' Lorna wanted to hear that all had gone according to plan, thereby further easing her own conscience.

Ruth, flushing a little, said, 'I didn't come back in the truck. Some people I know, farmers at Yetton, fetched me back; I got home sooner that way, because the truck went all round the district dropping off girls, and they brought me home direct. I hoped you wouldn't mind.'

'Of course not; just as long as you arrived home safely.'

'Oh, yes, I was quite safe. Shall I carry in the breakfast now, Miss Lorna?'

'Yes, please, Ruth.'

After breakfast Lorna escorted her father to church. At a quarter to one, when they were home again and each taking a glass of Madeira in lieu of a pre-lunch sherry, Herbie rang. They arranged to meet at Winwold Beacon at four, walking there from their respective starting points. It was warm and sunny; they lay behind a hedge, on a groundsheet Herbie had brought with him folded over his arm like a mac, and made love, and this time there was no muddle.

At last Herbie said, 'Time to say goodbye. Duty calls.'

'At least we've had one whole marvellous afternoon forgetting about duty and war and all of it,' said Lorna.

'We certainly have.'

'It's never any good, in wartime, worrying about what comes next.'

'Meet what the next brings, when the next comes,' responded Herbie. Perhaps without knowing it he stared up at the sky as he spoke.

'Seems a sound philosophy.'

'I don't see how to get through this war any other way.'

XXII

Next morning, at the office, Buzz was still aglow with the success of the Gala Ball. 'Gee, it was great the way the British turned up wearing their family heirlooms!' He beamed in delight. 'Did you know one guy had on his grandfather's shoes? Isn't that sump'n? I tell you, when the British at last let their hair down, oh boy, do they take some beating!'

'You can say that again,' said Herbie heartily, entering the office in time to catch this last remark. He grinned broadly and happily at Lorna behind Buzz's back.

Lorna, gently humming 'Moonlight Serenade' to herself, got to work on her files. Herbie, in his office, could be heard having a busy morning on the phone.

At lunchtime Lorna took a snack lunch with Buzz and the Red Cross girls. Buzz said: 'I don't know if it's reached you yet, but it's coming through on the grapevine there's going to be a big one flown tomorrow.'

'Oh?' They all turned enquiring eyes upon him.

'Yeah,' said Buzz. 'Seems it's to be a kind of anniversary occasion. Seventeenth of August was the start of the Eighth Bomber Command missions from England, remember?'

'First birthday,' said Amy May. 'We'll hope the war will be over before there's a second one.'

'Seems there's plenty of crazy nuts around wanting to go on this birthday celebration,' said Buzz. 'People all over camp are talking about how they'd sure welcome a chance to be in on it. From what I hear, several ground-duty officers are taking part as tourists. There's a joke they'll be put in Purple Heart Corner.'

'They're saying it's Berlin,' said Angie.

'That would make it one of the big pinnacles of the war,' said Amy May. 'An all-time high for sure.'

There'd been talk all summer of Berlin coming up some time.

The atmosphere of tense excitement mounted all afternoon. Although security was always strictly observed and the destination of a forthcoming mission kept a close secret, there was no attempt this day to disguise the fact that the Eighth was on the brink of something pretty momentous.

Herbie had left his office. It was not until five o'clock that Lorna heard his voice and knew that he had returned; presently he put his

head round the door. He said: 'You've no doubt learned, like everyone else, that there's quite a big mission scheduled for tomorrow.'

'Yes. There's a lot of speculation going on.'

'Well, don't encourage it. You and the others in the aeroclub do
your best to dampen it down; get things on a lower key.'

'We'll do our best.'

'It's been coming up for quite a while, this anniversary. No need
to go over the top about it now it's here.' He walked to her desk
and fiddled with the things on it in the way he had. He picked up
a glass paperweight, deep raspberry red and when held to the light
apparently full of bubbles. 'How clever,' he said.

'It comes from Venice.'

'You seem to have brought back some good things from Venice.
Party dresses, paperweights.' He placed the weight carefully back
on the desk. 'I must get moving,' he said. 'Everyone wants to talk
to me all at once. No time for you.' He gave her elbow a hard
squeeze that was almost painful and managed a smile. 'Don't forget
me,' he said, and left.

Lorna hadn't been feeling particularly happy at the prospect of
a big one on the morrow, but now she liked it even less: the way
Herbie had fiddled with the things on the desk; had fiddled with
the paperweight; least of all had she liked the 'Don't forget me'.

Fursey Down for the rest of that afternoon and into the evening
was ahum with excited people saying that three hundred Forts
would be going to Berlin next day and boy, would that put the
Germans in the place right where they belonged.

The Red Cross workers tried to discourage the talk, but there
was little point in making the attempt. Presently news got round
that crews had been put on standby; that was, ready to fly next
morning at five.

A Bombardment Group contained four squadrons; each of
which was expected to be able to provide at least six aircraft and

crews for any operation. To judge from the talk in the aeroclub that evening, about twenty-six bombers would go out from Fursey Down on the morrow.

The tension mounted all evening. The message 'OK fellows, hit the sack early tonight' was passed around among the crews. There was an atmosphere of suppressed excitement with an undercurrent of something half-fearful; a recognizable mood of premonition.

Presently Lance appeared. Lorna was alone at the rear of the canteen fetching a supply of hard candy. When she saw Lance she said: 'Shoo! You aren't supposed to be in here, and well you know it. The bar counter is your limit.'

He came up to her, looked at her intently and said: 'I've come to kiss you good-night.'

He put his arm round her, drew her gently towards him, gave her a lingering kiss, looked at her again, and walked out.

Lorna felt a cold finger of fear reach out and touch her. She returned to the bar; Angie said something to her, Lorna didn't know what. Angie said: 'Are you OK?'

'I reckon so. Yes, I'll be all right.' Lorna made an effort to pull herself together.

Angie said: 'I'll fix you a coffee.'

The numbers in the bar had thinned out considerably, though it was not yet nine. The boys sat around talking in an inconsequential sort of way, some drinking a Coke, some a beer. Gradually, by ones, twos and threes, they drifted away to bed. They would be awakened between one and two next morning, probably without having had much sleep. Take-off was scheduled for five-fifty.

Long before ten the aeroclub was empty except for the Red Cross personnel. The place which a mere forty-eight hours previously had throbbed, sparkled and scintillated as the scene of the Gala Ball was now engulfed in a strange haunting stillness. Waiting for tomorrow, thought Lorna fearfully. Her companions felt it, too.

Presently Buzz said: 'You girls call it a day and get some rest. I'll close the shop.' They said good-night to him thankfully, and went their ways.

Lorna set her alarm for four-thirty. She slept intermittently; hearing in the distance the rumble of Fortress engines as the planes were moved or tested by the ground crews getting all ready for take-off time.

When her alarm at last went off Lorna rose promptly, dressed, made herself a quick cup of tea and pedalled off in the dark, up to the Beacon. The morning was cloaked in cloud; she realized that it was unlikely the bombers would set off on schedule. The eastern sky was barely showing dimly through the cloud when Lorna reached the Beacon top. Wrapped in muffler and windcheater she watched the light seep in through swathes and curtains of mist so heavy she knew that departure of the mission would certainly be postponed.

She returned home, walked the dog, had breakfast and pedalled away to Fursey Down. The low cloud and mist still blotted out visibility, and the Forts were still grounded. She arrived at the airfield to find the crews waiting at their planes on the hardstands, ready for the signal that didn't come.

Angie reported that, wherever the target might be (and this had been kept shrouded in mystery successfully, despite all the talk), the crews, it was rumoured, had not thought much of their destination.

Lorna went into her office and did her best to concentrate on making a start with her day's work.

Gradually the mist dispersed. At last, shortly after eleven, the bombers received the long-awaited signal to fly. It was fifteen hours since they had first been put under standby orders; a brutal nervous ordeal which could not, thought Lorna, make a propitious start for the mission.

The sun was striking through the white fog, and the runways had become visible. Suddenly a great roar of sound burst from the waiting bombers; everything, ground included, began to shake. Lorna went outside to watch; she found Angie and Amy May there, too, and stood with them. One by one the Forts rolled forward from the hardstands and along the runway towards take-off point. Lorna was able to distinguish *Star Stripper*; she was some distance off and there was no hope of being able to pick out Herbie in the cockpit. Lorna thought of all her other friends in other crews; it was impossible to imagine how they would be feeling at such a moment. 'Mighty relieved to be away at last, I guess,' said Amy May.

At take-off point each Fort hesitated, summoning a final burst of full power, then moved forward with ever-gathering speed, the engine roar becoming a full-throated scream. Faster and faster went the bomber, fighting and struggling to rise, the ground a blur beneath the wheels; the scream became desperation, and then the Fortress was airborne; the ungainly struggler was abruptly transformed into a regal creature of soaring splendour.

Fortress after Fortress took off; Lorna was reminded of a flight of swans beating and struggling and straining to lift clear of an expanse of water and then at last rising magnificently to be revealed as *conquistadores* of the air.

Effortlessly, it seemed, the bombers found their assigned position in the Group formation and began their long upward climb into the clouds. The watchers on the ground returned indoors. Twenty-six planes had set off; they wondered how many would return.

The day passed with incredible slowness; it felt like a day that went on for ever. It was not until towards six o'clock that the first of the returning bombers was heard in the distance. It came in slowly, dropping the dreaded scarlet flares. The survivors of the badly knocked-about crew, speechless with exhaustion and moving like robots, were only able to say that it had been the worst day ever.

Gradually, one by one, other planes came limping back, almost all dropping scarlet flares. Piecing together the fragmentary information they provided, it was possible to form some idea of the day's fighting. The scheme to celebrate the Eighth's first anniversary in England had been on a lavish scale. There had been two missions, flown separately but strategically planned in conjunction; the one to strike at the Messerschmitt factory at Regensburg, the other, parallel mission to bomb the ballbearings plants at Schweinfurt. The Fursey Down Group had been part of the force despatched to Schweinfurt.

The late start had disturbed the timing of the combined strategies and prevented Allied fighter escorts from showing up as expected. The Luftwaffe had appeared in the sky in hordes, commencing their attacks on the Forts near Antwerp and continuing without a break all the way to Schweinfurt and all the way back to the coast. It had been a day of intense unremitting battle. The only satisfaction was that the target had been well and truly bombed and that claims for German fighters shot down were high.

The homing Forts continued to come in, with longer and longer intervals between, all evening. By ten at night nine bombers were counted missing, excluding those which, because of damage to the aircraft, or the serious condition of the wounded on board, or both, had had to touch down at some other airfield nearer the coast.

Star Stripper put in no appearance, neither was there any news of her. Lorna told herself that she should not have expected differently. With her tragic bad luck throughout the war so far, why shouldn't this blow, too, fall upon her? Somehow she managed to check her tears and finish her stint of duty at the aeroclub for the evening. Miss Glaister, who was on duty there, too, offered to drive Lorna home. 'You're looking quite washed out; you don't want to cycle all that way back in the dark tonight.'

Lorna decided to accept Miss Glaister's offer and go home with her. 'Phone me and tell me if you get any news of *Star Stripper*, Buzz,' Lorna said. Buzz, who himself seemed to have wilted several inches into the ground over the past few hours, replied: 'Sure thing, kid. I will.'

Lorna and the Good Egg walked out to where the car was parked. Lorna was opening the door to get in when she heard Buzz calling her name. He was lumbering across the open ground towards her; she half-ran, half-stumbled to him. 'Yes? What's happened?'

'Just had a call. Herbie's touched down in *Star Stripper* at an RAF airfield near the coast; he has severely wounded crew on board, including Jimmy Yeo, and he wanted them rushed to hospital without waiting to get back here. *Star Stripper*'s pretty badly knocked about, too. Seems it's a marvel they reached England at all.'

Lorna found herself without words. She clung a little to Buzz, and he clung a little to her. Then she thanked him, said goodnight, and returned with Miss Glaister to Fursey-Winwold.

Herbie rang Lorna at eleven; he apologized for the lateness of his call. Lorna, who had been sitting up in the hope that he might telephone, without really believing that he would, replied that the lateness of the hour didn't matter. 'It's so wonderful just to hear your voice.'

'It's to say I'm alive, just about,' said Herbie. 'We had three dead on board, five injured and one dying, and the ship herself sinking fast.'

'How's Jimmy? Did you get him back in time?'

'No. He died while they were putting him in the ambulance.'

Jimmy had been Herbie's closest friend at Fursey Down. Lorna could think of nothing to say to this one, so she left it.

'Are you OK, Herbie?'

'Yeah, I guess.' She could hear him draw a deep breath. 'I always wanted to know what the battle of Waterloo was like – you know, that nice close-run thing. Now I think I do.'

XXIII

The days following the Schweinfurt raid were melancholy ones for Fursey Down; the empty beds in the barracks, the empty places in the mess, the empty seats at the briefings spoke, more keenly than words, of the losses 'Herbie's Worst' had suffered. Ten Forts from Fursey Down had been lost with their crews; Tex the trumpeter was among those who hadn't returned. Lance Vogel had been brought back dead in a shattered *Daisy May*.

Sixty Forts in all were missing after the twin missions to Regensburg and Schweinfurt; the previous high had been twenty-six, on the Kiel raid of 13 June. Thirty-six B-17s of the Schweinfurt force had failed to return.

The Fursey Down survivors were not surprised by what had happened. 'When we went to the briefing and they uncovered the chart showing the mission's route and we saw it going deep into the heart of Germany, with no chance of fighter protection ... well, that was the moment we all started to yell. All the boys were asking the same question – what goddam idiot at HQ had dreamed that one up as an anniversary celebration?'

Herbie and Lorna managed a week's leave together; they went to Cornwall, staying at a tiny old manor house converted into a private hotel, near Tintagel. They were immensely discreet; travelling separately, to meet up at Camelford. Herbie was in mufti and calling himself Professor Blenmire; Lorna, likewise in civilian tweeds (and wearing her grandmother's wedding ring), was Mrs Blenmire. ('But we aren't on our honeymoon, Herbie; we don't want to rouse any *mushy* interest in us.' 'Oh, of course not,' agreed Herbie, trying to conceal his amusement at Lorna's vehement tone. 'Just is,' he added, 'under the circumstances I don't think we'll convince anybody we've been married all that long'.)

Lorna, over the past few weeks, had done a lot of thinking about Herbie and herself, and made up her mind on three points. In the first place she was not going to think at all about his being a married man. In a war like this one family ties fell into abeyance: a wife a thousand miles and more away could not be expected, by any rational reckoning, to maintain the foremost role in the life of a partner who had gone off to war. Lorna knew that her mother had never expected her husband to give detailed accounts of what he had been doing during his periods of absence; he was a soldier, and she had been a soldier's wife, and soldiers' wives did not ask questions.

Well, perhaps Herbie's wife would understand this and perhaps she wouldn't. Lorna, having thought about her, and her place in things, and having concluded that, as things stood, Herbie's wife didn't enter into it, firmly consigned the real Mrs Blenmire to cold storage. There was a war on. This was the ETO.

Lorna was pretty certain that Herbie didn't expect to survive to return to the States. In a world of fragmented chaos one clung to any plank of comfort one could lay hands on: she and Herbie had lain hands on each other, for the present. This time next week he might no longer be alive. And this was the second point Lorna now made up her mind upon: she would never think about how long she and Herbie might or might not have together. She would try never to dwell upon time at all. 'Meet what the next brings, when the next comes.' In other words live for the moment. It might be the only moment ever.

One third point she resolved upon. She was not going to feel guilty about herself and Herbie. Lorna was good at feeling guilty; introspective by nature, she spent a lot of time feeling guilty about this, guilty over that, or simply wondering whether she should feel guilty. She could truthfully say that under normal circumstances she would never have dreamed of having an affair with a married man; it just wasn't in her code. But war changed everything. Life in its every aspect had become a desperate battle for survival. Somehow or other, one had to keep going. One had to stay afloat. Planks of comfort, she repeated to herself; and not just of comfort, either, but of vital necessity if one weren't to collapse under the sheer weight of things.

As it turned out, the other people staying at the Cornish hotel were pleasant civilian types who took happily to the company of 'those nice Blenmires'. Nobody seemed to nurse the slightest suspicion that Lorna and Herbie weren't really the married couple they claimed to be.

The manor house stood at the head of a narrow little combe leading down to a tiny rocky beach where Lorna and Herbie once or twice swam until they discovered a big rock basin of their own, deep enough to dive into. They wandered along cliff paths for tireless miles, the sea crooning, gulls calling. They visited Tintagel and inspected the ruins of King Arthur's castle. Herbie bought himself a copy of *Morte d'Arthur*. 'I've always meant to read this.' They hired bikes and explored the countryside inland, bowling along narrow lanes between hedges permanently bowed before a wind which was more often there than not. But most of all they clambered down the steep cliff faces by the interlinking rock terraces, to find refuge on some ledge where tufts of thrift trembled with the dried heads of June's flowers and the samphire beds smelt of salt and semen. The guillemots and razorbills who had roosted there earlier in the season had all gone out to sea, but the gulls were still there, cross at being disturbed; their ungainly speckled fledglings watched Lorna and Herbie as they made love in their cliff fortress perched high above the rocks where the surf broke and cormorants sunned themselves while the Atlantic heaved and murmured.

Every dawn they were woken in their beamed Tudor bedroom by the gulls calling in the thick sea mist that enshrouded the cliffs till the sun came through. Herbie couldn't sleep after five; 'The boys are going out now,' he would say. He and Lorna dressed and walked hand in hand on the cliff, keeping well back from the edge until the mist had dispersed and they could see where the land ended and space and ocean began. By that time it was the hour to return to breakfast.

Sometimes, out on these early-morning walks, Herbie would speak about Schweinfurt. 'It was a real battle. There's a lot of fighting that isn't true battle, like this guy Arthur and his knights, always on the scrap; a lot of our missions have been fighting our way in and fighting our way out, but you couldn't call it battle. Schweinfurt was different. It was a proper pitched battle; certainly fought on the move, because you can't stay in one place in the sky, but there was a definite place where they were gathered, expecting us. And there were plenty of them; the Germans had vectored pretty well every fighter they had in the west: they had made up their minds they would put paid to us and our Forts that day.'

'Were you expecting them to be expecting you?'

'We anticipated some tough opposition, yes, but not of that intensity all the way. There was never any real let-up; it was fantastic. They kept it up like a three-ring circus, every step. They fought flat out to break us; we fought flat out to hold formation and reach our target. That's one reason why it made me think of Waterloo; the British in those squares, the French throwing in everything they'd got.'

'Did they throw in the Imperial Guard?' Lorna's great-great-grandfather had fought at Waterloo, and the family had never ceased discussing it ever since. Waterloo, for the Washbournes, was one of the great ancestral memories.

'I don't know about their Imperial Guard, but they brought Gruppen in from all over; they had fetched them from over two hundred miles away, which tells how big a show it was. And, like I've said, it was a very close thing. They were out to smash us and, by nation, they almost did.'

'Did you think they might?'

'When it was happening, d'you mean? Well, I make it a rule not to think that way, ever; it never helps. And, in my own case, once Jimmy had caught it I had to take over the controls – I was flying co-pilot, you see, and after that there was certainly no time for thinking.'

'Poor Jimmy.'

'Yeah, his face was splatched all over the cockpit. The right waist-gunner was most blown in half. The ball-turret went, with the gunner inside. Everything started to blow. Yet somehow that ship held. And somehow the formation held. And we dropped our load on Schweinfurt, and plastered it good. *And* got back to England.'

They were sitting on an old stone wall near the cliff edge, over-looking the sea. Lorna thought of the Spanish Armada riding up that way; the lofty ships with their gun decks, supposing themselves invincible.

'It was a battle all right,' said Herbie. 'I'm glad, in a way, I was in it. You don't get to be in a real battle like that every day. You read about 'em; but, shucks, reading gives you no idea. Schweinfurt will go in the books, and people will see it as one of the big battles of this war. They won't be able to visit the battlefield, though, because it was in the sky. That was the darndest aspect – all happening in the *sky*.'

*

255

Their week together seemed, in one way, to be magic and to go on for ever, while simultaneously it whirled past and before they knew it they were packing their bags and Herbie was saying: 'Duty calls!'

'I'd have to go back anyway,' rejoined Lorna, trying to make the best of things. 'I can't leave poor Mrs Cuthman to cope single-handed with Father any longer.'

Ruth Cuthman had gone fruit-picking, not announcing that she was going until the eve of her departure, which had also been the eve of Lorna's departure for what she had said was to be a week's cycling in Cornwall with Bunty (who had cheerfully agreed to be named as an alibi). Ruth's decision, at this junction, to remove herself from home could not have come at a more inconvenient moment, but she had been adamant. 'It's patriotic, going fruit-picking,' she had said earnestly. 'It helps the war effort, and if I'm going now's the time to go. I'm entitled to a fortnight's holiday with pay, and I'm making it a working holiday. I can't see much wrong with that!'

'Well,' Lorna hadn't wished to appear too much of a curmudgeon, 'I hope you'll meet a lot of young company, girls of your own age, and have a jolly time. Only don't stay away too long, will you? A fortnight's your limit, remember.'

'Oh, I'll not stay away longer than that.'

But when Lorna returned home to The Warren she found a post-card, sent from the other side of the county, saying that Ruth would be taking an extra week or two continuing to help with the fruit harvest. She was working for a farmer who paid her well, and she was with some other girls, very nice, and not to worry about her.

'I'm a bit disappointed in Ruth, I must confess,' said Lorna, in conversation with Miss Glaister. 'I feel she's let me down over this fruit-picking spree.'

'They don't see it as going on a spree,' rejoined the Good Egg. 'Fruit-picking, potato-gathering; it's considered patriotic, a way of helping with the war effort while they're too young to be called up.'

'I know, that's what Ruth said,' responded Lorna resignedly. 'Still, I hope her patriotism won't keep her away too long.'

'Another week will see her home again, no doubt,' replied Miss Glaister comfortingly.

Conversation with Titus Swann was less reassuring. 'Best make up your mind to it, Miss Washbourne,' he said. 'You'll not be seeing Ruth Cuthman again for a good while to come.'

'What d'you mean, Titus? She's only gone fruit-picking. That won't keep her away for ever.'

'Depends what's meant by fruit-picking,' retorted Titus drily.

'All the girls of her age go fruit-picking nowadays. It's their way of doing something to help the country,' said Lorna, rather sharply. She wasn't going to have Titus being disparaging about Ruth. 'Always throw the worst possible light on everything, don't you, Titus?' added Lorna. He turned away with a grunt; Lorna marched off in the opposite direction with a toss of her head intended to make it clear she had no time for him.

Nevertheless the seeds of a niggling anxiety for Ruth were now sown in Lorna's mind.

A letter from Violetta helped to take Lorna's thoughts away from the distracting matter of Ruth's fruit-picking:

Dearest Lorna,

Hear from Mother that you're just back from a cycling holiday with Bunty in darkest Cornwall. Never thought of you as an ardent cyclist, devoting precious holiday time to the sport! Rum, too, that Bunty, that week you were supposed to be away together, sent me a letter postmarked Hampstead!

Never forget that I am the daughter of authors of

whodunnits, and was fed on red herrings from the cradle upwards. I can guarantee to be able to spot a red herring from a mile off. However, don't worry; I won't breathe a word to a soul that I think that cycling tour of yours has a fishy smell.

Unlike you I don't go in for enigmas and their variations and so shall say, without beating about the bush, that *I* have just spent an utterly wizard illicit few days in the Lake District, on the shores of Ullswater. It didn't rain, except for one day, which we spent in bed, anyway: rain is sometimes a good excuse for doing the most marvellous things!

Our affair has been going on for several months now, and I am happier than I ever imagined possible! I really do know now what loving someone in *complete understanding* really means. Perhaps you have never been lucky enough to love anyone in this way. Maybe you never will. It's all a matter of being lucky enough to meet the *right* person (what is known as a truism, with a vengeance!).

Otherwise I still find my job pretty engrossing; human beings are a rum species and you do learn some most extraordinary things when you're a Welfare Officer. I have some choice anecdotes for you next time we meet. Hope that won't be at too distant a date. *Do* let me hear more about that 'cycling' orgy.

Yours to a cinder as the popular saying goes,
Violetta

Lorna wrote back:

OK, Sleuth,
So it wasn't a cycling orgy with Bunty!
I trust you with that secret, just as you have trusted me

258

with the illicit spree on the shores of Ullswater. How fearfully romantic you make a rainy day sound! Well, it never rained at Tintagel; we had all those magnificent cliffs to ourselves, sometimes in mist, and when the mist cleared, in sunshine. It's a wonder we never rolled off the edge into the sea below.

Oh, Violetta – how far away St Hildegard's seems now, doesn't it?

October: the cloudy weather that had enshrouded the past month gave way to bright days glowing with gentle sunshine and autumn colours. The first of the falling leaves began to drift down from the trees; Michaelmas daisies bloomed in gardens.

A card arrived from Ruth posted from Marden in Kent. It bore no address and was brief: she was keeping well, doing nicely, and busy helping with the apple harvest. Home soon.

'And high time, too!' exclaimed Lorna. Patriotic fruit-picking might be, but Ruth was needed back at The Warren. Things were becoming fraught once more at Fursey Down, and Lorna had little time to spare for the extra household chores which fell on her shoulders during Ruth's absence. Replacements for the crews lost at Schweinfurt had now arrived; one way and another this made a lot of extra work for administrative and Red Cross staff.

The arrival of the crews coincided with the tail end of the cloudy weather which confined missions to 'milk runs'; invaluable, of course, as kindergarten for the newcomers. They flew relaxedly by day, chick-chased at night. Looking at them, so bright and brash and eager, it was impossible not to think of all those other bright, brash and eager faces that had gone before. Among them Lorna thought of Lance. And thinking of Lance reminded her of Vic Wendell; she hadn't seen him around since her return from

Cornwall. She anxiously enquired after him. Amy May, a great romantic at heart, rolled big eyes.

'He's out camping, all his spare time.'

'Camping? Who with?'

'Camping' was a euphemism for taking a local girl out into the bushes.

'Some girl he's gotten sweet on; real spoony he is, the other boys say. He's built her a little cabin in the woods. Says he's going to marry her. Don't you think that's wonderful – Vic Wendell found himself a steady at last?'

'Jerks the heartstrings,' responded Lorna drily. She always found Vic amusing company, but she couldn't imagine any right-minded girl taking him seriously, nor Vic being genuinely serious about any one girl for that matter.

The cloudy weather now gave way to the bright cloudless days of a late Indian summer. The Fortresses were suddenly flung into a frenetic bout of rugged long-range sorties over Germany. Three days of offensive cost the Eighth some eighty-five bombers in all; five from Fursey Down. The atmosphere of the aeroclub took a deep dive into gloom. The old hands, over the past weeks, had begun to forget Schweinfurt and had recovered their spirits, seeing that catastrophe as something that couldn't happen twice. They were finding they'd been wrong. The young replacement crews, for their part, with their 'milk runs' and chick-chasing, had convinced themselves that being posted into 'Herbie's Worst' (now reckoned as one of the crack groups) was just one big bonanza. This disastrous weekend, ushering in October, came as a hideous awakening.

On the following Wednesday evening when the crews received their standby orders for the morrow, Lorna felt a tense atmosphere steal over the aeroclub like a cold fog creeping up from the ground on a winter's night.

Herbie rang her after she had arrived home. He rarely indulged in calls to The Warren. He said: 'I think I should tell you the mission tomorrow calls for a maximum effort. I'm flying on it; so keep your fingers crossed for me. And for us all, come to that.'

'Yes, Herbie, I'll do that thing for you,' said Lorna, making up her mind to be very brave.

'That's my girl. See you.' And he rang off. When Lorna rose from the little chair beside the phone her knees were shaking under her.

The planes took off next morning in a heavy thick world under low cloud with trailing mist. Lorna heard them go out, but did not try to look; it was not a morning for seeing anything. When she arrived at Fursey Down the bombers could be heard overhead, above the cloud. 'It's bright sunshine up there where they are,' said Buzz. But that was about the only bright thing Lorna heard anyone say that day. A rumour leaked out that the target was Schweinfurt again.

Sixteen Fortresses had flown out from Fursey Down. Amy May went round organizing a crossing of fingers; people to cross two fingers on each hand. Some found little things like this comforting; it helped get through the day. Lorna didn't find it awfully helpful; this day nothing helped her.

The fog was seeping down again when at last the sound of returning bombers was heard. The evening was cold and raw. The aircraft drew nearer; the runway lights were switched on. One by one four bombers staggered in, each dropping red flares. Lorna, Angie and Amy May stayed busying themselves in the aeroclub; they could not steel themselves to go outside after they saw the first dark shapes in the sky, and the flares. What seemed an age afterwards Buzz Cabrini came in to tell them that among the survivors, in their usual charmed manner, were Herbie and Vic Wendell. Herbie, though unscratched himself, had gone to hospital to be with the wounded. 'Everyone will want to fly with those two guys from now on,' said Buzz. 'Everyone that's left to fly, that is.' Of the sixteen Forts that had flown from Fursey Down that morning, only the four had returned.

Of the total of 291 Forts which had taken off on the raid, only thirty had returned undamaged. Sixty had been shot down. Heavy damage had been done to the target, and as usual an impressive number of enemy fighters had been claimed by the gunners of the B-17s: a tally of 288, all told. But again, as usual with fighter claims, there was a strong element of propaganda for public consumption, and those close to more accurate sources of information did not enthuse. The number of German fighters claimed by the American heavies during the five major air battles of October, culminating with 'Black Thursday', 14 October, amounted to what would have been the annihilation of the German fighter force. 'The answer to those claims, for your ears only,' said Herbie to Lorna later, 'is that useful RAF one: "It's in the plural and they bounce."'

The weather once more became cloudy and unsuited for day-light visual bombing deep into Germany. The 'killer strikes', as they had come to be called in the aeroclub, had drawn to a halt.

The crews, understandably, didn't conceal their relief. Herbie, spinning in his chair, growled at Lorna: 'They just don't realize. There's this goddam invasion of Europe due to come up, and we're two, three months behind hand with our planned destruction of German airpower. That's the hard fact.'

'Perhaps the weather will improve again, Herbie. You know how it comes and goes in Europe.'

'It's not just the weather. The truth is, the Germans have con-trol of daytime skies. Their fighters have learned to break up our bomber boxes, using rockets and mass concentration of attack. Without long-range fighter protection our heavies just haven't a chance. You can't sustain for ever prohibitive losses like we've had this fall. The self-defensive daylight-bomber strategy has been explored to the limit, and it's had it.'

Lorna said nothing. Herbie spun and spun again.

Part Three

MOMENTS OF TRUTH

XXIV

Autumn slowly transformed itself into winter. Lorna expected Ruth Cuthman to return any day; indeed, wondered that she had not already come home. She'd heard nothing since Ruth's last card.

Lorna caught herself dwelling on the serious possibility that Ruth had no intention of returning, but had seized the opportunity to escape from home in order to sample what seemed a more entertaining way of life elsewhere. She had never disguised the fact that she would much rather work on the land than at The Warren, and Lorna by now was nursing the strong suspicion that Ruth had, at any rate for the time being, found herself some seasonal job on a Kentish farm. Mrs Cuthman, too, agreed that this was more than likely.

'But, that said, you would have thought the girl might trouble to drop us another postcard, just to say she's all right,' sighed Lorna to Jeffrey one evening, when she was seeing him out at the front door, he having called round to have a chat with her father.

'She's probably a bit guilty about not having returned, and that holds her back from writing,' said Jeffrey. 'I shouldn't worry about her too much. She'll be home for Christmas. Strays always head home for Christmas.' He gave Lorna an encouraging grin.

She tried to share his optimism.

There was abundant evidence of the kind of life some girls in search of fun and adventure were drifting into. Stories abounded of how, at some of the American camps, the GIs were importing prostitutes, paying their fares from London and installing them in the Quonset huts. These 'shack rats', as the men called them, were not professionals of the famous so-named 'Piccadilly Warrior' class, but girls, some of them looking barely in their teens, who had taken to prostitution among the Yanks as an easy source of income combined with what they saw, at least initially, as having a good time.

Not that Lorna envisaged a fate of this extreme sort for Ruth; she didn't. Ruth's natural good sense, careful upbringing and fundamentally straight nature ruled that out. Nonetheless it was pointless blinkering oneself to the fact that wartime Britain was a dangerous place for the innocent and unwary. Keep hoping it will be as Jeffrey says, and she'll be home for Christmas! Lorna said to herself when she felt an attack of worrying about Ruth coming on. Home for Christmas; probably as unconcerned as if she hadn't been away for weeks, months!

Christmas came; but no Ruth. Only a greetings card; this time posted in Bedford. It bore a brief message, 'Joined the Land Army. Lied about my age. It's a great life. See you. Luv Ruth.'

'I guessed as much,' said Mrs Cuthman resignedly. 'Where there's a will there's always a way, and she's been Land Army mad from the start. Well, it's better than her roaming round on the loose, doing casual farm labour. At least they'll have her name on the books.'

'As you say, at least she's joined a proper organization,' agreed Lorna. To herself she sighed sadly, 'After all these years of being so close, to gallivant off like this and join up!' Yet in a way it was understandable. Boys had been lying about their age and joining up since time immemorial, so why shouldn't girls, now that they were claiming equality with men?

'Once she's found her feet in the Land Army she'll head home on leave to see you,' said Jeffrey, in his usual reassuring manner, when Lorna showed him Ruth's card.

Lorna laughed a little shortly. 'If she does time her prodigal's return for the New Year then I'm afraid I'll be away; I'm going up to London to welcome in nineteen forty-four with Bunty.'

To Bunty Lorna had written rather differently: 'Don't breathe a word of this to anyone, but Herbie and I are spending the New Year in London together. He won't tell me where we shall be staying; it's to be a surprise. Three days: New Year's Eve, New Year's Day, and return to Fursey Down the day after, by evening train. Only, if I may, I'd like to tell Father I'm spending it with you.'

Bunty replied by return of post: 'Of course. I've told you before, any time. But my, that sounds fun. Better than Rainbow Corner, where I've been invited by the Flopper.'

Herbie, shown this letter, said, 'We might see Bunty for a meal or something when we're in London. You're always saying she's like a sister to you.'

'She's my greatest friend.' Lorna hesitated, not sure what he'd say to the idea that had crossed her mind. 'Of course, the time to take her out would be New Year's Eve. On the other hand, you mightn't want that. I know you've planned for us to have a special time together.'

Lorna had told her father what she had told Jeffrey; that she was seeing in 1944 with Bunty. Lorna didn't like lying; if Bunty spent New Year's Eve with Herbie and herself, then that would mean that Lorna, basically, had spoken the truth.

'Yeah, well . . .' It was Herbie's turn to hesitate. Then: 'She's been a good friend to us both, providing you with alibis. And we might feel more Christian, giving her an evening on the town, rather than leaving her to dunk doughnuts at Rainbow Corner.' He paused a moment more, then grinned at Lorna. 'Hell, what are friends for if not to celebrate New Year with? Specially at a time like this. And, anyways, we'll have the rest of the weekend to ourselves.'

'She has this highly eccentric, but rather amusing – at least, in short doses – friend she sometimes goes out with. I've met him; he's a perfect gentleman and all that – Hungarian-Jewish, I think. I mean he'd be quite all right for one evening, probably be very good fun. Well, what I'm saying is, why don't we make it a foursome?'

'Say, that's a notion! Why not?'

The idea was put to Bunty; she in turn put it to Theodor Kaufmann, and the thing was arranged.

Bunty dropped Lorna a hasty note: 'Ring me when you get to London. Suggest I try to book for an early show to start the evening and break the ice. Leave that to me. Bunts.'

Lorna made a bid to have Violetta along with them, too; plus any escort she chose to bring with her. 'I'd so love you to have a real taste of Miss Binkle's gals,' Lorna explained laughingly to Herbie. But Violetta's reply put that notion out of court.

Dearest Lorna

What a wizard notion! – to see the New Year in with you and your CO, and Bunty and her eccentric gentleman friend. I'd have loved to have been there, too; sweet of you to think of it, and thanks a million for asking. But, you see, I'm spending Christmas *and* New Year tucked away in darkest Dorset with *my* CO. We've managed to wangle this break together, and I need say no more than that I CANNOT WAIT!

Let's hope the weather is FOUL, that we have to stay indoors in our room all the time, and get snowed in, so that we can't return to duty and are forced to remain holed up and alone together for WEEKS! What a wonderful dream!

I've told the poor old parents, of course, that I shall be on duty over Christmas and New Year, so can't get to Fursey-Winwold. So remember that – little Violetta is ON DUTY. Puir wee beastie.

All for now – I have to write a report. Give Bunts all my love and have a wonderful evening dancing on the table and whooping it up. And think of me and my lovely CO in Dorset.

Hugs and mistletoe kisses,
Violetta

'Well, sorry not to meet her,' said Herbie, when Lorna showed him this letter. 'And her CO, too. I take it you've never met him?'

'No. Violetta's such a lovely girl she might well do what so many beauties do and make a beeline for some really ugly mug. On the other hand, she says he's lovely! Still, that may merely be a figure of speech.'

'I hope so,' rejoined Herbie, laughing. 'And maybe I'm glad, after all, we shan't be meeting him. A lovely guy doesn't sound my kinda territory.'

Lorna and Herbie travelled to London on separate trains; he went ahead and was there to meet her when she got off her train. He was in uniform, she in her smartest town clothes – now becoming a little out of date, for she had had them since before the war, but still very wearable. Indeed, she looked good, and he eyed her most appreciatively.

'Where are we going?' she asked.

'Surprise. Surprise. You won't know till you get there.'

He had booked them a suite at the Dorchester. Lorna was overwhelmed.

'But, Herbie, it will have taken a year's salary!'

He burst out laughing. 'It'll be worth it. I want it to be a time we'll always remember.'

There were flowers for her, a big box of candy, a bottle of Worth perfume, and champagne.

'But where did these things come from? It's like fairyland!'

'Oh, I fixed things.'

'Mr Can Do.'

'Let's have some champagne.'

They toasted each other; the champagne was chilled to perfection, and the bubbles chased one another frivolously. Lorna felt that everything would go to her head very quickly and quite delightfully.

'I guess I should wait until later before I say this,' said Herbie.

'Say what?' Her heart fell to somewhere below her knees. He was going to tell her that this was goodbye; next week he was being posted thousands of miles away. She steeled herself to take it well.

Herbie, holding his champagne glass in one hand, fiddled with some random objects on a small writing table with his other hand. 'I've been thinking a lot about this,' he said, 'and I think some time we should get married.'

'Married!' Lorna felt she couldn't be hearing him aright. 'But you're married already, Herbie.'

'I know. But not like this.'

'But, Herbie darling, we're not married.'

'No; but I'd like us to be. I want us to be. We should be.' He dropped down on the sofa beside her, and tipped his champagne into her skirt and down her stockings.

'Hell, now what've I done?'

Lorna dabbed at her wet skirt with her handkerchief. Herbie said: 'Look, I know I'm married, and by rights I shouldn't be asking you, but you're all I ever dreamed of. I mean it when I say I can't manage without you. I can't imagine trying to live without you after this. My marriage has never been anything out of the way; never a real success. With you it'll be so different.'

'What about your children? Don't they need you?'

'They're managing without me now OK by all accounts. I've never been at home that much at a stretch, you know. Posted here, posted there, and Margy – that's my wife – she's never liked moving around, so much of the time she's stayed put.' He paused. 'I shouldn't be talking like this. I'm not doing this very well. I'll try to start again maybe.'

'No, no, I'm listening. Just carry on.'

'Lorna, I'd like you to say something, instead of just telling me to carry on.'

'Herbie darling, I don't know what to say.'

'Gee, all you have to say is yes or no!'

'Herbie, I don't think this is the kind of thing we can rush into.'

'You're damn right we can't. There's a war that will go on for years, and I have to get a divorce. But if we could go round the corner and be married tomorrow, what I'm asking you is, would you do it?'

'You know I would.'

'And one day, when we're clear, will you?'

'Yes, Herbie.'

'Jeez,' he said, running his fingers through his hair, 'that was a rough run if ever was.'

Lorna said, laughing rather shakily: 'Colonel, you can pour me a little more champagne.'

They drank some more champagne. 'I had it planned,' he said. 'I had it planned what to say, real good. You know, to sweep you off your feet. And I didn't say any of it.'

'Never mind; say it later. I'd love to be swept off my feet.'

'Are you very wet? That was so clumsy of me.'

'In a minute or two I'll undress and we'll find out, shall we?'

'Now you're talking, kid.'

Not long afterwards Lorna exclaimed: 'Oh lor, I haven't rung Bunty!'

'Too late now.' And it was.

Ultimately Bunty was telephoned. She said: 'Did you miss your train or something? You had me worried. I've booked a box for four for *The Lisbon Story*.'

'Sounds great. What time?'

'Six-thirty. At the Hippodrome.'

If they rushed, they'd just make it.

'Why in hell did we ever agree to do this?' said Herbie.

'You wanted to feel more Christian, don't you remember?'

'Always a mistake.'

'You'll feel good about it later, darling.'

'It'll count with St Peter, you reckon?'

'We should think where we'll eat after the show.'

'I have. While I was waiting for your train to show up I reserved a table at the Écu de France, which Major Shaw highly recommends. He's a food buff.'

'You were lucky to get a table there.'

'Another party had dropped out. Look, we must get a move on. Why *did* we agree to all this?'

It was an awful scramble, but they arrived at the Hippodrome just in the nick of time for them all to be in their box just as the second warning bell rang.

The Lisbon Story, a musical, at that time was the most popular show in town. It starred Patricia Burke and had two highly animated Polish dancers called Alicia and Cheslaw. Quite why it should be so popular was a bit of a mystery: it told a story loosely connected with the war in an escapist kind of way; the music was pleasant but nothing memorable, apart from a song about a fisherman called Pedro. The foursome in the box were determined to enjoy themselves, however, and applauded enthusiastically at the end of each act. Even Theodor Kaufmann refrained from being critical.

He was looking amazingly smart in a sharply cut dark suit with a natty white pin-stripe, a dazzling white shirt, a deep crimson tie in heavy silk, and mother-of-pearl and gold cufflinks. His hair had been freshly shampooed and rakishly styled to stand up on end with even greater verve than usual; his moustache was trimmed. His gold-rimmed spectacles glittered. He himself laughed, grimaced, craned his head to see, threw back his entire body in amusement, clapped loudly, at one point cheered the dancers. 'Bravo!' Lorna found him really rather more amusing to watch than the show itself.

After the show they walked to L'Écu de France, groping their way through the crowds of Leicester Square and Piccadilly into Jermyn Street. Bunty said: 'Gosh, if it's like this now, what's it going to be like at midnight?'

The dinner was admirable; it was possible to forget that there was a war and rationing. Wine and excitement made Theodor increasingly animated and witty. Bunty, looking very pretty in a pre-war low-cut black crêpe de Chine shift dress scattered with black sequins, laughed a lot and was obviously enjoying herself. As for Lorna (in her dress she had worn at the Gala Ball), she was blissfully happy. Herbie looked youthful and relaxed. Everything was great.

Theodor told stories about his youth; his climbing exploits in the Tyrol, his sailing exploits on various lakes, seas and rivers, his ski-ing, his skating, his shooting, his dancing. 'The strength of my ankle to which I owed my agile grace was phenomenal.' False modesty was not one of his sins. 'When I skimmed on the ice chance onlookers spontaneously exploded.' Bunty threatened to explode at this one, but he continued undeterred: 'How to describe my dives, my swoops, my daredevilment?'

'Sounds like you should have been in the air force, too, Theo,' said Herbie.

'No, no, I stuck to the ice. No pie in the sky for me.'

Bunty and Lorna laughed until tears sparkled in their eyes. These anecdotes intoxicated them. Lorna, realizing that Theodor was particularly exerting himself to impress Bunty, wondered if the undoubted effect he was having upon her was really the one he hoped for.

For dessert they ordered an ornate charlotte russe, a work of art as it reposed on the dish. 'I wonder if it tastes as good as it looks,' sighed Bunty, like a happy anticipatory child.

Theodor said, taking up his spoon and wagging it at her, 'Aha! The proof of the pudding is in the consummation.'

'I must remember that one,' said Herbie.

After they left the restaurant they took a walk in St James's Park; it was a cold night, but they were all too merry to feel it. In the open park, away from the shadows of tall buildings, the moonlight silvered the frosty mist rising between the trees; the lake glimmered mysteriously. Theodor flung back his head and declaimed with bravura:

> 'Quanto e bella giovinezza,
> Che si fugge tuttavia!
> Chi vuol esse lieto, sici;
> Di doman non c'e certezza!'

'And what does that mean?' asked Herbie.

'The old old truth in yet another form; gather your rosebuds while ye may,' replied Theodor, adding breezily: 'I am lucky to be at home in so many languages.'

'Well, I guess it's good advice for the eve of nineteen forty-four,' said Herbie. 'It's going to be a year for moments of truth.'

It was now time to go to Piccadilly Circus; the place to be when midnight struck.

Crowds of people were thronging the streets leading to the Circus and more crowded in all the time. A babble of voices filled the air, loud American predominating. The prostitutes stood in every doorway, on the street corners, lingered on the pavements; each with her own beat; the famed Piccadilly Warriors plying their flourishing trade with the GIs; picking up clients and walking away with them, some not very far before obliging with their services, to judge by the sounds coming from the narrower shadow-filled side-streets. The blackout curtained and screened, concealed and yet accentuated the extraordinary goings-on. The GIs groped and stumbled, the glowing tips of cheroots here and there punctuating the dark; a crossfire crackled of greeting and response: 'Hey, soldier.' 'Say, babe.' 'Hi there, Big Boy.' 'Evenin', lady.' The night was charged with sexual excitement; little stabs of electric torchlight, furtively flicked on and off, glimmered here, glimmered there; appeared, vanished; the tide of GIs seemed endless.

Herbie clutched Lorna closely to him; he said: 'Well, if this doesn't beat all. You hear about it, but . . . ' Bunty, determined not to become separated, gripped Theodor's arm as he regaled her with tales about the *poules* in the Paris of his youth. 'Very different from this London riff-raff, I assure you.'

In Piccadilly Circus itself the atmosphere suddenly changed. The crowd gathering here was not sexually predatory; genial spirits of all nationalities, come to celebrate the New Year, jostled cheerfully together, joking and laughing in the dark, round the base of the sandbagged and boarded-up statue of Eros, God of Love. 'Oh Love, what crimes are committed in thy name!' exclaimed Theodor dramatically, waving his arm and accidentally striking a stranger on the head. 'Watch out!' said a very English voice. Bunty got the giggles.

Herbie stopped, secured the attention of Theodor and Bunty, and said: 'Say, pay attention. If we become separated, which we may well be, the plan is after midnight we go back to the Dorchester for dancing and early breakfast. Keep that in mind and see you there if so happen we lose each other.'

'Aye aye, sir,' said Bunty.

'I've got it. I've committed it,' said Theodor.

Midnight drew near. English, Scots, French, Poles, Americans, Canadians, Australians and the Metropolitan Police mixed together freely; the police in a mood exceptionally benign. As midnight struck from distant clocks a spontaneous outburst of cheering, hugging, kissing and handshaking seized the crowd; strangers suddenly flinging their arms round one another, all in the dark and unable to see, but all enthusiastic in their desire to greet the New Year with a display of warmth and goodwill for their neighbours. Cries of 'Happy New Year' in every kind of voice and accent rose to the skies. It was all so different from what was going on in the neighbouring streets that it seemed in another world.

Lorna exchanged a fervent kiss with a tall Scot smelling of whisky, supposing it to be Herbie. 'Verra nice,' he said. 'And a happy New Year to ye, lassie.' Herbie meantime was being embraced and kissed on both cheeks by a Frenchman saying something rapid and emotional. Bunty, clasped by a suddenly tearful Theodor breathing Happy New Years down her neck, was caught from behind, pulled away and kissed by someone she thought was a sailor, who in his turn was hugged by someone else. Bunty, by now a little bewildered, stepped heavily back on somebody else's foot. 'Oh, I am so sorry I hope I didn't hurt you but Happy New Year all the same!' she exclaimed all in one breath.

'Say, Bunty, that you?' said a voice she had not expected ever to hear again.

'Waldo!'

Lorna and Herbie, trying to struggle from the crowd, suddenly heard Theodor's unmistakable voice. 'Waterloo! Waterloo!' he seemed to be repeating to himself aloud.

'No, no, Theo,' cried Lorna, grabbing hold of him. 'We're going to the Dorchester; it's nowhere near Waterloo. Have you Bunty with you?'

'I have met my Waterloo!' intoned Theodor dramatically, and then was gone again, swallowed up in the dark mass of people.

Neither Bunty nor Theodor surfaced at the Dorchester. Herbie and Lorna danced and early-breakfasted alone, and went to bed with the intention of not getting up again in too much of a hurry.

XXV

Bunty and Waldo gravitated, without quite knowing how, into Regent Street, up which, clinging to one another in a kind of daze, they stumbled in the dark, bumping into people and being bumped into. They fell off a kerb, tripped up another, collided with someone lurching off the kerb they had just tripped up.

A taxi halted a few yards from them, they heard male American voices of passengers getting out of it. Bunty found herself being pushed head-first into it, and then Waldo fell in after her. Rather like their last taxi ride together, she thought.

'Where are we going?' asked Bunty.

'Mignonette's flat.'

'Who's Mignonette?'

'A woman I know; American, lived in Paris, now she's working over here. She's whooping it up with an old flame at present and, being the understanding type, she's loaned me her apartment while she's away.'

He began feeling in his overcoat pocket for something. Bunty said: 'I trust you're not going to produce a cheroot.'

Waldo broke into laughter. 'You remember that?'

'Who could forget it?'

'And still she comes back for more! You're game, kid, you're real game.'

He was still fumbling in his pocket. 'I think I've lost them.'

'Lost what, Waldo?'

'The keys to Mignonette's flat.'

'That's a helpful start.'

He felt around some more. Then: 'Found them. I was searching in the wrong pocket. My, that's a relief! I'm not very good with keys.' He put his arm round Bunty. 'Let's relax.' They started a long kiss.

After a bit he said: 'You're beautiful. Have we met before?'

'I hope so. I never kiss strangers.'

Waldo sighed romantically. 'This is going to be the best night of our lives. Guaranteed perfection.' He began kissing her again.

The driver called over his shoulder to them: 'Behind Middlesex Hospital, innit?'

'Where's he taking us – hospital? I didn't ask for any damn hospital,' said Waldo. 'We may need it by the time we're through with one another, but at this stage certainly not.'

'Don't worry,' said Bunty. 'He's merely trying to get his bearings.'

'Have to get them without me helping him any,' replied Waldo. 'It's the first time I've been to the flat myself.'

'We'll find it, guv,' said the driver. 'All things are possible.' Presently he stopped and spoke over his shoulder again. 'I've fetched you within a stone's throw of where you want. You can't miss it.'

Waldo paid the cabbie, who drove away leaving them looking into a small narrow cul-de-sac, very dark and uninviting. 'Do we have to go down there?' asked Bunty apprehensively.

'It seems so. A kind of test of our determination, I guess. We'll mean something to one another after this, kid. Come on.'

Hand in hand they groped their way down the cul-de-sac, past little terrace cottages squeezed together.

'Which number do we want, Waldo?'

'Twenty. Flat Two.'

'Have you a torch? We'll never find it without one.'

'Torch?' Waldo sounded contemptuous. 'I've been trained to see in the dark.'

'I think I'll stop here while you look around.'

Waldo stumbled and tripped and peered into doorways. Bunty hugged herself to keep warm and wondered what had prompted her to this lunacy in the first place.

After a bit Waldo, fumbling around a few doors distant from her, said: 'I think this must be it.'

Bunty cautiously picked her way through the gloom to where he was standing, fingering a key-ring he had taken from his pocket. 'Choice of two keys. And I reckon whichever one I try first will be the wrong one. Like a bet?'

'Waldo, just open the door. I'm freezing to death.'

'I'll warm you up, kid, once we're in.'

He fumbled to find the keyhole in the dark. Next the key wouldn't fit; it was the wrong one. 'What did I say?' from Waldo. Bunty, her teeth chattering, hopped from one foot to the other, trying to get up some circulation.

At last Waldo had the door open. They stepped into total darkness smelling strongly of a combination of cat and minestrone soup. 'There must surely be a light switch somewhere.'

'I'd be careful, Waldo. We can't be certain the blackout works, and we don't want to be run in by some prowling ARP warden accusing us of showing a light. Can't you feel your way?'

'Mignonette said up the stairs, door on left of landing. Simplicity itself, once I've found the stairs.' There was a heavy thud as he fell over. 'Found them.'

'Tell me how to find them. Which direction?'

'You don't have to try. Just take one step forward and they'll trip you over.'

'This is all quite ridiculous.'

'If a year goes on as it begins, nineteen forty-four is going to hit an all-time high in inspired lunacy, I guess.'

'Oh lor.' She began feeling her way after Waldo. She thought to herself: Inspired lunacy about sums it up.

'Here's the landing,' he said, after they had cautiously mounted several treads of a narrow staircase. 'Now, feel for a door. Somewhere to the left.'

They felt around, patting the hard cold surface of a wall. Bunty said at last: 'Don't let this go to your head, but I think I've found it.'

'Say, I think you're right. Gee, now we're going places.' There was the sound of him unlocking the door. 'Eureka. A light switch, too.' And, so saying, Waldo switched on.

For a moment they had a view of a bed-sitting-room, nice and bright with posters and painted furniture and lively striped curtains pulled back from the windows.

'Quick, turn the light off, Waldo, turn it off!' Then, as he made no response, Bunty leaped to the switch and turned it off herself. A blackness, infinitely darker than anything that had gone before, engulfed them.

'For crying out loud,' said Waldo. 'You gone crazy?'

'The curtains aren't drawn. D'you want us to be run in?'

'Right now I don't want anything except you. Where've you got to? Say something to point me in your direction.'

'I thought you were trained to see in the dark?'

'Don't make cheap jokes at a friend's expense.' He knocked into something. 'Gee, this is terrible. Suppose she collects Ming?'

Bunty, subsiding into the giggles, collided into something herself. Losing her balance, she toppled over. Then: 'Waldo, I've found the bed!'

'Stay put,' said Waldo. 'Just leave the rest to me.'

Several hours later Bunty heard Waldo's voice from a long way off saying: 'My, that's a relief.'

'What is?' she asked dazedly.

'It's you.'

The dim light of a wintry morning revealed Waldo propped on his elbow, staring down at her. 'It might not have been,' he said.

'Who d'you think it was?'

'You could've been anyone. Picking a girl up like that in

282

Piccadilly Circus in the pitch black, it was risky. I thought I'd got it right, but looked at in the cold light of day, when I woke up, suddenly the riskiness of it hit me. I didn't dare peek at you for a moment.'

'Next year you'll think twice before you try that again.'

'The same goes for you with me. I might have been the wrong guy.'

'You sounded like you, Waldo, all along. And you acted like you, too.'

'How'd you know what I'd act like?'

'Feminine intuition.'

'What, how I'd act all night?'

'I knew you'd be great.'

'Come to that, I knew you'd be great, too.'

Bunty wrapped her arms round him and hugged him. 'It was pretty remarkable, though, when you come to think about it.'

'I've never had such a night. I've never known such a girl.'

'Yes, that, too; but what I meant was, it was remarkable the way we bumped into one another like that, among all those crowds of people. Sort of like the hand of Fate. Don't you think?'

'Not really. I phoned Kenilworth Lodge to see if you'd come out with me, and Mrs Wells told me you'd gone to the theatre with Theodor Kaufmann, and he had told her that you'd be in Piccadilly Circus at midnight. Couldn't be plainer.'

'But it was extraordinary the way we were standing right next to each other in the dark, don't you think?' Bunty was determined to bring Fate into it somehow.

'Not really. Once I'd heard the well-known Kaufmann voice declaiming about Love what crimes are committed in thy name I knew whereabouts you must be standing, so I made for it.'

'Trained to see in the dark.'

'You've noticed?'

'Anyway,' said Bunty presently, 'I did tread on your foot.'

'Yeah yeah. I reckon that was meant.'

Presently Bunty asked: 'Why did you stay away so long without writing, Waldo?'

'There was no way I could have written. War isn't for keeping in touch. You just have to face it – in war people drop out of one another's lives. If they're very lucky, they may drop back in again.'

'How long will you be around this time, Waldo?'

'I've no idea.'

'Shall we be able to see each other?'

'While I'm around? Yes, I'd think so. If you want.'

'If it's what you want, too.'

'Certainly is.'

When Bunty reached home she took David's portrait down from the mantelshelf, sighed, kissed it, and put it away in her drawer.

Bunty and Waldo spent as much time together as possible, which wasn't really all that much. She had her bus schedules; he was working long and irregular hours. Fortunately Mignonette continued to be absent from her flat, which meant that Waldo and Bunty had that as a refuge. It would have been difficult otherwise, for he couldn't take her to his hotel, and she couldn't risk having him spend the night at Kenilworth Lodge. 'Mrs Wells would never stand for that. She's absolutely insistent that all her guests must be respectable.' Bunty added: 'I suppose she has to be.'

But one Friday afternoon in mid-February, which they each happened to have free, things went a little haywire. It was a wonderful afternoon of crisp cold air and sunshine; they went for a tramp over Hampstead Heath to Ken Wood and back to Bunty's flat for tea, after which they proposed going into town to the cinema, and afterwards to Mignonette's place. They had their walk; they had their tea; but then they ended up in Bunty's bed.

At eleven they recovered their senses sufficiently to have a practical talk about what they should do.

'I'm entitled to have you to tea, Waldo, and I'd be very surprised if anyone has noticed that you've stayed on, even if they noticed you come in in the first place. But I think if you tried to creep away now . . . '

'Best leave it till tomorrow morning, you think?'

'If you sneak away now, ten to one you'll meet somebody coming home late. Whereas if you leave about half-past five in the morning. Or say five o'clock . . . '

'Oh, I'm like a mouse when I want to be.'

'OK, then. Be like a mouse tomorrow morning.'

That settled, they subsided back into bed.

At some hour – she didn't know when – Bunty woke up with Waldo gasping in her ear: 'What's that terrible noise?'

Bunty jerked awake. 'It's the sirens sounding an air-raid warning.' The horrible wail, like a demented banshee, rose and fell on the air repeatedly. Then at last it stopped and everything was very still. 'What happens now?' asked Waldo.

Bunty said: 'I don't suppose anything much will happen. There haven't been any air raids on this country for two years, and I can hardly think they're going to start up again. It's probably a false alarm.'

Shortly afterwards they heard footsteps coming from the top floor and going downstairs. 'That's people going down to the air-raid shelter in the basement,' said Bunty.

'Should you go?'

'Don't be silly. Absolutely nothing's happening. They're just being nervous.'

They lay in the dark, Waldo with his arms round her. She could hear the regular beat of his heart under her right ear. Everything was as still and tranquil as it had been before the alert.

'What's the time?' she asked him sleepily. He raised his right wrist and looked at his watch that had a dial which showed in the dark. 'Just before one.'

'We've got hours together yet,' she murmured happily.

From somewhere in the distant sky came the low heavy throbbing of a plane.

Their senses instantly became strangely alert. The throbbing drew nearer. 'Is that one of theirs or ours, d'you suppose?' asked Waldo.

'How can one say?'

More people were going downstairs, rather hurriedly.

The throbbing faded again. Then once more it drew nearer.

'It sounds like more than one, don't you think?'

'Hard to say.'

The throbbing became loud and ominous with a hard thudding undertone which seemed to bruise the sky.

'D'you think that's a German?'

For answer there was a fearful crash of anti-aircraft fire from the nearby battery on the Heath. Bunty and Waldo clutched one another convulsively. 'That's a German OK for sure!'

And now people from all over the house were going down to the shelter and calling to one another to come quickly. They heard Theodor hasten from his room and run downstairs.

The guns crashed out again. The windows rattled, the whole house seemed to shake. The plane, or planes, seemed to be right on top of them.

'You best go down, Bunty honey. It's not safe for you to stay here.'

'What, and leave you? Certainly not.'

'Look, I can't go down; it'll give the game away and compromise you, but you must go down, and fast,' said Waldo urgently.

'Darling Waldo, I am not going to leave you, and there's the end of it.'

From some distance away came a heavy explosion that was not the sound of gunfire and which made the ground shudder and the entire house shudder with it.

'That must be a bomb,' said Bunty.

'You reckon?'

Another salvo of ack-ack guns. 'Dear me,' said Bunty, 'this is hotting up.'

At that instant there came a heavy pounding on Bunty's door, and Mrs Wells's voice at its most piercing pitch: 'Mrs McEwen, Mrs McEwen, come down to the shelter! Bring that young man with you. Both of you come this instant, I insist!'

'Oh lor!' said Bunty.

The voice came again, accompanied by more thumps on the door. 'Come down immediately. D'you hear me? You're risking your lives staying up here.'

The bomber's thudding seemed right overhead again. 'She's right, you know,' said Waldo. 'Come on. We're too young and beautiful to die. And she knows I'm here anyway.'

They disentangled themselves from the bed and began to dress. The racket from the ack-ack battery was deafening.

'Are you putting *all* your clothes on, Waldo?'

'Of course. We must look respectable. We've been sitting up talking late.' He was dressing at record speed.

Bunty hurriedly donned slacks, sweater, socks, shoes; brushed her hair, applied her lipstick, and finally put on her overcoat and scarf and collected her handbag. Waldo took up his cap and overcoat. Outside the sky seemed to be splitting in half. In spite of everything they paused for a moment to look each other up and down and laugh.

'We do each other credit,' said Bunty.

287

Then they closed the flatlet door behind them and hurried down the stairs. The door to Mrs Wells's basement flat was open; they hurried down her stairs. 'This way,' said Bunty. They let themselves out at Mrs Wells's private exit and tumbled into the dark outside to be greeted by the sound of shrapnel falling round them like hail. Searchlights stabbed and roamed across the sky; bombers droned in all directions.

Waldo exclaimed admiringly: 'Say, this is the real McCoy!'

'Come on, you loony!' Bunty pulled him down the steps leading to the shelter, illuminated by a murky blue light. They could make out a narrow tomb-like chamber containing two rows of camp beds in which huddled weird-looking occupants. An equally strange apparition, in trousers and a padded jacket and with what appeared to be a fantastic helmet on its head, stepped forward towards them saying severely: 'Tempting Providence is no way to behave when bombs are falling.'

It was Mrs Wells, though what she had on her head Bunty couldn't imagine. However, brushing her wonder aside, Bunty said, in her best social voice: 'Mrs Wells, let me introduce my friend Captain Stein. Waldo, this is Mrs Wells.'

Waldo extended his hand. 'Delighted to meet you, Mrs Wells. This is a real pleasure.'

Mrs Wells, obviously a little taken aback, limply shook Waldo's proffered hand and said: 'Ah.'

There came four violent explosions, one after the other. Then Mr Parsons's voice said: 'Stick of four. In the direction of Finchley Road, I'd say.'

'Do you think so?' said Theodor. 'I would have said a little further to the east.'

'West Hampstead, for sure,' said Miss Amhurst.

The din of ack-ack fire made further conversation impossible for several moments.

Mrs Wells offered Bunty and Waldo deckchairs. They sat down side by side. All was silence for a while. Then Mrs Parsons said: 'Quite out of the blue, too.'

'Yes,' said Mrs Wells. 'Quite out of the blue.'

'Two years since they last tried it.'

'Yes, two years.'

The drone of the bombers swelled in volume. 'Here they come again,' said Mrs Parsons.

'Yes, here they come again.' From Mrs Wells.

'They like us tonight,' said Miss Amhurst brightly.

'Too much,' said Theodor.

A thin high whine of sound, rapidly growing louder and closer, scythed downwards as though with Kenilworth Lodge as its target. Waldo grabbed Bunty's hand and held it tight. The explosion was near enough, but not so near as it had sounded it would be.

'Close,' said Mrs Parsons.

'Heath Street,' said Miss Amhurst. 'Tube station perhaps?'

'Fitzjohn's Avenue,' said Theodor.

'Frognal Way,' said Mrs Wells.

'No, no, Fitzjohn's Avenue,' repeated Theodor decisively.

Then more ack-ack fire.

At last the all-clear sounded: a sustained unwavering blast from the sirens that was little less unnerving than the warning. The shelterers gathered themselves together and returned to their flatlets.

Bunty decided to beard Mrs Wells, who, seen in the light of her own well-lit flat, proved not to be wearing a helmet but a dome of curlers piled high, with a pink tulle hood over them. Bunty said courteously but firmly to Mrs Wells: 'I hope you will raise no objection, Mrs Wells, but I am taking Captain Stein up to my flat to give him breakfast before he leaves.'

Mrs Wells assumed the expression of one who suffers but can do little about it. 'You know the standards I set for my guests, Mrs

McEwen. This is a respectable household, and even with a war on I don't expect those standards to slip. I hope that you and Captain Stein have not let those standards slip.'

'Far from it, ma'am,' said Waldo, who was standing behind Bunty. 'Mrs McEwen and I have kept our standards way up.'

'I'm delighted to hear it,' said Mrs Wells.

'Mrs McEwen is a most respectable young lady,' pursued Waldo. 'I regard myself as highly privileged to be allowed to visit a respectable young lady like Mrs McEwen.'

'Yes, Captain Stein, but one in the morning is rather late to be visiting a young lady.'

'Not when she's a respectable young lady like Mrs McEwen. I reckon I can visit Mrs McEwen at any hour and she'll still be respectable. Respectability', said Waldo, 'isn't timed by the clock.'

'True,' said Mrs Wells, inclining her curler-clamped and tulle-enwrapped head graciously.

'Mrs McEwen', said Waldo, 'is a lady and an ornament to Kenilworth Lodge.'

Mrs Wells inclined her head again.

'Which you, ma'am, being a lady yourself, will have recognized,' said Waldo.

'Just so,' said Mrs Wells, grimacing a smile which said she conceded defeat.

'Breakfast, I think?' murmured Bunty brightly to Waldo.

Mrs Wells smirked and wagged her head and showed them out, and they returned to Bunty's flat.

'You well and truly settled her hash!' exclaimed Bunty, eyeing Waldo admiringly.

'It wasn't that difficult. And I'm certainly not going to have her saying you're not respectable. Come to that, I'm not going to have her saying *I'm* not respectable, either.'

'I'm sure she'll never dare say another word against us.' Bunty opened up her kitchenette and stared thoughtfully into it. 'I can give you potato cakes with carrot ketchup.'

'Sounds delicious. But I'm not eating your month's rations?'

'No, no. Potatoes and carrots aren't rationed.'

She busied herself with cooking. Waldo watched her. Then he said: 'Have you ever thought of getting married again?'

Bunty, who wasn't expecting the question, said slowly: 'Well, I suppose I shall think of it again some day, but certainly not while this war's on. I've been a war widow once, and that's enough.'

'But if I asked you again, after the war, that would be on?'

'Wouldn't your family want you to marry a Jewish girl?'

'My parents wanted me to be a violinist. They wanted me to be a scholar. They've wanted me to be, or do, so many things, one more disappointment isn't going to be all that much of a surprise. They expect me to disappoint them; in fact I figure they'd be disappointed if I didn't. Would your family object to me being a Jew?'

'I can't see how they could. They pride themselves on being utterly without prejudice of that sort. My mother especially.'

'Our families appear to be no obstacle. All we have to do is survive the war.'

'Maybe we'll be lucky. We survived last night. And I shall look back on that as a close thing.'

'You will? I'll remember last night as a near miss.'

Bunty laughed happily. 'Some would say we deserve one another.'

Waldo presently walked away down the hill, proposing to catch an early train from Hampstead station. A little later Bunty went off to start her day on the buses. The streets echoed with the sound of glass being swept from pavements, of ambulance bells ringing and fire-engine bells clanging. Clouds of dust filled the air; there was an acrid smell of burning. Craters gaped where buildings had stood, and over great piles of debris the rescue teams clambered and dug, while stretchers and big bags lay ready nearby. Nurses and policemen, firemen and ARP wardens were everywhere; dusty-looking people with grim grey faces who had been working all night and would continue to work long into the day.

The raids continued for several nights; it was rumoured because the Allied top brass were gathered in London planning the approaching invasion of Europe. The air raids stopped as suddenly as they had begun, but as everyone said: 'When we start invading in earnest, then the fun's bound to begin again for us here.'

XXVI

The exceptionally cold winter prolonged its snow into late February. Roads and railways remained blocked. No word had reached Fursey Down from Ruth since her Christmas message that she had joined the Land Army. 'She's got herself well dug in, wherever she is; expect her now when we see her,' said Mrs Cuthman philosophically. Lorna agreed. 'I think that's the only attitude to adopt.'

To Jeffrey, however, she expressed anxiety. 'All very well, but we still haven't a clue where she is. No address, though she must know we want to keep properly in touch. Scrappy little messages out of the blue from time to time aren't good enough. I never realized she was that casual and uncaring in her feelings for us.'

He, as usual, was optimistic. 'Be thankful, Lorna, that wherever she is she's found a place where she's obviously busy and happy. As for not caring for you, of course she cares: looks on you as a sort of sister, mother and fairy-godmother combined. It's simply that she's having, as she says, a great life on the land; probably too busy to write – these old farmers work their Land Army girls like stink, you know.'

'Maybe I can trace her through the Land Army,' sighed Lorna, still troubled.

'Give her a chance, before you start going to those lengths. Like I said earlier, once she's found her feet she'll head home to you, first day off she gets, to tell you all about it.'

His cheerful manner had its effect; Lorna allowed herself to fall in with his view of Ruth's absence. After all, she did send cards and messages home, which was more than many truants troubled to do. She hadn't forgotten them at The Warren, and sooner or later she'd come back to see them, just as Jeffrey said.

One Sunday afternoon, all sparkling snow and sunshine, Lorna, unable to resist such a beautiful day, set out after an early lunch to take the dogs for a tramp. She walked them up to the Beacon and then down the hill to cut across the lower end of Fursey Down where there was no airbase and the landscape was what it had always been. They followed a pleasant old cart track to a group of farms and cottages; here Lorna paused for a moment to eat an apple and enjoy the atmosphere of another time, another world. Then she continued walking, looping back by a bridle-path across some fields. She reached the outskirts of a wood; the bridle-path continued into it, among the trees, and Lorna cheerfully followed it.

The sunlight shone between the coppice trees, throwing blue shadows on the sparkling snowy ground; the branches of the trees were adorned with plumes of white snow and prism-coloured droplets of water fell from them as the snow melted in the sunlight. The twigs and next spring's buds had a pewter sheen. The dogs scampered happily ahead, kicking up the snow as they went; Lorna, looking at the ground, could see fox prints in the snow; the animal had not travelled in a straight purposeful line but had been out for an idle sniffing ramble, inspecting this, considering that.

Interested in the fox tracks, Lorna had been slow to notice that her bridle-path had become lost beneath layers of hewn coppice. At last realizing this, she began making a detour. To the left, towards the edge of the wood, the ground became miry and unpleasantly squashy; Lorna headed for drier ground, further into the wood, whistling for her dogs as she went. They came running and soon were ahead of her again.

Here the coppice turned into mature beech wood and grew more forestlike; the light seemed to be caught in the branches overhead, and everything was cold and shadowy and very still. There was no path in this part of the wood; Lorna had to pick her own way among the trees.

This way, that way, further into the wood. Then suddenly she saw what was unmistakably a little half-cabin, half-wigwam, built of branches and sods. There had been a low doorway with old sacking over it, but this had subsequently been blocked with branches on the outside; as if whoever had used the cabin had closed it up and gone away. The little edifice, though rather tumbledown now, because it had been left standing empty and neglected in severe winter weather, must have been a neat backwoodsman's job when newly constructed.

Looking at it, Lorna suddenly remembered Amy May's remarks about how Vic Wendell had built a little cabin in the woods for some girl he had 'gotten . . . real spoony' about; to quote Amy May, 'Says he's going to marry her'. Might this possibly be Vic's love-nest, abandoned when the cold weather had set in? Shut against possible intruders, but waiting to be used once more, perhaps, when warm weather returned and camping out became a pleasure again?

The little alfresco habitation filled Lorna with a sentimental melancholy. She was fond of Vic; he was a brave young chap and always lively and amusing. She knew nothing of the girl he had lodged with in this cabin, but one could imagine them in the green warm days of summer, or on moonlit nights, sharing a forest idyll, lost to the rest of the world. Lorna tried to conjure the sound of their laughter together, the smell of the smoke from their camp-fire. For a moment she thought she captured the feel of it all; a time as genuinely idyllic for the little ball-turret gunner and his sweet-heart as that time in Cornwall had been idyllic for herself and Herbie.

Lorna was seized with an urge to see what the cabin was like within. Overcome by curiosity she began pulling aside the branches that had been placed blocking the entrance. A final tug, and the branches fell from the doorway, letting the light into the hut. Some of the sod roof fell in, too, hiding part of what was in there, for which Lorna was thankful.

On the ground, mostly covered by a stained and sodden old blanket, was the huddled form of a girl; a bit of green and red cotton stuff- it seemed the skirt of her dress – showed from under the blanket. Almost all of her was hidden by the blanket and the fallen sods, but at the end nearest the door there protruded two blue-black, mildewed, partly gnawed to the bone things that had once been feet.

Lorna stood in horrified amazement, rooted to the ground, star-ing at the body under the blanket and the black gnawed feet. She was aware that her heart was pounding and her knees trembling. Suddenly, all she wanted was to get away from this dreadful place as fast as she could. She struggled back out of the tangle of sods and branches and looked round for her dogs. Put them on their leads and get out of this wood without an instant's delay! But the dogs were nowhere to be seen.

Then she heard them yapping in the distance, in that high-pitched way which meant they had found something that excited them. Following their tracks in the snow, Lorna discovered them at a badgers' set, sniffing at the entrances, one large hole in particular. The more adventurous of the two little terriers began worming her way into the hole; Lorna dropped down on all fours in the snow and hauled her out. The terrier, half-crazed by badger scent, kicked and struggled. In the middle of this scrimmage Lorna's eye caught a glimpse of a bright red object lying a short distance into the hole. Wondering what ever it could be, she pulled the terrier clear of the hole, reached in, grasped the red object and fetched out a handbag.

Although it was muddy, worn and mildewed, she recognized it as the bag she had given Ruth as a present, and which Ruth had received with the joyful exclamation, 'I'll never part with it. It's just what I've always dreamed of having, a red handbag like this.'

Somehow or other, Ruth and the handbag had become parted.

Unless, of course, this was not the handbag that Lorna had given Ruth, together with a red pigskin wallet, but a similar one belonging to somebody else, though it would be a remarkable coincidence if such were the case.

There was only one way to find out, and that was to look inside the bag to see if its contents, if any, identified it as Ruth's. The clasp had become rusted and difficult to undo, but after a bit of a struggle Lorna got the bag open. In it were a ration book and an identity card; one glance at them showed that they were in the name of Ruth Cuthman. The ration book hadn't been used since early October.

There was no money in the bag; the red pigskin wallet was missing. There was an old comb, a powder compact, a well-worn lipstick and a little mirror.

The question was, how had Ruth's bag got into the hole? Then, worming its way into Lorna's inner eye's vision came the green and red cotton material of the skirt of the girl lying under the blanket in the cabin. It seemed vaguely familiar. The material itself now seemed to move closer into Lorna's mental view; yes, it was the same material as the dress Ruth Cuthman had made for herself out of Miss Cusk's curtains.

Even so, Lorna couldn't believe that this meant more than that another girl had used similar material for making a dress. Lorna stood holding Ruth's handbag in her hands, with a vision in front of her eyes of Ruth bending over the kitchen table, cutting out the dress pattern, saying that Miss Cusk had given her the old curtains. 'A kind body, is Miss Cusk.'

Things began to fit together, whether Lorna wanted them to or not. Ruth's dress material worn by the body under the blanket in the cabin; Ruth's handbag in the hole near to the cabin.

Lorna looked once more at the handbag. On one side of the bag the inner lining was split along the top, she now noticed. Knowing how things had an annoying habit of slipping down inside damaged linings of handbags, Lorna inserted two fingers and explored the recess. As she had half expected, she felt something there and had soon extracted a season-ticket case of cardboard and Cellophane; instead of a ticket, the case contained a small photograph of Vic Wendell.

Lorna drew a deep breath. She was appalled by what she had discovered; but now she had discovered it she couldn't undiscover any of it again.

Vic and his cabin in the woods; Ruth the girl in the cabin; his photo in Ruth's handbag.

Questions began to bombard her shock-benumbed mind. Why was Ruth dead in that cabin? Hadn't she gone to Kent, apple-picking, and after that had she not joined the Land Army? They had received those postcards, that Christmas card from her. How in the world could she have ended up here: lying dead in the cabin, covered over with a blanket?

And why was she dead? She could, of course, have died from

natural causes. But, whatever the cause of her death, someone else had blocked up the cabin entrance from outside, while Ruth was lying inside either dead, or dying. There was no way in which Ruth, from inside that cabin, could have blocked that entrance in the way it had been blocked.

And why was the handbag in the hole? Had Ruth, when she was in the shack, used the hole as a safe place in which to hide the bag, rather than keep it in a not awfully secure little hut? And why had she stopped using her ration book in mid-October, when, to judge by her postcard, she had gone to Kent?

Perhaps she had left her handbag in the hole by mistake and had had to obtain a new ration book, a new identity card? But that always necessitated proof of identity, and filling up forms: Ruth had never written back home asking for her birth certificate or anything. Yet she couldn't have joined the Land Army without means of identification.

And this string of questions asked, the biggest remained: if indeed she had joined the Land Army and was living and working on a farm miles away, how had she finished up in that cabin, to die there, and lie there a forgotten corpse, under that blanket?

It was all baffling and horrible, beyond anything Lorna had ever known.

It had never, ever, crossed Lorna's mind, at any time, that Ruth might have been the girl camping out with Vic in the woods. The realization now came as an utter shock to her.

She felt sick and dizzy; her already trembling knees suddenly became so weak that she wondered for a moment if she were going to faint. But then she told herself it was no good passing out now, all alone in a snowy wood late on a wintry afternoon. So, with a desperate effort, her hands shaking so badly she could scarcely control them, she put the dogs on their leads, clutched Ruth's bag tightly under her arm, and began hurrying away as fast as she could, forcing herself to step out in spite of legs which felt as though they had turned to pulp.

She rediscovered the bridle-path and followed it forward to where it brought her out on an open road on the further side of the wood. Here the walking was much easier.

The day was now growing late. The afternoon light was waning and snow was starting to fall again, softly at first and then faster and faster, with a growing wind behind it. Lorna knew her way and was well on the road; there was no chance of her becoming lost, but there were still several miles between herself and Fursey-Winwold. She was wet and cold, the evening was black and wild, with night coming on fast. She could hear the Forts returning from their milk run; their loud throbbing rumble droned above the sound of the wind. Lorna thought of Vic up there with his guns, homing safe and sound no doubt as he always did. She thought of Ruth, or what was left of Ruth, lying under the blanket in the rotting little cabin in the wood.

At this thought Lorna found herself shuddering violently, and the poor little wet dogs, shivering as they trotted along beside her, looked up at her in anxiety.

She had a heavy feeling that this was all her fault; she had failed to keep an eye on Ruth at that fateful Gala Ball. Lorna had never quite believed the tale that Ruth had been driven home that night by nice farming folk; more and more Lorna felt convinced that the girl had been escorted home by Vic, and that was how all this had begun.

At last a bend in the road brought Lorna to the outskirts of Fursey-Winwold. Lorna intended going straight to Jack Hoppett, the village police constable, to tell him without delay about the discovery of Ruth's body and to give him the handbag. But the constable's house was locked up; he was out, doubtless gone with Mrs Hoppett to visit her sister, it being Sunday evening.

Lorna stood in the whirling snow, half frozen to death, shivering and pondering on what her next step should be. Phone the police at the main police station in the nearest town, she supposed. She didn't want to do the telephoning from her own home, where her conversation might be overheard; she was anxious that Mrs Cuthman, at this stage, should not be abruptly shattered with news of what had happened to her granddaughter. There was no telephone kiosk in the village; public calls might be made from the post office, but that was closed on a Sunday evening. Her neighbours would all have let her use their telephones, but this meant that the discovery of Ruth's body would be known all over the village in no time. A village was the last place for discretion.

Jeffrey, it seemed to Lorna, was her only hope. He had a telephone in his surgery which would be perfectly private, if he would let Lorna use it, and she guessed that if she explained the need for privacy he would probably be obliging. Of course she wouldn't mention Ruth to him.

However, she wasn't hopeful about finding Jeffrey at home. He was probably passing a cosy evening with cronies in the pub.

The blackout meant that at night you could never tell whether anyone was at home or not. But footprints (now becoming snowed over), looking large enough to be Jeffrey's, led up to his front door. This seemed promising. Lorna climbed the flight of steps herself and banged on the knocker. Jeffrey's dog began barking inside the house. Then the door opened, and Jeffrey (simultaneously having a struggle with his hallway blackout curtain) said: 'Hello. Who is it?'

'It's me, Lorna. Please may I make a phone call?'

'Of course,' he said, though sounding surprised. 'Come in.'

Lorna emerged from the folds of the blackout curtains, which were strung across the hall immediately behind the front door, and followed Jeffrey down the hallway, dimly lit by a blue-shaded light.

Previously Lorna had never been further into the house than the waiting room and the surgery.

Jeffrey showed Lorna into a sitting room cum study: cheerfully lit, book-lined, with comfortable furniture, a desk littered with papers and a roaring log-fire. The change from gloomy hall to glowing room almost stunned Lorna. Meantime Jeffrey exclaimed, in accents of genuine horror: 'My dear Lorna, what have you been up to?'

Lorna, between chattering teeth, managed to gasp: 'I took the dogs for a walk.'

'Here, take that wet coat off.' He pulled off her coat; Ruth's handbag fell to the floor. 'You're blue with cold and shaking like a leaf,' said Jeffrey. 'Where the hell have you been, the North Pole and back?'

'No, I . . . I . . . It's not the cold, Jeffrey. I've been for a walk in Stanley Wood and I've found a body. I think it's Ruth.'

Lorna made miserable gulping sounds and groped out a hand towards Jeffrey. He scooped her into a tight hug and subsided with her on to the sofa by the fire. 'You poor little thing, you,' he said. Lorna gulped more, against his shoulder. He was large and solid, like a comfortable seat in a tree. The dogs, who adored Jeffrey, jumped on the sofa and cuddled appreciatively against him. They licked Lorna's face. Their sopping-wet coats and their licks restored both herself and Jeffrey to their senses. 'Get down, drat you!' The dogs, rolling reproachful eyes, half fell, half dropped on to the floor. 'Let me fetch you a good whisky,' said Jeffrey, relinquishing Lorna and going to a cupboard.

Lorna said shakily: 'I'm OK now. It was just for a minute. I'm sorry.' She added: 'I better take my boots off. I'm making a terrible mess, and so are the dogs.'

'For God's sake stop fussing about things that don't matter. Sit and drink that.' He handed her the whisky; Lorna sipped the whisky while Jeffrey pulled off her boots. Then he took the dogs outside and wiped them. Then she heard him giving them biscuits. Then he came back into the room and said, 'Another whisky?'

'Oh, Jeffrey, I don't know why you're so kind.'

'I sometimes wonder that myself.' He noticed the handbag on the floor, bent down and picked it up. 'That's Ruth's,' said Lorna. 'It has her ration book and identity card in it. I found it down a badger hole. After I'd found her dead in a hut.'

Jeffrey put the bag carefully on the desk, handed Lorna another whisky, poured himself one and sat down opposite her. 'Now tell me exactly what happened, from the beginning, slowly.'

Lorna told him. When she had finished neither of them spoke for a minute or so. Then Lorna said, 'Someone must have shut her in when she was dead or dying. She couldn't have shut herself in like that. Even if she died a natural death, or took her own life, somebody put all those branches across the door and shut her in.'

Jeffrey poured them more whisky. 'There'll be an autopsy; that'll make it clearer what really happened.'

'I still can't help feeling it was my fault.'

'Don't be daft. How could it be your fault?'

'I invited Ruth to the Gala Ball and that was where she met Wendell and this all began.' Lorna sipped whisky miserably, her forehead crinkled in perplexity. She said, 'He must have taken her camping in the woods during the time I thought she was fruit-picking. Camping with him, in between fruit-picking. But I still can't fathom how, once she'd joined the Land Army, she managed to get back here back in the woods again . . . She might have spent Christmas with him, I suppose, but in a hut in the woods, in the snow?'

'You can't hold yourself responsible for Ruth's behaviour,' said Jeffrey. 'How she behaved was her look-out. I'm afraid the Ruths of this world get what they ask for.' He continued, 'And I should be careful what you say along those lines, Lorna – about Wendell's probable involvement with her, I mean. You don't want to implicate the chap from the word go. She knew plenty of other Yanks besides Wendell. Come to that, it's not fair to blame it on the poor bloody Yanks; she could have been having it off in that hut with all and sundry.'

'Jeffrey, that's a beastly way to speak!' Lorna, her eyes suddenly brimming with angry tears, glared at him in resentment. 'You don't say things like that about people who are dead. Ever. And particularly you don't say things like that about Ruth. She wasn't like that at all. Not one little bit.'

'I'm sorry. I should be more careful what I say to you.'

'Not just to me, to anybody. Ruth obviously went camping in the woods with Wendell; and according to his buddies he spoke of marriage to her. The poor girl undoubtedly thought he was serious. He certainly meant something to her; otherwise she wouldn't have . . .' But here Lorna broke off short. She was about to say that if Wendell hadn't meant something to Ruth she wouldn't have carried a photo of him in her handbag, but Lorna suddenly had two thoughts cross her mind; one, that Jeffrey possibly had a sound point in warning her to be careful about implicating Wendell at this stage when nobody even knew how Ruth had died; and the other, that she had not yet told Jeffrey about Wendell's photograph discovered inside the bag. Perhaps she should keep this discovery to herself for the moment, until she had done some hard thinking.

Jeffrey said: 'You'd better get home, have a hot bath and a change, then I'll run you over to the area police station, rather than wait around for old Hoppett to open up his Toy Town copper shop. This is obviously going to be a CID job. I'm afraid there may be rather an unpleasant time ahead.'

'I'm afraid so, too.'

Jeffrey said hesitatingly: 'One thing I think it might be wise to do. Try to put through a call to your CO type at the camp, Colonel Blenmire, and let him know what's happened and that you're reporting it to the police. They're bound to put Fursey Down high on their visiting list, simply because it spews out so many chaps over the surrounding countryside. Blenmire, I'm certain, will appreciate a tip-off, instead of having all this drop on him without warning like a ton of bricks.'

'I hadn't thought of that, but you're probably right.'

Jeffrey glanced at his wrist-watch. 'I'll call round for you in about an hour, shall I?'

'Please. That'll give me time to have a bath and change and have a word with Herbie, if I can get hold of him.'

Lorna, as she lay in her bath endeavouring to soak some warmth back into her body, tried to clarify the now rather chaotic thoughts jostling in her mind. She wanted to be clear-headed, if she had to make a statement to the police.

The more she pondered, the more uncomfortable she felt about handing over Ruth's bag to the police with Vic's photo inside it. Supposing Ruth had been murdered; the presence of Vic's photo in the bag would undoubtedly be seriously prejudicial to him. Did he deserve this?

On the other hand, in the interests of what might well prove to be a criminal investigation, it would be very wrong to tamper with the contents of Ruth's handbag, which should be handed over to the police exactly as it had been found.

When Lorna telephoned Herbie he had only just returned from a weekend staff conference and sounded dejected and weary, as such conferences nearly always left him. He listened to what Lorna had to tell him and then commented rather coldly, 'I can see that the police have to know about this, and it may be true that Wendell, and perhaps others from this camp, were from time to time out in the woods with the girl, but, supposing she hasn't died a natural death, or maybe killed herself, which we don't yet know, I fail to see that any of my men are necessarily implicated in her death.'

'Nobody is saying that they are; all I'm pointing out is that, under the circumstances, the police are bound to turn up at this airbase somewhere along the line and probably sooner rather than later, asking questions.'

'Well, let them come along and ask questions. They're entitled to, just so long as it doesn't all get in the newspapers and the men here aren't further smeared by the moralists of this world.'

She could tell that he was angry.

'They can't gun for Wendell without evidence,' he continued.

Lorna cut in: 'Nobody's gunning for Wendell. But there's evidence that he was with her from time to time, Herbie. It was a known thing that he was camping out with her.'

'And who else besides camped out with her?' said Herbie. 'A girl like that can't be reckoned on to have only one guy in her life, you know.'

'Oh, I know,' responded Lorna coldly, ironically quoting Jeffrey. 'These little girls get what they ask for.'

'They do, too.'

Lorna saw that Ruth's name was going to be mud. But just as there was nothing to prove that Vic Wendell was in any way responsible for Ruth's death, neither was there valid reason for Ruth to be spoken of as if she had been no better than a shack rat, available to all and sundry!

Lorna said, 'It's odd, isn't it, that when these chaps go chasing after girls every night they're described as Lotharios, but the girls they have their fun with are called whores.'

'The girls are paid for it.'

'What evidence have you that Ruth was paid? In any case, is selling so much more reprehensible than buying when it comes to a deal like that? I can't see the difference myself.'

Herbie made no reply to this one. Instead he said, 'I think you had better take a day or two off. If the police decide to pester you with questions, as I'm pretty sure they will, it's best you should be away from this camp when they do it.'

'Probably a sound idea.'

'And, when they question you, don't bring Wendell's name into it unless you have to. No need to feed them ideas. Let them do the detective work. He's a first-rate gunner and a decent little guy. It's only hearsay he had anything to do with the girl, in any case.' And with an abrupt 'Good-night' he rang off.

Lorna's thoughts tilted first this way, then that. Hand over the photo; don't hand it over. She liked to see herself as the decisive sort; but really and truly, she told herself, she always had to be pushed into a serious decision. Now the push came; the sound of Jeffrey's car in the drive. He had come to take her to the police. No more time for dithering.

Ruth's handbag lay on Lorna's dressing table, ready for her to pick up. Lorna took it, opened it, slipped her fingers behind the torn lining, removed the photo, concealed it under a little clock on her chest of drawers, picked up Ruth's bag again, snatched up her own handbag and ran downstairs. She took her Burberry raincoat from the hall cupboard, hurriedly put it on and presented herself to Jeffrey. 'I'm all ready,' she said.

XXVII

Lorna spent a sleepless night racked by thoughts of Ruth. The police had put Lorna through an interminable questioning, finally taking a detailed statement from her. In this she had made no mention of Vic's name. When asked about Ruth's free-time social activities Lorna had been able to say, truthfully, that Ruth had never mentioned having had boyfriends or of going out with Americans from Fursey Down; her talk had been exclusively of local girls she had known, while her postcards sent home while she was fruit-picking spoke only of 'nice girls' she had met.

The detectives wanted to see the postcards; they also wished to see the Christmas card with Ruth's message that she had joined the Land Army. It was agreed that Lorna would let them have these.

Lorna always breakfasted early, whether she was due to go to Fursey Down or not; but this morning, having the day off and therefore with no reason to hurry, she lingered over her coffee as the misty early light outside gradually strengthened. She was breakfasting alone; Mrs Cuthman, as yet still in ignorance of Ruth's death (the news would have to be broken to her this day, a task which would fall to Lorna and which she was dreading), was in the kitchen preparing the General's breakfast of scrambled dried egg on toast. The time was just after eight.

Suddenly there came a tap on the dining-room window. Lorna looked up; she saw a man's face peering in at her and recognized Vic Wendell.

She went to the window and opened it. 'Vic, what are you doing here?'

'I want a word with you, some place quiet,' he said. His manner was both furtive and urgent.

'I'll let you in. We can talk undisturbed in the study.'

'I don't want to come in the house.'

His tone was so emphatic that she realized there was no point in arguing.

'I'll put my coat on and come out,' she said. She closed the window, slipped on a coat and outdoor shoes, and joined him in the garden.

'Let's find some place where we can't be seen or overheard,' he said.

Lorna, shivering slightly in the cold air, led him through a gate into the vegetable garden, screened and sheltered by high stone walls. The ground where neat rows of vegetables would flourish later in the season was now bare and frosty; small espaliered fruit trees stood against the walls, like prisoners with their hands up before a firing squad.

Vic took a pack of Lucky Strikes from his pocket, offered one to Lorna, put one between his own lips, and lit them both from the same match. Lorna drew on her cigarette, inhaling deeply – a wartime way of smoking which went with taut nerves and apprehension.

Vic said: 'The Colonel spoke to me last night. He told me Ruth had been found and she was dead.'

Lorna made no reply. She thought it best to let Vic do the talking for a little. But he, after this initial remark, was silent. She glanced at him; his face had a grey pallor and was puckered in a frown that was close to a grimace of physical pain. At last he resumed: 'The Colonel said she'd been found in a kinda little cabin in the woods. He didn't say who found her. He said it wasn't known why she was there, or how she died. He told me the cops had been informed, and he guessed I'd be among those they'd ask questions, because it was generally said I'd known the girl. Then he told me not to say anything right then to him, or to anyone else, but to go to my quarters and think what I'd best say to the cops when they questioned me. He said if, when I'd thought it over, I wanted to talk some more to him about it I could. But he said, too, "Not to rush this thinking, see? Just think, quietly. No need to panic."'

'Sensible advice,' commented Lorna, thinking to herself that it sounded typical of Herbie.

'So then I thought,' continued Vic, 'I thought I'd come to see you, because you might've heard how she'd been found – I mean, who found her – and know some more about it all than the Colonel, seeing that you live here in the village and belong. Folks who belong talk to each other. You might know who found her, for a start. And who told the police.'

Lorna said: 'Well, there's no point in beating about the bush. It was I who found her. And told the police, too.'

Vic shot Lorna a look of horrified dismay.

Lorna continued, 'I was taking the dogs for a tramp through Stanley Wood. I ran across this little shack. When I looked inside . . .' Her voice faltered.

Vic said slowly, 'I guess that was a bad moment.'

'It was.'

For a while they stood side by side leaning against the wall, smoking in silence. The morning light grew. A cock pheasant called from a neighbouring field.

'She must have been dead some time, Vic.'

'I reckon so.'

After a few moments' silence, Lorna said, 'What I can't understand is how, or why, she came back here camping in the woods once she had joined the Land Army.'

'She never joined it.'

Lorna stared at him, wondering. 'How d'you mean? I had a Christmas card from her, saying she'd joined the Land Army and it was a great life. I still have it. I can show you.'

'She didn't send it. I did. She was dead by then.'

'Vic, what *are* you saying?'

'See, this all looks real black for me, I know.' He paused, picking at a piece of lichen adhering to the wall. 'She never went fruit-picking, not at any time. She told you she was going fruit-picking, sure enough, but she never; she came camping with me.'

'But I had those cards.' Lorna had so pinned her faith on the cards, as evidence that Ruth was fit and well and working happily in some distant part of the country that she found it impossible to relinquish this touching confidence in the cards in a matter of moments. True, Lorna now knew that Ruth, far from being fit and happy in a distant job, was lying dead; but this said, the cards themselves were real and remained as evidence that Ruth had paused for a moment in her giddy fling, to think of The Warren and those she had left behind.

'Sure thing, you've had cards,' replied Vic. 'We went on a trip together so she should send you that first card and throw dust in your eyes. She never fruit-picked,' he repeated. 'The whole time she was with me, camping. Said she'd rather be with me than with anybody else in the world.' His voice had become broken with tears; he struggled to get it level again.

'And then?' asked Lorna, trying to sound as gentle as she could.

'We went on camping, me building her cabins, then moving to some other place and building another. She liked to go from camp to camp, kinda like a travelling Indian.' He paused for a moment, struggling again. 'We knew, come winter, we'd have to give over camping. She said, maybe if you'd have her, she'd come back to you for a spell, until we married; we figured we'd marry in the spring and set up camping together again. She seemed real pleased about marrying me; asked all about my home folks, said she'd love to meet them and settle in the States.'

Another silence while they smoked. The cock pheasant called again. A thrush, reckoning spring was just around the corner, sang a few tentative bars of rejoicing.

'I built her another cabin; the last one of the season, we reckoned. The cabin you found her in. She said it was one of the nicest.'

Another brief silence.

'I had a spell flying missions most every day; didn't see her best part of a week. When I went to the cabin next, I found her lying there under the blanket. Had her head stove in.'

It was Lorna's turn to cast her companion a glance of horror.

'There was no sign who'd done it; no footmarks, nothing. Ground was dry; weather was good, no rain. She'd been dead, I judged, 'bout twenty-four hours when I found her. I could see all this looked real bad for me; I'd be the fall guy. I covered her right over with the blanket; that was all. Touched nothing else. Left no fingerprints.' He added: 'Her feet stuck out bare when I pulled the blanket up over her head. Her feet showing didn't matter. I wanted her face covered.'

Lorna tried not to visualize the scene. Vic's voice continued, in a sort of monotone, more convincingly distressed than if he had resorted to histrionics. 'I piled boughs and greenery all over the cabin outside; it hid it real good at the time, because there were still leaves on the trees and bushes. I knew you had no coyotes here, or wolves, but I didn't want her touched by nothing, not even a mouse.' Lorna had a sudden vision of those dreadful gnawed feet. Probably rats; maybe a fox. She was glad Vic hadn't had to see them.

'I planned to go back and bury her some time, but then I just couldn't get myself to do it; couldn't bear to look at that again.'

'While you were camping with her, did anyone else visit her besides yourself?'

'Not that I knew. She'd known a number of the boys one time; but after she took up camping with me they dropped off. She was only wanting to see me.' He repeated: 'She said she'd rather be with me than with anyone else in the world.'

He had another struggle with tears, then he resumed. 'After I found her dead I wrote that second card you had. Copied her writing and posted it in Marden, where I knew there was good apple-picking. Christmas, I posted you that card from Bedford.

311

That, I thought, should see the end of it; at least for a good time to come, and I mightn't still be around by then. I said, when I covered up her body and shut up the shack and left it all alone and forgotten, "Well, the guy who notched this one up won't be confessing." And with the poor kid seemingly gone in the Land Army, who would come looking in the woods?'

Lorna hesitated. 'And her handbag?' She remembered that Americans called it a purse. 'What did you do with her purse?'

'I never found her purse. I did look around for it, but it was gone. That's what made me think for sure some no-good had broke in upon her. Broke in, killed her, made off with her purse.'

'You should have reported all this to the police right away, Vic.'

'Go to the cops? That would have been like sending myself to the chair. Everything pointed to me. Leastways, nothing pointed away from me.' He gave a contemptuous snort. 'Would the cops believe there was I camping with this girl and so then I stayed away a few days and when I came back I found her murdered? Who'd believe that one?'

'They might've believed it if, like I say, you had told them right away. They'll be less inclined to believe it now, because of the covering-up you've done.'

'Supposing, when I first found her, I'd 'a told you: "Ruth's dead in the cabin I built her, someone's brained her, but I had nutt'n to do with it." What would you have said to that one? Bet you'd never have believed it!'

'You're telling me now, and presumably you expect me to believe it.'

'Maybe you will, maybe you won't. But I just gotta tell someone.' He lit a fresh cigarette from the stub of his first. His hand was shaking. He repeated: 'It's gotten so I must tell someone.'

'You'll have to tell the police, Vic, exactly what you've just told me. Go to them, and tell them.'

'Think they'll believe it?'

'It'll mean that they won't think of you as the sole suspect; there'll be another man to think about who might have done it. I'm sure it will help your case if you come clean. You see, they're going to know that you were camping out with Ruth. Pretty well everyone at Fursey Down knew you were camping with a girl, and some must have known who that girl was.'

Vic shifted around uncomfortably. The sweat was glistening on his forehead.

Lorna said: 'I've been asked by them to let them examine those cards. If two were written by you, forging Ruth's handwriting, which I'm sure one of their handwriting experts will spot without much difficulty, it'll bear out your statement to them.'

'It'll bear out I did what I said in the matter of the cards but I could still be the one who killed her.'

'Yes. You could.'

'You believe me when I say I wasn't the guy who killed her?'

'Yes Vic. I believe you.'

Suddenly she felt very cold, and quite exhausted by the conversation. She said: 'I must get indoors, Vic. I'm turning into a block of ice.' She began moving towards the gate. 'Get back to Fursey Down, Vic, and have a word with Colonel Blenmire. Tell him everything you've told me, then tell the police.'

He followed her to the gate. She opened it and let him pass through first. 'Good luck, Vic,' she said, and held out her hand. He took it mechanically, held it, then let it drop. 'So long,' he said. 'See ya.' He sounded as though he knew he'd never see her again.

She watched him walk away; then she went into the house. Without delay she took the two pieces of the torn photo of Vic and consigned them to the heart of the red-hot coke in the Aga.

XXVIII

Lorna, having burned Vic's photo, sat down for a few moments to prepare herself for what was coming next. Mrs Cuthman was upstairs making the beds. When she came down Lorna would have to break the news to her of Ruth's death.

This, when the moment came, proved to be far less gruelling than Lorna had anticipated. Mrs Cuthman took the news stoically. 'I should've remembered what happened to her mother at the same age. Any excuse to be off with a chap, that was Florrie. Might have known Ruth would be tarred by the same brush. I should've kept a better eye on her.' She waited for a moment or two, as if getting her breath back. Then she said, 'I must get over to Florrie. Break the news to her before anyone else does. If I go now I'll just catch a bus.'

Lorna tried to persuade her not to rush. 'You're more shaken by this news than you think. Have a little sit-down for a moment and a cup of tea. You can catch the next bus.'

'Florrie will need me,' retorted Mrs Cuthman. 'I shall get all the sit-down I need on the bus.'

Walking back to The Warren, after seeing Mrs Cuthman on to her bus, Lorna repeated to herself again and again: 'I should've kept a better eye on her. All very well for Jeffrey to say I'm not to blame for what has happened, but I should've kept a better eye on her.'

In mid-afternoon Detective Sergeant Plommer, who had taken the statement from Lorna the previous evening, called to collect the cards. As Lorna led him into the house he said: 'I'm afraid there's been foul play in this case, Miss Washbourne, though I think that won't come to you as altogether a surprise, after what you saw yesterday. In fact the case is now being treated as a murder. We may call in the Yard.'

Lorna said nothing; she could not think of anything adequate to say.

She gave Mr Plommer the cards; he scrutinized them in hard concentration. 'Can you identify these as being in Ruth Cuthman's handwriting?'

The writing was schoolchildish; plain round-faced letters each standing singly rather than flowing fluently one with the next. The writing on the first card seemed to reveal more spontaneity than the others. Lorna, staring at the cards, said, 'They all look to me to be very like Ruth's hand, though now you come to ask me I do think that maybe the writing on the first seems, for some reason, to be slightly different from the others.'

'These are the only communications she sent you while she was away?'

'Yes.'

Without further comment the sergeant placed the cards in a long buff envelope and put this in the briefcase he carried.

He had a police constable with him; they asked to be allowed to examine Ruth's bedroom. Lorna agreed to this and sat waiting downstairs while they went to the bedroom. When they came down again Sergeant Plommer said: 'We'll be coming back shortly, if we may, to try for some fingerprints. We may get some of her prints from something in that room, in spite of all the beautiful polishing you've been doing.' He added wryly: 'Cleanliness may be next to godliness but more often than not it doesn't help the job of the police.'

'I wasn't expecting to find myself helping the police,' retorted Lorna, her tone as wry as his.

'And we'd like to take your prints, if you've no objection. You see, no doubt her handbag now carries one or two of your prints, besides, we hope, some of hers, and we need to know which are which.'

'Of course.'

The interview was over. She showed him courteously out of the house and down the path to the garden gate.

She now heard her father's voice calling her; providentially he had been taking his afternoon nap during the Sergeant's visit. Lorna was anxious that the General should be kept in ignorance of Ruth's death for as long as possible; Lorna had told him that Mrs Cuthman had nipped off to Ipswich because Florrie was in trouble and needed her, but had not specified the trouble. He had taken the news philosophically. 'Don't worry, we'll survive on our own without her till she comes back.'

She gave him his tea and chatted with him as a dutiful daughter should. By the time she had the tea things cleared away she had to begin preparing supper: toad-in-the-hole made with sausages Jeffrey had kindly given them, he having been paid in sausages for removing a dew claw from a farmer's collie. Lorna, as she beat the batter for the pudding in which the sausage 'toads' would hide, did some more agonized thinking about Ruth and Vic.

To her mind, the account he had given her that morning of the happiness of himself and Ruth together and the thunderclap experience of returning to the shack to find her murdered, resulting in his very natural reaction not to go to the police but to attempt to do a cover-up which had now failed owing to Lorna's own discovery of the body, had all been stamped with the ring of veracity. Lorna could only feel that if Vic went to the police with that story they would, like herself, realize that he was speaking the truth. The one thing jeopardizing their acceptance of his statement would surely be her own idiotic handling of the thing. She had taken the advice of both Jeffrey and Herbie, 'Don't implicate Vic at this stage.' It had been the wrong advice.

She would have to eat humble pie and tell Sergeant Plommer what she had done. Which would not be an enjoyable experience. She wondered uncertainly whether trying to hide evidence from the police carried a prison sentence. In her mind's eye she saw herself locked up in a cell.

Supper started with carrot soup. Lorna served it in her beloved Wedgwood tureen. She felt she needed something to lift her morale.

After supper Jeffrey called in to chat with the General. Lorna left them together while she prepared a cheese and onion flan for lunch on the morrow. After that she prepared coffee and egg sandwiches for her father, Jeffrey and herself; her fowls were laying splendid numbers of eggs at present. Later on, when she was washing up at the kitchen sink, Jeffrey looked in to say good-night to her. He asked: 'How did poor Mrs Cuthman take it, when you broke the news about Ruth to her?'

'She appeared to bear up remarkably well, but I rather suspected it was because she was too shocked to be able to take the thing in properly. She insisted on going to Ipswich without delay, to her daughter; so off she went on the very next bus. She says she'll come back when it's all settled down. What she means by that I'm not quite sure.' Lorna added: 'I hope she won't be away for too long.'

'So do I, for your sake,' said Jeffrey, picking up a clean tea towel and starting to dry things without being asked.

After a few moments of random chat during which Lorna washed the Wedgwood tureen with infinite care and Jeffrey dried it with similar concentration ('This is a fine piece, Lorna'), she observed slowly: 'I'm not so happy about the police. I took your advice, which Herbie repeated when I phoned him, not to implicate Vic Wendell by mentioning him at this stage, and now I'm not so sure it was good advice, because Vic came to see me this morning and gave me what struck me as a completely honest account of what happened to Ruth, and resultantly I'm now of the opinion I *should* have mentioned Vic and his association with her.'

'Why is that?'

Lorna gave Jeffrey a brief outline of what Vic had told her that morning. She concluded: 'He absolutely convinced me that he was speaking the truth. Somebody else killed her, while he wasn't there. Some ghastly prowler. Someone like that.' She paused to rinse out the coffee pot with particular care. 'It's easy to be wise after the event, but I should have made it absolutely plain to the police that Vic was devoted to Ruth, as she was to him, and that she died because she had the misfortune to have some awful homicidal maniac – you know the sort I mean – come across her cabin while she was asleep, or he in some other way caught her unawares, and he attacked her. It needn't have been for any particular reason; just a violent unprovoked attack. You do read about such things.'

Jeffrey replied cheerfully: 'Yes, you do. But I'm sure if there'd been a homicidal maniac prowling about round here we'd all have heard about it. It's the kind of thing that would certainly set the whole district abuzz. Titus would certainly not miss out on a homicidal maniac, that's for sure.'

'But people mightn't necessarily know about him, Jeffrey. There always has to be the first victim. Maybe Ruth was that first.'

Jeffrey, looking unconvinced, started drying a milk jug. He said: 'It'll be a difficult case to unravel. As I said last night, though you didn't like it, Ruth knew plenty of other chaps besides Vic, and heaven alone knows how many of them visited her in that shack.'

Lorna replied coldly: 'Vic certainly didn't think anybody else visited her. He said she used to know some of the other boys, but now all she wanted was to be with him.'

'He wouldn't know who visited her when he wasn't there, would he?' returned Jeffrey, giving a fancy finishing flick to the jug.

'In any case, I'm not altogether convinced that Vic was right when he said she used to know some of the other boys,' retorted Lorna. 'As far as I could see, and she was living under my very nose, she never knew any boys at all until, under cover of going fruit-picking, she went off camping with Vic. He may think she'd known one or two other boys before him, but I'd never seen her with a boyfriend, that's for sure. Plenty of girlfriends she went out with, in the way girls of that age do; otherwise she was curled up in a chair reading, or taking the dogs for a walk by herself.'

Jeffrey passed his hand across his forehead. 'Really, Lorna, in many ways you beat me.'

'How d'you mean?'

'You just don't notice things, do you?'

'How d'you mean, I don't notice things? What don't I notice?'

Jeffrey heaved a heavy sigh. 'Someone's bound to tell you in the end, so I might as well.'

'Tell me what?'

'That Ruth was on the game.'

'On the game? What game?'

'Great Scott, Lorna, where have you been all your life?' Jeffrey looked at her with a strange expression, she thought. 'I shall have to take you in hand,' he said.

'Oh!' said Lorna slowly, light dawning on her. 'You mean . . .'

'Precisely.'

'But she lived here with us. How did she manage . . . ?'

'When she took your dogs for a walk, muggins. And no doubt during those times when she'd kidded you she was out with other girls. She had a sort of little one-woman knocking shop in the old barn where the Invasion HQ used to be.' Jeffrey paused. 'You do know what a knocking shop is, I suppose?'

'I can guess what you mean.'

'Did a roaring trade with the Yanks.'

It was now Lorna's turn to look at Jeffrey with a rather strange expression. 'How d'you know all this, Jeffrey?'

'I can assure you I never patronized her,' said Jeffrey, amused by the look she had given him.

'I didn't suppose you would.'

'It was common talk at the Queen's Head. Pubs are the place to learn what's going on.'

'I never go to a pub.'

'No, I know you don't. That's your trouble. I'll have to start taking you to the occasional pub. Educate you.'

It was now Lorna's turn to heave a heavy sigh. 'Do they really know *everything* that's going on?'

'I can guarantee they know everything about everyone in this village.'

'Including you and me?'

'Why, what have we been up to?' said Jeffrey, laughing.

'Now, you see, you're not being serious again. I didn't mean that, as well you know.'

'They know, everyone knows, that you are a very nice young lady who had no idea what little Ruth was up to; which was why nobody enlightened you. As for me, I don't think it matters very much about me. So long as they call upon me when they need a vet, that's all I'm worried about.'

'D'you think the police will know all this?'

'If they don't already, they soon will.'

'I told them Ruth never had any boyfriends, and as far as I knew never went out with Americans.'

'That'll keep 'em laughing.'

She began putting the china away in the cupboard as Jeffrey handed it to her, item by item.

'I was wondering if I should confess to them that I hadn't entirely been speaking the truth and that . . . well, you see, Jeffrey, Ruth had a photo of Vic in her handbag, and I took it out and burned it.'

'My eye, Lorna, we shall have you ending up in clink!'

She looked at him anxiously. 'You are pulling my leg, aren't you?'

'Of course. Only don't be surprised if, next time they see you, they ask you some rather pointed questions.'

Lorna gazed sadly round the kitchen, thinking of Ruth curled up in the chair reading; Ruth at the table cutting out the material for her red and green dress. 'I'm certain Ruth never meant any wrong. I'm sure she never ran what you call a knocking shop. I'm sure she saw them all as friends.'

'D'you honestly not know what goes on?'

'Of course I know.' Lorna thought of the shack rats. 'Of course I know,' she repeated. 'But it just is I don't believe that Ruth, in spite of whatever everyone says, was really like that. She was a dear little thing.' Her voice shook.

'I better get along home; it's late. If I were you I'd call it a day too. You're looking quite flaked out; take a sleeping pill and have a decent night's rest. Fretting won't fetch Ruth back to the land of the living. And you know, she did rather let you down, didn't she? You and poor old Mrs Cuthman.'

Lorna said nothing except a weary 'Good-night, Jeffrey. Thanks for calling. And once again thanks for those sausages.'

After he had crunched away and closed the garden gate behind him Lorna stood a while in the garden, smelling the smell of spring on the night wind and thinking of Ruth, and of Lance and Vic turning up at The Warren, come to see a girl they'd heard about at the camp, and pretending at the last moment, when Lorna opened the door and said who she was, that they must have made a mistake with the address. But of course they had had the right address. She had been the wrong girl.

So, Ruth had kept her well and truly in the dark about socializing with the Americans. But, that said, to begin even to suggest that Ruth had 'been on the game', to use Jeffrey's revolting expression, running a one-woman 'knocking shop' ... No, a thousand times, no!

The next morning, before it was light, a great armada of Fortresses flew over. Lorna, drinking an early cup of tea, heard their thunder and, going outside, peered into the darkness; light snow blew across her face as she strained her eyes skyward. She wondered where they were heading for; probably an important target, as it was such a heavy force: one of those big missions which all too often took a toll on the crews. She wondered if Herbie were up there, and she shuddered and hurried back indoors.

At ten-thirty, through the powdery snow showers that blew intermittently across the landscape which yesterday had breathed of early spring, Sergeant Plommer arrived with a fingerprint van and a small team of experts. He took Lorna's fingerprints himself while his companions busied themselves upstairs in Ruth's bedroom. Sergeant Plommer was chatty. 'There'll be a post-mortem this afternoon,' he said. 'That should tell us a bit more than we know at present: the inside story.'

He smiled encouragingly at Lorna; she began to wonder if he had made this abrasive remark with the intention of upsetting her, eroding what he saw as her obstructive self-confidence.

'Now, if you'd just press your fingers on that pad, Miss Washbourne. That's right. And now on this sheet of paper ... I'm sorry fingerprinting is such a messy business.'

Lorna thought to herself: All of it, the whole Ruth thing, is a messy business.

Sergeant Plommer was speaking again. 'From our own enquiries, there's no doubt that for some time now she'd been consorting with American servicemen.'

An indignant protest rose to Lorna's lips on behalf of Ruth. But she had the sense to realize that outraged indignation wouldn't carry far with the CID. So she said, in the most reasonable voice she could manage, 'It doesn't follow that Ruth was necessarily killed by someone she knew. It strikes me, Mr Plommer, that she was more likely killed by a complete stranger; someone who came across her in that cabin unawares.'

'That's always a possibility, of course.' He sounded guarded.

'She may have been camping out, as they call it, very happily in that little shack, with some chap she was genuinely very fond of, and he of her. And then some ghastly interloper came along when she happened to be alone . . .' Lorna noticed a smile twitching Mr Plommer's mouth and she broke off, saying, 'I suppose it's impossible for you to give this case a romantic interpretation like that.'

'In our job you learn never to rule anything out as impossible. It may well be that the poor girl did have one chap she was particularly sweet on, as you suggest. But she was seeing a lot more than just one man, Miss Washbourne.'

Lorna remained silent. Mr Plommer continued: 'We haven't had any cases of serious attacks on women reported in this district; rather than some homicidal maniac roaming around, it's far more likely she had an awkward customer turn up; someone who made perverted demands she didn't want to meet. The real pros know how to deal with those sort of clients; these little girls, being amateurs at the game, all too often don't.'

Lorna felt herself flinch, and hoped it had escaped his notice. But it had not; he changed his tone to one of a man of extensive experience kindly putting things in perspective for an innocent. 'Cases like this, Miss Washbourne, are happening all the time: these little girls are ten a penny nowadays; part of the wartime scene. Not surprising when you remember that there's tens of thousands of servicemen, all sorts and sizes, all nationalities, bad 'uns alongside the good, at present assembled in this tight little island, awaiting the day when we invade Hitler. Men show up in their true colours under these conditions. You get a spate of little girls making hay while the sun shines, and some of them are bound to come to grief.'

It all sounded cut and dried, put like that.

'Most of the time, from a police point of view, finding the man concerned is like looking for a needle in a haystack,' concluded Sergeant Plommer. 'This time, though, we may get off to a better start. At least, we now have the name of one of the chaps she knew, from Fursey Down. Not that the girl was necessarily murdered by an American. But in the cases of girls found dead near camps – British, Canadian, Yank, any camp – the killer is usually from that camp. These things are part and parcel of war, I'm afraid. The squalid side they don't mention in official histories.'

So, thought Lorna, officially Ruth had ceased to be Ruth, an individual in her own right, and had become a sordid little ten-a-penny character from the darker pages of history. War from time immemorial, as Sergeant Plommer had just kindly spelled out, had bred its camp followers, its shack rats, tagging along behind every army from the legions of Imperial Rome to those of the present hour. Ruth, little round-eyed rosy-cheeked Ruth, with her friendly ingenuous smile, was now to be reckoned one of that ageless, time-less tide of squalor.

Sergeant Plommer, for his part, was now smiling at Lorna one of his pleasantest smiles. 'Thanks for co-operating with those prints, Miss Washbourne. It's much appreciated. And don't forget, if anything crops up you think I should know, or you recall any-thing you think might be remotely helpful, any little thing – the most trivial-seeming things often turn out to be jolly helpful – just give me a ring at the station.'

Soon he and the police van drove away, with everyone on board politely repeating thanks for the co-operation.

Lorna had cautiously told her father that Ruth had now been so long absent from home that the police had started enquiries after her. 'They like, if possible, to keep tabs on all these girls who go fruit-picking and, once gone, stay away.'

'Very sensible,' rejoined the General. 'And reassuring to know that even in wartime they trouble about such things.'

All afternoon Lorna could not keep herself from thinking morbidly about the post-mortem which Sergeant Plommer had said would be taking place. She wondered, too, if Vic had by now been interviewed by the police. Of course he might have flown on the mission; in that case the police would have to wait till the morrow.

It was all horribly upsetting. The war was sufficiently awful in itself, without having this additional ghastliness.

The afternoon began to wane; the fields enclosed themselves in misty cold. Lorna by now had something else to worry about: she was anxiously waiting for the sound of the returning Forts. At last she heard, in the distance, the labouring, all but groaning engines of struggling aircraft; they came in ones, twos and threes at sporadic intervals, flying ominously low over the last fields between themselves and home, like great wounded birds straining to regain their roost before collapsing. The mist had become a rolling white fog; out of it the stricken Forts loomed, to struggle in full view for several long moments and then dwindle away, once more engulfed in mist, leaving a wake of tortured sound to throb on the air.

Miss Barker arrived on her weekly round of the village, collecting for National Savings. Lorna, who so far had counted nine returning bombers, had to try to forget the Forts and to attend to Miss Barker.

Angie phoned just after eight that evening; she was full of mingled pride and distress. 'Just hear this, Lorna honey! The target was Big B itself. Just imagine!' Big B was Berlin. 'They're saying over seven hundred of our heavies went out. But it's been a real rugged day; heavy casualties.'

She paused for breath; Lorna, her end of the phone, was holding hers, dreading what might come next.

'We sent out twenty-four of "Herbie's Worst"; so far ten haven't returned,' continued Angie, adding quickly: '*Star Stripper*'s just touched down, made it on one engine. And there's still hope that some of the others may make Fursey Down yet, so keep your fingers crossed.' Then she dropped her voice and said: 'Oh, and there's other news, too, which I'm not supposed to tell, and it isn't good at all; but you'll hear it soon enough, no doubt, and so I'll tell you now. It seems that something terrible has happened to that girl Vic Wendell camped out with. The police have been here, questioning people. They're still here right now, questioning the boys.'

Lorna asked: 'Where's Vic?'

'*Daisy May Two* is one of the birds not back yet; she's reported having ditched in the drink.'

'Vic was flying in her today?'

'Sure thing. But there's a good chance they'll be rescued, so keep your fingers crossed for that one, too.'

Lorna thought it might be better for Vic if he weren't rescued.

She spent the rest of the evening on tenterhooks. Just before eleven Herbie phoned. 'I thought you should know we've had the police here, and they're mighty interested in talking to Vic.'

Lorna gave a loud sigh into the telephone.

'And Vic flew on *Daisy May Two* this day,' continued Herbie, 'and she ditched in the drink on the way back. I've just had a call from RAF rescue to say they have her crew safe – except for Vic. He's missing.'

'Oh, Herbie!' She didn't know whether to sound glad or sorry.

'One of our boys says Vic jumped earlier on; saw him jump and his chute open while they were still over France. The others can't confirm. It's all impossible to unravel at this hour tonight. But one thing's definite: Vic's missing, officially lost in the drink.'

Lorna drew a long breath. 'Perhaps it's for the best. Poor Vic. I absolutely believed him when he said he didn't kill poor little Ruth.'

'The rest of his crew are with you there. That's why, for your ears only, he's missing.' Herbie paused. 'If his chute brought him down intact in France, then he'll either evade, with the assistance of the French Resistance, or be taken prisoner by the Krauts and spend the rest of the war in one of their prison camps. If he's put in prison camp, he'll be bored to hell, but he'll come out safe the other end. If he evades, he'll doubtless have all manner of adventures but, being Vic, ten to one he'll come through. Vic,' concluded Herbie in his best cryptic tone, 'always has been a lucky guy.'

With Vic officially missing, presumed drowned, much of the heat seemed to go out of the police investigations. The police continued with their enquiries, but there was no more talk of calling in the Yard.

Before long Titus Swann came with the news. 'The police are calling it a day, by all accounts. They can't make any headway with there having been a second feller involved, and as they never thought much of that idea in the first place it stands to reason they won't want to waste any time further than they need.'

'I don't call trying to catch a poor little girl's brutal killer a waste of time,' retorted Lorna.

'A girl like that's not worth spending time on, alive or dead,' replied Titus roughly.

Lorna changed the subject. 'You know where I want that spinach planted, don't you Titus?'

Lorna complained to Herbie: 'I think the police should persevere a bit longer with trying to find Ruth Cuthman's killer. They're showing a remarkable lack of concern in not doing their utmost to bring a brute like that to account.'

'They're convinced that Vic was her killer, and equally they're convinced that he's at the bottom of the drink. Which is lucky for us, for if they do manage to unearth another suspect they'll undoubtedly decide he comes from this outfit, seeing that everyone looks in the direction of Fursey Down when there's any trouble. Good rule: always blame the Yanks.'

Lorna, knowing that this was a sore subject with Herbie, said no more. It would have been easy for her to have quarrelled with him over this business of tracing Ruth's killer: he, naturally, thought first and foremost of his 'outfit'; showing no concern for what Lorna saw as the prime necessity of bringing Ruth's murderer to justice. Lorna had tried to put this to Herbie, only to receive in reply the inevitable 'Well, girls of that sort kinda stick their necks out, don't they?'

Even Angie and Amy May, who might have been expected to show at least a tinge of sympathy for the girl, simply as one of their own sex, echoed the 'Well, she invited something of that sort, you must admit, Lorna'.

'I don't think she had any idea she was inviting being murdered,' said Lorna.

'It's always dangerous for a girl to take up that way of life,' said Amy May. 'And they know it, too.'

'But you were all gooey-eyed and sentimental when you first heard about Vic camping out with a girl and getting spoony over her,' retorted Lorna.

'Yeah, but we thought she was a regular kinda girl. If we'd 'a known what she was, we'd 'a said: "Vic, think again before you get in that deep." There's girls and girls. You know that as well as we do, Lorna.'

'And you think it's OK for a girl like her to be found murdered?' asked Lorna.

'Not OK, Lorna honey, but not all that sur-prisin'.' Amy May shook her head. 'I declare, it's real sad that that girl of Vic's met that dreadful dreadful end, but sur-prisin' – no, it *hain't*.'

Lorna sent Violetta a long account of the whole thing, written indignantly in defence of Ruth and ending with an exclamation of disgust: 'The more one sees of men . . . !'

Lorna looked forward to a long and sympathetic reply, but instead all she received was a one-line note: 'Who in hell wants to see anything of men? V.'

Oh heavens! gasped Lorna to herself. It could mean but one thing; Violetta had broken it off with her 'lovely' CO. I wonder what went wrong? She seemed to be ecstatic about him!

There was no way of finding out. Perhaps Violetta, in due course, would unburden herself in another letter.

Meantime, on a lovely April afternoon, Ruth's funeral took place, attended only by her mother and grandmother, Lorna and Miss Barker. The Reverend Barker, who conducted the service, referred to Ruth as 'this poor unfortunate child'. The interment took place in a deserted corner at the northern end of the church-yard: a place traditionally reserved, in rural England, for suicides, unbaptized infants and other 'unfortunates'.

XXIX

The Thames glittered in the spring sunshine. An enormous assembly of Fortresses roared overhead, the sound and sight of them obliterating all else; their devastating presence bringing the city far below them to a halt while everyone gazed. Bunty and Edie, on their way to have lunch together, drew to a standstill, to tilt their faces to the sky.

When they could hear themselves speak again Edie said: 'Was you in London when old Goering's lot came flying up the river, just like that, to squash us flat?'

'Yes,' said Bunty, 'I was.'

'Never forget that to my dying day,' said Edie. 'Those of us that come out of it alive was lucky.'

'We certainly were,' agreed Bunty.

'Well, now the tables are turned,' said Edie. 'That's what Churchill promised, one day the tables would be turned. Serve 'em bleeding well right, too.' The girls watched the Forts dwindle and lose themselves in the sky. Edie said, with a derisive grin: ''cos old Hitler's still got his secret weapon up his sleeve, hasn't he?'

'If you believe it,' replied Bunty with a derisive smile of her own.

'Lot've old codswallop,' said Edie. 'Thinks he can frighten us with talk. All he's got left now, talk, I reckon.' She added: 'Homer figures the war will be over by Thanksgiving Day.'

'When's Thanksgiving Day?' rejoined Bunty. 'I can never remember.'

'Same as our Christmas, isn't it?' replied Edie vaguely.

'I don't think so,' said Bunty. 'November, I think, but I'm not certain.'

'Same as our Guy Fawkes?'

'Good heavens, no; nothing to do with Guy Fawkes. I do know that.'

'Well, anyway, Homer says it will be over by then.'

The two girls intended to have their meal at a British Restaurant Edie had discovered not far from Lupus Street. 'They say they're ever so good. And I'm fed up with the depot canteen,' Edie had said persuasively. And as Bunty had never tried a British Restaurant she had agreed to experiment with one.

British Restaurants were cafeterias where you could obtain cheap meals that were by all accounts wholesome and filling.

Eddie and Bunty found they could have a first course described as 'meat and two veg', followed by jam roly-poly suet pudding, bread and butter, and a cup of coffee, all for elevenpence. The bread and butter and the coffee arrived with the first course. The meat, heavily camouflaged with a packet gravy, was difficult to connect with any specific animal. The 'two veg' were boiled potatoes and boiled carrots. However, the girls were far too hungry to be critical.

'How is Homer?' asked Bunty, as they settled down to their food.

Edie replied: 'Oh, all right. I don't know when I'll be seeing him again, but I expect he's all right. Homer generally is.'

'Why don't you know when you'll be seeing him again?'

'Well, he's gone off. They're all going off, aren't they.' She said it as a statement, not a question.

'Where are they going?'

'They don't tell you that. Just tell you they've been moved. If you're unlucky, you never hear another word from them.'

'Have you heard another word from Homer?'

'Oh, Homer's different. I shall hear from him in the end. I dare say it'll take some time; he's not much of a hand at writing. But I shall definitely hear from him.'

'Where d'you think he's gone?'

Edie, forking up a large mouthful of potato and carrot, said: 'How'd I know? It's kept secret. They're being got ready for the invasion.'

She made it sound like turkeys for Christmas, thought Bunty. Eyeing Edie ruminatively, she asked: 'D'you miss Homer?'

'Yes, I do. We had some good times together in the back of that old truck.'

Bunty stared hard at Edie's neck, but the lovebites had faded. It must have been a week or two since she had last seen Homer.

'Well, you said Homer didn't have a one-track mind, but it seems to have been a one-truck mind instead,' said Bunty, finishing off her veg.

'Got to have something to take your mind off the war,' rejoined Edie, 'and sex is the only thing left that's not rationed.'

'I hope you take good care of yourself, Edie.'

'Oh, I don't take no risks,' said Edie buoyantly. 'Always lie straight with my legs together.'

'Good heavens!' said Bunty. 'D'you really think that works?'

'Proved it, haven't I?' replied Edie.

'Can't be much cop for Homer.'

'Homer takes what comes,' said Edie tranquilly. 'Shall I fetch both our roly-polys? Save you getting up.'

The pudding was decidedly stodgy, but at least it was filling. After it they each smoked a Camel cigarette.

'Mum didn't take to Homer.'

'I'm sorry about that.'

'He didn't take to her, neither.'

'Difficult,' murmured Bunty, wondering what her parents would think of Waldo Stein, and his parents of her. Then she reminded herself of her resolution never to think about after the war, and what might be. Don't tempt Providence.

Edie sighed and tapped her cigarette ash into her saucer. 'It's a rum old go,' she said philosophically.

In the evening Bunty went with Waldo to dine and dance at the Savoy (from the ridiculous to the sublime, she thought to herself). They loved dancing together, and Bunty, who always enjoyed being taken to the Savoy, kept repeating happily: 'This is the best evening ever. Don't you think this is the best evening ever?'

'I'll tell you tomorrow morning.'

They returned to their table and their dessert. Waldo said: 'I've been thinking about after the war. I shall study law in Paris, and then devote myself to helping to build the new Zionist state. How would you feel about that?'

'Waldo darling, don't *ever* talk about after the war!' Bunty looked at him with troubled eyes that slowly filled with tears.

Waldo was seized with consternation. 'Gee, honey, I only made the—'

'I don't want to hear one *breath* about after the war. It's tempting Providence.' She dabbed her eyes with her table-napkin, fighting back the tears.

'Darling, please don't,' begged Waldo. 'I only said the itsiest bitsiest little thing about it, not enough to tempt anything.'

'Never say a *thing* about it, Waldo. There's one lesson I have learned from this war, and that's not to build plans for the future.' She finished dabbing her eyes and then stared ruefully at the table-napkin. 'Damnation, I've smeared mascara all over it.'

'Give it me.'

She handed him the table napkin. He folded it carefully and put it in his pocket. 'I'll keep it for our wedding day,' he said. 'To mop up our tears of joy.'

After the Savoy they took a taxi to Mignonette's flat. Next morning, when they left, Bunty asked him, laughing: 'Now, don't you think that was the best ever?'

'Let's put it this way: it'll take some beating.'

When they said goodbye at Oxford Street Tube station Waldo said, as he always did: 'I'll phone you as soon as I find a free moment.'

Bunty replied, as she always did: 'Sure thing, kid.'

A few days later, when she got home from work, Mrs Wells produced a registered letter for her. 'The postman let me sign it on your behalf.' Bunty thanked her and took the letter upstairs. It was from Waldo and contained the keys to Mignonette's flat. The note read: 'Just to tell you I'm being moved. I don't know when I'll find myself back in London. Expect me when you see me, as they say. I enclose Mignonette's keys; she'll be away a good while longer, the rent for the apartment is paid, and it seems a pity to leave it standing empty all the time. So, if you want to use it, do. It would be nice to imagine you sometimes lying in that bed and thinking of your boy from Odessa.'

The weeks passed; spring changed into early summer. Everyone knew the invasion was due to begin any day; expectancy trembled in the air, daily life vibrated with the sensation of imminent and most intense drama. The weather was warm and sunny. 'Just right for the job,' said Mrs Moxton. Then, abruptly, it turned gusty and cold. 'Ike will be swearing,' she said.

Mrs Wells invited Bunty and Theodor to join her in a raspberry cordial in the evening after supper. 'The fifth of June, my birthday. I was a June baby, a June bride and, alas, a June widow. But not all on the same day.'

'That would have indeed been a *tour de force*,' said Theodor.

They toasted her health in the cordial. 'To many more returns, Mrs Wells! May you live for ever!' Theodor raised his glass and bowed to her; she smirked and nodded graciously. Bunty said, 'Happy birthday!' and kissed Mrs Wells, who laughed and said, 'Oh, thank'ee, m'dear,' and went rather pink, though whether from pleasure or from cordial it was difficult to say. The cordial was unexpectedly heady.

Presently Mrs Wells glanced at her watch. 'There's a news bulletin coming up and I'd rather like to listen to it. If you don't mind, I shall switch on the wireless set.'

She crossed the room, pausing for a moment to peer into the garden rapidly subsiding into twilight; it had been a rainy, windy day, and gusts of unsummery air frilled up the leaves of the standard roses and tossed the last of the heavy heads of white lilac.

'"Rough winds do shake the darling buds of May,"' intoned Mrs Wells, taking one of her occasional random flights into Shakespeare. 'Only now we're in so-called "flaming June"!' she added with an ironical laugh. 'Let us hope it quietens down for the merry men of England when the time comes for them to cross the brine. Half of whom are Americans this time, in any case, except I do feel that in a moment like this they become Us. All pull together!' She turned away from the window to switch on the wireless. 'Let's hear what the BBC has to tell us, shall we?'

They turned expectant faces towards the wireless, but all they heard were salvoes of crackling noises. 'Atmospherics,' said Mrs Wells disgustedly. 'And just when you really want to know what is going on!'

Theodor whispered in a loud aside to Bunty: 'Something wrong with her set.'

'Nonsense,' said Mrs Wells. 'Everyone is prone to atmospherics. But it's maddening to have them at a time like this.' She picked up the *Radio Times*, which she always kept inserted in a hand-tooled leather binder, and with it dealt the wireless set a sudden hefty *thwack*. A voice immediately leaped out at them *fortissimo*: '. . . and there can be no assurance that with the passage of time we shall . . .' Then came a further eruption of atmospherics, followed by abrupt and total silence.

'All quiet on the Western Front,' said Theodor.

'It's broken down,' said Mrs Wells. 'It always does when the news hots up, so of course it does it now when we've reached the high point of the war. I shall have to call in a man, first thing tomorrow morning.'

It was in the dense cold dark which immediately precedes earliest light that Lorna rose, dressed, took out her bicycle and set off for Winwold Beacon. She had gone to bed before ten the previous evening to allow herself almost five hours' sleep, but she had scarcely slept a wink in fact; the night had throbbed with RAF bombers and a strange pulse of excitement which seemed to come on the wind.

Just before eleven she had heard muffled steps and voices in the lane; the Home Guard setting out on a night patrol in the interests of national defence at this vital hour.

The intermittent rumbles and growls of Forts being moved on their hardstands had only heightened Lorna's half-fearful, half-thrilled anticipation of the morrow: 6 June 1944. Overlord.

At Fursey Down the build-up for the launching of Operation Overlord had made Lorna think of the construction of some massive pyramid, rising day by day higher and higher; built not of stone, but of squadrons of Forts, stacked one on the other, squadron by squadron. Each prime mission that was flown was larger than the last: the stacked Forts reared up, tier upon tier, and, as they flew, seemed to be carrying the sky with them. Lorna imagined how, for those unfortunates below, when the Forts reached their target and fell into line for the bombing run and the bombs began to drop, the whole sky must seem to tilt and crash down.

The date for Overlord was a closely guarded secret; even the name, Overlord, was supposed to be known only to those in command. But in a tight community like Fursey Down it was impossible to maintain secrecy for long: over the months during which the place had been operational a kind of telepathic atmosphere had grown up which defeated strict observance of secrets, however trivial; with Overlord, a fully maintained secrecy proved impossible. The very *raison d'être* for Fursey Down had been the making possible of Overlord; to a lesser or greater degree everyone at the airfield was personally involved. Fursey Down knew that the spring and summer of 1944 would see Overlord, and as the year grew everyone could feel Overlord inching nearer and nearer;

everything tingled with approaching Overlord; the Fortresses themselves, as they stood immobile on the hardstands, emitted a static signal which reiterated 'Overlord. Overlord.'

So, when Overlord arrived, all Fursey Down knew, without being told, that this was it.

Angie asked Lorna: 'Say, are you gonna be here to see them off in the morning – wave them goodbye and good luck? It'll mean real early, mind; they'll be away with sunrise, I guess.'

'I'll be on time.' Lorna would not have missed this take-off for all the world.

She set her alarm for half-past two, and within fifteen minutes of rising she was pedalling through the pre-dawn darkness smelling of wet grass and late hawthorn blossom making for Fursey Down to join the throng of people gathered on the tarmac to see the Forts take off.

The pallid light was eerie; suddenly there seemed to be a lot more people than were actually present. The crowd waited in a hushed expectancy that was solemn. A green flare shot into the air, to hang motionless as if suspended by an invisible cord. Simultaneously from the distant control tower came an answering green flare. At once all the Forts stationed ready on the hardstands started up their engines; a salute of roaring tumult shook the dawn.

One by one the huge gun-bristling monsters rolled forward. The nudes sprawled across their fuselages gleamed like echoes of fantastical dreams. Lorna spied Sergeant Matlak standing not far from her; he was staring hard at the line-up of his lovelies moving forward into Overlord's mighty dawn. Unashamed tears glittered in his eyes.

At the head of the bombers moved *Star Stripper*, delicately removing her flimsy bra; 'Real provocative and yet she's got class.' The places where her old wounds had been patched were invisible at this distance. She was flying lead bomber for 'Herbie's Worst'

337

that day. Herbie, as CO, sat in the copilot seat: at the controls sat *Star Stripper*'s pilot, Captain 'Whizz' McKinley. *Star Stripper* taxied towards take-off point, where she paused for an instant, as if hesitating. Then, with a sudden burst into full power, the bomber began roaring up the runway; gathering speed, jolting and recoiling in bounds from the rough runway surface, faster and faster, to metamorphose in a blur of frantic sound and movement – no longer man-made machine but a living creature in its own right which hurled itself from the runway and soared, immeasurably beautiful, into the sky.

The people on the tarmac burst into a glorious cheer. From Winwold Beacon came an answering cheer; a crowd of villagers could be seen bounding about, waving like mad. The second bomber had already wheeled into position and in an instant was in turn shrieking up the runway. One after another the Forts took off; the cheering accompanied them in a steady pennant of sound, everyone on the ground shouting their heads off, tears running down their faces. This was the moment Fursey Down had sweated for, suffered for, that so many had died for.

Lorna, choked with sobs, watched *Star Stripper* steadily climbing upward, with the long line of other bombers following. And she thought of all those other young men who had flown out from Fursey Down on other mission mornings and were no longer here to see this greatest mission morning of all: Lance and Vic, Jimmy Yeo, Tex the trumpeter, Barney Coster of *Rosie's Roosters* . . . But individual names became swallowed and lost in the throng of young fellows who had flown out from Fursey Down never to fly again; yet who, suddenly and mysteriously, now seemed present and flying out with the rest this morning.

The final bombers rose into the sky. On Winwold Beacon the villagers were executing a crazy dance; wild whoops of joy spun down to the airfield. People there began hugging one another;

Lorna and Angie clutched in tearful embrace, then Amy May flung her arms round them, next the three girls subsided into a bear hug with Buzz. 'Oh, gee, oh, gee, isn't this what you've just lived for?' sobbed Amy May.

Bunty lay engulfed in deep slumber. Then she began dreaming of great air battles, in which she herself was taking part in a huge silver plane. The bombers streamed round her, like dark rivers converging; the noise they made was that of heavy cataracts plunging over gigantic cliffs. Then the dark bomber streams turned into shining rivers and twined together like enormous serpents. Suddenly Bunty was no longer in the plane, part of the battle, but was sitting on the edge of an immensely high precipice, watching the aerial fighting going on above her, the planes that were shot down spinning into the depths below the precipice. Her head drummed with the sound of the thousands of aircraft. Then she woke up to discover it was daylight and the noise of the bombers was real and every bit as tremendous as it had been in her dream.

She jumped out of bed and ran to the window, to find herself gazing into a green and silver dawn and the whole world vibrating with the tremendous thunder of the planes. She opened the window and craned from it; high, high above she could see more bombers than she had ever seen before, or had imagined possible, flying in formations across the sky. They flew steadily forward into the growing light of day, and more and ever more came on behind them. Bunty said aloud to herself: 'This is it. The invasion has started.'

It was not quite five o'clock.

She ran to the drawer where she kept David's portrait, took it out and carried it to the window. 'Darling, you mustn't miss this,' she said.

She was far too excited to try to recapture sleep; she placed

David's portrait on the table, facing the window, made herself tea and drank it listening to the never-ending tide of bombers.

At ten o'clock a passenger who boarded Bunty's bus at Victoria Station said that Eisenhower had broadcast half an hour ago and had said it was D-Day and Allied troops had landed on French beaches and all was going according to plan. Everybody immediately started calling it 'D-Day', though nobody had the faintest notion, it seemed, of what the 'D' stood for.

When Bunty came off duty she found Edie waiting for her. She said: 'Let's have a cuppa. I want to talk to you.' She looked peaky.

Bunty said: 'You seem as if all the excitement's been too much for you.'

'Let's find ourselves a nice quiet corner,' responded Edie wearily.

They found a secluded table for two, Bunty fetched cups of tea, they lit Lucky Strike cigarettes and drew the deep breaths of those who have had an exhausting day.

'I've fallen,' said Edie.

'Oh lor, Edie,' Bunty groaned in commiseration, then added: 'But I did warn you, didn't I, that your method of prevention sounded pretty dicey? Lie straight and keep your legs together.'

'It worked all right.'

'If it worked, why are you pregnant?'

'Because I got caught in a situation where I couldn't lie straight, let alone keep my legs together.'

'Did you?' It was no use telling Edie it wouldn't have made an atom of difference.

'Gymnastics,' said Edie. 'Homer's idea. Wanted a change.'

'In the back of the lorry?'

'No. In a blooming jeep. I never have liked jeeps. Nowhere to put yourself.'

Edie stirred her tea moodily, inhaling her cigarette smoke.

'Does Homer know?'

'How can he? Don't know where to write to him, do I?'

'Hasn't he written to you yet?'

'Not yet, no.' She sighed. 'Not the keenest of writers, Homer, best of times. I reckon, if they've sent him over there, I'll be a bleeding grandmother before I hear from him.'

'Where did you write to him last?'

'Some camp,' said Edie vaguely. 'But that's quite a while back. He's gone from there. Don't you remember I told you he'd been moved?'

'But that was weeks ago. And you were telling me how well your system worked.'

'That was before I cottoned on to what the jeep had done to me.' Moodily she gulped more tea and said: 'If it was you, would you keep it?'

'What, the baby? Now, Edie, don't you start talking like that!'

'I can't think what Mum will say.'

'Well, I don't suppose she'll be exactly chuffed.'

'If I get rid of it, she'll never have to know.'

'I don't see how you can take a decision like that off your own bat,' said Bunty.

'How d'you mean?'

'It's Homer's child as well. He might be tickled pink to know he was going to be a father. He might like to think' – Bunty's voice trembled slightly – 'that he was leaving something of himself behind. Some people do feel like that.'

'Gawd knows how many Homer's leaving behind,' said Edie grimly.

'Oh, come on, Edie. You were bonkers about him, don't you remember? You can't put *all* the blame on Homer.'

'It was him who insisted on us doing it in that jeep.'

'You can't blame the jeep, Edie.'

'Well, something has to be to blame, doesn't it?'

When it came time for them to part Bunty said: 'Don't do anything rash, Edie.'

'Me? I've done all I can think of to do to myself. Pills, slippery elm bark, skipping, cold baths, meths, running up and down escalators. Only thing I haven't tried is getting someone to jump on me, and that's only because I can't think who to ask.'

'Well, don't ask me,' said Bunty. 'You go home and apply for your extra rations and go ahead and have the baby.'

'All very easy for you to talk,' sighed Edie, rising wearily from her chair.

'When did you learn for sure, Edie?'

'This morning. Stayed off work and went to the doctor. Shan't forget D-Day in a hurry, shall I?'

XXX

On the evening of D-Day everyone gathered round their wireless sets to hear the news and listen to the voices of the Allied leaders and soldiers: the King, President Roosevelt, de Gaulle, Eisenhower, Montgomery, all spoke; the news from the landing beaches was better than anyone had dared to hope, the great crusade for liberation and democracy had been launched and would now, with God's help, sweep across Europe, carrying all before it. This was the message. Bunty kissed David's portrait and got into bed. She felt worn out.

D-Day was followed by D-plus-One, D-plus-Two, and so on. Fresh waves of troops were sent across the Channel in endless succession; the armadas of bombers roared over the sky by night and by day. Everyone lived for the news bulletins.

Bunty had a telephone call from Lorna. Herbie had been promoted to a Staff job, which meant they'd see him no more at Fursey Down, but before he took up his new post he and Lorna proposed spending a few days in London together. 'Not the Dorchester this time, but some nice quiet little hotel where we can be comfortable and happy,' explained Lorna. Perhaps Bunty, with her knowledge of London, knew of some place that she could recommend?

'What about Mignonette's flat?'

'Never heard of her,' replied Lorna. 'Who's she?'

Bunty described Mignonette's flat; Lorna said it sounded perfect. It was decided that Lorna should meet Bunty on the evening of Thursday, 15 June; they'd have dinner together, and Bunty would give Lorna the keys. Lorna would have a night alone at the flat, spend next day making it nice and have everything ready when Herbie joined her on Friday evening. 'We plan to have a weekend to beat all weekends. After which he'll go to North Africa for a bit. It'll be hell for me, being without him, but at least I shall know where he is and that he is, comparatively speaking, safe. I shan't have to live on tenterhooks all the time; at Fursey Down I never knew whether he'd still be alive in the evening to sign the letters I'd typed for him in the morning.'

'Every cloud has a silver lining,' responded Bunty. To herself she said: God, what a frightful cliché! But, like so many clichés, it did convey precisely what she meant.

And now a letter arrived for Bunty from Violetta.

Dearest Bunts,

Just a quick line to say I'm due in London for a few days on a course – this time, how to make our female square-bashers more aware of the contemporary world around them re social issues, politics, the post-war scene and their part therein, and other little things like that. Getting ready for the golden years of peace ahead, in short; towards which we are all straining. What's the betting it will be the biggest letdown in history?

But what I'm really wondering is can we manage a glimpse of one another during while I'm in town? Do let me know, soon as poss, if there's an evening you'll be free. I shall have a friend with me in London, and as we love spending our spare time together (shared interests and inclinations, and all that) – well, I shan't want to take up too much precious free time spending it with someone else, even when that someone else is you! But, that said, I should hate to go back without having had one evening of chinwag with you – so let's try to fix *something*.

In hopes of seeing you soon.

Luv as always,

Violetta

Bunty, thinking how well things sometimes work out, arranged for Violetta, Lorna and herself to meet at the Café Royal on the Thursday evening and, in the spirit of St Hildegard's and friendship, invited Megan along, too.

Lorna and Bunty met a little ahead of the others. Bunty gave Lorna the keys of Mignonette's flat. 'I've had some happy times in that flat,' said Bunty, as she handed them over, 'and I can only hope you and Herbie will follow suit.'

'I've no doubts on that score,' replied Lorna, dropping the keys in her handbag.

Bunty gave her friend a deeply sympathetic look. 'Poor Lorna. I'm afraid you're going to miss him sadly.'

'He says he'll do his utmost to wangle seeing me again before too long.' Lorna continued firmly: 'In any case, I'm not going to beef about losing him, because I've been so wonderfully lucky, having him survive all those terrible missions the way he has. It'd be flying in the face of Providence to start complaining now, when he's being moved to a place that is going to be far, far less dangerous for him. I shall just dwell on how fortunate we've been, and think of the lovely times we've had together, and pin my sights on all the wonderful things I'm sure the future holds, once this beastly war is over.'

'Let's hope!'

'Wonderful things if Herbie and I are together; yes, I'm sure there'll be. And I'm going to believe with all my heart and soul that we *shall* be together, because believing is half the battle.' Lorna spoke with unusual vehemence for her; that English coolness of style and delivery once cultivated by her was no longer her hallmark. Bunty thought to herself that being with the Americans had changed Lorna a lot; she had loosened up, come to life in a way she had never done before. 'Relax and let your hair down, babe.' Lorna had let her hair down. It suited her.

'You'll carry on with the job at Fursey Down, I suppose, even though your boss has gone?'

'I've no choice, have I? That's the job I've been directed into for the duration. Anyway, I wouldn't wish to switch to any other; I've thrown in my lot with the Yanks, and with the Yanks I'll stay.'

At this point Megan appeared. There was the usual St Hildegard's explosion of kissing and exclaiming and laughter.

'Let me get you a drink, Flops.'

'No, no, let me get you ...'

They sorted out who'd buy this round of drinks and then settled down to chat.

'And how's life treating you, Flops?'

'All seems amazingly quiet at the moment actually, now that most of the GIs have gone off to France. Poor young fellows.' Megan's expression, always maternal whenever GIs were mentioned, now became more motherly and concerned than ever.

'Playtime's over,' said Bunty.

'I guess so. Now their war's for real,' sighed Megan.

'Violetta's late showing up,' remarked Lorna, glancing at her wrist-watch.

'Can't tear herself away from that chap of hers,' said Bunty.

'Which chap is that? Not the type she was on about, hot weekend and all that, when we were all in town together last time?' asked Megan. 'Has she still got him in tow?'

'Dunno,' shrugged Bunty. 'But she certainly made it clear to me, when we were organizing this evening, that she only had a limited amount of time at her disposal to spend with us: has someone else in town she'd much rather be with.'

'One loses track with Violetta,' said Lorna. 'She was – at least, according to the rapturous letters she sent me – having an amazingly torrid affair with some officer or other last summer, and I think she was carrying on with the same bloke into the New Year, but the last I heard of her she said she was through with men, so somehow or other that *affaire d'amour* must have come unstuck.'

'Violetta through with men!' exclaimed Bunty with a peal of laughter. 'That'll be the day!'

'Sounded highly categorical, she did,' said Lorna. '"Who wants anything to do with men?" she said.'

'When was that?'

'Five or six weeks ago.'

'She's found herself another chap since, then,' said Bunty merrily. 'Men grow on trees for Violetta to pick, no doubt.' She added, changing to a more serious key: 'Let's face it, with this war on, and her fabulous looks, one can't imagine Violetta ever being without a man in her life for long.'

'My observation of all these carryings-on is that they usually end in a mess,' said Megan. 'And, in any case,' she repeated, 'I know

346

nowadays everyone is very free and easy, but somehow one doesn't expect one's own friends to . . . well, be all that free and easy.'

Bunty and Lorna exchanged glances. Then Lorna said gently: 'I thought you'd grown up, Megan.'

'I think I have,' replied Megan thoughtfully. 'I don't believe anyone could live through this war and not grow up. But growing up doesn't mean I've lowered my personal standards.'

Bunty said: 'Well, it does you great credit that you feel like that, Flops; but I think, none the less, that what Violetta does with her private life is none of our business. We've been joking about her, I know, but in all seriousness I think she can be left to live her own life in the free time left to her by the bloody war. And that goes for everyone else, too.'

Here the conversation ended, because Violetta herself arrived on the scene. 'There's the dear girl now!' exclaimed Lorna with a happy smile. Then the smile faded. 'Damn, she's fetched another ATS type along with her!'

'Whatever for?' growled Bunty. 'She knew this was going to be a St Hildegard's reunion!'

Violetta advanced towards them, even more *soignée*, elegantly groomed and scintillatingly beautiful than when they had last seen her. Her looks had developed a touch of the voluptuous, thought Lorna, like a peach at the moment of perfection. The young woman following her was equally immaculately groomed, in the mould of the new ATS top brass: slim, tremendously trim, with clean decisive features, hair expensively and dashingly shingled, an unobtrusive yet faultless *maquillage*; a uniform tailored to perfection, beautiful hand-made brogues in gleaming red-brown leather; an arresting snap about her lively facial expression, her observant eyes, vivid smile, and precise and athletic movements. She might have posed, with complete confidence, for a recruiting poster, excepting that most people, reflected Lorna, couldn't have hoped to look like her in a month of Sundays of trying.

As the pair drew close to the three other young women, who were staring, fascinated, at this demonstration of studied military glamour, a delicious breath of Worth's Tabac Blanc hung in the air; though which of the pair wore this subtle touch of scent it was impossible to decide. First it seemed to come from one, then from the other. It was a delicate statement of hidden femininity, which, in combination with the uniforms, the faultless brogues, the shirts and ties and short crisp hair, conveyed a lightly disturbing eroticism.

Violetta, her eyes dancing, crooned: 'I hope you don't mind, darlings, I've brought Chips with me. She's heard so much about you all, she says she can't bear to go any longer without meeting you.' Then, adopting a more formal tone: 'Let me introduce Senior Commander Chipperfield.' Then back to informality again: 'Chips, here you have them at last – the trio you've heard so much about: Lorna Washbourne, Bunty Bastable and Megan Thomas. Lorna and Megan, as you see by their uniforms, are both serving in the American Red Cross and both by way of turning into real Yankee girls.'

'How d'ye do's', hand-shaking, laughter, and from Chips an 'Oh, please, just call me Chips!'

Lorna said, with the slightest hint of sarcasm: 'Let a Yankee girl go get you two British Army types something to drink.'

Violetta and Chips each asked for a dry sherry. Bunty said naughtily: 'Anyone care for a Lucky Strike?'

'It's the way she keeps her fringe and eyelashes from growing out of hand,' Violetta explained in a loud stage whisper to Chips. 'She singes them off periodically with Lucky Strikes.' Violetta then leaned forward to peer at Bunty's eyelashes. 'They seem to have grown again nicely,' she said.

Bunty lowered her eyelashes demurely to display their luxurious regrowth. 'Bounced back as good as ever,' she said modestly.

Lorna had a sudden instant of poignant memory. Ruth's long, thick, straight eyelashes, dropping down like a pair of little sun-blinds over Ruth's ingenuous round blue eyes every time she lowered her lids, exactly like the doll Lorna had once had: you tilted her back and she lowered her lids and said 'Ma-ma!' – Lorna had always pretended the doll was her baby sister and said 'Lar-na!' Somewhere she still had what was left of that doll, loved to a point of losing arms, legs and most of her hair. Then, as Lorna had grown a little older, she hadn't needed a doll for a baby sister, because she had had Violetta as let's-pretend sister.

And now here was Violetta turning up with Chips who some-how, in these mere first moments of introduction, struck Lorna as being on much closer terms with Violetta than she herself, the let's-pretend sister, had ever managed to be. Lorna had never been of a jealous disposition, but suddenly she felt herself strongly resenting Chips.

Chips had now produced a silver cigarette case containing Players and was offering it first to Violetta, now to Lorna, who jerked herself back from a Memory Lane of Ruth, eyelashes, china dolls and let's-pretend sisters and, like Violetta, accepted a Players cigarette. Chips lit them with a black and silver lighter, then lit one for herself. As she did this she remarked: 'I must say how privileged I feel to be here amongst you St Hildegard's gals.' She had obvi-ously heard all about Miss Binkle! Chips continued: 'I do hope you'll forgive me for gatecrashing your cosy foursome like this but, you see, it's absolutely true what Violetta says: having heard so much about you all, I simply couldn't miss an opportunity to meet you!'

'By the end of the evening you'll be thankful only one of us chose to join the Army, that's for sure!' retorted Bunty, laughing. She had stuck to smoking her Lucky Strikes, but was now inserting them into a long ebony cigarette holder which she gestured with, in between drawing on the cigarette. 'One has to be different in this world of wartime uniformed monotony,' she drawled in her Gertie Lawrence voice, winking at Lorna, who could only suppose that Bunty had brought the holder along in the first place to tease Violetta.

Megan, conversationally, asked: 'Does this course you're on, Violetta, allow you time to enjoy yourself in town a bit, or is it one of those tightly scheduled things where you never have a minute to yourself?'

'We've managed to find time for a fair amount of fun, haven't we, Chips? A couple of shows, and some jolly little dinners together, and Sunday morning we're going to the Guards Chapel at Waterloo Barracks; it's a special service – Waterloo Day. Should be a rather marvellous occasion.'

'Sounds wizard!' exclaimed Megan, adding wistfully: 'How I'd love to go to that! But I suppose it would be impossible for me to get into.'

Chips's expression suddenly became that of a person who has had a bright idea. She turned to Violetta. 'Why don't we take Megan to the service with us? American Red Cross – I'm sure she'd be welcome.'

Violetta said, 'Wizard notion, Chips. Let's do that thing.'

'I'd absolutely adore it!' exclaimed Megan eagerly.

Bunty muttered to Lorna with a grin, 'There she goes, floppin' again!'

'And after the service, Megan, we're thinking of going to Richmond to tramp in the park. Would that appeal?' said Chips.

Violetta said quickly: 'Chips old thing, don't force Megan to come on one of our route marches if she doesn't want!'

'I'd love to come,' said Megan, 'but I'm afraid I'm on duty at the Rainbow Club in the afternoon.'

Violetta, with a relieved expression, murmured politely, 'What a pity.'

Bunty asked: 'You a great walker, Chips?'

'Love it!' responded Chips enthusiastically. 'Fortunately Violetta does, too; she and I have had some marvellous walks together, haven't we, Violetta?' And Chips looked at Violetta with sparkling eyes.

'Absolutely wizard!' agreed Violetta, sparkling back at Chips.

'Where d'you do your walking?' enquired Megan.

Chips replied: 'We had a superb holiday in the Lakes together last summer. Ullswater. Lovely spot and grand for walking. And we managed a few memorable days in Dorset over Christmas, in spite of wintry weather.'

'Absolutely memorable,' echoed Violetta dreamily.

Vagrant half-forgotten lines from Violetta's letters surfaced in Lorna's mind: 'I have just spent a few days in the Lake District, on the shores of Ullswater. It didn't rain, except for one day, which we spent in bed ... rain is sometimes a good excuse for doing the most marvellous things!'

'I'm spending Christmas tucked away in darkest Dorset with my CO ...'

Megan was asking Chips, 'D'you go walking with a party, or just by yourselves?'

Violetta's letter murmured its echoes in Lorna's ear: 'Our affair has been going on for several months now ... "

'Oh, just by ourselves!' Chips was telling Megan. 'We both loathe walking with parties. All that jolly mob stuff: get enough of that in the Army! Not for us when we take a break.'

Violetta's letter: 'I'm happier than I ever imagined possible! I really do know now what loving someone in *complete understanding* means.'

Bunty was saying, 'I never knew you were that keen a walker, Violetta.'

'I never knew that you and Lorna were keen cyclists, come to that,' retorted Violetta.

'Lorna's the crazy keen cyclist, aren't you, Lorna?' said Bunty. Once again she was being naughty. 'I'm just an old buddy, ped-alling along, pedalling along; you can always rely on me!' She rolled her eyes and pulled a face; Violetta began laughing.

Megan said: 'You're all so marvellously enterprising! My last leave I spent either sitting by the Serpentine, reading Agatha Christie, or going with Yank friends to Hampton Court and Canterbury for the day.'

'Nothing wrong in that,' said Chips. '*Chacun à son goût.*' One of Violetta's favourite expressions. As she spoke she shot Violetta a quick glance from her attractive ever-so-slightly slanting green eyes.

Violetta laughed back. The two laughed as if they shared a secret. Which, thought Lorna, no doubt they do. That one-line note: 'Who in hell wants to see anything of men?'

Lorna told herself that she had been fearfully dumb. Violetta had spoken repeatedly of having an affair with her CO. So, as she was in the ATS . . .! But Lorna, wrapped up in having an affair with her own CO, had automatically visualized Violetta's CO as male.

Lorna gazed pensively at Violetta. Nothing that she had ever known of Violetta had prepared her for this. Lorna felt that she had lost her totally.

If Violetta had had an affair with a man, there would not have been this sense of loss, because no mere man could ever penetrate a female friendship. He might, inspired by chagrin, chisel away at its exterior surface, inflicting minor dents and scratches, but he would never get inside. A Chips, however, was quite a different proposition. Hadn't Violetta written: I know now what loving someone in *complete understanding* truly means?

Lorna had always thought that she and Violetta, close and trust-ing confidantes since childhood, had known and understood each other through and through, but now she knew they hadn't – or, at least, she hadn't known Violetta. Violetta had made discoveries about herself which Lorna had never guessed at.

Violetta, feeling Lorna's eyes upon her, switched the general conversation to the safe jolly old ground of St Hildegard's. 'I wonder how La Binkle is.'

'Still running her secretarial college at wherever it was she evacuated it to; I forget exactly where, but no doubt it's all going strong,' said Bunty. 'Real Rock of Ages, La Binkle.'

'Must be getting to look a bit like a rock herself by this time,' said Megan.

There was an explosion of chatter and laughter: St Hildegard's! Mrs Plessey with her gramophone and the 'Turkish March', *thump* thump-thump-thump, *thump* thump-thump-thump (never to be heard now, or even thought of, by Lorna without an echo of the sledgehammers of Fursey Down). Miss Trott with her dots, dashes and shun hooks. Madame Bonnard-Krutz in her velvet hats, pearl chokers and, in winter, heavy fur cape and complaints of the weather: 'Ah, ce mauvais temps!' Miss Binkle over all.

'You really can't imagine *anything* shaking her!' said Lorna.

'The Rock of Ages,' repeated Megan.

'Show me a gal unobtrusively but decisively made of rock,' said Bunty. They all laughed louder than ever.

Chips listened, and laughed as much as any of them.

'It must have been fun,' she said. 'You make me wish I'd been there, too.'

'Bloody good fun, and bloody *bloody* hard work,' rejoined Bunty.

'My dear Bunty,' said Lorna in her Binkle voice, 'where *have* you been – riding on the buses?'

'A gal may travel by bus, but she must never let a bus leave its mark on her,' said Megan.

'Your trouble, Bunty, is that you are incurably flighty,' said Violetta.

At dinner Chips insisted on ordering and paying for the wine. When they all parted at the close of the evening she and Violetta went off to their ATS officers' club, where they were staying; Megan set off for Cromwell Road; Bunty and Lorna walked up Regent Street together, to Oxford Circus. Bunty said to Lorna: 'And what did you make of that?'

'Well, Bunts, we agreed earlier on that Violetta's private affairs are entirely her own business, so let's leave it at that.'

Before they said good-night to each other Bunty and Lorna arranged that Lorna should bring Herbie walking on the Heath on Sunday afternoon, and they would call in at Kenilworth Lodge, pick up Bunty, and after their walk all three go into town and have dinner together.

This organized, they found Lorna a taxi, the recent departure of so many Yanks having made this possible for the British once more, and Bunty then returned to Hampstead, while Lorna was driven to Mignonette's.

Bunty, earlier in the day, had been to the flat, had tidied it and had put up the blackout – 'So that you won't have to grope around in the dark when you first get there,' as she had explained to Lorna. Lorna had brought a sleeping bag with her; she need not trouble about airing bedding the first night. She looked round the flat and decided that it was perfect as a love nest: a big single divan bed that was large enough for two people interested in close proximity; a nice little bathroom with a modern geyser for hot water; a trim little kitchen. Bunty had dusted and tidied, and had even left a bunch of carnations in a vase with a note propped against it: 'Have a good time!'

Lorna decided to take a hot bath and then turn in. She had just got into the bath and was luxuriating in the hot water when she heard a shattering explosion some distance away. This was followed shortly afterwards by the air-raid sirens sounding their wailing alert. Lorna, who had never been in an air raid before, wondered what she should do. Bunty had warned her that the house had no basement; the nearest air-raid shelter was a flat-roofed brick edifice, known as a 'surface shelter', two streets distant. None of this had worried either Bunty or Lorna; they had neither of them thought of air raids as being on the cards.

A bit dismayed, but not unduly nervous, Lorna continued to lie in her bath. Then she heard a plane travelling fast with an unusual boombling sound. Next moment there was a deafening crash of ack-ack guns bursting into action from every battery in and around London, from the sound of it. Then a short silence, after which shrapnel began falling, like metallic rain, upon the roofs and pavements outside. Then came another shattering crash; the house shook. Until this moment she hadn't really believed in any of it. Now the uncomfortable feeling that the house might come apart with her being blown into the street naked, in the bath, prompted her to leap from the water, snatch up a towel and rapidly rub herself dry. Instead of putting on her nightgown she dressed again in street clothes. This made her feel less vulnerable.

She sat in the bed-sitting-room smoking a cigarette, and listening to the racket of the guns and the explosions of, she supposed, bombs; though she could hear no bombers overhead, only, occasionally between the sound of the ack-ack fire, the boombling of single aircraft which didn't really sound like any aircraft she had heard before. She was not a Blitz veteran; she had no previous experience of being under bombardment and was not in a position to judge whether what was going on was all that unusual. She lit a second cigarette, and then a third, and prayed that the raid would soon come to an end so that she might go to bed and get some sleep.

Then she heard one of the boombling aircraft, flying low and rapidly, coming closer and closer. Abruptly the engine cut out. Silence followed; there came a low clear swooshing sound passing over the roof-tops, and next a tremendous explosion, shaking the building and close enough for her to hear the sound of glass fragmenting in all directions.

Lorna said: 'This is no joke.' She took her sleeping bag and spent the rest of the noisiest part of the night huddled at the foot of the stairs in the sleeping bag. When at last an 'all clear' sounded she went upstairs, fell on the bed and slept like a log, and then the warnings were sounding again.

She spent the day putting finishing touches to the flat and wondering, as she did so, how much time she and Herbie would really want to spend in it if things continued as they were. Explosions, ack-ack fire and the boombling of the little planes went on all day. There was no mention of what was happening, either in the papers or on the BBC; from talking with a man selling fruit from a stall on the corner of Coventry Street, Lorna learned that they were being attacked by pilotless planes sent by Hitler. 'That secret weapon he's been on about so long.' The planes, said her informant, cut out when they reached London, and exploded when they hit the ground. The ack-ack was trying to shoot them down. All this he had learned from a friend in the ARP. 'They've been expecting them.'

Herbie arrived in the evening. 'What's all this the cabbie's been telling me?' he said.

'You'll soon find out,' replied Lorna.

They went up the stairs smelling of cat and minestrone. Lorna showed Herbie the fiat. 'Gee, this is cunning,' he said. He went to the window and surveyed the street below and the vista of roofs. Suddenly, in the distance, they saw a tiny plane flying low and very fast. It drew closer, making its strange doodling bumbling sound as it flew. Herbie flung open the window and leaned out to get a better view. Lorna shrieked and clutched him. 'Herbie, are you mad?'

'It won't drop on us. The cabbie told me it has to cut out before it drops.'

The plane passed right over them: a light blue-green in colour, with a long plume of bright scarlet and orange flame spurting out behind it. It passed out of sight; Herbie said: 'That was a sure enough good view.' Then the sound of the plane stopped short; they stood looking at each other, and the explosion came and the house shook and part of the bathroom ceiling came down with a thump and Lorna screamed and flung herself at Herbie.

He said: 'One way and another this promises to be an exciting weekend.'

XXXI

Megan, like the rest of London's Blitz veterans, instinctively adopted the view that the pilotless planes were one more menace which old hands would take in their stride.

She spent Friday working at the office and in the evening went to Rainbow Corner as usual. She spent the night, as she had spent the previous one, constantly disturbed by bangs and by ack-ack fire from Hyde Park; these guns were almost more of a disturbance than the pilotless planes themselves. On Saturday morning, on the way to work, she passed a scene of carnage and disaster which was, she thought, as bad as anything she had seen during the height of the Blitz: a double-decker bus had been blown to bits and all the passengers with it; ambulance men were gathering up pieces of people and putting them in big paper sacks. The place where the pilotless plane had landed had been cordoned off; but the bits and pieces had been scattered over a wide area. The houses on either side of the road had been blown down; the rescue teams were at work, and National Fire Service members were hosing the great heaps of debris to settle the dust while the rescuers tried to find and reach people buried beneath it all.

Megan was in the office all morning. As it was Saturday she was able to take the afternoon off, and she went to the hairdresser. In the evening she went to a Red Cross colleague's birthday party. The pilotless planes continued to come over in waves. The ack-ack batteries tried to shoot them down. There was no escape from the racket of the guns.

Megan, thanks to the birthday party, didn't get to bed till late. For a while she was kept awake by the noisy night, but then she fell into heavy slumber and when she woke up she found to her dismay that she had badly overslept. She would have to hurry to be in time for the service at the Guards Chapel. At high speed she dressed herself in ARC uniform, polished her shoes, made sure she had money for the offertory, and scampered downstairs.

The Guards Chapel at Wellington Barracks, next to Birdcage Walk and St James's Park, would be crowded this morning with Guardsmen, including many distinguished officers, their families and friends, for it was the annual service commemorating the battle of Waterloo, when Wellington had defeated Napoleon, and for the Guards it was always a solemn and impressive occasion. Normally Megan would not have thought of trying to attend it, but under the wing of Violetta and her senior commander things were rather different.

Getting to the barracks wasn't easy that morning; Megan was obliged to take a roundabout route, thanks to a large area having been cordoned off because of devastation by a flying bomb (as Londoners were now calling the *ci-devant* pilotless planes). By the time she reached the chapel the service had begun; the place was crowded, and Megan could get no further into the building than the entrance. By standing on tiptoe and peering between the heads and shoulders of the people standing in front of her, she could just glimpse Violetta seated with a group of other ATS officers. If Megan had been on time, she would have been seated in there, too, with the main congregation, instead of being barely squeezed across the threshold of the building! And tears of mingled disappointment and self-annoyance came into Megan's eyes.

The first lesson was being read. Megan's mind wandered a little; she thought to herself that many of those present at this morning's service would have had ancestors fighting in that battle 129 years ago to this very day; only yesterday, in terms of British history. How she wished she were further into the chapel, that she might be able to see properly the faces of men and women whose great-grandfathers and great-great-grandfathers had served at Waterloo! This was what history meant, thought Megan.

The lesson ended, the *Te Deum* began. A band of Guardsmen provided the music instead of an organ. Megan was overcome by the beauty of the sound of that band. The congregation started to sing. 'We praise thee, O God: we acknowledge thee to be the Lord.' Megan's ear caught the sound of another of the wretched flying bombs in the distance. 'All the earth doth worship thee: the Father everlasting.' The sound of the flying bomb grew steadily louder; the congregation ignored it, and Megan, too, gave herself to singing the *Te Deum*. 'To thee all Angels cry aloud . . . ' The ack-ack battery at this point opened up a shattering salvo directed at the flying bomb, now almost overhead but its own sound drowned out by the guns, the resolute strains of the band and the equally resolute voices of the congregation. 'To thee Cherubim, and Seraphim . . . ' All in one stroke there was an overwhelming roar and crash of sound and the world was full of everything falling and collapsing, and Megan simultaneously felt herself whirled into blackness. The next she knew, she was lying under some bushes against some railings, with pieces of paper falling slowly around her in a shower, fluttering down through a thick yellow fog.

She lay too dazed and shaken to try to move. She could hear distant shouts. After a while the fog began to clear and figures moved in it. Then a young Guardsman was stooping over her and calling to someone else: 'Here's one!' A stretcher materialized; Megan was placed on it and carried away. She managed to raise her right hand and saw that for some reason it was quite black and streaked with very wet-looking blood. She closed her eyes and tried to pray.

She was put in an ambulance; there was the sensation of being driven somewhere. Then she was in a building, with nurses round her. Hospital, she thought numbly.

She was asked for the name of a near relative who could be contacted and told what had happened to her. Megan had no relations apart from one aunt miles away. Then she thought of Bunty and so gave her name and address as her sister. After this Megan was given some kind of injection, which almost instantly plunged her into insensibility.

Lorna and Herbie arrived at Kenilworth Lodge on Sunday afternoon to have the door opened to them by a distraught-looking Mrs Wells, who, clutching hold of Lorna, began without preamble: 'I'm afraid it's distressing news, Miss Washbourne. Mrs McEwen isn't back yet, and St George's Hospital is on the line. Mrs McEwen's sister, though I'm not quite sure how she *can* be a sister, but they said Mrs McEwen's sister, a Miss Megan Thomas, has been taken to the hospital injured by a flying bomb.'

'Megan!' exclaimed Lorna, leaping up.

She hurried to the phone and had the news confirmed to her: a

Miss Thomas had been brought in as a flying-bomb casualty and had given Mrs McEwen's name as her sister.

'I'll come right away,' said Lorna. Explanations would only waste time.

Leaving Herbie to tell Bunty what had happened, Lorna, without further delay, raced off to St George's Hospital at Hyde Park Corner. Here she was directed to one of the wards and led by a nurse towards a bed enclosed by screens.

The nurse moved aside a screen, and Lorna found herself standing beside a bed, looking down at a small, smut-engrained, grey-headed child with a blue and black swollen face, bright scarlet scrapes and abrasions where it wasn't blue and black, and raw puffy lips. She had a dressing on her right eyebrow, and her right arm and hand were heavily bandaged. She lay with her eyes closed. Lorna, horrified, stooped over her. 'Flops darling!' Then, looking up at the nurse: 'Is she very bad?'

'Not in danger,' said the nurse, 'but with severe shock and some nasty cuts and abrasions.'

'What exactly happened to her, do you know?'

'She was at the Guards Chapel this morning. One of those devilish contraptions landed fair and square on it and flattened the place. Somehow or the other she seems to have been blown clear; almost everyone else has been killed, or else frightfully injured, they're saying.'

'Oh, no!' gasped Lorna.

She found herself sitting on a chair. The nurse was bending over her solicitously. 'Let me give you some water.' She poured water into a tumbler from a carafe on the bedside locker.

Lorna said, sipping the water: 'I'm sorry to be so silly. I felt rather dizzy for a moment. You see, Megan was at the chapel with another great friend of mine. And now you have me terribly worried about her.'

'How tactless of me. I do apologize.'

'You couldn't have known. Don't give it another thought.' Lorna put down the tumbler; her hand was shaking. 'How frightful this all is,' she said.

'Ssh. She is coming round,' whispered the nurse urgently. She bent over Megan, who was staring up from the bed with bewildered eyes. 'Don't try to talk,' the nurse said. 'And don't worry. Just accept that you've been lucky beyond belief.' She pressed Megan's uninjured hand reassuringly and straightened up. 'I'll fetch Sister. She'll like to know you're taking notice of things again.' She disappeared between the screens.

Lorna, making an effort to pull herself together, leaned over Megan and kissed her. 'Well, Flops, God was surely on your side today.'

Megan tried to smile, but couldn't.

The ward sister appeared; she smiled at Megan and said in a cheery tone: 'So we're back with the world again, are we?' She felt Megan's pulse. 'The doctor will see you in a little while, but I think you'll do fine.'

Lorna was then left alone with Megan. Lorna held her hand; Megan attempted to speak, but couldn't. Lorna said: 'Don't try to talk, Flops love. Simply try to rest. Everything's going to be all right.'

Soon afterwards Bunty arrived, still wearing her clippie's uniform and looking upset. There was more kissing and telling Megan not to worry and not to try to talk and how lucky she had been. Then Sister brought a doctor in to see Megan, and Bunty and Lorna had to leave. Sister said: 'If you phone tomorrow, we may have a better idea when she can go home.'

Bunty said: 'She had two companions with her in the chapel. How can we find out about them? Would they have been brought in here, too, d'you suppose?'

'There's an enquiry desk downstairs you should ask at,' replied Sister. 'They know more than I do.' She suddenly looked very weary.

Lorna said, as she and Bunty walked away down the long ward: 'It seems that a lot of people have been killed, or else badly injured, at the Guards Chapel, Bunts.'

'So I heard, from someone on my bus who had been in Green Park when it happened. Apparently the Hyde Park ack-ack battery shot the thing down and it landed . . . well, you know that. But if Megan is OK . . . '

'That's what I keep telling myself, Bunts. No doubt they were all three sitting together when it happened, and if one of them has survived, a bit battered but intact, the other two have probably been equally lucky.'

'Let's head for that enquiry desk.' They did so; and found themselves joining a long queue.

As they waited, Bunty said to Lorna: 'Herbie's gone back to Mignonette's; I told him we'd find him there. But I don't want to be in the way, as it's your last evening together.'

'Don't be silly. Besides, it may take us longer than we think to track down Violetta and Chips. They may not be in this hospital at all.'

'Maybe they're not even injured, but back at their club and Violetta's trying to contact us to tell us she's safe. You keep our place in the queue while I try phoning her.'

But Bunty soon returned, shaking her head. 'No word of them there since they went out this morning.'

Slowly they shuffled their way, step by step, to the desk. Nothing was known there about either Violetta or Chips. Lorna and Bunty were advised to try the police. 'Casualties have been taken to other hospitals as well as this one; the police will know which they are.'

The police named several hospitals to which rescued injured

from the Guards Chapel had been taken. They also gave a special telephone number to ring for those enquiring about the victims of the disaster. The girls were advised to wait till next day, when the picture would be clearer. Meanwhile they should remain at home near the telephone, in case they received a call from a hospital or from the ATS.

'We shan't be contacted,' said Bunty to Lorna. 'It'll be the Stackses who receive any calls of that sort.' She added: 'D'you think we should alert them the Chapel has been hit, in case they haven't yet heard?'

'I'd think not,' said Lorna. 'Not yet. We don't want to worry them unduly. There's nothing worse than that. And, speaking of worrying people,' she added, 'we'd best get back to Mignonette's. Herbie, I'm sure, will be wondering what's happened to us. We need a drink, a bite to eat, and a chance to think quietly for a while.'

'Good wheeze,' agreed Bunty. 'We'd best go by Tube; it's safer underground.' She had had some hair-raising moments on her bus over the past three days.

The Tube was crowded with people all in agreement with Bunty. The stations were being used as shelters again during the night, as they had been used in the Blitz. The shelterers slept on the platforms; some in bunks that had been fixed up against the wall at the back of the platform, some on the platform itself. They had brought bedding with them, and food. A white line about four feet back from the edge of the platform marked the point beyond which the shelterers could not take up any more room. It didn't leave a great deal of space for travellers using the trains.

The people were still in the stage of preparing for the long night ahead; they busily arranged their bedding, tried to settle down the children, and having got themselves organized broke into excited talk, swapping their flying-bomb stories. Their cockney voices crackled on the air, together with gusts of raucous laughter. There was a lot of blaspheming, too, of a serious sort. Despite the laughing, people weren't finding flying bombs funny.

It was almost seven when Lorna and Bunty arrived back at Mignonette's flat, to be greeted by an extremely anxious Herbie. 'My, I've been worrying about you two girls. These wretched things have been going off bang in all directions.' He added: 'I've packed your bag, Lorna, and if we step on it we'll get you on that evening train back to Fursey-Winwold.'

Lorna stared at him aghast.

'And miss our last night together!'

'That's what I want to avoid – it being our last night together,' said Herbie. 'You'll go back home, I'll go stay with friends out of town. It's tough, but at least it guarantees us a further lease of life; there'll be other nights. If we stick around here, I wouldn't like to take bets on that.'

'But Herbie . . .'

'Come on, honey,' said Herbie. 'Let's get moving.' He made towards the two bags, hers and his, which he had placed ready for departure.

'Herbie, I can't possibly leave like this.' Lorna's tone was crisp and cool. 'For one thing, Bunty and I have to find out what has happened to Violetta. I can't walk off not knowing whether one of my best friends is alive or dead. And then there's Megan; it's all very well for the hospital to say she's not dangerously injured – and compared with many I suppose she's not much hurt – but when she leaves St George's she can't be expected to return to Cromwell Road on her own. Something must be done about her.'

'So what do you propose?' asked Herbie rather testily.

'I propose remaining in London for a day or two, until Megan is discharged from hospital, and then I shall take her down to Fursey-Winwold. We've bags of room at The Warren. She can stay with us until she's fit again.'

'Well, all that sounds pretty clear-cut, I guess,' said Herbie. 'I just wasted my time packing those bags.'

'You do see, don't you, Herbie, that I've no alternative but to stay here?'

'I see you've made up your mind to stay,' said Herbie. 'You have an alternative, but you won't take it.'

Bunty, who had seated herself in an armchair and was trying to look as if she wasn't present at this interesting clash of wills, now intervened. 'Will you stay on here, Lorna, or come back to Kenilworth Lodge with me?'

'She'll spend tonight here,' said Herbie. 'Where she'll spend tomorrow night, if she's still alive to spend it, will be her decision. I shall be on my way to the safety of the Mediterranean Theatre of War.'

'Where will you be tonight, Herbie?' said Lorna.

'Here with you. If you won't jink, I can't jink. We'll just have to stay in formation and take what comes.'

'Well, we'd better go and find some dinner,' said Bunty. 'Not too far away, and where we can use the telephone without being trodden on by the chef. And get there by Underground. I suggest the Euston Hotel. It's not exciting, but—'

'Oh, forget the excitement,' said Herbie. 'I'm all for a dull life.'

After dinner they sat in the hotel lounge and drank coffee, and then Lorna went to the phone to speak to the Stackses. There was no reply; she made two further attempts, but without success. 'They've probably gone away for the weekend,' she said at last to Bunty. 'Unless, of course, the police have already contacted them and they've come dashing down to London to Violetta.'

'We're getting nowhere fast,' said Bunty. 'What do we do now?'

'Leave it till tomorrow,' said Herbie. 'More will be known tomorrow, I guess.'

They left the hotel; Bunty took the line to Hampstead, Lorna and Herbie to Goodge Street. As they walked the short distance to Mignonette's they heard a flying bomb coming fast and, looking up, saw its tail of flame racing like a meteor across the dark sky; the rest of the little plane was invisible. It passed out of sight behind the roofs and chimneypots; in a short while its engine cut out, and a few seconds later they heard it explode.

'Real pretty,' said Herbie.

'Better than fireworks,' said Lorna.

When they got indoors and were up in the flat Herbie picked her up and laid her on the bed and said: 'Well, if we die, we die.'

Several eternities later, when they had at last fallen asleep and then had woken up simultaneously, Lorna turned her head towards the window, noticed a sky faintly pallid with earliest light and said: 'We never did the blackout before we went to bed.'

'Oh, shouldn't we have thought of that!'

Lorna wondered if Waldo and Bunty had had wonderful nights like this. Then came the interruption of the sound of a flying bomb charging at top speed in their direction. The engine cut out; at the same instant a searchlight sprang up in the sky and fingered across it, seemingly groping for something directly above the house, and as the beam swung round there was a long rippling shudder skimming over the roof-tops and terminating in a terrific explosion. The door blew open, the glass fell out of the window into the street, and with it the glass from every window in the neighbourhood, from the sound of it. The plaster fell in chunks from the ceiling. In all directions heavy things were dropping and falling. Herbie pulled the covers over their heads; they lay clutching each other. Things quietened. They asked one another: 'Are you hurt?'

By some miracle they both seemed uninjured.

For a while they lay quite still, without moving or speaking. It might have been a few minutes; it might have been longer.

At last Lorna said: 'That shudder. The Angel of Death.'

'I've heard her many times,' said Herbie, 'but never as spooky as that.'

Voices sounded in the street. People were opening front doors and calling from windows. Lorna said: 'We'd best make a move of some kind; try to find out what's happened.'

The air was full of plaster dust. It made them both cough. It also rendered the dim light of early morning even dimmer. They couldn't switch any lights on because of their lack of blackout. Herbie, cautiously swinging his legs out of the bed and putting his feet to the floor, said: 'Everything's deep in fallen plaster.'

Lorna peered into the murk. 'What did we do with our clothes last night? D'you remember?'

'Shed them on targets of opportunity, as officialdom puts it. In other words, rid ourselves of them as fast as possible, at random. In this case, on the floor. Which means, they're buried.'

'But, Herbie, that's ghastly! What are we to do? I've nothing else to wear. I made a point of travelling light.'

'So did I. And mine's a new uniform, I might tell you. A new uniform, to impress my new command, when I show up, which will be some time in the next twenty-four hours. It's gonna take me that long to dig it out.'

'This is like a nightmare.'

'Your idea, lady. You wanted a last night together. Don't say I didn't warn you.'

'But, Herbie, it was worth it, wasn't it?'

'It sure was. Worth tunnelling through plaster from here to eternity. And I mean every word of that.'

This said, retrieving their clothes and, worse still, putting them on was an experience not to be relished. Herbie's jacket, which it turned out he had slung over the back of a chair, would recover with a good brush; but his trousers, found in a ball under a foot of plaster, would need expert valeting service and more to restore them to something resembling their former appearance.

They couldn't get into the bathroom because the ceiling had fallen in there and had blocked the door. They tried to wash some of the plaster dust off themselves at the kitchen sink, but the water-supply had been affected and the thin trickle that came out of the tap was of little use and merely made them look streaky.

They stood surveying one another in the growing light of a day which outside was chaotic and inside the flat equally so.

Fortunately the bags Herbie had packed in readiness for the hasty departure they had not made remained unopened, and from these they were able to provide themselves with plaster-free items of underwear, and hairbrushes to clear their hair of some of the dust. Lorna had a pair of sandals she could put on instead of the grit-engrained shoes she had finally dug from the chaos. She also had a chiffon dinner dress, but this she preferred not to put on at this hour; it looked even more odd than her plaster-smeared navy-blue corduroy suit.

It was decided that Herbie should go to his officers' club, have a shower, and see what he could do to borrow a pair of trousers. 'I don't see why you want to alter your appearance really, darling, however,' said Lorna. 'Think what a dramatic entrance you'd make, turning up in North Africa and saying you'd been flying-bombed.'

'I just don't like show-offs, that's why.'

Then they started laughing, and couldn't stop.

They had to shut the front door on all the mess in the flat and leave it. It was decided that Herbie must take the first taxi they saw; he hadn't all the time in the world. They were walking up Mortimer Street when they saw one; Herbie had to chase after it to stop it. He hung from the window waving goodbye as it drove off; Lorna stood on the pavement and waved back. Then the feeling of being alone hit her like a brick wall falling on her, and she wondered for a moment if there had been another flying bomb.

She went to Kenilworth Lodge; Bunty had not yet left for work, and greeted Lorna with a shriek of alarm. 'We're both of us all right,' said Lorna. 'We nearly bought it; but a miss is as good as a mile. Herbie's gone to North Africa, and I've come to beg for a hot bath and some clothes I might borrow. Oh, and a bed for tonight.'

'What sort of state is Mignonette's flat in?'

'The most God-awful mess you ever saw in your life.'

Bunty was then obliged to hurry away on duty. Lorna, after a bath and some breakfast, tried phoning the special enquiry number the police had given her the previous day. It was engaged. She rang some of the hospitals where Guards Chapel casualties had been taken, but nothing was known of Violetta and Chips. Lorna returned to trying the special number; still engaged.

She made herself a cup of coffee and thought about Herbie, who by now would be airborne, heading for Africa. The feeling of growing distance between them, like an ever-widening crevasse, an extending void splitting them apart, overwhelmed Lorna with a sensation of bereftness so acute that it was actual pain. Attempting self-control Lorna reminded herself of what she had said to Bunty; Herbie would be far safer in North Africa than he had ever been at Fursey Down. And in the distant future, as yet far off but one joyous day to be reached, they would be together again to part no more. She must wear a brave face during this period of desolate emptiness, lengthy as it threatened to be.

With this resolution she put Herbie from her mind and tried the special enquiry number once more.

This time she got through. A firm female voice (doubtless that of a member of the stalwart WVS) explained that it was feared that few survivors would now be recovered from the ruins of the chapel; the roof had fallen in on the congregation, burying everyone under massive blocks of masonry. This said, Lorna was asked for descriptions of Violetta and Chips, for the Stackses' phone number, and her own at Kenilworth Lodge.

Lorna made more coffee, lit a fresh cigarette and seated herself by the open window, staring, without really seeing, down into the summery flower-filled garden. She told herself over and over again that Megan, Violetta and Chips had been together at the Guards Chapel and that, since Megan had survived, there was every chance that Violetta and Chips would likewise be among those fortunate few to come out of the incident alive.

Shortly after midday a call came from the Enquiry Post: the bodies of Violetta and Chips had been dug out from under the masonry.

Lorna stood numbly by the window, watching a small group of sparrows that had appeared, to hop and peck and twitter among themselves on the lawn.

Violetta was the first of the St Hildegard's gang to go, thought Lorna. How many of them would be left by the end of the war? Anyone, at any time, might find themselves in the front line and under fire, as they were now. 'All a matter of chance.'

And then it hit her that she would never see Violetta again, and Lorna threw herself down on Bunty's bed and cried until she could cry no more.

XXXII

By the end of the week Megan, though still pretty shaky, was discharged from the hospital; the continuing flood of casualties from the flying bombs made the pressure on beds too great for patients to be detained any longer than was absolutely necessary. Lorna took her down to Fursey-Winwold; Megan stood the train journey better than Lorna had feared she might, but she was glad to be helped into bed when she reached The Warren and given her supper on a tray. Later, when Lorna went to say good-night to her, Megan sighed, 'This is absolutely heavenly, to find myself here like this. I can't begin to tell you how much I appreciate it.'

'Don't try to, Flops. Go to sleep and enjoy a good long quiet night's rest. At least, as quiet as the Forts will allow.'

'Is that what that rumbling noise is, like thunder?'

'Yes. The ground crews are working on them, preparing them for tomorrow's missions.'

'I've only seen them flying over London.'

'Here we live with them all the time.'

After Megan had fallen asleep Lorna took her dogs for a walk in the gathering twilight. As she returned she met Jeffrey, walking his dog. He said: 'The village will be relieved to see you safe back. The news about Violetta has shaken everyone, and we've all been keeping our fingers crossed for you while you've been in London, I can tell you.'

'I hope you were able to prevent Father from worrying too much about me, Jeffrey. I was relying on you to feed him a diet of funny stories to buoy up his spirits.'

'Not a lot to be funny about at the moment, I feel. Still, I've tried to take his mind off things as much as possible.' Even Jeffrey sounded subdued. 'However,' he added, brightening, 'we've got you safe home again, and that at least is a plus thing.'

Lorna resumed walking along the field path; it was narrow at this point, and Jeffrey fell in behind her. The three dogs bounced in and out of the hedge, excited at the possibility of rabbits. Lorna, over her shoulder, asked Jeffrey: 'How are poor Dicky and Daphne taking it?'

'Dicky's fearfully cut up, as you can imagine.'

'And poor Daphne will be desolate!' Lorna added miserably: 'I suppose I had better visit her tomorrow and condole.'

'Daphne's not there.'

'Oh, where has she gone? Some quiet place where she and Dicky can be alone together for a bit, trying to get over it all, I suppose.' Lorna's tone was deeply understanding.

The path widened; Jeffrey moved level with Lorna and took her confidentially by the arm, drawing her close to him. 'No, no; nothing like that, I'm afraid. Truth is, Daphne's walked out on Dicky.'

'What?' exclaimed Lorna, staggered. Then, with a movement of distaste, she jerked herself as far away from Jeffrey as the path would permit. 'I don't like gossip, Jeffrey, as you know,' she said stiffly.

Jeffrey, not to be rebuffed, took her distinctly frigid arm again. 'This isn't gossip, it's fact. And I'm only telling you to prevent you wasting your time going to the Manor tomorrow to condole. And embarrassing Dicky. Not that Dicky doesn't rather deserve to be embarrassed. He's hardly been the soul of discretion, for the lady in question is always popping in and out of the Manor when Daphne's not there, or he's popping over to her. And people notice this.'

'What lady in question? You're talking in riddles, Jeffrey.'

'I'm trying not to make it sound like gossip.'

'Either tell me properly or don't tell me at all.'

Jeffrey stifled a half-sigh, half-groan. 'Well, start again then. Dicky, and everybody else in the village knows this but of course you won't have noticed it or as much as heard a whisper of it, but . . . now I've lost track of what I was saying.'

'Dicky.'

'Ah, yes, Dicky has been having an affair with Frisky, going on for two or three months at least. And . . .'

Lorna, in disbelief, interrupted: 'An affair with Mrs Friske?' She sounded, as indeed she was, amazed. She added, ingenuously, 'And there was Titus hinting to everyone that she was your mistress!'

'Titus is but a poor yokel oaf. That's the sort of thing he would think. No, no, Frisky being a vet herself isn't interested in fellow vets. For her the romantic novelist.'

'I can't imagine anybody finding Dicky romantic; novelist or otherwise.'

'What you have to remember, Lorna, is that both Dicky and Frisky are married types, and war gives the married a golden opportunity to get away from one another, meet new faces. And the grass is always greener on the other side. Frisky's escaped from her husband for the duration, and though Dicky's still stuck at home in the Manor, Daphne's dedication to her Red Cross means that he's virtually grass-widowed. She's out all the time, and he's as good as forgotten. And then up turns Frisky, and Bob's your uncle. Daphne, naturally, was the last to know, apart, of course, from your incredibly innocent self. And when Daphne found out she made the traditional scene and walked out. Where to, Dicky hasn't a clue.'

'But, Jeffrey, *somebody* will have to discover where she is and tell her!' Lorna was wearing her Binkle look, demanding action. She continued: 'Imagine how she'll feel if she returns home and learns, out of the blue, that Violetta is dead!'

'I agree. It's hard to imagine a worse situation.'

'I'll have to have a word with Dicky,' said Lorna grimly.

'Best not to get involved, if you ask me. I believe there's a sister, and contact is being attempted through her.' They walked a little further in silence. It was now almost dark.

'Poor Daphne,' sighed Lorna at last, ruminatively. 'There she was, up in arms about the way the Yanks were carrying on, and never thinking to keep an eye on her own husband.'

Jeffrey said: 'There's poetic justice embedded in that, I feel.' His wry tone reminded Lorna of Herbie's when he was passing a comment on something or somebody. Lorna, without consciously realizing it, drew closer to Jeffrey and allowed him to tighten his clasp on her arm.

They arrived back at The Warren. 'Are you coming in to pass the time of day with Father?' she asked.

'If you promise to save me from Mrs Cuthman's nettle nightcap, yes.'

'What on earth is a nettle nightcap?'

'She's been experimenting with it while you've been away. You drink it hot, with a little milk in it. It keeps you up all night.'

'One of her old herbal remedies.'

'Guaranteed to cure some condition you've never heard of in your life, let alone had; such as the thin rheums or the tetters. Ever had the tetters, Lorna?'

'No, Jeffrey, I haven't. And I don't think I would much like to, either.'

He could never remain serious for long, she thought. But undoubtedly he had a cheering effect upon Father.

Megan, too, had a cheering effect upon the General; they took to one another immediately. Come to think of it, so did Megan and Jeffrey. The Warren suddenly became quite a jolly house.

Daphne returned home. She didn't show herself in the village at first. Lorna and Megan decided that it would only be right and proper for them to call on her. It was a melancholy visit, but Daphne said it was sweet of them. Daphne told them about the funeral. Chips's parents were in Kenya, and they had written to say that they would like her to be buried with Violetta, as the two had been such good friends. The funeral took place on a beautiful day at the end of June; it was a moving occasion attended by a contingent of ATS. Mr Barker preached a special sermon, and an ATS bugler sounded the Last Post over the grave, which was a double one, because the two had died together as friends and comrades and should therefore lie together at rest, as Mr Barker had said in his sermon. Megan and Lorna stood by the graveside clutching each other and fighting their tears.

Afterwards, they visited Ruth's grave. Megan, when earlier told Ruth's story, had responded with a sympathy very different from the usual reaction. 'Poor, poor little soul!' Now, by the graveside, Megan unselfconsciously dropped on her knees and said a prayer for Ruth. Lorna remained standing, gazing pensively at the roses and lilies from her own garden, placed in a vase on the grave; she put fresh flowers there twice a week.

Two of her friends now lay in this graveyard; one a girl of her own age, the other a few years younger. Each had died a terrible death. Lorna – miraculously, she felt – still lived: but, whenever her mind turned back to it, she felt a numbing chill as she remembered the moment when the Angel of Death had shuddered over Herbie and herself, touching them with the breath of her long-drawn icy sigh. Had shuddered – and passed over and on. For Violetta, and for Ruth, there had been no passing over and on. And so they lay here.

Fortunately, reflected Lorna, war left you little time in which to grieve or give yourself to open displays of emotion. Everything combined to hustle you on, carry you forward, whether you wanted to go or not. The strains of 'Lead Us, Heavenly Father, Lead Us', sung at the funeral of Violetta and Chips, had scarcely faded before they were replaced by the swinging blare of Glenn Miller. He and his Army Air Force band were now in England; the band broadcast on the radio and gave live concerts up and down the country at AAF and RAF camps and hospitals, and to huge audiences of service personnel in London. Throughout the summer his sound vibrated as a background to the roar of the bombers and, in London and the so-called Bomb Alley (the route by which most of the flying bombs approached the metropolis), with the chugging bumble and the crashes of the robots.

The band came to play at Fursey Down. Lorna invited Megan along to hear it. The concert was held in a hangar decorated in red, white and blue as it had been for the famous Gala Ball.

After the concert there was coffee in the aeroclub. Lorna had already introduced Megan to Angie and Amy May; they had all four sat together during the concert. Lorna wanted Megan to meet Buzz Cabrini, who had allowed Lorna to invite Megan to the concert in the first place. Buzz right now was caught in a crowd of jostling people all trying to talk to him at once. Meantime Angie, from the back of the canteen, was signalling wildly to him as if in dire need of help.

Lorna managed to reach him and tap him on the shoulder, saying: 'Buzz, I'd like you to meet my friend from Rainbow Corner.'

He half-slewed his head round, cheroot in his mouth, his face glistening with perspiration. It was not a good moment for introductions. 'Waddya?' Everyone was seething round him. He said: 'Lorna sugar, mustya? Can't ya leave it to some other time?'

'I just wanted very quickly for you to say hello to my friend you kindly let me fetch along this evening. You remember I told you she was injured at the Guards Chapel.'

Megan still looked pale and fragile, her hair framing her face in a loose halo of ringlets, her eyes behind the chic green specs wearing a slightly otherworldish expression, as though part of her was not fully restored to everyday life. Buzz glanced casually over his shoulder with an automatic half-smile. 'Hi,' he said, nodding affably, without really identifying the person at whom he was nodding. He then turned away to resume his struggle towards Angie. But almost simultaneously, as if physically struck by an urgent double-take, he swivelled to look at Megan again. 'Gee!' he uttered to the privately much amused Lorna. 'She's no more'n a kid! What's a little doll like her doing fielding flying bombs anyways? There oughta be someone taking care of her.'

He jostled through the crowd to reach Megan, removing the cheroot from his mouth – an exceptional courtesy for him. 'Hi,' he said again, holding out his hand to her and smiling in a manner that was a combination of the paternal and the bashful. 'I'm Buzz Cabrini.'

'Megan Thomas.' They shook hands.

People shoved and struggled round them, trying to reach the coffee bar or else endeavouring to move away from it. Someone biffed Megan in the back, jolting her against Buzz in turn. He put a protective arm round her. 'Let's get you outa here before you're trampled. Waddya say to a coffee in a quiet corner, hey?'

Without waiting for a reply Buzz propelled her into the rear of the canteen, where the crowd didn't penetrate. He politely beckoned Lorna to join them; this, after some breathless squeezing and wriggling, she managed to do. The three of them sat down at the little round table where the Red Cross girls had their coffee and snacks in privacy. Angie now brought Cokes and cookies. Buzz said sardonically: 'Well, Megan, I guess this seems kinda quiet after Rainbow Corner? We rusticate here, y'know.'

Lorna, when seeking an invitation for Megan that evening, had explained to Buzz that she was ARC and worked at Rainbow Corner. Glenn Miller played strictly for services personnel.

Megan said, looking at the jam-packed scrimmage in progress on the further side of the counter: 'I wouldn't want to be here on a busy night.' She smiled at this little joke as she spoke. Buzz smiled at her smile.

'Oh, you'd get so you could handle it, same as the rest of us,' he said. 'It's personality that counts. That's so, isn't it, Lorna?' Without waiting for Lorna to reply, he switched back to Megan. 'And how did you enjoy the concert?' he asked her, devouring her with his eyes.

She said: 'I loved it. And I loved the way you'd decorated the hangar, too. It all felt so festive and special. He must have liked it himself. Hasn't he said how much he liked it?'

'Why not come ask him? He's in there right now, signing autographs. You like to come and meet him? Like him to sign you his autograph, huh?' Buzz made as if to jump up.

'It looks such a scrum to get to him. I think I'd rather stay here, and have *your* autograph,' replied Megan, laughing.

'D'you hear that?' said Buzz to the world in general. Then, to Megan: 'First minute I get to spare, peaches, I'll start those writing lessons.'

Megan laughed. Lorna and Angie stared at Buzz.

Then Lorna said to Angie: 'What was it you wanted Buzz for in the first place, Angie? You looked as if it was fearfully urgent.'

Angie said: 'It was a spider in the sink; but the panic's over. It's gone down the plug-hole.'

'Sensed me coming,' said Buzz. 'Like I was explaining, it's personality that does it. Even a spider crumples when it learns Cabrini's around.'

'It looked kinda timid when it heard me call your name,' said Angie.

'*Slunk* to that plug-hole, I bet? Couldn't get away fast enough?'

Somebody else called: 'Buzz! Buzz!'

'Have to say goodbye; I'm in demand. Guess this time it's big game on the rampage,' said Buzz, rising from the table. He took Megan's hand. 'This has really been a pleasure. If I'm around town any time and I look in that little corner place of yours, maybe you'd let me stand you a ham sandwich?'

'Love it,' replied Megan, looking, Lorna thought, a trifle dazed.

'See ya, then.' And Buzz shoved away into the throng.

Megan asked: 'Is he always like that?'

'He's a real sweet guy,' said Angie. 'He's the kinda guy who never laughs at a girl who's scared of spiders, and that I call real sweet.'

'He's always the exuberant type,' said Lorna. 'But tonight I must say he does seem unusually high.'

'It's the Glen Miller sound,' said Angie. 'That sound makes you high. I feel real high myself.' She gave her head a playful little shake, as if to clear it.

'What a nice crowd to work with,' said Megan when they got home. 'We're so lucky to work with the Yanks, you and me, Lorna. They're so very nice to be with.'

'Yes, we're lucky to be with them,' responded Lorna. She almost sounded smug in her contentment at her lot. 'And', she added, 'I'm extra lucky to be on Fursey Down with the Forts.'

Lorna and Megan were invited to dine by Whizz McKinley and Buzz Cabrini at the Pheasant. It was good fun, with something calling itself Chianti to drink with their dinner. They became merry; Buzz, especially, was in tremendous form.

The Pheasant had a big shrubby garden that went down to the bank of a canal. Megan found herself in the twilight among the shrubs on the canal bank with Buzz. The smooth water looked black in the twilight. They found a rustic garden seat; it wasn't awfully comfortable, but Megan was glad it was not the sort of thing to encourage relaxed attitudes: Buzz, perhaps because of the Chianti, was becoming alarmingly amorous. Megan wished she hadn't allowed herself to become separated from Lorna and Whizz.

She and Buzz sat down. He put one arm round Megan's waist, and with his other hand began fondling her knee. She started to think she would have to say something stiff and English. His fingers roamed from the top of her knee down to underneath it and began to feel gently up the inside of her thigh. 'Really, Buzz . . .' But at this point he suddenly snatched his hand away and gave himself a tremendous slap on the neck.

'Jeez,' he said, 'this country's short on bugs, they say, but those you do have are quality.'

He restored his hand to her knee. Megan took his hand in a firm grip and placed it on his own knee. He seemed on the point of remonstrating, but then, 'Yow!' and removing his hand he had round her waist he gave himself another slap, this time above his left ear.

Megan at the same time felt something bite her on the face. 'It's a bad place for midges by this canal, I reckon,' she said. 'Perhaps we'd better go back in.'

'I'll try smoking. These little fellers don't tolerate smoke. D'you object to me smoking?'

'I don't object to you *smoking*, Buzz. I *do* object to your creeping your fingers up my leg.'

'I was kinda hoping you might figure it was just one more bug.'

'There wouldn't be much point in that, would there? I mean, you thinking I thought you were a midge – bug, as you call them.'

Buzz sighed heavily and lit a cheroot. 'I had the feeling you weren't that keen on my hand.'

'Well, you know how it is, Buzz. We Red Cross hostesses aren't to be touched.'

'Sure thing; but that's a different ball game from you an' me, wining and dining together an' . . . for *chrissake*.' He gave himself another slap, this time on the other side of his neck. 'I reckon these insects must stick themselves up for vampire bats.' Megan began to giggle. 'There *is* a difference, you know,' resumed Buzz. He put his arm back round her waist.

'Between midges and vampire bats?'

'Nope. Between no-touch hostesses and a girl you're taking out.' He gave her waist a squeeze. 'See, I wouldn't do that to a hostess.'

'I would hope not.'

He squeezed her harder. 'You wouldn't mistake that for a bug, would ya? Squeezin' bug. Hitherto unknown variety of bug.'

'Buzz, please.'

He threw away his cheroot and put his face close to hers, looking at her lips. 'A kissing bug?'

'I don't . . . '

'You might kinda take to it. You never know till you try.'

'I honestly don't think . . . '

Buzz sighed again, removed his arm from round her waist and said: 'Well, I was gonna invite you to spend a weekend with me at a nice place I've found near Tooksbury, but I reckon I'd be wasting my time asking.'

'You would.'

'I was afraid so.'

'It isn't that I don't like you, Buzz. It just is, I was brought up very old-fashioned. A ring or nothing. That sort of girl.'

'A ring-or-nutt'n girl, huh?'

'That's it. Not much fun, I'm afraid.'

'You got the right credentials for a Red Cross hostess anyways.'

'Oh, yes, I've the right credentials for that.'

'A pity,' he said regretfully. 'Well, let's get back inside before we're eaten.'

When they arrived back in the coffee lounge they found Lorna and Whizz there, deep in conversation. Megan had been wondering how Lorna was making out with Whizz.

After more coffee and general chat the girls were taken home to The Warren. 'Poor Whizz,' remarked Lorna lightly, as she let herself and Megan into the house, while the buggy drove away with a final farewell toot, 'pouring out his troubles to me; the hard, hard life of a CO. He doesn't know what hard, hard times are.' She sighed, and then turned to Megan with a smile. 'How did you make out with Buzz?' She added: 'He's taken a great fancy to you, you know. Though whether he's quite *your* type . . . '

'I don't think he found me what he'd hoped for,' replied Megan. She sounded weary. 'It's no good these chaps asking *me* to spend weekends with them. I mean, that's not my code. Whether he's my type or not doesn't signify; I just don't spend weekends with men. Full stop.'

'Well, you have your principles, Flops, and so you'd best stick to them.'

'I shall. But I would like to think that not everyone considers me a freak.' She sounded upset.

'I suppose in a way you *are*, Flops. I mean, not many people have managed to cling on to those sort of principles in this war. But, that said, I reckon you're one of those people who *do* cling to their principles.'

'Yes, I reckon I am. And I reckon it's a bloody misfortune. But it's too late to change now.'

They said good-night and went to bed.

Meanwhile Bunty wrote to say that the first week of July had brought more flying bombs than ever. 'Night and day; they never seem to stop. It's worse than the Blitz, and that's saying a real mouthful! Do try to persuade Megan to stay on with you as long as possible. She's had a real pasting, and should continue to take things easy while she has the chance.'

But Megan herself didn't see it that way. She announced that the time had come when she really must get back to London.

'But Flops love, I'm sure you don't need to rush back like this. Don't tell me your office in Grosvenor Square can't spare you a little longer,' urged Lorna. 'And, as for Father and myself, we love having you here. You've settled in so well. Can't we have the pleasure of your company for a few more days at least?'

'It's sweet of you, Lorna darling, and I do so much appreciate all your kindness, but I really must get back.'

'Then at least move into another flat. That top-floor place of yours is a death trap.' She had given this advice to Megan before, but Megan always replied, as indeed she replied now: 'Where you live doesn't matter. Look at my mother and how she was killed out in the country, while I'd remained in London. If it has your number on it, then it has your number on it.'

The General said: 'In a way that's true. But you did get rather knocked around, you know, and to ask for another dose quite so promptly is, I'd say, speaking as an old soldier, unnecessary. Give it another week or two. Before long our chaps will have captured the launching sites and these things won't be coming over any more.'

'But that means I shall have been here a month!' And she sounded dismayed.

She repeated this to Jeffrey in the evening when, at Lorna's behest, he urged Megan to extend her stay. 'But, Jeffrey, if I remain here much longer, I shall have been here a month. I can't take all that time off. I'm pretty well OK again by now, you know. They'll think I'm sprucing if I stay here much longer.'

'Do they give you an annual holiday?'

'Yes. A fortnight.'

'Have you taken it yet?'

'No. I was planning to take it in the autumn.'

'Ask to have it now. To extend your sick leave. I'm sure they can't object to that.'

'Jeffrey, how clever you are!' exclaimed Lorna admiringly.

'I was wondering how long you'd have to know me before you noticed that.'

Megan said: 'It's a good idea, but I'm afraid I'm going back, all the same.'

'Why?' said Jeffrey.

'I don't know if I can make you understand. You and Lorna aren't Londoners. You belong here, but I belong to London. I don't feel I belong here at all. I really do feel I should get back to where I belong. Especially when London's going through such a dreadful time.' She hesitated, and then added: 'I know it probably sounds jolly silly to you, but I feel London needs me there to take care of it.'

'London,' retorted Lorna grimly, 'isn't a blooming lost GI.'

'I can very well understand what Megan means,' said Jeffrey. 'My parents live in London. I was brought up there. I wouldn't want to live there now; I'm a true countryman at heart, but at the same time I hate to think of poor old London being battered about the way it is.'

'Jeffrey.' Lorna didn't want him to talk like that.

'Megan's a real Londoner,' said Jeffrey, 'and she feels her place is in London in its hour of need. If she wants to go home, I don't think we should try to persuade her not to, Lorna.'

'But, Jeffrey,' hissed Lorna, 'you're going back on me.'

'I'm not going back anywhere. It's Megan who's going back, to London.'

'But I asked you . . . Oh, what's the good of talking to you!'

'Now that I've heard what Megan has to say, I realize that you asked me to do the wrong thing. She should go home.'

'You haven't been flying-bombed, Jeffrey; *I* have. It's madness for anyone to stay in London if they don't have to. And Megan doesn't *have* to go yet.' There was a pause during which none of them spoke. 'Jeffrey, please. Back me up on this one.'

'It's up to Megan,' said Jeffrey.

Megan said, 'It's very sweet of you both to be so concerned for me, but I'm going back.'

'I don't think Jeffrey's concerned for you one bit. He's not concerned for you, and he doesn't give a fig for me.'

'I think he does, though, really – don't you, Jeffrey?' said Megan, smiling at Jeffrey.

'I'm certainly concerned for you, Megan,' replied Jeffrey, 'but Miss Washbourne's demand for a fig puts me in a fix. I haven't seen a fig since the outbreak of war.'

'Oh, funny,' said Lorna.

'I just love hearing you two together,' said Megan, laughing.

After Jeffrey had returned to The Firs, and Lorna and Megan were preparing to put the dogs in their baskets and to go upstairs to their own beds, Megan said: 'Jeffrey worships you, doesn't he? I've always wondered about your romantic interest in this war, Lorna. I knew you must have someone; everybody has someone, except me, and I reckon somehow I'm the sort who never will have anyone. Some people just don't. I'm quite resigned to it. In any case, I've been far too busy with my job and Rainbow Corner to light on anyone special. But I knew you must have someone somewhere. And now I've met Jeffrey I'm so glad it's him. I like him *very* much. He's absolutely right for you.'

'Good heavens, Flops!' exclaimed the staggered Lorna. 'You couldn't be more wrong.'

'Oh?' said Megan, sounding far from convinced.

'And I'm sure you're equally wrong about you never finding anybody. You've turned into a very attractive girl, Flops.'

'Well, maybe I do from time to time attract a few people. But, you see, I have to be attracted by them, too, don't I, for it to work? And they'd have to share my peculiar principles. So I reckon I'm doomed to be left on the shelf.'

'Don't despair. It'll hit you some day, Flops.'

'Heavens, Lorna, don't talk about being hit! I'm going back to London!'

'Well, you scored a direct hit with Buzz Cabrini, Flops. He hasn't stopped talking to me about you since he met you.'

Megan gave a rather brittle little laugh. 'Dear me! Well, I can see he's a nice enough chap, but he's not *my* cup of tea. I don't like fat men who smoke cheroots. Anyway, he'll stop talking about me now, that's for sure, after the way I turned him down last night.'

'Then let's hope a thin non-smoker turns up for you, Flops. You never know what's round the corner!'

Next morning Megan said her goodbyes and thanks to the General with tears in her eyes. 'You've been so wonderfully kind to me. I can never say thank-you.'

'Come again whenever you feel like it,' he responded. 'You'll always be most welcome.'

Lorna accompanied Megan to the station and put her on the train. 'I'm not even going to *try* to say thank-you to *you*,' said Megan as they hugged one another.

'You don't have to. Father and I both mean it when we say, if you want to come again at any time, just come. And promise to take great care of yourself, Flops love. At least as far as you're able.'

'I'll do my best. Duck every time I hear one heading in my direction!' laughed Megan, bravely determined to depart in high spirits at all costs.

But back in London, waiting with her case at the station taxi rank, she sniffed apprehensively; already she could smell stale high explosive and dust and death on the air, just like the old days of the Blitz.

When she arrived home in her flat she telephoned Bunty, to tell her that she had returned. Bunty, who was just about to go on duty, greeted Megan with a dry 'It's a good thing you're in the habit of praying, Flops. You'll find yourself doing it a lot now you're back in the Smoke.'

XXXIII

Hampstead was well peppered with flying bombs; the nearest to Kenilworth Lodge fell not far from the East Heath ponds, fortunately exploding on open ground. Leaves were stripped from the trees and bushes lay strewn on the ground as if by a green autumn. Window panes were shattered in distant houses; broken glass made the pavements crunchy.

Kenilworth Lodge stood undamaged. But, though the house itself seemed impregnable, disaster struck one of the inmates: poor nice little Miss Amhurst quite literally vanished; obliterated when the bus she was travelling to work in was blown to pieces. There was no funeral, because there was nothing left of her; a quiet little memorial service was held instead. Her brother and sister-in-law came to it, and afterwards removed her belongings from her flatlet.

Mrs Moxton arrived one morning looking an odd charcoal colour. 'I been washing myself all night, but can't get clean. I'm better than I was at the start, though; before they got the soap and water to me, I was black as Newgate's knocker.'

'But what happened?'

'What happened? Why, what you expect to happen these days, didn't it? One of them things landed at the end of the next street. Knocked down the end of a whole row of houses. How many dead, I don't know. Our ceilings came down and turned Edie white as a marionette show with plaster, and the rest of the blast came down the chimney and smothered me with soot.'

'Is Edie all right?' asked Bunty anxiously.

'Well, if it brings on a miss in her case, it won't be a calamity,' replied Mrs Moxton philosophically, adding: 'But I don't suppose it will; these things never happen when you want them to, only when you don't.'

Meantime the Allies were advancing across France. On 25 August, Paris was liberated. Ten days later Bunty received a letter from Waldo. He wrote that he was in Paris; it was the most wonderfully exciting experience of his life to be there at this time of liberation. One day he would tell her all about it, and what he had been doing since they had last seen each other. 'I know you say it is tempting Providence to speak about "after the war", but, soon as the war is over, I'm going to bring you here.'

Bunty kept this letter in a pocket of her clippie's uniform, and every now and again she would slip her hand into her pocket and feel it. When she replied to Waldo she didn't tell him about the flying bombs, or the fate of Mignonette's flat, or anything of the dark times they were now living through, but of how she dreamed of being in Paris with him when the war was over and done.

With the advance of the Allies more information reached England about the numbers of European Jews who had been deported to concentration camps. A black question mark hung over their fate: terrible stories circulated about the numbers who had already died from the appalling conditions.

The Schwartzes continued to smile politely and chat in a remote social sort of way when occasion demanded. Otherwise they sunned themselves in silence in the garden, or took long strolls together, arm in arm, still in silence.

Theodor put on a brave show of high spirits when in company. He played a great deal of tennis and once a week went to Belsize Park to indulge, as he put it, in a bridge supper. Some evenings he and Bunty, when she was not on duty, walked on the Heath, dropping in for a drink at the Holly Bush before going home. Alone with Bunty, he would occasionally hint at his growing deep concern for his mother. 'She is old. There can be no hope of her surviving concentration camp. None whatever.'

'As she is old, she'll probably be allowed to remain at home in peace,' said Bunty, anxious to help keep his spirits up.

Theodor's invariable response to her attempted optimism was to shrug a huge despairing shrug. Then they would talk about something else.

Summer passed; the flying bombs continued unabated. Government spokesmen explained to the grim-faced civilians living in the target areas that it was just a matter of everyone hanging on until the advancing Allies captured the launching sites. Londoners, and the denizens of Bomb Alley, gritted their teeth and hung on.

Bunty, as she wryly commented in a letter to Lorna, hung on both literally and figuratively. Riding on her bus platform, clinging with one hand to the pole which passengers held as they mounted or dismounted from the bus, with her other hand screening her eyes against the glare of the bright summer sunshine, she endlessly scanned the sky above the roofs and chimney pots. This was the way all the London clippies now rode: ever on the lookout. She and Gus Harris had had several close shaves with flying bombs, but so far they had gone unscathed.

So it was just one more flying bomb that Bunty spotted early one afternoon; travelling, thank God, away from their bus. With relief she watched it go, steadily distancing itself; yet it was a relief tinged, as usual, with guilty feeling: 'All very well for me, but what of the poor unfortunate people it's ultimately going to fall on?'

She had plenty of time to watch the thing; her bus was caught in a procession of buses which, as sometimes happened, had formed during the midday rush and were now moving slowly and sedately along the traffic-congested thoroughfare. Bunty followed the robot craft with her eyes. She heard the engine cut out, the missile began to glide, gradually losing height; then it suddenly toppled forward and dived down behind the skyline. Bunty waited for the explosion, bracing herself against the anticipated, though providentially distant, bang. But instead there was a violent and much closer explosion; the bus slewed round in the road, Bunty was hurled from her platform into the interior of the bus, landing literally in the lap of one of her passengers. Vehicles were skidding, colliding, mounting the pavement. Screams, shouts, utter confusion.

Another flying bomb, its engine cut out, had glided towards them in silence and unnoticed, to fall and explode further along the street. Their own bus was far enough back in the procession to be shielded from the worst of the blast by the vehicles in line ahead; Bunty's passengers were shaken, but nobody seemed seriously hurt. The clippie of the bus immediately ahead of them could be glimpsed giving first aid to one of her passengers. Her driver, evidently the stolid type, was seated in his cab, staring at what was going on in the street, obviously of the opinion that there was not much he could do to be of help so he might as well stay where he was. Gus and Bunty went to have a word with him.

He didn't notice them approach; Gus rapped on the cab window to catch the man's attention. Viewed from a distance he had looked perfectly unhurt; but now, as they peered up at him, they saw that his throat was gashed, all but severing his head. The windscreen was shattered; streams and spurts of bright red blood ran and trickled everywhere. Bunty had never seen so much blood. She gave a gasp and clutched at Gus's arm. He stood staring at the dead driver, then he said to Bunty: 'You get back there and tell that conductress of his what's happened, while I fetch some help. Don't let her see him, and don't let on to the passengers.'

Bunty walked back the length of the bus. The clippie was emerging from it. She said to Bunty: 'I need an ambulance for one of my lot. Meantime my driver's sitting there in his cab, enjoying a front-seat view of what's going on. Just like a man, innit? I'm going to give him a piece of my mind.'

Bunty laid a gentle arm round the girl's shoulders, to steady her against the shock she was about to receive. 'I hate having to tell you, but he's dead. Pretty well had his head cut off. I wouldn't go to look.'

The clippie turned pale, and sat down on her bus platform hard. 'You got a smoke?' she asked. Bunty gave her a Lucky Strike.

Gus returned to the bus with a Civil Defence rescue worker. The dead driver was removed from his cab; Gus was directed by a policeman to drive the bus a short distance up the road and then to divert into a side street and park the bus. Looking tense, Gus climbed into the blood-smothered driver's cab and moved the bus away as directed. Bunty returned to her own bus. She said to her passengers: 'Sit tight. We'll be on our way again in a moment.' Then she seated herself on her bus platform and smoked a cigarette herself, drawing on it, needing all the nicotine she could get.

Gus Harris returned from driving and parking the other bus; he had the driver's blood on his own uniform and hands, and looked as shaken as Bunty was feeling. 'Our turn to move on now,' he said. He put his head in the bus and spoke to the passengers: 'The road's blocked a bit further on, so we're having to make a detour; we'll try not to take you too much out of your way. Sorry about this. You should all thank your lucky stars you weren't two or three buses ahead of this one. They've all copped it proper.'

He then climbed into his cab and started up the bus.

They drove a short distance up the roadway. On either side, on the pavements, lay dead and dying people as if on a battlefield; which in a way, thought Bunty, indeed they were. Fire engines, ambulances, doctors, nurses, rescue teams, police were everywhere. The passengers on the bus couldn't really see out of their sticky-netting-covered windows; nor, it seemed, did they much wish to see – they sat still, in silence. Bunty, on her platform, saw far more than she wanted to see. Then Gus swung the bus into a side street, directed by a police diversion, and pretty soon they had left that battle area and were skirting another one, where the first flying bomb Bunty had spotted had fallen on a block of flats.

As the bus eventually drew up outside the Lupus Street depot another flying bomb flew overhead, to cut out and glide with a long drawn-out swishing sound, exploding the other side of the river among streets of small houses.

Gus put a comradely arm round Bunty's waist and drew her into the canteen. She could feel him shaking almost as badly as she was. 'Well, gal,' he said, 'we made it so far. Let's hope our luck holds.' They sat drinking tea, smoking, and eyeing one another in stunned silence; unable to believe that what they had just been through was true.

From the start of the flying bombs Bunty had fully realized the danger she was in, travelling all day every day in a bus in central London. In their canteens the crews endlessly exchanged appalling flying-bomb stories, all too often involving people they knew. 'Hear about that direct hit on that trolleybus on Wanstead Flats?' 'Hear about that bus sliced in half up the Elephant?' 'Hear about those four buses and trams clean disappeared into nothing at the Oval, rush hour, and all the people with 'em?'

But it was not till now, this afternoon, when Bunty had found herself staring at that dead driver in his cab, that the imminent possibility of her own death had struck her with a force which literally robbed her of breath for several seconds. She told herself grimly that she must make arrangements so that, if she were killed, somebody would write to tell Waldo.

That evening Bunty wrote to Lorna giving her Waldo's address in Paris and explaining:

This is Waldo Stein's address in Paris; he can be contacted through it, though he says he isn't necessarily there all the time. Waldo and I are engaged, though we've kept it very

393

quiet; it's inviting disaster to advertise these things in wartime, and the only reason I'm telling *you* now is because London's become such a frightfully dangerous place, especially if one is working on the buses, that I want you to have his address so that if anything happens to me you'll let him know. I haven't told my parents or anyone else about him yet, only you, so keep it strictly confidential. I feel a bit like one of those tommies in the last war, writing home before going over the top, but there it is; that is what we've come to.

Lovingly
Bunts

XXXIV

Megan sat at the enquiry desk of a deserted Rainbow Corner, knitting a pair of socks intended as Comforts for the Troops, and wondering if anyone would show up over the next hour or so and, if they didn't, whether she might be allowed to go home early.

Over her head the huge arrow still pointed: 'New York 3271 miles.' Who wanted New York? It was to the Rhine that all the GIs were now heading. 'The Rhine 100 miles' should be the sign for the Allied armies right now, she thought. Perhaps, tonight, less than a hundred miles; they advanced at remarkable speed, further each day.

The flying bombs were still coming over in shoals. Those Americans still in Britain didn't come to London unless they had to, and if they had to be in the metropolis they didn't linger around town after their business day was over. As enemy bombers were no longer anticipated, the blackout had been replaced by something less Stygian called the 'dim out'.

Megan knitted away. The deserted Rainbow Club had a spooky feeling about it; she concentrated on the heel she was turning in cross stitch. Then someone came in at the main entrance. A capaciously proportioned Yank officer, cheroot in mouth, amiable smile on his face, strolled up to her desk. 'Hi,' he said. 'How's the non-touch hostess? Still non-touchable?' It was Buzz Cabrini.

'Guaranteed,' responded Megan, smiling back at Buzz. There was something about Buzz that made it hard not to smile at him, despite all the things she found tiresome about him.

He propped himself against her desk and stared up at the arrow. 'New York three-two-seven-one miles,' he said. 'Sounds tempting, but I guess it's too far to go for supper. Where would you suggest that's a little nearer where we are right now?'

'Depends the sort of place you want.'

'Oh, you know: nice, with a touch of style, where a fella and a girl can eat and dance. Where d'you like to go?'

'It's not where *I* like to go, it's where the girl you're taking with you would like to go. You should ask *her* that.'

'What I'm doing. Where d'you like to go?'

'Are you asking me to come out with you, Buzz?' She was genuinely surprised. After that last evening together!

'I'm off to Paris day after tomorrow, and you're on duty here tonight. What about tomorrow evening?'

'Great,' repeated Megan, reminding herself of what Bunty had once said: that if you turned down an American's suggestion of spending the night with him after an evening out he'd nevertheless ask you out again, no strings attached, some other time; whereas a Britisher, once you'd said no to bed, wouldn't bother with you any more.

Buzz, next evening, took Megan to the Mayfair to dine and

dance. Like many large people, he was surprisingly light on his feet; he danced really well. He was in every way a most attentive escort; determined to give Megan a good time. He even went to the length of refraining from smoking for the entire evening – a real demonstration of his desire to please.

As they ate chicken Kiev between dances, Megan said: 'What are you planning to do in Paris, Buzz?'

'That very thing: planning. After this war there'll have to be some kind of Allied Occupation in Germany; and where there's US troops then there's Red Cross. Various schemes are already under discussion; the talking's taking place in Paris, so to Paris I'm going for a week or so. Pity you can't come with me. They all say it's a nice place. You been to Paris?'

'I've never been abroad. My mother and I were hoping to have our first Continental holiday the summer war broke out. The day we'd booked to go turned out to be the day Hitler invaded Poland.' She laughed ruefully.

'Where's your mother now? Living with you?'

'I wish she were. No; my mother's dead. Killed by a bomb during the Blitz.' She hurried on firmly. 'Have you a mother?'

'I'd be kinda unique if I'd gotten here without one,' riposted Buzz, taking up a forkful of Brussels sprouts.

'Tell me about her. Where does she live?'

'She's widowed, lives in Brooklyn. She's obstinate; won't listen to any kind of reason; very devout; makes her own pasta. I'm her youngest, her baby; it's pretty trying, keeps me away. A guy can't play along with that for ever.' He shook his head and ate more chicken. 'Once a year she goes to St Louis, to visit her sister. She has another sister still lives in Italy, in Bologna. Before I head back to the States, I have to get to Bologna to visit her, else my name will be mud all round. How I get to Bologna is a problem my mother isn't interested in. She's mad I haven't already been there; doesn't understand there's fighting going on. She says: 'It's just a step to your Aunt Concetta, once you've crossed to Europe.' See, she thinks Fursey Down's next door but one to the Vatican; she's upset I haven't yet set foot in St Peter's, Rome. Let alone Bologna. She says: 'You have all those airplanes at your camp. What's stopping you?' '

'I'm surprised at you, Buzz. What *is* stopping you?'

'Yes, it *is* silly of me to pass up the chance. All those swell day-trips I could make – Berlin, Cologne, Hanover, Hamburg. Give myself a real good time.'

'Have you any brothers or sisters?'

'Six brothers, two sisters. We're quite a family.'

'Gosh!' exclaimed Megan. 'I should say you are!'

'How about yours? Any more at home like you?'

'I've no family at all, apart from one unmarried aunt in Dorset whom I haven't seen since war broke out. We correspond at intervals.'

'Only one aunt?' Buzz sounded genuinely shocked. 'Nobody else? My, that's deprived. What happened to them all, for mercy's sake?'

'My father and his two brothers were killed in the last war; the two brothers weren't married. My mother's brother was killed, too; he left no children. That thinned us out. His widow died in the post-war influenza epidemic.'

Buzz shook his head in commiseration. 'Bad,' he said. 'Real bad.'

'But I have Lorna and Bunty. They're as good as sisters. Wonderful sisters.' Megan's little face kindled with appreciation of Lorna and Bunty.

'Lorna's a great girl,' agreed Buzz. 'You can't go wrong with her as a stand-in sister. She's a honey.'

'Well,' said Megan, raising her wine glass, 'here's to hoping it won't be too long before you're able to visit your Aunt Concetta, Buzz.'

'Here's to the war being over by Christmas,' said Buzz. 'Which,' he added, 'it's looking pretty certain it will be.'

If Megan had learned one thing, it was that Americans were incurable optimists. But over by Christmas! This was optimism gone mad.

Buzz, reading her expression, said: 'Like a bet?'

'You'll lose it.'

'Bet you a fish-and-chips supper at the Ritz, Christmas Eve.'

'I don't know about the Ritz, but I am willing to make it a fish-and-chips supper.'

'I'll keep you to that. Care to dance again?'

They danced, Buzz holding her close. Megan felt she couldn't object; holding a partner close was all part of dancing.

When the evening was over Buzz said: 'I'll see you home, honey.'

'You don't have to worry, Buzz; thanks all the same. Cromwell Road is more out of your way than you think. And I'm perfectly OK on my own.'

Before Buzz could make any rejoinder there came the sound of an extraordinary double explosion, deafeningly loud; the first explosion being a sharp *crack!* and the second, which followed hot on the heels of the first, being a drawn-out heavy rumbling rushing noise, as of a huge train travelling at speed through a tunnel.

Megan, on hearing the first explosion, dived for the pavement, Buzz in his turn landing on top of her. The air seemed to close in on them, then was sucked out again. For a few moments they lay in a dazed tangled heap; then they unwound themselves and helped one another to their feet.

Megan said: 'Whew! That was no ordinary flying bomb.'

'This is no ordinary evening, babe,' rejoined Buzz, adding: 'C'mon, let's find ourselves a taxi before the sky really falls in.'

Megan allowed herself to be put in a taxi; Buzz climbed in beside her. Although she would not have said so, she was thankful to have him with her; there had been something decidedly unnerving about that double explosion: her head was still ringing and she felt oddly weak in the knees. She was even compliant when Buzz put his arm round her and squeezed her close to him; there was a comforting reassurance in contact with his bulk.

They rode along in the taxi without speaking; Megan still feeling dazed and disjointed. Then she became aware of a tentative hand creeping its way up inside her tunic. She jerked from him. 'Buzz!'

Buzz heaved a long weary sigh. 'Still the no-touch situation? Even after that roll with me on the sidewalk?'

'Red Cross ruling, remember.'

'You sure have me wadjya callemses with my own wadsit, don't ya?'

'Hoist with your own petard, you mean?'

Suddenly the driver drew his taxi to a halt. 'Can't go no further. Police notice. Road's blocked. Diversion. Something's up; or, more like it, come down with a wallop.' He peered through his windscreen into the gloom.

'Don't worry. I can walk home the rest of the way from here,' said Megan.

'Hope you'll find you still have a home at the end of the walk,' responded the driver encouragingly.

Buzz paid the driver; the taxi departed, leaving Megan and Buzz standing in the dark. He said: 'Which direction now, honey?'

'Buzz, I think I must make it perfectly plain that you aren't coming any further than my front doorstep.'

'Have it your way, kid,' responded Buzz amiably – too amiably,

Megan thought. She sensed a disturbing confidence exuding from him, as from one who felt himself to be almost home and dry.

Megan began walking, stepping out as briskly as she could in the dark. Buzz kept pace beside her. Suddenly he tripped over something; Megan grabbed his elbow to save him from falling. 'Gee,' he said, 'this burg's a great place for kissing the sidewalk. Don't get carried away, Cabrini.' Megan took a small torch from her bag; the pavement was strewn with scattered bricks. They walked forward cautiously; broken glass crunched under their shoes. Ahead of them in the darkness they could hear voices calling to each other; shouts. Somewhere a terrified child was crying. The pavement disappeared under a tide of rubble. An ambulance passed them, its warning bell stabbing the night as it jolted over the debris-littered ground. The air smelt acrid with brick dust and cordite. More shouts, screams; they stood bewildered in the rubble, sensing, rather than being able to see, that where there should have been houses now there were none.

Torches gleamed, as attempting rescuers peered and groped in a shattered world. Megan, in the futile hope that its firefly glimmering would reveal more of the nightmare landscape, flickered her own little torch; she could barely discern a vast emptiness where once her house had stood, alongside other houses now also totally vanished.

'Any sign of that front doorstep of yours?' said Buzz.

'It looks like everything's gone.'

'Reckon you were lucky to be out at the time, honey.'

'Yes.'

Further words failed her. She stood speechless, engulfed by blankness.

Her little torch faintly picked out two Civil Defence men carrying a big heavy sack between them; the sack dripped a trail of blood. The men plodded past, and crunched away out of view.

Buzz put his arm round Megan and without speaking they picked their way back towards the spot where they had been earlier deposited by the taxi.

'I guess I can go to Katie,' said Megan. 'I could go to Bunty, only Katie's much nearer. There'll be a spare bed in her hostel, I've no doubt.'

'You best come back with me to my hotel,' said Buzz. 'It has a deep shelter.'

'So has Katie's hostel.'

'For chrissake, I'm not gonna rape you, you know!' His patience had deserted him.

Megan said: 'Oh Buzz, dear Buzz, I know you're not. But you see, Katie's American Red Cross, and works with me, and—'

Buzz cut in with a kind of groan: 'Jeez, another no-touch dame! Ain't one enough?'

'Buzz, I think Katie would be best; I really do.'

'OK, have it your way, sister.'

They walked on without further conversation, and at last reached a street with traffic moving along it. A taxi appeared; Buzz hailed it. It drew up; Buzz helped Megan into it. 'What's the address you want?' he asked. Megan told him; he told the driver.

They found Katie on the point of going down to the hostel air-raid shelter. Megan explained what had happened. Meantime a shoal of flying bombs came doodling over the roof-tops; crashes sounded in all directions. It was decided that Buzz had better come down to the air-raid shelter, too, rather than attempt to return to his hotel.

The shelter was lit by the usual eerie bluish-green lamps; there were the usual rows of camp beds, now almost all occupied. They found three vacant ones at the further end of a row and took possession of these. Katie had lent Megan a dressing gown to wear over her undies. Buzz removed his jacket, tie and shoes, rolled himself in a blanket, and in dour silence lay down on his bed and feigned instant sleep. He was obviously smarting from Megan's insistence upon going to Katie, rather than trust herself to him. She began to feel rather ashamed of herself. She could understand why Buzz felt affronted.

She fell wearily into the camp bed between Katie and Buzz. Katie kissed Megan and tucked the blanket round her. 'Now you get some sleep. You're looking real peaky.'

Katie lay down on her bed; went to sleep. Megan, unable to sleep, lay still, listening to the breathing of the slumberers all around her. At intervals came the sound of a distant crash, and the shelter floor reverberated with the vibrations of the explosion.

Megan began telling herself once more how lucky she had been. Miraculously lucky. If she hadn't been out for the evening!

Suddenly she began to cry. Until that moment she had had no sensations whatever of wanting, or needing, to cry; she had remained astonishingly self-possessed, amazing even herself by her calm and collected behaviour. But now she thought of the flat that had always been her home; of her mother; of the photograph in the living-room taken of her parents on their wedding day; of a father she had never known but had been able to believe in simply because there was that photograph to show that he had been real. And she thought, too, with a pang of childhood sentiment, of her old teddy bear, her mascot, seated on her bedroom window-sill. All vanished. Gone for ever. Nothing tangible left any more of her entire past. She buried her face in her pillow, attempting to cry low key and bury the sounds of her sobs. She mustn't wake people up. It was silly to cry like this, but she couldn't help it.

Suddenly a hand, from the direction of Buzz's bed, began feeling her arm; he was reaching out, feeling for her hand with his. His hand felt around; she took it in hers, clung to it. He squeezed her hand hard; sympathy came from his warm large grasp. It was the wrong thing, so far as Megan's tears were concerned; she began to snuffle and sob worse than ever. Her tears were soaking into the pillow; her nose stuffed up, she couldn't breathe; her struggles to weep unobtrusively were proving useless; she made choking noises. Oh God, she'd wake everyone up!

Abruptly Buzz rolled off his camp bed and lay down on hers on top of her, putting his arms round her, in a big surging movement of total sympathy, impossible for him to restrain or for her to repulse. He kissed her wet face. There was a sudden cracking of wood, the bed gave way beneath their combined weight and they went down with a violent thud to the floor, wrapped in each other's arms. Katie in the next bed woke startled, exclaiming: 'Hey, what's happened? Have we been hit?'

People were all sitting up in bed, exclaiming in alarm: 'What's happened? Have we been hit?'

The subdued lighting afforded Megan and Buzz some degree of camouflage; obscurity made it possible for Buzz to pick himself up and bundle back on to his own bed, while Megan struggled from the wreckage of hers.

'How did that happen? Oh, Megan, poor you!' Katie, all sympathy, was out of her bed in a trice and helping Megan to her feet. People all began asking at once how had it happened. Was Megan hurt?

Buzz stole Megan a look; she scarcely dared to return his glance. She was afraid now not of crying but of laughing. 'I guess you better have my bed,' he said. 'I can lie on the floor. I'll be OK.'

'But Buzz . . .,' objected Katie. 'You'll catch cold on the floor, honey!'

'I'll be perfectly fine.'

Megan transferred to his bed; he arranged himself on the floor beside her. People lay down again, slumber once more descended on the shelter. Megan, who had struggled with tears, now became triggered by exhausted nerves into a fit of wild giggles. Once more she buried her face in the pillow; she shook with laughter. From the floor came strange sounds from Buzz. He, too, was fighting off a terrible spasm of mirth. Megan reached down her hand and touched him; he grabbed it; they squeezed each other's fingers. Then laughter burst from them both, loudly and simultaneously. They couldn't stop. Everyone woke up again. People began to say 'Sh!' and complain. Megan managed to gasp: 'We can't help it. It's nervous reaction. We've been bombed by one of those new things with double bangs.'

'We're suffering from shock,' said Buzz.

They lay for the rest of the night with Buzz reaching up to clutch Megan's hand, which she, lying precariously on the edge of her bed, reached down to him. From their fellow shelterers came heavy breathing, snores. Occasionally there was a distant crash and rumble: Hitler's secret weapons pursuing war without end. At last Megan drifted into bitty uneasy sleep which in turn sank into the profound oblivion of total exhaustion. When she woke up Buzz had gone.

XXXV

Next morning Megan returned to Cromwell Road and had a day-light view of the enormous crater which now gaped where once her home had been. She didn't linger long; having fully taken in the extent of the havoc, she went to the Incident Enquiry Post to register that nobody need be digging in the rubble for her. Then she returned to the hostel where Katie lived, and arranged to have a room there.

She sat on the divan bed, staring forlornly at the walls, the fittings, the furniture; everything modern and perfectly comfortable, very much more up-to-date, indeed, than anything she had had in her own flat, but all perfectly featureless: nothing that she could look at and say, 'That is part of my own life, it belongs intrinsically to me.' She felt lonelier than she had ever felt in her life before; lonelier even than when her mother had died. Then there had been personal objects to reinforce memory: the clock her mother had wound every night, the utensils she had used in the kitchen, her umbrella in the stand by the front door. It had been possible still to touch things her mother had touched, sit on the sofa where her mother had sat, look from the window at the view her mother had looked at. Now all had been obliterated, as though none of it had ever been. One double bang; and all had gone for ever.

The double explosions continued, and multiplied. Londoners learned that they were rocket bombs; the second instalment of the secret weapons Hitler had promised. They were fired from The Hague and travelled through the stratosphere, taking less than four minutes to arrive on target in London. The famous double bang was a combination of the sonic boom (often heard as a sharp *crack!* rather than boom) as the missile re-entered the troposphere and the impact explosion, with a strange aftermath of rumbling and rushing, which was popularly said to be the sound of the rocket rushing through the air – heard after the explosion because of the speed at which the rocket travelled, faster than sound.

A spate of postcards arrived for Megan from Buzz in Paris. The first showed a view of the Eiffel Tower, and on the back of it Buzz had written: 'Paris OK – but you being here would improve it some.' Megan put the card on her mantelpiece; apart from her clothes and toilet things it was her only personal possession in the world.

The next card was a view of the Arc de Triomphe, and the message read: 'All fine and dandy here. Glen Miller arriving any time now, but I'd rather it was you.'

Megan with a half-smile, half-sigh, placed this second card alongside the first.

The third card showed a view of the Place de la Concorde and read: 'Lotsa people in Paris, as you can see, but Meg it's lonesome all the same without *you*.'

In mid-December the Germans launched a massive counter-offensive in the Ardennes. The war was definitely not going to be over by Christmas. The next postcard from Paris was of Notre Dame and said: 'You win the bet, Meg. Wish you hadn't. I'd have loved it to be a Victory Christmas spent with you.'

Nobody, mused Megan, had ever called her Meg before. The St Hildegard's lot had called her the Flopper, and that had turned into Flops (and she loved them calling her Flops), but everyone else, even her own mother, had called her Megan.

The next postcard showed a view of the Louvre and said: 'Shall be here for a working Christmas – me and Glenn Miller both. If I see him, I'll beg that autograph for you.' Then came a drawing of Buzz on his knees begging Glen Miller for his autograph.

Megan felt a small stab of jealousy at the thought of Buzz being in Paris for Christmas. Normally she never thought twice about other people perhaps enjoying themselves more than she did; she had been brought up to regard envy as a sin and to count her own blessings, to thank the Lord for what she had received and to be truly thankful for it. But now she found herself thinking how lovely it would be to spend Christmas in Paris; a Christmas free of rocket bombs, in a city that had known no blitzing or bombardment and did not smell of death and destruction as London was smelling now. And then she reminded herself that it was London's pride not to have capitulated to the enemy, not to have been occupied by the Germans. London hadn't had to be liberated; London had stood free from start to ... well, not finish, because the war wasn't finished yet, but it had never given in to the fiercest bombardment, and still wasn't giving in, and never would. And she was proud of being a Londoner who had stuck to London all the way through. So 'Good old London!' she said to herself as she crossed Piccadilly Circus past the boarded-up statue of Eros on her way to Rainbow Corner. That was where she would spend Christmas. And she'd make up her mind to have a real good time and not give a thought to Buzz swinging the festive season away to the strains of Glenn Miller's band in the shadow of the Eiffel Tower.

But, as it turned out, Glenn Miller's plane was lost on its way to Paris; quite how, it was not known. The death of this man who had become an integral part of the wartime scene cast a definite shadow over Christmas merrymaking, and if a Miller number were played people didn't dance, but cried instead.

Buzz's Christmas card had nothing to do with Paris but was a good old-fashioned one with snow and holly and Christmas bells. Under the printed Christmas greetings he had written: 'It's going to be a tough one all round, I guess. Still, Meg, here's to dreaming of you—' There was a picture of Buzz in bed, fast asleep, with a loud 'Zzz' to indicate his snoring; while Megan, depicted as a vision hovering over his head, sang 'Silent Night'.

Bunty spent Christmas on duty, watching out for flying bombs as she rode back and forth across London. Rockets you could do nothing about; they just arrived out of the blue, and that was it!

She and Megan made a date for a Café Royal supper a few evenings into the New Year. The weather had turned fiercely cold; the coldest winter on record for seventy years. There was a fuel shortage, with power cuts; London seemed to have become one long, dark, frozen, dismal winter night. Bad news came from the Western Front, where the Germans had broken through the American lines.

Edie had had her baby – a boy. Bunty, before going to the Café

Royal, visited Edie in hospital. Mrs Moxton impressed upon Bunty that Edie was known at the hospital as 'Mrs Moxton, young Mrs Moxton'.

'She wears a ring,' explained Mrs Moxton Senior, the true Mrs Moxton. 'After all, who's to know? I see it as the one good thing about this war – it's let Edie out of the mess she got herself in. She need never tell the kiddie it hasn't got a father; she can tell it that its father was killed in France before it was born. Between you and me, I think Edie's lucky to have come out of it what she's describing herself: a widow. That Homer wasn't much cop, and that's a fact. She's better off without him, far. It would've been no bed of roses, married to him. And think of having to live in America! No thanks!'

It had been planned that Bunty would be the child's godmother. She and Edie had had much discussion as to what the child should be named. If a girl, she would be either Marlene or Nova. But a boy presented greater difficulties. Edie spurned the name Homer, considering it 'poor' that she had never heard another word from the father of her expected child; on the other hand, she said that she would like the boy, if boy it proved to be, to have an American name, 'to remind me who his father was'. But 'That said,' added Edie, 'I hope it won't be a boy, for a boy's more likely to take after its father, and last thing I want is a second Homer on my hands.'

The child, now it had arrived, was a boy.

Bunty turned up at the hospital with flowers for Edie and a matinée jacket (knitted by Megan, who excelled at such things) for the infant. Bunty was shown the baby, who looked just like any other baby, though Edie was claiming that he reminded her of her own late maternal grandfather. 'Definitely the same nose.'

They began once more discussing what the child should be named. The matter was now more urgent than it had been hitherto.

'I been thinking of Chuck,' said Edie.

'Why Chuck?' asked Bunty.

'Well, Homer chucked me and the kiddie, didn't he?'

'Oh, Edie, you can't call the poor little thing Chuck for that reason. Besides, Chuck isn't a real name, I'm certain. What about Virgil? Goes with Homer.'

'Virgil doesn't sound right for a boy somehow.'

'Ezra? That's very American.'

Edie shook her head.

'Washington? Jefferson? Franklin?'

'Isn't Washington a town?'

'Yes, but it's named after George Washington. Their first President.'

'Jefferson would do. And Franklin. They can be shortened to Jeff or Frank. But you can't call a kiddie Wash. Wouldn't be fair on the child.'

'Franklin Jefferson, then? Franklin Jefferson Moxton.'

'Bit of a mouthful. Still, I reckon it'll have to do.'

After having settled this Edie gave Bunty a graphic account of all she had gone through bringing Franklin Jefferson into the world. 'I'd never have another one, tell you that. Worse than tonsils ten times over; twenty times. So you watch out.'

Finally Bunty kissed Edie and left, to join Megan at the Café Royal.

She took a bus; it was odd riding on a bus as a passenger and not as its clippie. Bunty sat thinking about Edie, and how she would manage bringing up Franklin Jefferson on her own. She spoke of returning to work on the buses as soon as she could, leaving the child in the care of an elderly neighbour. 'I'd rather it was Mum; but she can't afford to give up her job. Still, I dare say it'll all work out somehow.'

Bunty tried to imagine how she herself would cope with the

situation, supposing she were in Edie's shoes. The most important thing would be to try to treat it all as philosophically as possible—

A sudden tearing, roaring wind and everything became bright lights. Then nothing but screaming pain.

Megan sat in the bar of the Café Royal waiting for Bunty to arrive. She was almost twenty minutes late. Still, this was nothing to wonder at nowadays; London was disrupted by the rockets, and it was almost impossible for anyone to arrive anywhere punctually.

When Megan had been waiting an hour she decided that the time had arrived to begin to feel a little concerned. She went to the phone and put through a call to Kenilworth Lodge. Megan had visited Bunty at Kenilworth Lodge on several occasions, and had been introduced to Mrs Wells, so when that lady answered the phone Megan didn't have to waste time saying who she was. She explained why she was ringing. Mrs Wells said: 'I met Mrs McEwen just as she was going out; she said she was first paying a visit to Edie Moxton, who's had a baby, and then meeting a friend for supper.'

'Yes, that was me. And I've been here at the Café Royal for over an hour waiting for her to turn up.'

'Perhaps you should give her a little longer, though I'm surprised she should be as late as all that,' said Mrs Wells, adding unnecessarily: 'I hope she's all right. You never know what's going to happen these days.'

'I'll give her another half-hour, and then if she hasn't turned up I'll go back to my hostel and give you another ring from there. I can't think what else to do.'

'I can't suggest anything else. If she does turn up, please give me a tinkle and let me know. You've got me worried.'

Megan returned to the bar, ordered another drink and waited another half-hour. A Polish officer with a glass eye tried to pick her up; she politely but firmly turned him down. When the half-hour was up she went back to her hostel, after having left a message for Bunty with the barman just in case Bunts did turn up in the end.

By this time Megan was really anxious. She telephoned Mrs Wells as arranged; Mrs Wells erupted into a shrill distracted gabble: 'I'm very sorry, Miss Thomas, to have to tell you this, though I dare say you had it at the back of your mind like I did. Mrs McEwen's been blown up. She's in Middlesex Hospital, and her condition's serious; she's being operated on. I've given the hospital the phone number of her parents. The hospital says not to try to visit her, but to telephone tomorrow morning. That's all there is to say for now.'

Megan could find no words, except to murmur: 'Thank you, Mrs Wells. I'll keep in touch.' Mrs Wells rang off; Megan closed her eyes and prayed hard for Bunty.

Jeffrey was just about to put on his overcoat and step into a night of blinding snow storm, to grope his way home, after an evening of chatting with General Washbourne, and Lorna was washing up the supper things to rest Mrs Cuthman (who since Ruth's death had begun to show her age), when a telephone call came through from Lady Bastable, Bunty's mother. The police had rung the Bastables to say that Bunty had been injured in a rocket incident and had been taken to Middlesex Hospital. Could Lorna possibly go up to London, to Bunty? wondered Lady Bastable.

'It's a tremendous lot to ask of you, Lorna dear, I'm well aware of that. But, you see, we're still away from home, spending the New Year with Humphrey's aged aunt, and we've all gone down with flu. Aunty and Humphrey are in bed with the wretched bug. I'm still on my feet; have to be – somebody has to nurse them. Getting to London at the moment is an utter impossibility. But I know how Bunty often speaks of you as being like a sister to her and, if she can't have her mother at her bedside, at least she can have a sister.

That is, if you're willing to go to her, which I trust and pray you will be.'

Lorna exclaimed, 'Poor darling Bunty! How simply frightful! Of course I'll go. I'll leave immediately.' She glanced at her wrist watch. 'If I start now I can catch the ten-eighteen.'

She raced back to her father and Jeffrey. 'Bunty has been seriously injured by a rocket bomb, and Lady Bastable has asked me to go to her in hospital as both parents are down with flu. If you could drive me to the station, Jeffrey?' 'What, *now*?'

'If we leave promptly, I should catch the ten-eighteen.'

'Lorna, have you seen what kind of night it is outside?'

'Jeffrey, I wouldn't ask you if it weren't terribly terribly urgent.'

'Well, I'll do my best to get you there if you insist on going, but personally I've never heard anything so daft in my life; it's one hell of an awful night. Can't you leave it till tomorrow morning?'

'No, I can't; Bunty needs me.' With which Lorna charged upstairs to throw a few necessities into a bag while Jeffrey, with a shrug of resignation, went to fetch his car.

They started off. Mist and whirling flakes enclosed them; snowdrifts were banked high on either side of the road. Some heavy vehicle had been along it earlier, leaving good tyre tracks, but these were now becoming rapidly covered over. The snow fell faster and faster, the flakes whirling in the car's dimmed headlights like demented swarming bees. Beyond the flakes the roadway and drifts blurred into a blanket of whiteness. Jeffrey snarled: 'Does that stupid Bastable woman know what she's asking you to do, I wonder? Turn out on the worst bloody night of the year, and into the bargain make yourself a target for rocket bombs with a good chance of sharing Bunty's fate.'

'Lady Bastable would go herself if she could, Jeffrey.'

He gave a contemptuous snort, leaning forward to peer ahead, tense with concentration. He muttered: 'I must have been flaming mad to agree to this!'

The car forged slowly and perilously onward. The whirling snowflakes twisted and spun, taking over the sky; the world on which they fell was rapidly disappearing. Lorna had a terrifying sensation that she, and Jeffrey, and everything on earth, faced imminent obliteration. She exclaimed: 'You're right. This is really pretty fearful.'

'Thanks for telling me. I'd never have known.'

Self-reproach engulfed Lorna. He was right, of course; they should never have set out on such a night. It was all her fault; she had talked him into it. Fearfully wrong of her. And, even if they did reach the railway station in safety, how would he drive home again? Suddenly she had terrible visions of Jeffrey buried in his car under the snow, frozen to death. She said, seizing him urgently by the coat sleeve, 'Jeffrey, promise me one thing. If you do get me to the station, don't on any account try to drive home again. There must be someone who'll put you up for the night.'

'I'll fix something, don't you worry. Now leave go my arm and let's concentrate on reaching the bloody station, not on how I'm going to weather the storm.'

They reached the station just in time for Lorna to catch the train by the skin of her teeth. Jeffrey helped bundle her into a carriage. She leaned out of the window and for some ridiculous reason extended her hand to him in the formal style of a polite young lady saying goodbye. 'Jeffrey, I can't begin to say thank-you ...'

'Don't be bloody daft. You're on the train, that's all that matters. Let's hope things aren't as bad as they sound with Bunty.'

She clung to his hand as urgently as she had earlier clung to his coat sleeve. 'Promise you won't try to drive home. It's far too dangerous.' She stared hard into his eyes, seeking assurance that he'd do as she asked. 'Don't worry,' he said. His voice had gone rough. 'I'll live. Don't *you* get blown up.'

But she needed stronger assurance than that. 'Jeffrey, *promise* me, *please*,' she repeated, staring even harder at him. Abruptly he reached up, pulled her face down to his and gave her a kiss hard as her stare into his eyes. Their mouths glued together, a current of desperation ran through them both. As if struck reckless with despair, they ignored the guard's piercing blast on his whistle and waving of his flag; they remained glued. The train began to move. They were literally wrenched apart. Lorna fell backwards on to a seat. 'Gosh!'

Dazed, she sat gingerly massaging her fingers which he had squeezed to near pulp while kissing her. She wondered if any bones were broken. Her mouth felt bruised; her ribs were sore where she had been pulled leaning out against the window frame. Her head swam slightly and her eyes pricked with tears; whether from pain, or cold, or her confusion of feelings, or what, she couldn't have said. She felt exactly like the old saying 'pulled through a hedge backwards'.

The train gathered speed; a blast of icy air reminded her to close the window. Outside the night was a whirling mass of flying snow. Her crushed right hand just about functioned as she hauled up the window by its thick leather strap and secured it and then pulled down the blackout blind. After which, she once more fell back in her seat and resumed massaging her hand.

She couldn't quite understand what had happened, or how it had happened. Then she found herself thinking of that kiss Lance Vogel had given her, the evening before the Schweinfurt raid. 'I've come to kiss you good-night.' He had known he'd never see her again.

Perhaps she and Jeffrey had been kissing one another the same kind of good-night? It would be understandable; both caught in a blizzard of wartime awfulness, and herself heading for the Front Line.

Then, with a jab of betrayal, she remembered how, in her last letter to Herbie, she had sworn she wouldn't go to London again till all danger of rockets was over. He had written begging her to promise him this. Everyone asking everyone else to promise to take care of themselves, in a world where nobody could any longer promise anything . . . She drew another sigh.

It was well past midnight when the train reached London, steaming slowly into Liverpool Street station, cavernous and dimly lit, its platforms empty and echoing, and the few trains that were on the move uttering odd clanks and loud sighs. Lorna, aware that there would be no public transport at that hour, steeled herself for a long and unpleasant walk to the hospital. She was astounded, and grateful beyond words, when she found a taxi outside the station. The driver was friendly and sympathetic, in the way of wartime Londoners. 'Somebody you know copped it from a rocket, duck?' he said, when she asked for the hospital.

'Yes. My sister,' said Lorna. It was easier to say her sister.

The driver replied: 'Just fetched a lady to the station to catch a train. She's been to the London Hospital; her sister's died in there from one.'

They arrived at the hospital. Lorna paid her fare and tipped the driver the money she knew he'd expect for such late-night service. 'You saved my life,' she said. 'I was afraid I was going to have to walk.'

He replied grimly: 'I probably did save your life, and all. Nobody wants to walk about in London more'n they need, these days. Not that you can't cop it in a taxi, too.' His voice took on a new tone, flat with hatred. 'Whoever invented these rockets,' he said, 'should be hacked into little pieces, live. And so I hope they will be when all this is over and we have the buggers at our mercy.'

Lorna was startled; during her wartime visits to London she had hitherto been impressed by the absence of this kind of talk among people who had suffered so much, but there was no mistaking the loathing and contempt here, beneath the cold flatness of the utterance.

She arrived at the hospital and was directed which ward to go to. On the big landing outside the ward were people like herself: relatives and friends of those who had been injured by rocket bombs. Some were weeping, while others tried to comfort them; others sat, or stood, motionless and speechless, with grimly taut faces clenched in the presence of calamity.

A nurse conducted Lorna to the night sister in her office. Lorna explained who she was and why Bunty's parents could not be there themselves. When she had finished her explanation Sister said without further preamble: 'I'm afraid Mrs McEwen has lost a leg. They had to amputate it to release her; she was trapped under the wreckage of her bus. At the moment she is dangerously ill; she lost a lot of blood. But she's young, strong and basically a healthy creature, and she should pull through.'

'Does she know yet that . . . ?' Lorna edged away from saying more.

'She's under heavy sedation at present. I don't think she will remember much of what happened, when she begins noticing things again.'

Lorna was taken to see Bunty. The long shadowy ward echoed with sounds of suffering and distress; people sobbing, people crying out in delirium or pain. Lorna knew that she was in a field hospital close to the front line and the wounded in the beds were from a battlefield.

Several of the beds had screens round them. The nurse conducting Lorna up the ward led her to one such screened bed; from it came a long shuddering moan that didn't sound like Bunty at all.

Having had the experience of visiting an almost unrecognizable Megan after her encounter with the flying bomb, Lorna was prepared for an unrecognizable Bunty, but she had not been prepared for a human form that bore no resemblance whatever to any specific individual but was purely a symbol of intense suffering. Although under sedation, Bunty still gave these occasional shuddering moans, which more than anything made Lorna think of the shudder of the flying bomb passing low over the roof of Mignonette's flat: 'The voice of the Angel of Death.'

Lorna sat motionless by the bed, staring dumbly and numbly at a blotched and swollen face which was not Bunty's; any more than the voice that moaned was Bunty's.

How long she sat there, Lorna did not know. Her mind travelled back to those days at St Hildegard's: that thumping of the typewriters in time to Mozart's 'Turkish March'; those conversations about the coming war as they ate their lunch-hour sandwiches. Bunty with lively talk of her intention to 'entertain the troops behind the lines'. Her experiments to look and sound like whichever stage star she was worshipping at the moment; 'dropping her voice', developing a throaty gurgle; rouging her cheeks up to her hairline, pencilling in Marlene Dietrich eyebrows. Miss Binkle's dire warning: 'I fear, Bunty, that you appear to be a gal who tends to the flighty side.'

Bunty moaned again. Lorna didn't dare to make contact with her by touching her, in case of further hurting her. She concentrated on trying to get a message through to her, 'Hang on, Bunty, hang on!' but Bunty simply continued to moan.

Violetta had been swept away. If Bunty were to follow, that would leave two of the original St Hildegard's set of four. And, of those remaining two, one, the Flopper, had had her own close brush with death. And Lorna, that night in Mignonette's flat, had had destruction poised over her, too. It was all a matter of whether your number was on it or not; a game of chance, played in the dark, and nobody's luck could be expected to hold indefinitely.

Presently a nurse came round the screens and said to Lorna gently: 'I think you should leave her for a while now, dear. Come back to see her again later; perhaps this afternoon.'

Lorna gave Bunty a last lingering look. 'Hang on, Bunts!' she whispered. She followed the nurse into the ward. In the Sister's office a note was made of Lorna's address and telephone number; she gave these as Kenilworth Lodge. Then she left the hospital and found herself in the street. It was not yet five o'clock, still dark, and snowing. She felt almost too tired and bewildered to know what to do next, but it was silly to stand in the street in the snow, so she went back inside the hospital, found a telephone and put through a call to Kenilworth Lodge, though she didn't really expect anyone to answer at such an hour; but after the phone had rung for quite a time Mrs Wells answered it. Lorna explained where she was, and how she would like to use Bunty's flatlet for a while. Mrs Wells said: 'Come back as soon as you can find a bus or a train; knock on the door to my own flat, and I'll give you breakfast.'

Lorna reached Kenilworth Lodge at half-past six. Mrs Wells, as good as her word, gave her a big breakfast of dried egg scrambled, some peculiar bacon in funny little strips that came, according to Mrs Wells, from Canada in tins and took all your points for a month but was profitable in fat, and some fried potato cooked in the said fat. Lorna declared that *any* bacon was a beautiful change. Then they had a long sad talk about Bunty, and agreed that you couldn't do more than hope for the best. Lorna tried to ring Fursey-Winwold, to be told that all the telephone lines were down because of the snow. However, she managed to send the Bastables a telegram. Finally Lorna rang Megan, before getting some sleep.

In the afternoon Lorna and Megan sat either side of Bunty's bed. She didn't recognize them, but lay moaning; between moans she muttered to herself. Further along the ward a woman gave short sharp screams at irregular intervals, and in another bed someone was crying.

Over the following days Lorna spent most of her time at Bunty's bedside, watching her friend fighting her way back from the dark place in which she had so nearly foundered.

One evening, after returning from the hospital, Lorna decided she had better drop a line to Jeffrey, to let him know how things were going. Their fraught drive in the blizzard to Fursey-Winwold station and unexpectedly dramatic farewell had now become assimilated by Lorna as part and parcel of wartime's generally frenetic landscape, with its fantastically heightened chiaroscuro: danger, violence, excitement, irrational behaviour; with emotional outbursts and encounters, like volcanic eruptions, allowing temporary relief from endless stress, strain and exhaustion. It was important not to let the overwrought behaviour of herself and Jeffrey, that desperate blizzarding night, disturb the tenor of what fundamentally had become a most comfortable and comforting neighbourly relationship.

Dear Jeffrey,

Bunty is still in a somewhat dicey state, but slowly improving. She'd lost an awful lot of blood by the time they'd got her out from the wreckage of that bus; they had to amputate her leg to get her out. I don't think she will have any memory of it; we'll hope not, anyway. She's having longer periods of consciousness now; can't speak yet, but she knows I'm with her, and I think that's helping her to pull through. I shall stay here with her as long as my CO at Fursey-Down will let me; I'm living in her flat in Hampstead.

You were marvellous the way you got me to the station driving through that fearful night. I still feel horribly guilty about asking you to turn out in such conditions. Nobody has written to tell me you were dug out of the snow a frozen corpse, so I reckon you arrived home safely in the end. I must confess I was worried stiff about you at the time. Comfort yourself with the thought that, as I say, having me with her does seem to be helping poor darling Bunts.

I know you'll keep an eye on Father for me. And try to keep an eye on yourself, too! Some of those old farmers of yours, way out in the sticks, must be buried feet deep in snow and difficult to reach. So take care.

Not quite sure yet when I'll be back. But I'll keep you all informed.

Lorna

Jeffrey replied with a postcard which looked as if it had been dropped in the mud.

Thanks for your letter. Hope Bunty continues to make good progress. Yes, I survived the blizzard. The station master and his wife put me up for the night. I once neutered a cat for them and so they took me in like an old friend, God bless 'em. I didn't like the way the cat looked at me, though. He would have left me outside to perish, given the chance. Repeat take care of yourself and don't *you* get blown up. JB.

Lorna laughed at the bit about the cat and then hurried off to the hospital to sit by Bunty's bed, holding her hand and smiling at her whenever she opened her eyes.

XXXVI

Gradually Bunty edged her way out of danger and darkness and grew stronger and increasingly aware of what was going on around her. She took the loss of her leg most terribly well, Lorna and Megan agreed admiringly; she was a wonderfully brave girl, good old Bunts! She was even able to make a joke about it when Edie Moxton visited her. 'Well, you soppy old haddock,' said Edie affectionately by way of greeting to Bunty, 'this is a nice way to carry on, losing a leg.'

'Fortunes of war,' replied Bunty. 'Some win, some lose. You win a baby, I lose a leg.'

The Transport Board told Bunty that, once she had her artificial limb ('The Government provides me it free, it comes under war damage,' said Bunty) the Board would find her a secretarial job. She feared she would have to give up her flatlet at Kenilworth Lodge because it was on the first floor and she would be unable to climb the stairs; but the Parsonses, when they came to visit her at the hospital, remarked, without Bunty so much as mentioning the subject, that they would be perfectly happy to move up into her flatlet if she would care to move down to theirs.

'Everyone is so kind,' said Bunty to Lorna.

Theodor brought her books and magazines. Mrs Wells visited with home-made biscuits flavoured with fennel seeds. The Schwartzes brought her a jigsaw puzzle of the Tower of London. Gus Harris came, with a card signed by everyone else at the depot. He was disappointed that Bunty couldn't remember anything of what had happened. 'It's a waste of experience,' he said. Bunty was thankful she couldn't remember, though she could understand what he meant.

Megan and Lorna visited her every evening without fail; Megan fitting in the visits between leaving work and going on duty at the

Rainbow Club. This meant she missed supper, but anything for the sake of dear Bunty! The three girls laughed and chattered; Bunty remarked that, in a funny way, it was like a taste of St Hildegard's imported into Middlesex Hospital.

When Bunty had been in the hospital for a fortnight she was told she was to be transferred to another hospital, outside London, in order to release her bed at the Middlesex for some other rocket or flying-bomb victim. When sufficiently recovered she would be sent to a convalescent home, where she would learn to walk on crutches; then she would be allowed home for a week or two, and then she should be ready to be fitted with an artificial limb. 'And as I'm awfully lucky, as my amputation is below the knee, everyone assures me that I shall be able to learn to walk again without too much difficulty,' she informed Lorna and Megan buoyantly.

'She really is some wizard kid,' said Lorna to Megan, as they walked to Tottenham Court Road Underground station together, their visit over. 'I'd like to think I could face up to a disaster like that with her courage, but I doubt it.'

'Same here,' rejoined Megan.

At Tottenham Court Road they parted, heading in different directions. Lorna, rocking along in the Tube train bound for Hampstead, took Herbie's latest letter from her handbag and reread it for the umpteenth time. Still stationed in North Africa, he had been enjoying a brief furlough to Marrakesh. 'I'm going to take you there some day, Lorna my lovely. You'll fall for it, just as I fell for it. Though it would all have been so much better if I had had you with me.'

He was expecting to be moved to the Pacific theatre of war. 'It'll be all over in Europe by midsummer. Then all we'll have to do is polish off the Japs, and my convinced opinion is that the USAAF will bring things to an end much sooner than anyone thinks.'

Back where they'd come in, thought Lorna. The USAAF going to beat the Japs in record time the easy way. Like they'd been going to beat the Germans. Well, all honour to the Eighth: they'd hung on like grim death, and fought their way through the bad times, and now they were out on top, but it hadn't been quick and it hadn't been easy. Why should it be different in the Pacific?

But Herbie was an optimist on all fronts. He spoke with complete confidence in their future together. 'After the war, and repeat that isn't as distant as you may think, I'll get the divorce, and you can get divorces real quick in the US, as I've said before, and before you know where you are you'll be in the States, and we'll have started our wonderful new life.'

Lorna put the letter back in her handbag and slipped into a daydream about that wonderful new life with Herbie.

The next evening she paid a last visit to Bunty in the Middlesex. Megan had not yet arrived. Lorna sat by Bunty's bedside, holding her hand and chatting. 'We shall miss these evenings together,' said Bunty. 'For me, they've been a real silver lining to this cloud.' Then she added, her cheerful tone changing to one of deep sadness: 'I shall have to write to Waldo to tell him what has happened, and say to forget about me. I haven't felt like writing to him so far, but now I'm better I must do it. You can't allow a chap to find himself stuck with a girl with only one leg.'

The expression of haunting sorrow and suffering which momentarily settled on Bunty's face suddenly gave Lorna a glimpse of the real stricken girl behind the buoyant façade which Bunty usually gallantly maintained. So Bunty's gaiety and buoyancy were truly no more than a front, an act, but did this in any way make her less courageous? To Lorna, Bunty's normal display of lightheartedness in the face of disaster seemed all the more admirable simply because it *was* an act. Poor brave Bunty! And poor Waldo when he received

that letter! Lorna said: 'If I were you, Bunts, I wouldn't write immediately. Things are pretty chaotic on the Western Front just now,
and you always say you don't know precisely what it is that Waldo
gets up to, but you suspect it's something a lot more dicey than
simply being intelligent, and you don't want to send him an upsetting letter like that when he may be in a nasty crunch. I'd leave it
till a little later.'

'It's not fair on him not to let him know right away, Lorna.'
Bunty had clearly made up her mind; Lorna said no more. Poor
darling Bunts, what a letter to have to write! Breaking it off for
good and all with a chap she truly loved.

Bunty changed the subject. 'I wonder where Megan is. She's
usually the punctual type. I hope she's OK.'

Lorna, who was thinking exactly the same thing, replied: 'Don't
worry. There's still time for her to turn up yet.'

But Megan didn't turn up.

Megan returned to her hostel room after the day's work with just
enough time to spruce up a little before dashing off to visit Bunty.
She freshened herself up and was just putting on her overcoat when
a call came through from reception to say that Megan had a visi-
tor waiting to see her downstairs: a Captain Cabrini.

Buzz back from Paris without any warning. Good heavens!

He was standing in the middle of the otherwise empty visitors'
lounge, looking incredibly smart in a spit-and-polish sort of way
and holding a bunch of red roses. He struck Megan as being exceptionally formal and unusually nervous. 'Hi, Meg,' he said. He
handed her the roses. 'Thought you might like these. They come
from Paris. Fetched them over myself, today.'

'From Paris?' Megan stared at the roses as though they were a
miracle. 'How fabulous,' she said. She could scarcely believe in
them: roses from Paris in wartime London!

'You got time to come and have supper with me? That fish 'n' chips at the Ritz I owe you?'

'Buzz, I'd love to, but I'm supposed to be on my way to visit Bunty McEwen in hospital. She's been rocket-bombed; lost a leg. And it's her last night in London; she's being moved into the country tomorrow. I simply can't miss seeing her this evening.'

'Poor kid!' Buzz looked shaken. Megan guessed that in Paris he had begun to forget what wartime London was like. 'How did that happen?' he added.

'She was on a bus. You don't have to be doing anything out of the way to get blown up in London these days.' Then: 'I might have time for a quick, very quick coffee before I dash away.'

'Sure thing. Let's have that, then.'

Megan handed the roses to the reception desk, asking if they might be put in water awaiting her return. Then she and Buzz made tracks for an American-style coffee bar a few streets distant. As they walked she said to him: 'Have you finished what you had to do in Paris, Buzz?'

'For a while, but I'll be going back there soon. Like to come with me? It'll be my new headquarters; I shan't be returning to England again.'

Back where they came in, thought Megan. Only this time she cared, really cared about having to say no. 'Buzz, you know what I . . .'

'Yeah, you're a ring-or-nutt'n girl.'

'I'm afraid so.'

'You still are? Not changed your mind?'

Megan suddenly realized how much she wished she could change her mind, but it was no good. For better or worse she had been brought up on those bloody principles. 'I guess I can't change, Buzz. I wish I could. Believe me, you'll never know how much I wish I could! But, you see, I can't.'

'I'm mighty relieved to hear it,' said Buzz. They had stopped walking as if by mutual agreement and stood facing one another on the pavement. He went on: 'The way things have worked out, it wouldn't be any good otherwise. American Red Cross is strictly ring-or-nutt'n when it comes to its officers pairing off with members of the opposite sex. Uncle Sam has high moral tone. You've noticed that, no doubt.'

Megan didn't know what to make of this at all. She supposed he was pulling her leg.

'Well, anyways, what I'm saying is, if you do feel you'd like to come back to Paris with me, it will have to be wearing a ring, else I guess there's no future for us as upright downright representatives of the Land of the Free.'

'Buzz, exactly what are you trying to say?'

'I'm asking you to marry me, I guess.'

'D'you really mean it?' She couldn't disguise her amazement.

'Look, Meg, this isn't the kinda world you can play around in till the cows come home. As the war goes on and you learn more about it, that feeling of all the time in the world diminishes some. I used to think I'd live for ever; marry when I was about eighty, say; seventy, if it had to be a shotgun wedding. But I've changed my mind; reckon I'm gonna grow old gracefully from now on, if I'm given the chance. If you'd care to keep me company, that'll sure be fine and dandy by me ... Only, you'll have to marry me, Meg, for I'm American Red Cross and in a strictly no-touch situation unless officially wed.'

Megan managed to say: 'Oh, Buzz, I ...'

'You mean you will? You really will?'

'I reckon so. If that's what *you* really mean.'

They stood on the pavement hugging each other. There was no one in sight, though it wouldn't have made any difference had there been.

Buzz said appreciatively as he paused between kisses: 'London's so nice and quiet, now these rockets are around.'

'They're certainly one way of having the place to ourselves.'

'Our own street.'

'Yes. *Private* street.'

This dark narrow street with narrow-faced old houses; one of an infinity of narrow London streets, a street which she and Buzz suddenly and magically found themselves owning. They stared up and down it, as if they had neither of them seen a street before.

A violent double bang, apparently about two miles distant in the direction of Marble Arch, made them start and cling to each other more tightly than ever. 'Jeez,' said Buzz. 'Now who says we don't own hot property?' He suddenly stopped, as if remembering something. 'And talking of hot property – that darn ring!'

He began feeling in his pockets. Megan said: 'Have you actually bought a ring?'

'Yeah. Nothing stops Cabrini once he gets stuck in.'

'Suppose I'd said no?'

'I'd 'a kept it for the next girl.'

He took the ring from his pocket and slid it on her finger. A sparkle of light gleamed from it. He said: 'Like to have a proper view of it? I've got a torch.'

'It *feels* perfectly lovely, Buzz.'

'Yeah, but it'd be kinda nice to see it, too.' He shone the torch.

It was a diamond and sapphire ring. 'It's absolutely beautiful!' Megan could just about find the words.

'That's OK, then.'

After a minute or two they began walking again. Then it was Megan's turn to stop as if remembering something. 'There's just one snag, Buzz. I'm a Protestant, and I imagine you're a . . . '

'Far as I'm concerned, it don't matter a darn. My mother will probably disown me; but that don't matter a darn, neither. If we have children, that may take some thinking about, and you may have to make concessions; but that's what life's about, concessions. See,' he added, 'I been making concessions to you about this no-touch situation . . .'

'Have you, Buzz?' she teased. 'I can't say I've noticed it.'

'Gee, honey, when you find out what I'm really like!'

'You'll have to ease me into it, Buzz.'

'Yeah, well, I kinda figure it will be the other way round.'

They began walking on a little again. Then they stopped once more. They asked each other: 'Where are we going?'

'It's too late for that hospital now,' said Megan. 'They'll be turning all the visitors out by the time I reach there.'

'Let's go some place and dance. Celebrate.'

'Yes. Let's paint the town red.'

By the time Lorna had arrived back at Kenilworth Lodge she had worked herself into a state of acute anxiety over Megan: usually the most reliable girl in the world, never late for anything. Her failure to turn up at the hospital could mean only one thing: she had met with disaster.

Lorna had come to terms with the conviction that few she closely loved would survive this war unscathed – if, indeed, they survived it at all. But when the crunchy moments actually came, like when the Forts had returned dropping red flares and she hadn't known whether a flare was for Herbie or not, or when Megan had been injured at the Guards Chapel and Lorna had been called to her bedside, followed by that terrible business of trying to discover what had happened to Violetta, and then learning; and then that other crunchy night she had rushed to London to Bunty in hospital – when these moments were actually upon her, like some wild beast on her back, its black breath enveloping her, no resolution on her part to show a proper fortitude could save her from feeling as though she were dissolving to pulp, while a pitiless taloned paw clawed her belly. This was fear; fear for those she loved: so much more truly devastating than simple fear for herself.

Now once more she felt that fear; dreading what had befallen the Flopper, dearest darling Flops, who had already had the sort of brushes with death that made your flesh crawl when you thought about them. All very well for Flops to repeat philosophically that if it had your number on it . . . and if it didn't it didn't. How many times could you play the numbers game with bombs and get away with it? Lorna asked herself.

A rap on the door. Mrs Wells calling that Lorna was wanted on the telephone.

This would be it. Once more a summons to a hospital; once more a dash to a bedside to gaze down at an unrecognizable . . . Or perhaps, even worse, she was about to be told that Flops . . .

Lorna hurried downstairs to the phone booth in the hall. She lifted the receiver that waited for her like a doom-heavy mouth. 'Hello. Lorna Washbourne here.'

Megan was at the other end of the line, oddly breathless and quite unlike her normal self. 'Lorna! Oh, Lorna, I've been hit. Hit like you said. D'you remember, Lorna, how you said I'd be hit?' The Flopper's voice sounded high and trembly.

'Oh God!' groaned Lorna. 'Flops darling! Are you badly—?'

'It's Buzz Cabrini, Lorna. We're out on the town, celebrating, right now. We're engaged!'

Lorna closed her eyes and leaned against the side of the booth. She didn't know whether to laugh or to cry. At the other end of the line the Flopper repeated on a steadily rising note: 'Lorna. D'you hear me, Lorna? Buzz and I are engaged!'

Lorna, pulling herself together, shouted back: 'Hoddog, kid! Thatsa stuff!'

429

Then she hung up the receiver; leaned against the side of the booth again. Aloud, she said to nobody in particular: 'One's friends shouldn't give one frights like that!'

Next morning Lorna caught the train to Fursey-Winwold and on the morrow was back at work on Fursey Down. Buzz, too, had returned to the aeroclub. Lorna, finding herself dunking doughnuts with him at midday, said: 'Congratulations, Buzz.'

'Meg said she'd told you. Said you said, "Hoddog, kid! Thatsa stuff!" She was glad you approved.'

'I think she's a lucky girl; and you're a very very lucky guy, Buzz.'

'I sure am. Know that,' said Buzz, with the smug satisfaction of the newly, and happily, betrothed.

'She's a very remarkable girl, you know, is Flops. Meg, as you call her.'

'She's a marvellous kid, but I spotted that the first moment I set eyes on her.'

'Yes, you did. That's true.' Lorna thoughtfully dunked her doughnut. 'Did you ever think, though, that you'd end up wanting to marry her?'

'Never imagined I'd want to marry anybody till she came along. But then, when I found out she was a ring-or-nutt'n girl and, what's more, really meant it . . . See, a lotta girls tell you that, but with a little trying you can break 'em down. But she really meant it and stuck to it. First, when I found she meant it, I thought: Oh shit. It was a pity, but there's plenty other girls who'll weekend with a guy. But then I met her again, and we had that evening together and it was real nice, and I took her home in a taxi and I thought I'd have another try, though she was far from encouraging.' Buzz dunked some more doughnut, with a pensive expression on his face. Lorna waited for him to resume.

'When we got to where she lived, and I was getting all set to make another bid . . . well, we found the whole place blown apart. Any other girl woulda had the screaming heebie-jeebies, but she, she took it like a trooper. And still she wouldn't soften up; wouldn't come back with me to my hotel. Said we had to go to Katie. Another no-touch Red Cross girl. So we went to Katie. And ended up in the air-raid shelter there, in rows, on camp beds. It wasn't till she guessed we were all asleep, and she thought we'd never know, that she at last let rip and started to cry. Well, that kinda creased me. I just moved over on that bed with her. I didn't want her that way; I just wanted to show her she'd really gotten hold of someone who cared, or perhaps I should say someone who cared had gotten hold of her. Next thing, the darned bed gave way. Jeez, did we go to the floor with a crash!'

'Megan never told me a thing of this!' exclaimed Lorna.

'Well, after that things got kinda hysterical. She got into my bed; I lay on the floor. We held hands most all the night; it took me a fortnight to get my arm back down into its normal position. But on that plane to Paris I was thinking to myself: This wasn't any old two-bit milk-run sorta thing. This girl wasn't any kinda broad; this girl was a lady. She had class. She had style. She had lotsa things I wanted. But, most of all, she kinda . . . well, I don't know how to put it.' Buzz waved his doughnut bemusedly. 'Well, it all kinda hit me. Maybe you don't understand what I mean, but . . .'

'I understand,' said Lorna.

'It hit me.' He dunked the piece of doughnut, then whooshed it into his mouth. 'OK, so I guess I'll lose my freedom; freedom to prowl. But, shucks, I've prowled around like a blooming tom cat for years. I'm worth a million in warm memories and sore pads. I'm not denying I had my good times on the tiles, but now I've met her . . .' He sighed ruminatively and shook his head. 'Like I told her, time's come to grow old gracefully.'

'And you'll take her back to Paris with you?'

'Yeah. Marry her here, and take her back to Paris. And then, I guess, along with the Allied Occupying Forces we'll be sent to Germany. Hell, I don't mind where I go, though, just so long I got her with me.'

Lorna sighed. You would never have thought of Buzz as the romantic type. How wrong could you be?

XXXVII

Megan and Buzz fixed their wedding day for 15 April. 'Who knows, the war may be over by then,' said Megan. Suddenly, and incredibly, it did seem as if there were a real possibility of this.

The Allies had rolled back the German counter-attack in the Ardennes and had fought forward to cross the Rhine – a symbolic moment which took place the last weekend in March. Many people in Fursey-Winwold now had maps on their walls; on these they marked the Allied advance with little pins. Jeffrey had given the General a map and in the evenings the two men marked it up together, moving the pins forward; the General discoursing on the tactical implications of the Allied progress and the possible reactions of the enemy, while Jeffrey, when a particularly exciting gain of ground had to be notched up, indulged in a loud cheer. Setbacks provoked equally resounding groans. Lorna guessed that for each of them this was by far their favourite part of the day.

Lorna had never before been able to believe in the end of the war; it had been something towards which you struggled, and the harder you struggled to reach it the further away it withdrew, like Alice through the Looking Glass trying to reach the bulrush. But now it was truly coming, that moment of grand finale when the world would emerge from the years of wartime night into a glowing dawn of peace and promise. Victory: the downfall of Hitler and all that he stood for. 'Great is the truth, and it shall prevail,' as the Reverend Barker reminded them all in the sermon he preached on the Sunday of the crossing of the Rhine.

'I think it's wonderful to be living at this time, when everything is suddenly so full of hope and promise!' exclaimed Lorna that evening, when the map-marking had been completed for the day and she was serving her father and Jeffrey egg sandwiches and cocoa. Her eyes sparkled as she spoke. Yes, she added to herself, and the hope and promise of starting a new life with Herbie.

'Yes, it does feel pretty good,' said Jeffrey. 'We'll have to celebrate Victory in a big way when it comes. Should start laying our plans now, I suppose.'

'But of course we shall still have the Japs to beat,' said General Washbourne.

'Celebrating polishing off Hitler will be enough as a starter,' said Jeffrey.

'It'll be lovely if it could be over in time for Megan's wedding,' said Lorna. 'It'd be hard to imagine a more marvellous wedding present than the outbreak of peace!'

The wedding would be a very quiet one at a London register office, with lunch at the Savoy Grill afterwards. Lorna, Angie and Amy May and Tommy Taylor were the guests; Bunty, now on crutches, was about to be discharged from convalescent home but not in time for the wedding – a great disappointment. After leaving convalescent home she would come to stay with Lorna for a week or two.

Three days before the wedding President Roosevelt died; the funeral was fixed for the wedding day itself. It was too late to change the date, so everything went ahead as planned. As Buzz said: 'There are guys dying all the time right now, at what should be the start of their lives; Roosevelt's lived out the full span. He's been a real lucky guy; so let's give him three cheers and get on with *our* lives while we can.'

The day started for Lorna with a letter from Herbie. She read it on the train on her way to London. He wrote that he was returning to the States preparatory to being posted to the Pacific. 'I'd hoped to have a chance to be with you once more in England, before I left, but the ETO is folding so fast now that we're being moved out sooner than anyone previously thought possible. But perhaps it's best we haven't seen one another this time; saying goodbye to each other is always hell! In any case, it won't be all that long now, honey, before we're together for good, in the States. The most beautiful of GI brides! So long, then, sweetheart. I'll carry you in my dreams till we meet next time, and then I'll be damned if Uncle Sam, or anyone else on God's earth, will separate us again.'

Despite the fact there were other people in the carriage with her, Lorna gave the letter a surreptitious kiss. Never to be separated from Herbie again! It was a dream that was almost too good to be true. But it would come true; of this she was now certain.

She found Megan and Buzz looking as happy as she hoped, no, *knew* she and Herbie would look on their wedding day. The ceremony made herself, Angie and Amy May cry; the bride and bridegroom were pronounced man and wife; everyone started hugging and kissing everyone else. Then came the luncheon party, with American tearing high spirits, and toasts and non-stop gusts of laughter.

Gradually, however, as the luncheon wore on, Lorna ceased to feel happy. Suddenly she became overwhelmed by the realization (warded off by her, typically, to this last possible moment) that Megan's marriage meant that another of the St Hildegard's quartet was about to vanish. First a quartet, now a trio; this time tomorrow only two would remain, Lorna herself and Bunty. True, Megan would not be lost so irrevocably as was Violetta but, that said, who knew when they would meet again?

Lorna continued to laugh, josh, and drink toasts; but behind her lively façade she was increasingly feeling anything but festive. She wished profoundly that she had Bunty with her; they would have buoyed one another up.

At last the time for parting arrived. Buzz and Megan were spending the night in London; next morning they would be off to Paris. Everyone hugging and kissing; promising to see each other soon. Perhaps it would work out that way; perhaps it wouldn't. 'Goodbye, Flops darling. Mind how you go. Take good care of her, Buzz.'

'Sure thing,' said Buzz. 'Take care of yourself. Come and see us in Paris soon as you're able.' He gave Lorna an enormous hug. 'Yes,' echoed Megan, 'promise you'll come to Paris, Lorna, the minute the war's over.' They kissed; both in tears. 'Say goodbye to darling Bunty for me.'

'Yes, I will. See you again very soon, Flops love.'

Then Megan and Buzz got into a taxi and drove off laughing and waving, and Angie, Amy May and Tommy Taylor went off to spend the evening with American friends Lorna didn't know, and she went to Kenilworth Lodge where she was to spend the night in Bunty's flatlet and discuss with the Parsonses plans for their exchange removal.

Lorna, after her lavish luncheon, or what passed for a lavish luncheon these days, wasn't hungry; she made herself some tea and sat drinking it by the open window. In the garden, side by side in silence, sat the Schwartzes. Presently they came indoors. Lorna turned on the wireless. Roosevelt's funeral had been broadcast earlier that day; now the BBC rebroadcast an account of it for those who had not been able to listen the first time. Lorna was soon feeling increasingly miserable and depressed. The funeral was followed by an Ed Murrow news broadcast: the Americans, in their advance, had just captured a concentration camp; Murrow's account of what they had found there was so unspeakably awful that Lorna would have turned the broadcast off had she not felt painfully convinced that it was necessary to hear the truth.

And of course this wasn't the only extermination camp; there were others still waiting to be discovered. The sickening details the world had just heard would, she warned herself, be succeeded by others of a similar or perhaps even worse kind. What possible aftermath could result from all this? It was with embarrassment at her own inanity that she recalled her euphoric exclamation of only a few days ago: 'I think it's wonderful to be living at this time, when everything is suddenly so full of hope and promise!'

Through her open window came the sound of someone playing a Chopin nocturne on the piano. For a moment she supposed that someone was actually playing the piano; then she realized that the music was coming from Theodor Kaufmann's flat. Lorna remembered Bunty's tales of how he used to regale her with gramophone recitals; he must be playing the gramophone to himself now. She wondered if he had heard the Murrow broadcast; perhaps he was listening to the music as an attempted solacement.

Lorna cogitated upon whether she should knock on his door and exchange a few words with him after the music had ended. His mother – imagine how he must be feeling! Lorna wanted terribly to tell him she understood; but perhaps he would rather be left alone.

How *did* one behave after learning that a neighbour's aged mother had been put to death in a gas chamber? The English inclination was to do nothing, say nothing. Pretend it hadn't happened. 'But,' Lorna told herself, 'you can't pretend these things haven't happened. By pretending they haven't happened, we almost certainly guarantee that they'll happen again. And how do I look Theodor Kaufmann in the eye, next time we meet, if I insist on pretending that nothing has happened?'

When the music ended she crossed the landing and gently knocked on his door.

'Who is that?' he asked from the other side of the door.

'Lorna Washbourne; I'm here for the night, and thought I'd just say how d'you do. Bunty asked me to call, to give you her regards.' This was true.

After a moment or two he replied, still without opening the door: 'I'll be with you in a few minutes.'

Lorna returned to Bunty's flat, sat down by the window again and lit a cigarette. Presently there was a knock on her door; when she opened it Theodor stood there. His face looked swollen and blotchy. He said: 'Would you care to come for a drink at the Holly Bush?'

Lorna thought to herself: So he is the one who will do the pretending.

'If you would like it, I would, too,' she said, trying to smile.

They went out of the house and began walking up the hill. The evening light was waning into dusk; the lilacs in the front gardens were coming into bloom; birds sang. Lorna said: 'I loved that nocturne you were playing on your gramophone. At least, I supposed it was you.'

'That was my mother's favourite piece of music. My Uncle Leon used to play it to her.'

'I love Chopin myself . . .'

'It is nice of you to come out with me for a drink like this.' He took her by the arm. 'I greatly appreciate it. Of course, we Jews are not so amazed by these disclosures as you are. We have had our informants. I have been haunted by the thought of this for months. But now it is all confirmed as certain, what does one do? I could lie down and turn my face to the wall, but because they are dead do we stop living too? That would not bring my mother, or any of the rest of them, back to life again.'

They walked a little distance in silence. Then he resumed: 'My mother and my aunt, two old ladies, what did they do that was so wrong? Nothing. Apart from the fact that they were born. How inconvenient; how wrong of them. So annoying for other people. We Jews, however, are used to being told that we should never have been born; people have been telling us that since the dawn of history. And trying to kill us all off, to prevent us from being annoyances. There is nothing so new about Hitler; except that, being German, he has been so much more efficient.'

'Well, now that my mother and my aunt and millions like them are gone, is the world so much a better place? Is there more spare air to breathe? Space to move around? Will people feel happier? I doubt it. It is just one more nail in humanity's coffin. There is really no hope, you know. No hope at all.'

'I'm beginning to realize that,' said Lorna.

XXXVIII

Bunty, after leaving convalescent home, arrived in Fursey-Winwold to enjoy a brief stay at The Warren. Lorna had tea ready for her in the garden, like she had had that afternoon, three years ago, when Bunty had come to recuperate following David's death. Three years ago, when the bulldozers had been knocking down Weldon Court to turn Fursey Down into an airfield.

Three years ago when Bunty had paid her visit it had been June. This time it was May; early May, with bluebells in the woods, the hawthorn blooming in the hedges, the cuckoo calling like mad, the garden laburnums shaking their golden plumes, lilac scenting the air.

Bunty arrived, swinging across the lawn on her crutches, laughing.

Still putting on her courageous act, thought Lorna, and what an act! With tears in her eyes she hurried to embrace Bunty.

People everywhere, whose lives had been blasted by the war, were now putting on acts; some more successfully than others. The main thing was not to let the world at large see the wounds. Suffering was a private thing. 'There's too much suffering in the world today. For God's sake let's try to forget it,' said Bunty. 'Give ourselves a chance to know what it is to feel cheerful again.' She added, with a half-sigh, half-smile: 'The show must go on.'

When tea was over, and the girls sat smoking cigarettes, Bunty allowed herself to speak a little about Waldo. She had written to him: 'A fearfully difficult letter to write. I asked him not to reply.'

'And has he?'

'No. Best that he doesn't. I said to forget me. I mean it. I love him; and so I want him to forget me and find someone else to be happy with, who isn't stuck with one leg.'

'You told him that?'

'I told him that.'

Lorna gave Bunty a quick sympathetic kiss on the cheek. 'Poor darlingest Bunts.'

Bunty changed the subject. 'I was forgetting – I haven't given you the news about Ivo! He managed to escape from that POW camp and he's been in the fighting in Italy. Ma's had a long letter from him. He says he dreams of being back in England after this long long absence, though he's nervous he will find everything and everybody altered beyond recognition.'

Lorna made no comment. The last thing she wanted was Ivo trying to make a comeback in her life. Not that there was any chance of him succeeding; she had Herbie. And Herbie monopolized her heart and mind. Lorna had supposed that Bunty would fully appreciate this.

'He asked me to thank you for all those letters you sent him,' continued Bunty. 'He says it was only letters from home that kept him from going bonkers at one point.'

'Nice to know they helped,' responded Lorna, blowing smoke rings. She had taken to doing this since Violetta died; in a silly way it helped bring her back a little.

'To tell you the truth, I'd almost forgotten I had a brother,' said Bunty. She added musingly: 'D'you suppose, when all this is over, we shall be able to get back to things as they used to be?'

'I wouldn't have thought so.'

At this point Titus came into the garden to interrupt their conversation . . .

The Warren,
7 May 1945

My darling Herbie,

Today at three o'clock, while I was in the garden with Bunty (who is staying here a few days), Titus Swann looked in to tell us he had just heard that the German radio had announced unconditional surrender. As it wasn't officially confirmed, we didn't get too excited. I took the dogs for a walk; then washed some stockings and rinsed out a jumper. While I was making custard for supper, Bunty, who had been in another room listening to a Louis Kentner recital on the wireless, called to me that the announcer had just interrupted the broadcast to say that the unconditional surrender was confirmed, that Mr Churchill will announce Victory at three o'clock tomorrow afternoon, that the King will broadcast at nine o'clock tomorrow night, that tomorrow will be VE-Day, and it and the following day will be a holiday.

The village proposes to hold a thanksgiving service in the church tomorrow at midday, and a children's party on the village green if fine, and in the village hall if wet, the day after tomorrow. Otherwise the general feeling is that the big celebration will be kept for when we've beaten the Japs; for, until then, none of the chaps will be demobilized, and what is there really to celebrate about until they're on their way home again?

This household is now going to bed early. We're all worn out by the news. Wish you were here to help me celebrate – guess how.

L

(continued 8 May)

Now it's getting on for ten o'clock in the evening of VE-Day. We've hung out all our flags in this household; as has everyone else in the village – you've never seen so much red, white and blue in your life. We've had our victory service in the church – which wasn't a victory service at all really. Mr Barker said: 'We will kneel and thank God, not for victory, which isn't yet ours, but for deliverance from great evil.'

Apart from a glass of wine each at lunchtime (a bottle Father had been keeping specially for this occasion) we haven't done anything truly celebrative in this household. Jeffrey is having a sort of knees-up at the pub; he wanted Bunty and me to go along, but she doesn't feel up to that sort of thing yet, and I didn't fancy going without her. So we've been sitting quietly, talking about St Hildegard's and the old times.

It is just striking ten. This is the close of the day we have waited for, longed for, prayed for, fought for, six years. I was eighteen when the war started, and young for my age. Now I am twenty-four, and feel like forty.

I've always imagined the moment when I would sit down and write you a Victory Day letter. I thought it would be so great. But now it's come I'm afraid it's a very flat thing: complete anticlimax. I think the explanation is we've had just too much war; we're beyond celebrating because we're all worn out by what we've been through. Added to which there's the discovery of those appalling gas chambers; everyone's shaken to the core. Impossible to get up and dance, with those horrors at the back of one's mind.

Bunty says believing the war is truly over is the same as when you lose your leg: you know it's not there, but it still feels like it is! It'll all seem different, my darling, when we're together again. Then we *shall* have something to celebrate!

Loving you ever,

Lorna

The VE holiday over, Lorna returned to Fursey Down to resume her duties there. To her astonishment, she found everyone deep in plans to close the camp. Tommy Taylor, when Lorna expressed her surprise at the imminence of the departure, said: 'It's the Pacific now for the Eighth, for all-out warfare against the Japs. We're no longer needed in Europe. My reckoning is we'll be out of Fursey Down in a month from now, maybe sooner.'

Lorna's letter to Herbie had crossed with one from him. This, too, echoed the theme that it was the Pacific now for the Eighth.

Lorna Love,

It's definitely the Pacific, and any time now I'll be on my way. But, as I've told you before, I have the feeling we shall make short work of what's left of this one.

I've just been to see Margy and the kids. Once back in the States I had to see her, just to tell her it's all over between us. She took it surprisingly quietly. I think quite a number of her friends have been hearing the same hard truth from husbands who have returned home from the ETO. I felt a total heel, but she had to be told. All she said was: 'We've still got the Japs to beat; which gives you time to think again.' She didn't throw an over-reaction or bawl me out or anything. If she had, I wouldn't have felt so bad about it. But I had known it would be a hard thing to do. As to thinking again, she just doesn't understand how I feel about *you*.

The kids I didn't tell; she can let them know, by easy stages. They've not done too well while I've been away: failed with their grades, given Margy trouble – things like that. I guess kids need a father when they're young; but, that said, there should be a way of getting them to understand that parents sometimes stop loving one another, there have to be changes. Given time and careful briefing, they should be able to handle this one. It isn't as if they'll never see me again once we're divorced: I'll be entitled to have them visit me, take them out on the town – all that kind of thing; feel responsible for them and interested in them.

I'm thankful I've got this hurdle of breaking the news to Margy behind me. It was a rugged mission.

All for now, Lorna my darling. I'll write again real soon. Take care of yourself. I can't manage without you.

Herbie

Lorna was in the habit of reading Herbie's letters again and again, loving every word, but this one she found heavy reading and when she had finished it she folded it and put it away in her desk drawer and left it there.

Bunty departed, to go to Roehampton and have her artificial leg fitted. After that, she said, she would dedicate herself to a career of becoming a top-drawer secretary with a vengeance. 'Show me a gal with a wooden leg who is quietly but unobtrusively at the helm ... In short,' said Bunty, with something of her old twinkle, 'I see myself as a sort of Binkle-trained Long John Silver, running London Transport.'

'Dear old Bunts!' was all that Lorna could say.

The Fursey Down crews left in mid-June. There was a farewell party; Buzz came over specially to attend it. 'Can't have you saying goodbye to Fursey Down without me being present,' he said. He and Lorna sat nostalgically at the little round table at the back of the aeroclub canteen, dunking doughnuts, while the merrymaking went on around them. Lorna said: 'I suppose Europe is now what England was before all the Yanks crossed the Channel.'

Buzz shook his head. 'Nope. Not yet anyways. For one thing, there's a language gap there wasn't over here. *And* the girls aren't as generous with sex as the British girls. Maybe the Fräuleins will catch up, once we're in Occupation.' He paused to dunk some more doughnut. 'It was with the English that the Yanks had their big sex bonanza. Before the fighting began; before they made those landing beaches. You know, when people still believed that war was fun, and kinda chivalrous.'

Lorna started to laugh. 'Chivalrous?'

'Sex and swordplay, old style,' said Buzz. 'OK, laugh; but that *was* the old style, and that was how the boys all saw it at the start. That's how the boys here at Fursey Down saw it.'

'Well, I guess so,' said Lorna. 'At all events, I can see what you mean, though I can't say it struck me that way at the time.'

'Those young guys, "Herbie's Worst", they came over here with real high expectations. It was war, and war was a venture into something all new and exciting. Non-stop fighting in the sky, and you-know-what on the ground. It was the time of their lives. They were lives that weren't gonna last long anyway, and they soon knew it, but those boys sure made up their minds to live while they had the chance. "Herbie's Worst" doing their best.'

'In the sky and on the ground.'

'Wherever they were, they didn't cramp their style,' said Buzz, shaking his head and helping himself to another doughnut.

'The later waves, the ones that came over after D-Day, they've been different,' said Lorna.

'Yeah; good airmen, first-rate airmen, but lacking the style.'

'They've lived to finish their tours,' said Lorna.

'True. There's nothing like cold death round the next corner to promote a hot style in living.'

'Very true,' said Lorna, thinking of Herbie's similar remarks on the same subject.

Buzz poured them each more coffee. Then he said: 'There's gonna be a mighty lotta respectable people, both sides of the Atlantic, guys one side, dames the other, in the years to come, who'll find they've forgot what went on during this war. Lose their memories when asked. You'll see. It'll all get forgotten.'

'Not forgotten,' said Lorna. 'Kept quiet.'

'Kept very quiet.'

Buzz pushed his chair back and rose to his feet. 'Well, babe, for the last time in this aeroclub, care to cut a rug?'

At the end of the evening everyone present wrote their names in candle smoke on the aeroclub ceiling; a ceremony always performed by those lucky enough to have completed their tours. After the last name was written, they all joined hands and sang 'Auld Lang Syne'. As she sang, Lorna felt haunted; haunted by faces and voices lost for ever. Above all, though his was not a face lost for ever, she felt haunted by Herbie.

Early next morning the whole village assembled on Winwold

Beacon to wave goodbye to the Forts as they flew out. Lorna, at the airfield, stood with Buzz, Angie and Amy May, waving and waving as, for the last time ever, the Forts roared up the runways, clawed and screamed into the sky and then, supreme in their own element, climbed higher and higher into the clear June morning, at last to dwindle from view. Lorna stared after them till her eyes hurt; stared until she was gazing at an empty sky, where only the thunder of the departed Eighth echoed. Then that, too, was lost and gone.

For the next few days Lorna, Angie and Amy May worked at emptying and clearing the aeroclub. Buzz had returned to Paris; after they had said goodbye to him it really did seem that the world of Fursey Down had come to an end. At last the clearing-up was completed; the hour came when the aeroclub was as barren as an empty pantry. There was no coffee left to drink; no doughnuts left to dunk. All the furniture was neatly stacked; the posters and notices removed from the walls; the curtains taken down from the windows. The girls had left their little table at the back of the canteen so that they might sit there and smoke a last cigarette together. Above their heads on the ceiling the names in candle smoke were already fading slightly. But, long before they could fade entirely, the aeroclub would be demolished by bulldozers.

Angie and Amy May were to spend a day or two in London before flying back to the States. Lorna saw them off on their train. They hugged and wept and vowed never to lose touch with one another and that Lorna would visit them in the States and they would come back on sentimental trips to Fursey Down.

When the train had gone from view round the bend and there was no possibility of waving any more to Angie and Amy May, or they to her, Lorna returned home to The Warren. She took out her writing pad and went to her favourite corner of the garden to write to Herbie and tell him of the final hours of Fursey-Winwold as a bomber station. Of how they had had a farewell party and written their names in candle smoke on the ceiling; of how the Forts had flown out; of how the aeroclub was now emptied and cleared. Of how . . .

Instead, she wrote:

Dearest darling Herbie,

But of course you know as well as I do that we cannot do it. We can't do it to Margy and, above all, we can't do it to your children. Children need a father; not just to visit from time to time, to be taken out by him on the town, so that he can play at feeling responsible for them and interested in them. They need a proper father. And, if I know you, what you are talking about wouldn't satisfy you; you, too, need to be a proper father. And I don't think you will find you can leave Margy all that easily, either. You just aren't that kind of a man. And I'm not that kind of a woman – to break up a family, and then to suppose that I can go on to be perfectly happy and guilt-free. No, I'm afraid, darling Herbie, that we just can't do it.

What we had was perfect; but it was a wartime perfect. Now it's peacetime, and what went in war is no good for now. In a funny sort of way, wartime had something that peacetime can never have: a sense of needing, and being able to give understanding, that transcended barriers of what was right and what was wrong in the peacetime meaning of those things. But now we're back to peacetime, and you're needed by your family far more than you're needed by me. That doesn't mean I don't still love you; but it means I shall feel what you call a total heel if I don't let you go.

This is a dreadfully difficult letter to write, Herbie, but I know I am right to write it.

Dearest most darling Herbie, I shall always love you and never forget those out-of-this-world times we had together. Promise to think of me, too.

Think of me
most lovingly
Lorna

It wasn't a letter she had intended to write. It wasn't a letter she had even realized needed to be written, until she sat down to write it. She had done what she always did: warded off recognition of the hard truth until it could be warded off no longer. Or perhaps it was a case of what Jeffrey had told her: 'You just don't notice things.' She didn't notice them until they hit her. But surely, she had to confess to herself, not noticing them was partly because she didn't wish to notice them.

She had made up her mind, at the start of her affair with Herbie, that she just wasn't going to think about his being a married man. They had been in the thick of a terribly dangerous war; and war put everything in a totally different context from peacetime. But now the war was over, and everything had become switched back into a peacetime context. She realized that she and Herbie had planned to marry in what had been, truly, another realm: the realm of war, which changed and distorted everything. Herbie's wife and children hadn't entered into it; they had belonged to another sphere. But none of this applied any more; if she still went ahead in saying yes to Herbie's divorce and her marriage to him, three other people would be shattered like having a rocket land on them. This was the hard truth.

She took the dogs and walked them to the letter-box; she needed to post that letter before her resolution ebbed from her. The letter fell into the letter-box with a soft little flop: the falling of a leaf; a delicate sigh of relinquishment. Then she turned away and walked the dogs up to Winwold Beacon. Here she lay down on the ground where she and Herbie had made love that first Sunday afternoon. She pressed herself into the grass, as though courting the earth to swallow her up, and wept as she had never wept in her life before. Then, quieter at last, she lay on her back staring at the empty sky and giving herself to recollection.

Mignonette's flat. That last night together. That shudder: the Angel of Death. The bed, the floor, their naked selves smothered in fallen plaster.

'But, Herbie, it was worth it, wasn't it?'

'It sure was. Worth tunnelling through plaster from here to eternity. And I mean every word of that.'

But all the same, in spite of all that, you couldn't, *she* couldn't, smash his marriage. She was sure, from his last letter, that he, in spite of everything, in his heart didn't want it smashed. 'The kids ... Given time and careful briefing, they should be able to handle this one.' Back with the crews of his beloved 'Worst' – and knowing that there wasn't the time, and that, however careful the briefing, there wasn't a hope in hell that they'd be able to handle it and come out at the other end all in one piece. And Margy, she wouldn't come out all in one piece, either.

But, if Margy and the kids were to come out all in one piece, *something* had to smash. Her innermost being reiterated: Smash!

It was growing dark; the dogs, uneasy, were crouching beside Lorna, whining. At last she stood up, heaved a deep breath, and began walking home. The house was silent when she entered. The Wedgwood tureen stood before her eyes on the kitchen dresser shelf: a perfect piece, not as much as a chip or a crack after a century of time! She sprang at it, grabbed it off the shelf and hurled it to the floor.

For an instant, following the crash, and seeing the explosion of white porcelain around her feet, she felt engulfed by a wave of miraculous release, abruptly displaced by acute guilt; guilt coupled with anguished regret at the destruction of something so beautiful, so precious. She burst into violent tears, dropping to the floor to crawl, sobbing and wailing, trying to pick up the bits of a cherished possession smashed beyond any hope of repair.

XXXIX

After the aeroclub had been emptied everything was taken to the middle of the airfield and burned in great fires that went on day and night. All the food from the canteen and the PX stores. All the furniture and fittings. Burned, too, the equipment of the admin-block; the Quonset-hut barrack quarters, cots and curtains, bedding and blankets. All the equipment from the kitchens. Everything, going up in great funeral pyres of black smoke.

When the locals found out what was happening, there was almost a riot. Armed guards stood on duty round the clock to prevent pillaging. Lorna, her cheeks scarlet with indignation and her voice icy, said to the officer in charge: 'Was it your idea to burn all this?'

'It was not, ma'am,' he said. 'Orders from on high.'

'But who would give such orders, to burn food and furnishings and blankets, at a time like this?'

'We mustn't take a loss or give anything away. So what does that mean? That's the instructions. Not for us to argue with. It's from on high.'

'It must be bloody high!' exclaimed Lorna scornfully. 'So bloody high, they haven't a clue what's going on in the world at their feet.'

He said nothing. In all fairness to him, Lorna recognized, he couldn't. He stood impassive, his cheeks almost as red as hers.

Lorna, quivering with indignation, turned away. What was the use? As usual, the people responsible were out of reach. 'Out of reach, and out of touch,' said Dicky Stacks. 'Damn civil servants put in uniform and placed in charge of supplies. Cash-register mentality. I know the type. Find 'em everywhere.'

After the fires came the bulldozers thumping away, demolishing the hangars, the aeroclub buildings, the admin block; the office where Herbie had once sat and spun on his chair. The chair, together with all the other office furniture, had been taken out and burned.

Lorna went to the piano and began playing Mozart's 'Turkish March'. Her father, hearing her, said: 'I'm glad you're playing that jolly little piece again. It's always been one of my favourites.'

Presently she took the dogs for their evening walk. The demolition workers had gone home and the bulldozing had stopped till next day, and the evening was peaceful and quiet. The quietness of Fursey-Winwold, now that the Forts and the Yanks had gone from Fursey Down, often startled the villagers. There was something uncanny about it.

Next morning the bulldozers resumed their thumping. Lorna bottled raspberries and tried not to think. The postman brought a letter from Bunty, saying she wondered if Lorna, no longer tied to American Red Cross, could possibly go up to London to move Bunty's things from the first-floor flatlet to the one on the ground floor which the Parsonses were relinquishing for her? Mrs Parsons would do all she could to help; but to have Lorna there would be of unbelievable assistance. Mrs Wells said that Lorna might have Miss Amhurst's flatlet during her stay, if she wished.

Lorna leaped at the suggestion; she was only too relieved to have the opportunity to escape from Fursey-Winwold at this juncture.

Moving everything from the Parsonses' flat up to Bunty's, and the things down to the Parsonses' flat from Bunty's, was not all that complicated when done methodically. It was all ready in time for

Bunty's return. Theodor planned a little celebrative supper party for Bunty, Lorna and himself the evening of her return: he began preparing a fricassee. 'And, surprise, surprise, I have a bottle of Emu wine up my sleeve! How, do not ask! Simply be content that it is waiting there for the occasion.'

His face, during the weeks since she had last seen him, had become more heavily lined; his hair was turning white at the temples. He laughed, smiled, jabbered incessantly, all as usual, but the changes in his appearance spoke silent volumes.

On the afternoon of Bunty's return he came home early from the office in order to be present to receive her and, as he put it, 'help her install'. Bunty came walking in as if she had never lost a leg; the only tell-tale sign was an elegant ebony cane with a silver knob. 'Daddy gave it to me,' she said, waving it airily. 'It's Edwardian. Wasn't it sweet of him?'

Theodor bowed, smirked, kissed her hand. 'My dear Miss Clippie! Two-legged you were always enchanting, but one-legged you are devastating!' This made Bunty laugh so much that she lost her balance and nearly fell over.

Mrs Wells fetched up tea; real tea, 'the bona-fida cup that cheers, for this special occasion'. The Schwartzes produced a cake from a Viennese bakery. It was smothered with cream; 'No doubt made with liquid paraffin – how else, with the fat ration as it now is?' murmured Mrs Wells.

'Never mind,' responded Theodor in a similar discreet murmur, 'it will help us to go.'

'I hope not,' retorted Mrs Wells. 'It would be most rude to leave the tea party at this stage simply because you don't fancy the cake!'

Bunty went off into more gales of laughter. 'Oh dear!' she exclaimed to Lorna. 'I had forgotten what they were like!'

The Parsonses looked in; Mrs Parsons brought Bunty an embroidered tray cloth as a housewarming gift.

After the tea party was over Bunty was left to rest for a little and put her feet up, while Lorna joined Theodor in his kitchenette to help in preparing the festive supper. In addition to the fricassee (which smelt tempting enough for Lorna to be careful not to enquire about the ingredients; it spoiled nice dishes nowadays to know what people had put in them), there were potato croquettes, little tartlets with strawberries, a bean salad with a special dressing of Theodor's own invention ('A guarded secret,' he said, tapping the side of his nose with his right forefinger), Bavarian cream made without cream ('Aha, don't ask how; I won't tell you!'), cheese straws, pickled-herring salad, and little pancakes stuffed with pureed carrot disguised as apricot.

'I didn't know you were a chef!' exclaimed Lorna admiringly.

Theodor contorted his face to indicate modesty. 'Nothing. Nothing. Simply the good fortune to possess culinary flair.'

They cooked, tasted, chattered, bumped into each other, exchanged recipes, and drank a glass each of mint syrup with which Theodor was experimenting as a substitute for *crème de menthe*. 'If the war goes on long enough, we shall all become so good at this kind of thing . . .' He stopped himself short, rolling his eyes.

Lorna said gently: 'I know. I keep catching myself saying things like that, too.'

Bunty, told by Theodor and Lorna to rest while they prepared a snack supper ('Nothing out of the way,' said Theodor, 'rationing being what it is now – worse than during the war itself!'), stretched herself out on her divan and amused herself wondering what kind of a surprise Theodor had in store for her; she knew him well enough by this time to know that his deprecating 'Nothing out of the way' meant that he was producing something special.

She lay gazing idly at the weeping ash in the front garden; the tree, in its fresh June foliage, was a fountain of green. She had loved the view from her old flat, overlooking the back garden, but the front garden was very pretty, too, and the ash tree was a real bonus. As for this new flat itself, it almost, in every detail, resembled her old one. True, it wasn't her own old lair, her wartime pad where she ... But she switched her mind away from the things that had happened in her flat upstairs, and reminded herself firmly that she was starting a new life – that of a dedicated London career girl in a brave new post-war world. And, whichever flat she was in, this was still dear old Kenilworth Lodge, back under whose roof she already felt herself settling with a real feeling of homecoming.

The portrait of David stood on the mantelpiece; he had no rival now, and she doubted if he would ever have one again. Well, there it was. Compared with some, she had been a very lucky girl. One thing war did teach you, and that was to count your blessings.

She was beginning to feel drowsy; she still found walking with an artificial limb pretty tiring, though she was gradually becoming used to it. She had been assured that the day would come when she wouldn't notice that the wretched phoney leg wasn't really part of her; people even said that by next Christmas she'd be dancing on it – always providing, of course, she had someone to dance with!

Her eyes closed without her knowing it; she drifted into a doze, out of which she was jolted by the sound of Theodor bumping against her door with what was obviously, from the sound of it, a heavily laden tray. She must be careful to feign surprise, amazement. 'Theodor! What have you ...? Good heavens!'

She manouevred herself off the divan and hastened as best she could across the room to open the door for him. The first thing that greeted her eyes was not a laden supper tray, but an enormous canvas bag of the kind Americans called 'grips'. Holding the bag was not Theodor, but ...

'Waldo!'

The shock made her lose her balance. Waldo let go the bag and caught her as she fell. He kicked the door to behind him and carried her over to the divan.

'Waldo, didn't you get my letter about my leg?'

'Are you honestly that dumb? I fell in love with you, not with your goddam legs.'

Upstairs Lorna and Theodor arranged the food on trays. 'Herring salad and cheese straws to start with. Fricassee, beans and croquettes to follow. Finally the tartlets, the Bavarian cream and the stuffed pancakes. *And* the wine: there should be enough for a glass and a half each.'

'My goodness, Theodor, it does look a marvellous spread! You really are a wizard.'

'I wanted to make this an occasion, to show her how much we ... how highly ... well, how we ... at all events, to convey to her ...'

'Oh, Theodor, it most certainly will!'

They went downstairs with a preliminary tray of salad, wine and cheese straws. Theodor carried the tray, Lorna went ahead of him to open the door for him. Bunty's door was not properly shut, just closed to; Lorna pushed it open wide, and almost fell over a huge grip lying where someone had dropped it. On the divan Bunty and a large dark-headed young man in Yank officer's uniform were immersed in a complicated-looking embrace. Lorna and Theodor backed sharply and fell into the hall, closing the door behind them.

'Waldo?' queried Lorna.

'Precisely.'

They went upstairs to Theodor's flat. '*Eh bien*, let us eat,' he said. 'A nice little supper for two.'

'Don't you think they may want some later?'

'Look, as it was, there was just enough for three. To pretend it is enough for four!' He gave an expressive shrug. 'So now a glass of wine and some herring salad to start?' He added glumly: 'I've no doubt Waldo will be taking her to the Savoy, when they have, so to speak, got their breath back.'

The wine soon cheered him up, and Lorna, too, and they had a lively little supper, toasting each other and telling funny stories. They ate everything; as Theodor said, it was a proper-sized supper for two. There were a few pancakes left over. They had just reached the coffee stage when there came a knock on the door. Theodor opened it; Waldo stood there.

'Theodor, hello!'

'Yes, I live here,' said Theodor. 'Come in and meet Miss Washbourne, Bunty's great friend.'

'Lorna,' said Waldo. 'Bunty never calls her Miss Washbourne.'

'Meet Lorna.'

Waldo and Lorna shook hands. He was sunburned, looked much tougher than Lorna had expected from the description of him given her by Bunty, and had most of his left ear and two fingers of his left hand missing. He walked with a limp. Theodor said: 'What have you been doing with yourself?'

'Making sure that nobody will ever pester me again with requests to play the violin.'

'Nor dance with the ballet, from the looks of it.'

'The limp's supposed to improve; but I don't expect to grow new fingers. However, it doesn't matter . . .'

'How did you manage it?'

'Helping to blow up a train. Bunty and I were wondering if you would both care to join us in a glass of champagne? I've brought a whole load of goluptious goodies back with me from Fortress Europe.'

The bag in the middle of the floor now lay gaping open; from it spilled bottles of champagne, boxes of chocolates, of *petits fours*, of *marrons glacés*, silk scarves, bottles of perfume. This trail of largesse led to a table where stood further bottles of champagne, glasses, a cake smothered with *glacé* fruit, tins of *pâté*, biscuits, a Camembert cheese; with Bunty, her cheeks flushed and eyes sparkling, presiding over this bounty as a delighted hostess.

'Bunty!' Lorna, unable to think of anything more to say, ran to her friend and began hugging and kissing her.

'Oh, Lorna, isn't this . . . ?'

'It is!' agreed Lorna, tears of joy running down her cheeks on Bunty's behalf.

Theodor, shaking his head in smiling bewilderment, took both Bunty's hands in his. 'My dearest Miss Clippie, I am struck in a heap; like a dying duck in a thunderstorm you could knock me down with a feather! Nevertheless, that any man would be so flabbergastingly up the spout as not to return to you, oh no! Such a notion to me struck as a total non-starter from the word go!'

'Just what I've been telling her,' said Waldo. 'And some.'

'Well,' said Bunty, taking Waldo's arm and giving it a loving squeeze, 'he's talked me round to seeing things his way now; we're getting married and I'm going back to New York with him with as little delay as possible, because he says, and he's quite right and I absolutely agree with him, that in a world as uncertain as this one if you meet someone you love and know you want to be with, then don't waste time not being with them.'

'Be thankful you have been spared to be together,' said Theodor.

'Exactly,' said Bunty, giving Waldo's arm another squeeze. 'So, though it's all going to be a mad rush, you two must get out your glad rags and brace yourselves to be guests at our wedding.'

'To which we will now drink,' said Waldo, taking up a champagne bottle. Theodor intercepted him and took the bottle from him. 'Permit me, opening champagne has always been one of my tip-top accomplishments. Let me demonstrate how it is done by the dab hand.'

*

Next morning Lorna returned to Fursey-Winwold. Before she left, Bunty said to her: 'I hope you're doing the right thing, giving up Herbie. You can take being noble and self-sacrificing too far, you know, Lorna love.'

'I'm quite sure I've done the right thing, Bunts. Absolutely sure. It wouldn't have worked.'

Bunty looked, Lorna thought, a trifle embarrassed as she said: 'I do hope that you haven't . . . haven't, you know . . .'

'Know what?'

'Been building your hopes on Ivo.'

'Ivo? Good heavens, no! To be honest, I can't really remember what Ivo looked like.'

'I was just hoping that you weren't, because Ivo's written to say he's marrying a Russian girl he knows in Cairo. A divorcée. My poor parents aren't exactly thrilled by the news; they'd have much preferred it if he'd returned to you. But there it is . . .'

'Thank God for the Russian girl!' exclaimed Lorna. 'Last thing I'd've wanted would be Ivo on my doorstep. Not that I'm doubting he's as attractive as he ever was, but you simply can't turn back the clock like that!'

Bunty sighed. 'I always, privately, hoped that you and he . . .'

'You're a dear old sentimental thing, Bunts. And now you'd better start fixing a date for that wedding of yours, and stop worrying about me.'

Sitting in the train, watching the well-known landscape flash by, Lorna wondered if there would be a letter from Herbie waiting for her when she reached home. Suddenly she began asking herself what she would do if Herbie refused to give her up, as Waldo had refused to comply with Bunty's request that he should forget her. This was a possibility which hadn't previously occurred to Lorna.

She hoped to God that Herbie wouldn't try to get her to change her mind: having gone through all that trauma of realization and writing her letter (not to mention her smashing of the tureen), she knew she had no heart left for a reopening of the wound. Besides, her mind was made up. It always took her a long time to perceive realities; much longer than it took most people, who seemed able to see things clearly without any difficulty at all (or at least thought they did). But, that said, once she had had that long-delayed flash of insight, and had taken up her thoroughly considered position, then nothing could persuade her to change her ground. She had found her sticking place, and stick to it she henceforth would.

But there was no letter from Herbie when she arrived home at The Warren. Perhaps he was too upset even to answer her. Perhaps he had simply said to himself: 'To hell with her.' And that was that.

The bulldozers had finished their work on Fursey Down. Titus Swann informed Lorna that everything had been flattened. 'You should go up to the Beacon and take a look. You won't believe your eyes. The demolition chaps are having a last clear-up; carting the rubble away. Then we can all forget the Forts were ever here.'

Lorna told herself she would never go up the Beacon again.

When that afternoon's post arrived, there was a letter from Herbie. Lorna, trembling at the sight of it, carried it up to her bedroom in order to read it in complete privacy. As she opened the letter neatly with a paper knife (Miss Binkle had insisted that this was the only way in which one should ever open a letter) Lorna asked herself once again: What if Herbie refused to give her up?

As always when she read one of his letters, she could hear his voice as if he were speaking right next to her.

Lorna love,

You're right, as usual; we can't do it. Certainly not to the kids. Or, come to that, even to Margy. There are some people can do these things, and not turn a hair. It's our bad luck we're not made like that, you and me. As you say, back

459

of our minds we'd always have it gnawing at us: what we had done to those three innocent people.

But, equally, I can't bear to think what this will do to us. It feels like having the bottom of the world fall out. Like dropping into black eternity without a chute. I don't know, I really don't know how we're going to manage.

You're right: wartime has something that peacetime can never have. Though we used to think the war was a barrier in our way, the truth is without a war our love could never have been. We used to dream about our future together when peace returned, but if we hadn't been so darn starry-eyed, in that crazy way war makes you starry-eyed, we'd have known we couldn't last out when peace took over.

I hope, when we're over the worst of losing each other (if we ever do get over it), we'll find we are able to look back on it as *the* great good thing the war gave us, and thank Providence for it. Certainly I see it as the greatest thing in *my* life, and I most genuinely mean that! So thank you, Lorna my love, a thousand thanks, and bless you for ever.

But, gee, the rest is going to be a rough mission. I figure you'll weather it best. You're young, you're strong, you're full of the promise of life. With luck you'll find someone else, far better for you than I would be. Me, I'm past finding anyone else, and *never* another like you.

I've told the family I'll be back once the Japs are licked. So goodbye, my one and only Lorna. Repeat, we've taken the right decision, tough as it is; though, repeat again, I'm under no illusions about what it means for me. That period on Fursey Down, all those great young guys, and you lighting up my life, was the all-time high. Whatever happens to me from now on, however good it looks to outsiders, will be all downhill.

Herbie

As Lorna read, her eyes flooded with tears. They fell on to the letter and made the ink run. But, after these first tears, Lorna found she couldn't shed any more. Instead she began to ache; first in the head, suddenly and violently as though she had been struck with an axe, and then in every part of her body.

She read the letter again; the violent pain in her head seemed to affect her eyesight, the words jumped and jumbled together. She felt sick. She put the letter back in its envelope, groped her way to her desk and thrust the letter deep into the back of a pigeon-hole, well hidden by other papers. It was there for her to look at, if she ever wanted to look at it again; but, as she felt at this moment, she would never again wish to see it. It was carved into her heart, incised with a blade sharp as a razor, and her heart was bleeding from it. There was a great sore aching place in her chest. She knew now that a broken heart wasn't simply a romantic metaphor; it was a physical reality.

Yet this rupture with Herbie had been her decision. She kept telling herself this as she bathed her aching forehead in cold water and found herself aspirins. Her decision; and she had known it would be a killing one. Yet there it was; she had taken it. And now it was tough.

Presently she slipped downstairs, let herself out of the house without being noticed, and took the dogs for a tramp, well away from Fursey Down.

Of course she should have known it would end like this. Could only end like this. 'If we hadn't been so starry-eyed, in that crazy way war makes you starry-eyed, we'd have known ...'

She walked until she was tired and then sat down at the edge of a thick belt of trees, a windbreak. There was a steady breeze blowing, and every now and again it gathered itself into a gust and roared a little as it charged through the wood, challenging the trees; carrying Lorna back to another time, another place. Those broad rock ledges overhanging the sea, between Boscastle and Tintagel.

The waves crashing below like cannon fire, and booming in the caves, and the white foam exploding over the green water surging round the cliff bases, and flowering on the black rocks where the cormorants stood . . .

Presently she rose to her feet and marched the dogs back home in time for supper.

After supper she was sitting on the lawn, smoking a cigarette and blowing smoke rings and thinking of Violetta and Bunty and Flops and St Hildegard's, and what the war had done to them all, when Titus appeared. He walked across the grass towards her. 'Something for you, Miss Washbourne. Found on Fursey Down by one of the demolition workers. I thought you should be the one to have it, seeing as who it belonged to in the first place.'

He handed Lorna a small, battered, dirty something; it took her several long seconds to recognize it as the wallet she had long ago given Ruth, to go with the red handbag; indeed, Lorna would not have recognized it if it hadn't had the name, Ruth Cuthman, barely discernible, written inside it in marking ink. The wallet was no longer red, but a dull rusty colour. It was empty, and looked as if it had been so for a very long time.

'Where was this found, Titus?'

'Near where they knocked down all those Quonsets, miss. No saying how it got there, or who dropped it, or what.'

She sat silent for a while, turning the wallet over and over in her hand. Like a good countryman who understood the speaking voice of silence, Titus stood beside her, watching her without comment. At last she said: 'I suppose this clears Vic Wendell, wouldn't you say, Titus? If he killed Ruth, I can't imagine he'd be so daft as to carry her wallet, with her name on it, back to the camp and then go on to mislay it there.'

'Unless, miss, he hid it there, and when they pulled the huts apart it came to light.'

'We don't know which hut it was found in. We don't know which hut Vic was quartered in. We don't know if it was Vic who had the wallet in the first place. We don't know anything, except that this is Ruth's wallet and she was murdered.'

'Miss Lorna, if I was you, I'd just go on believing in Vic. It doesn't make any odds now; and, if you want to believe in him, believe in him. It's as likely that somebody else killed her and took her wallet as that Vic killed her; more likely, on the face of it. She'd been his sweetheart for quite a bit; if he'd wanted money from her, he could have got it any time. She most likely always had a good bit of folding money in that wallet, for she had plenty of what you might call customers . . .'

Lorna broke in with a reproachful 'Titus!'

He said: 'You're right, miss. Never speak ill of the dead. Sorry I said it.' He added: 'It's all well in the past now anyway.'

'I believe in Vic, and I'll go on believing in him, and I believe in Ruth, and I'll go on believing in her. As you say, it's all in the past anyway. And the past is the past is the past.'

'Can't well be anything else, can it?' responded Titus.

After he had gone Lorna sat for a good while longer, smoking, and holding the wallet in her lap, and thinking of Vic and Ruth in their cabin in the woods. If they, too, hadn't been starry-eyed, in the crazy way war made you starry-eyed, they'd have known their greenwood love couldn't last, either.

XL

An invitation arrived for Bunty's wedding, fixed for 15 August, just six weeks distant in time. The General said drily: 'I suppose they'll be off to the States afterwards?'

'I think that's their intention; at least, for a while.'

Thank goodness, Lorna thought to herself, that she had never told her father that she had intended going to the States. It would have shaken the poor old boy to the marrow; possibly might have given him another stroke. She had postponed breaking the news to him, and for once her fatal fondness for leaving everything to the last moment had proved the right course to follow. Her father had been spared all that trauma. He would never know now how nearly he had lost her!

But, even though spared this emotional disturbance, he showed a general despondency that caused Lorna concern. She spoke to Dr Murray about it. He paid regular routine visits to her father and now assured her that the General, though certainly depressed, was otherwise fundamentally in much the same state of health as usual. 'It's this flat now-the-war-is-over feeling that's affecting everyone. A combination of anticlimax and exhaustion. Not surprising. For six years every man jack of us in this country has been fighting for survival; not victory, but stark survival. We've been put through the mangle and we're showing it. It'll take donkey's years for us to recover from this one.'

Lorna agreed. You saw it everywhere; not only in her father. Jeffrey was another case in point; normally so cheery, full of lively talk and loud laughter, he had withdrawn into a morose shell, so utterly unlike his usual self that Lorna found it hard to believe he was the same young man. Not that they had much to do with each other nowadays; he seemed to be avoiding her, though she couldn't think why. All a part of *his* post-war depression, she supposed.

And hers? The days passed; she remained at present without a job, but was told that she might be redirected into industry. She busied herself about the house, gardened, took the dogs for long walks, and tried not to think about Herbie or, indeed, about anything else very much. She seemed never to be without a nagging headache, and that sore aching place in her chest where her once sound heart had been.

Bunty had invited Daphne and Dicky Stacks to her wedding; she had also invited Jeffrey. Lorna asked him if he thought he would be able to make it. He replied in his new short manner: 'Difficult to say with any certainty. I've accepted on the understanding I may not turn up when the time comes. Never know, in my job, when you're going to be called out to deal with some emergency.'

And off he went.

On 5 July a general election was held. Everyone in Fursey-Winwold seemed to suppose that the Conservatives would win, because they were led by Churchill. Lorna was not so certain. The night before the election, after Jeffrey had been chatting with her father (he and the General still seemed to find comfort in one another's company, even if not in that of anyone else), she said: 'Jeffrey, who do you think will win the election tomorrow?'

'Hard to say. Probably the socialists, I think.'

'D'you think that? I think so, too.'

'Do you?' He sounded surprised.

'Well, I know that an overwhelming number of civilians in this country are more indebted than they can say to Churchill, for leading them safely through this war. I mean, his leadership won the war for us, and history will see it so. But, that said, you can't vote for Churchill; you have to vote for a party, and the party Churchill will be leading is not one which inspires the majority of people with an awful lot of confidence, I think. Not today. There somehow has to be a change. I felt it when I was in London amongst all that suffering, all those terrible bombs. These things can't be. There has to be a change. A new way of looking at things.'

'I agree with you entirely,' said Jeffrey. 'However, we'll see what happens.'

'I think Father would have a fit if the socialists got in.'

'Yes, poor old boy, I think he would. However, to be hard, there are other considerations besides your father and whether he'll have fits or not.'

And with this Jeffrey brusquely cut the conversation short and let himself out of the front door into the night.

On 26 July they learned the election results, delayed because of the complications of getting in all the votes from the armed forces. There had been a landslide victory for the socialists. The General was shattered, but it turned out that almost everyone else in the village had voted for Attlee and the Left. Even Miss Barker said: 'The time is right for complete renewal of our social fabric. After all, that's what we've been fighting for: social justice.'

Jeffrey looked in to try to cheer up the General, who was horribly downcast. Lorna didn't join the conversation; her father had no time for discussing politics with one of her sex.

On 10 August the news was released that an atomic bomb had been dropped on Hiroshima and a second on Nagasaki. The destruction had been terrible, and it was expected that the Japanese would surrender at any moment. There were fearful descriptions of the blinding brilliance of the flash of explosion, the giant mushroom of cloud that curdled up into the sky, accompanied by an awesome rumble louder than the loudest of thunder.

Everyone became desperately dejected. Miss Barker said: 'All very well, this talk of the Japs being forced to surrender, but we shan't feel so perky when our turn comes to be atom-bombed, as come it undoubtedly will.'

'It will shorten things,' said Miss Cusk. 'The next war won't last six years.'

'I suppose that might be counted as a blessing,' said Miss Barker.

Lorna met Jeffrey. 'How d'you feel about these bombs?' she asked him.

'We're all done for now, aren't we?'

They looked at one another and then, without further conversation, each went into their own house.

The following day, Friday, shortly after noon, while Lorna was in the post office buying stamps, Dicky Stacks thrust his head in at the door and shouted that news had just come through that the Japs had surrendered. 'Come on, let's get across to the Queen's Head and celebrate this one!' he cried, seizing Lorna.

Everyone else in the village had the same idea: the Queen's Head was already crammed with frenzied celebrants, and more were swarming in all the time. The pub was in a tumult, with a forest of arms waving tankards and voices yelling and screeching, 'Here's to peace!' Others bawled 'Long live Victory!' Daphne Stacks was already in there, squeezed in a corner of the public bar with a knot of regulars; distinguished as such by their tankards, which were pewter instead of mere glass. Dicky was a regular; Daphne had become one since Violetta's death as part of her avowed intention to 'make a go of marriage'. Where Dicky was found, Daphne nowadays was sure to be found, too.

Lorna struggled through the general scrimmage to reach Daphne, while Dicky fought his way to the bar for drinks. Daphne's group, amazed to see Lorna in this setting, greeted her with raucous shouts. 'Come to let your hair down for once?' bellowed Dr Murray genially. Daphne, putting her face close to Lorna's, screamed: 'The day we've all been waiting for!' Whether she meant Victory, or Lorna's appearance at the Queen's Head, wasn't certain.

Jeffrey, squashed against the fireplace behind Dr Murray, stared morosely at Lorna over the rim of his, needless to say pewter, tankard.

Lorna, not for the first time, wondered what right he had to be so eternally glum these days. He hadn't the excuse of a broken heart, or a head that ached from perpetual loss. No; he was just giving way to self-indulgence in that after-the-war drop in morale that seemed to have afflicted so many people. He was a young man, fit as a fiddle, who had emerged unscathed from those six years which had scarred so many. He really should pull himself together. She shot him a cold look of distaste.

Next instant Dicky was thrusting an enormous pewter tankard at her. ''fraid it's cider. They've run out of beer.'

'What, already?' asked Jeffrey despairingly.

''fraid so.'

'What's she been given a pewter mug for?' asked Daphne, noticing Lorna's tankard. 'Since when has she been a regular in this house?'

Everyone began to laugh and shout 'Shame!' 'Make her hand it back!' 'She hasn't earned that!' and other witticisms. Dicky said: 'Turned over a new leaf, haven't you, Lorna? Be a fixture in here in no time.'

Everyone cheered. Lorna found herself, tankard raised, acknowledging toasts. 'Here's to the new fixture!' 'Here's to peacetime and barrels of beer!' 'Roll out the barrel for Lorna!' Lorna, trying to suppress the thought of how Herbie might be celebrating this moment ('I've told the family I'll be back once the Japs are licked'), waved her tankard and responded gamely: 'Here's to us all and the future!' The future; the bloody old future.

More cheers. Then they all began shouting attempted general conversation at one another. Lorna, who had no intention whatever of spending the rest of the day trapped in this bedlam, decided to creep away as soon as she saw the opportunity.

Her head swam, her ears rang with the din. The bar became more like the Black Hole of Calcutta with every moment that passed. The crowd spilled out into the beer garden at the back and beyond that on to the village green. Another crowd had taken over half the vil-

468

lage street. A comforting rumour made the rounds that the landlord had prudently put by a special stock of cider in preparation for this hour of victory. 'Let's hope it's true!' bawled Dicky. 'Pity it's not beer, though!' came the stertorous sigh from Jeffrey. 'There's been a war; haven't you noticed it?' screamed Daphne in merry retort.

More braying attempted conversation, punctuated by wild hoots of laughter. People all trying to talk about different things at once; chaos wasn't the word for it.

Dicky, one side of Lorna, was shouting to nobody in particular: 'Can't see any hope of shortages ending for some time, myself. You try finding a decent pair of scissors!'

Daphne, on Lorna's other side, was screeching at Jeffrey: 'Half the girls in the village seem to be crossing the Atlantic as GI brides!'

Dr Murray pressed Lorna's elbow to attract her attention. He was offering a vacant bar stool he had kindly discovered on her behalf. She said: 'Thank you. Though I warn you I'm leaving any time now.'

Jeffrey, peering at her even more lugubriously from over the top of his tankard, enquired, from necessity at the top of his lungs: 'Where are you sailing from?'

'*Sailing* from?' Lorna shrieked in astonished reply.

'Sorry. I suppose you're going by air, seeing that you've been more or less employed by them,' bellowed Jeffrey.

Lorna raised her voice to its fullest capacity: 'What *are* you on about?'

'Where are you off to by air, Lorna?' screeched Daphne, all agog.

'I'm not off by air to anywhere,' yelled Lorna.

Dicky gave a whoop. 'Another GI bride? Didn't know you'd joined their ranks, Lorna!'

Dr Murray's boom joined in. 'Lorna, this is news indeed!'

'I'm not off to anywhere!' Lorna's scream was frenzied. 'I can't imagine why Jeffrey . . .' She flung him a furious glance.

He rejoined in a bassoon-like *fortissimo*: 'I understood . . .'

'Well, you understood wrong! I tell you I'm staying here!' She leaped from her stool, brandishing her tankard in his face. For some reason he was able to make her angrier than any other man she had ever met.

He grabbed her arm and without ceremony bundled her out of the bar into the beer garden. It was as crowded as the bar, but not quite so noisy; the tumult of voices ascending into the open air, rather than rebounding back from a ceiling. Jeffrey, still gripping Lorna's arm like a vice, thrust his perspiring face into hers. 'D'you really mean that?'

'I can't imagine why you think that . . .'

Daphne, Dicky, Dr Murray and the rest of the group came tumbling out to join them. 'Whew! It's better out here!' gasped Dicky, adding: 'Who's murdered who?'

'Still both on their feet,' said Dr Murray. 'I'm putting my money on Lorna.'

Daphne shrilled, in wearisome repetition of her question: 'Come clean, Lorna. *Are* you off to the States?'

'For crying out loud! For the last time, I am not, repeat *not*, going to the States.' Lorna's exasperation had almost brought her to the brink of tears. She attempted to take a hold on herself. 'If you must know,' she continued, adopting her iciest manner, 'at one time I *was* contemplating going there after the war, but now I've changed my mind. That said, why a private concern of mine is in any way the business of you lot, I can't imagine. And now I must go home and give my father his lunch.'

She turned her back on them and began trying to force her way, not with any great success, through the press of people and towards the beer garden exit. Jeffrey overtook her and diverted her into a small side passage. 'Try this way. It's better.' Obviously he knew the premises like the back of his hand. He opened an unobtrusive door, and she found herself stepping into the street. He emerged after her.

She rounded on him with blazing eyes. 'You dolt. Now the whole village will be talking about how I was going to the States, and no doubt trying to guess who I was going with into the bargain.'

'As you're not going, who cares what they talk about?'

'I can't imagine how you got hold of the idea in the first place,' she snapped, her eyes full of angry tears again.

'Haven't you learned by now that in this village everyone knows everything about everybody? It's even reached the ears of your father that you're thinking of . . . have been thinking of . . .'

The hubbub of the village celebrations rose on the air, enclosing them in a vibrating circle of sound.

'He's been frightfully down in the mouth at the thought of losing you, poor old boy. Come to that,' added Jeffrey, 'so have I.'

Lorna, unable to find quite the right reply to this, retorted briskly: 'Well, you aren't going to lose me, so you had both better snap out of being down in the mouth. It's depressing for other people.'

Jeffrey said: 'I'll see you home.'

'I can see myself home perfectly well, thanks all the same. It's broad daylight.' He stood looking at her in a way that reminded her of a large, pleading and vaguely hopeful dog. She felt her own expression softening. She never could resist dogs. 'You go on celebrating, Jeffrey. We don't win a war every day of the week. I'll see you later.'

He ventured, with an increase of hope: 'I think there's going to be dancing on the village green this evening. Like to come?'

'Love to.'

She walked home feeling rather dizzy. All that cider. It wasn't till she let herself in at the back door of The Warren that she discovered she was still holding the tankard. She placed it on the kitchen dresser where the Wedgwood tureen had stood. It filled the gap pleasingly.

As she sat down to lunch with her father she realized her headache had gone. Even the sore place in her chest felt better. It could only be the cider; she should drink it more often.

She said cautiously: 'Have you ever thought, Father, that with the war over we might cast around for a less gloomy house to live? Here in the same neighbourhood, but with a sunnier aspect?'

He looked at her in the same hopeful way Jeffrey had looked at her. Then 'Why not?' he said.

Jeffrey phoned after tea. 'Heard the news? That talk of surrender was premature; the bloody war is still with us. Peace breaking out and all that was a false alarm.'

'I thought it was too good to be true!'

'Me, too. Bloody typical. The dancing's been cancelled of course. But, in any case, the evening would have been out, far as I'm concerned; I've had an emergency call to a prize Jersey that's blown up to twice her size and is threatening spontaneous volcanic eruption.'

'Then see you at Bunty's wedding maybe, if I don't see you before.'

'Yes. See you at Bunty's wedding. All cows permitting.'

He sounded quite his old cheery self again, even though the breaking out of peace had been a false alarm.

Next day Lorna tried on the frock she intended wearing for Bunty's wedding; a register office ceremony, but still calling for dressing up. The frock was a blue foulard, one that she was fond of, though she hadn't worn it for a long time. She had bought it in Paris just before the war; it had always been a flattering dress that had brought out the colour of her hair. But when she put it on this time it didn't do anything for her hair at all, nor did it fit so well; she had grown a lot thinner. But it was its failure to do justice to her pretty sandy-gold hair that disappointed her most. She stared at herself a long time in the mirror. Then 'It's not the frock that's letting you down, my dear,' she said aloud to herself. 'It's your hair. You're going grey.'

Grey at twenty-four? Surely not.

She peered more closely at her hair; overall it had lost colour and had become dreary, dowdy, dingy. 'Almost as if it still had plaster dust in it,' murmured Lorna. But also, no avoiding the truth, there were grey hairs.

On Monday she went up to London to spend a couple of nights at Kenilworth Lodge prior to Bunty's wedding; she intended to shop for a hat to wear for the occasion. To Bunty, who was looking blooming, Lorna said: 'D'you know I'm going grey? At my age!'

'Lots of girls of our generation are. It's the war.'

Next morning, without saying anything to Bunty about her intention, Lorna went into town and had her hair tinted as near as possible to what it had been at the start of the war; perhaps just a shade brighter, to give that extra fillip to her morale.

While she was under the hair drier an assistant gave her an *Illustrated London News* to look at. Lorna found herself staring at photos and fearful accounts of the atomic destruction at Hiroshima. 'I should have gone raving Titian,' she said to the assistant.

She bought a blue hat to go with the dress; it was dashingly trimmed with an emerald green bow. Then she went back to Kenilworth Lodge.

'Crikey!' said Bunty, when she saw Lorna's hair.

'I thought I'd put up a bit of resistance against decrepitude.'

'I'd say that was coming out fighting with a vengeance, Lorna.'

'Too red?'

'No. It's terrific.'

'Looks like it used to?'

'Well,' said Bunty, smiling lovingly at Lorna, 'let's put it this way: it's a brave step into the future.'

The Japanese surrendered at midnight that night. Lorna, awake next morning at half-past five, Flying Fort time, a habit she could not break, was drinking her early-morning tea when she heard the announcement on the six o'clock BBC news bulletin. She went straight downstairs to wake Bunty and tell her. 'Bunts love, your wedding day will sure be one to remember. The BBC has just told us today is to be known as VJ-Day.'

'And what in hell is VJ-Day?' asked Bunty, not yet fully awake.

'Victory over Japan. They surrendered at midnight last night.'

Without another word they flung their arms round each other and burst into tears.

The wedding was at eleven-thirty. The reception was held at Kenilworth Lodge, at Mrs Wells's insistence. 'I speak on behalf of the rest of my guests; like myself, they feel the dear child has come to belong,' she had told the Bastables. They had taken it in good part. So now the guests assembled in Mrs Wells's big living room and spilled over through the French windows into the garden. The room was lavishly decorated with bouquets of flowers; the garden, too, seemed to have put on a special display for the occasion. For a wartime wedding, a large number of guests had been invited; all contriving to look amazingly smart. As a surprise Megan and Buzz had managed to fly over to be present; Megan was looking very pretty in a pale yellow linen suit. Jeffrey arrived in a blinding white shirt and a light grey suit that had marks all over it. 'I shouldn't have tried to build the bonfire before I caught the train,' he said. 'I looked fine till then.'

'What bonfire?' enquired Lorna.

'For the Victory celebration tomorrow night. I'm the organizer. Have to have it tomorrow night; tonight's too short notice. You'll be there?'

'I hope so. I'll try to be.'

He was looking at her rather more intently than usual. Lorna thought: Oh lor, he's noticed the hair and doesn't think much of it! I bet Father won't, either.

'I like your hat,' said Jeffrey approvingly.

'Do you? That's nice to hear.' She decided to stick her neck out. 'And what d'you think of the hair?'

'Very nice.' He sounded casual about the hair.

'I've just had it done.'

'Looks very nice,' he repeated in the same tone of voice.

'Don't you notice anything unusual about it?'

'Can't say I do. It looks jolly nice, like it always does.'

'Nothing unusual about it at all?'

Jeffrey stared even harder, doing his best to notice something obviously because she expected him to notice something. 'Well,' he said at last, 'it looks sort of . . . cleaned up. I suppose you've spent a fortune having it specially shampooed? Anyway, whatever you've done to it, it looks very nice. All told you're absolutely ravishing. Real winner.'

'Well, thank you, Jeffrey. You've rather made my day.'

Perhaps if he thought it looked natural all the other chaps would too. She didn't much care whether women noticed she had had it touched up. Women were more broad-minded about such things than men.

Thanks to contributions from the rations of everyone at Kenilworth Lodge, a gift of eggs and two cold fowls from Lorna, a dazzling array of salads and savoury tartlets from Theodor, a side of smoked salmon (palpably black market) that had been mysteriously and anonymously donated (all Mrs Wells would say was that it had 'turned up just when it was needed'), and a hamper brought over from France by Megan and Buzz as a wedding present and containing a cake, a basket of apricots, pâté, cheeses, and half a dozen bottles of champagne, the wedding breakfast was quite the most lavish seen for years.

A so-named 'Buck's Fizz' (the chief ingredient of which was Mrs Wells's notorious perry champagne) had an astonishingly effervescent effect upon the gathering in no time at all. The reception became delightfully lively. People lost their inhibitions and began uttering indiscretions which promoted amusement and consternation simultaneously. Shrieks and guffaws of laughter filled the air. Mrs Parsons murmured to Mrs Moxton that it wasn't like any wedding reception she had been to before. 'Well, it *is* VJ-Day into the bargain,' retorted Mrs Moxton, 'so it's a double celebration, and when all's said and done everyone's got a lot to make up for, haven't they?'

Edie Moxton was among the guests, with Gus Harris and Mrs Harris. Gus confided to Lorna that driving a bus could never be the same without Bunty as his clippie.

'Gus thinks more of her than he does of me,' said Mrs Harris merrily.

Gus went bright red in the face. Lorna exclaimed tactfully: 'I'm sure that's not true.'

'Don't you kid yourself!' said Mrs Harris, merrier than ever.

Edie was equally full of beans; she announced that she'd been told to say nothing about it but she was soon taking over from her mother at Kenilworth Lodge. 'Mum's getting on; she says the time has come for her to stay home and keep an eye on my Frankie, and I'll go out to work. I shall enjoy coming here to Kenilworth Lodge.' She gave Lorna a broad wink. 'I'll take the whole place over meself one fine day, you'll see. Even Mrs Wells can't last for ever.'

Thankfully, Mrs Wells was beyond earshot of this one.

Everyone seemed to be telling everyone else their plans for the future; many people were proposing to go to the States. The Schwartzes were joining their son in Chicago. Waldo and Bunty were of course going to New York, before they came back to Paris. Megan and Buzz were going to visit his mother in Brooklyn, and would then be stationed in Germany. Somebody asked Theodor what his plans were. He replied, with one of his dizziest smiles: 'I shall be remaining in residence here. I am happy to say I see myself as entirely the Union Jack.'

Lady Bastable, who had never met him before, asked him in an almost awe-stricken tone of voice: 'Did it take you long to learn your English, Mr Kaufmann?'

Theodor raised his eyebrows and shrugged modestly. 'Basically the answer is no, Lady Bastable. Syntax-wise I found the language plain sailing, and I have always had a brilliant ear for idiom in any tongue. But I will confess that, with English, it required much practice before I could grasp my genders.'

Waldo, overhearing this, had an unfortunate choking spasm, and Bunty had to take him in the garden and pat him on the back.

Lady Bastable then turned her attention to Lorna, saying loudly and archly: 'A little bird told me you, too, were thinking of crossing the Atlantic, Lorna.'

Lorna replied, as coolly as possible: 'I did think of it at one point, Lady Bastable, but I dropped the idea. I'm afraid, like Theodor Kaufman, I'm entirely the Union Jack.'

'I'm running her up the flagstaff on the village green tomorrow night,' intervened Jeffrey. 'Spotlit. She'll look rather good, don't you think?' He was obviously awfully pleased with life.

Lady Bastable retorted, laughing: 'Oh, I see now I've been thoroughly misinformed!' and gave Lorna a roguishly knowing look which made her flush in her turn. What a silly woman Lady Bastable was! Not a bit like Bunty.

There followed the toasts, the speeches, the cutting of the cake. At last the young couple were driven away to catch a train to Cornwall; they were spending a short honeymoon at the old manor house where Lorna had stayed with Herbie. Lorna had suggested it to Bunty: 'It's a perfect place for a honeymoon.' Adding: 'I should know; I spent a blissful one there myself!'

When Bunty and Waldo had gone, the guests began departing, too. Megan and Buzz were the first of them to hurry off; they were returning to Paris that same night. Their exit triggered a general one. People drifted away in pairs and groups; the garden and the big living room gradually became silent and empty. Theodor approached Lorna. 'I know you will now be feeling rather lonely, as I am, having lost our dear Miss Clippie. Shall we join forces and go up to the West End to celebrate Victory together?'

Lorna, who had suddenly become agonizingly aware that she was now left, the last of the Hildegard's quartet, greeted his suggestion eagerly. 'What a splendid idea! Do let's.' She turned to Jeffrey, who, as he so often did at a party, was lingering longer than he should have done. 'Any chance of your joining us?'

'It's a tempting idea, but I'll have to shunt back to Fursey-Winwold. Get on with those Victory celebrations, preparation thereof. They've got to be something to remember.'

He paused, then repeated: 'You will be there, won't you, Lorna?'

'To be run up your flagpole? Oh, yes,' she responded blithely. He flicked her a look, and she suddenly became assailed by Freudian doubts about what she had said. The Buck's Fizz and the champagne were certainly proving a dangerous combination.

At last all the guests were truly gone; Mrs Wells made a pot of tea for herself, the Moxtons (who were staying on to help with the stacks of washing-up) and Lorna. They sat exhausted, but confident that the occasion, as Mrs Wells said, could not have been bettered. 'I say to myself, but even a West End hotel *couldn't* have put on a nicer wedding reception than that.'

Presently Theodor, looking very spruce in his navy-blue blazer with brass buttons and with a red, white and blue handkerchief tucked in his breast pocket ('My unobtrusive patriotic touch'), collected Lorna and they went into town. They strolled for a while by the lake in St James's Park; then dined, because Lorna wished it, at the Café Royal. Then they went out to join the crowd that had now collected in Piccadilly Circus; crackers went off round their ankles, squibs were thrown from windows, rockets (of the firework sort) burst overhead, their explosions making too many people jump unpleasantly. Then into Trafalgar Square – more squibs and crowds. Down Whitehall to Westminster Bridge; by now it was almost dark, and the trams, fully lit, scarlet and gold, heavily laden with cheering passengers, were coming over the bridge like elephants in a raja's procession of triumph. The lights along the Embankment reflected glitteringly on the Thames. Theodor and Lorna smoked a cigarette apiece, leaning on the parapet, marvelling at the scene. London had not been lit like this for six years.

They went into Parliament Square, where music was playing, and danced for the best part of an hour; not normal dancing, but mostly hand in hand with other people, in rings, skipping round and round, like children at a party. At one point, however, Theodor broke off and insisted on Lorna dancing a polka with him. After which they returned to St James's Park, now looking unbelievably pretty with the lake floodlit. Fireworks shot in showers into the sky, revealing the bushes to be full of copulating couples, all cross at being suddenly and ruthlessly illuminated. 'One shouldn't laugh,' said Theodor, 'but the whole thing is so very British.'

Then to Buckingham Palace, where they waited half an hour for the King and Queen to come out on to the balcony, which at midnight they did. The King was in naval uniform, the Queen in white. They waved to the crowds, the crowds cheered and waved back. This was repeated several times and was still going on when Lorna and Theodor both decided enough was enough and it was time to go back to Hampstead.

'It was a grand evening,' Lorna afterwards wrote to Bunty. 'Theodor says he will never forget it, and neither shall I. The flood-lighting was out of this world; the buildings of London, in spite of their battle scars, or perhaps because of them, looked utterly majestic. But, best of all, corny as it may sound, was the illuminated Craven A cigarette advert in Shaftesbury Avenue, and the globe on top of the Coliseum, chasing itself round and round non-stop in a whirligig of electric lights. For six years we hadn't seen these things, and we, like the rest of the people, were totally enchanted. We had all forgotten what pre-war London night-life used to look like. And how we all took it for granted in those days! I don't think I shall ever take anything for granted again.'

XLI

Fursey-Winwold village green, next evening, in the dusk, was a total contrast to the dazzling Victory-sizzling metropolis of the previous night. The weather had turned chilly and overcast. The scene was dimly illuminated by the few street-lamps considered necessary to a small community like Fursey-Winwold. The unlit bonfire round which the villagers had gathered rose in a black mound like a waiting funeral pyre.

Lorna, a little late on the scene, wondered where Jeffrey was. She didn't want him to think that she hadn't troubled to turn out. She saw Miss Glaister and asked her: 'Have you seen Jeffrey?'

'Yes, he's in the bus shelter. He's using that as his HQ, he says.'

'I do hope he hurries up and lights that bonfire,' said Miss Barker. 'It's not exactly warm, standing out here.'

Jeffrey's voice came over a Tannoy apparently situated in the bus shelter. 'OK, folks. The fun's about to begin.'

A ragged cheer went up. Lorna walked across to the bus shelter, a dismal little wood and concrete edifice, and peered in. There were two large cardboard boxes, Jeffrey and the Tannoy. Lorna managed to squeeze herself in. 'Hello, Jeffrey.'

'Lorna, how splendid! Come to be hoisted at the top of my flag-pole?'

Lorna ignored that one. 'What's in those boxes, Jeffrey?'

'Fireworks. Don't you touch them.'

'People want you to start the bonfire.'

'My intention.'

'What's that sort of black thing in the middle of the bonfire?'

'That? That's the Jap emperor.'

'The Jap emperor? But that's perfectly horrible. You can't possibly burn the Jap emperor, Jeffrey.'

'Why not? Everyone's longing to see the Jap emperor go up in flames.'

'I think it's the most repulsive idea I've ever heard.'

'Well, if you don't like it, you can go home, can't you? You don't have to stay and watch.'

'Oh, shut up arguing, you two, and get on with it!' shouted Dicky Stacks. 'We want these Victory celebrations before the next war breaks out!'

Jeffrey tried to switch on the Tannoy. It was already switched on. 'They heard all that,' he said to Lorna.

'Heard all what?'

'You and me and the Jap emperor.'

'Come on, Jeffrey, it's starting to rain!' shouted Dicky.

Jeffrey advanced to the bonfire and set fire to it at several points; it ignited slowly. A lurid red glow gradually spread over the company. They all stood staring solemnly at the bonfire in silence. The spots of rain turned into a fine drizzle. Jeffrey said to Dicky: 'Lend me a hand with the fireworks, would you?' Several people started trying to light fireworks; few of them lit, and when they did they burned lop-sidedly and died slowly with a nasty smell.

People began to laugh and ask Jeffrey where he got them from.

'I should forget them,' said Dicky. 'You've obviously been landed with a dud lot.'

'The bonfire's nice; burning up quite well now,' said Miss Cusk encouragingly.

The landlord of the Queen's Head brought out what he said was hot spiced punch. People drank it with experimental sips. 'Not bad,' said Dicky. 'Basically cider; but beggars can't be choosers.'

Jeffrey said to Lorna: 'You'd better wear my jacket. You're getting soaked.'

'I didn't expect it to turn out like this.'

There was a sudden frightful explosion. A red-hot man-sized missile shot out of the bonfire, flew straight at Lorna, missed her by inches and fell blazing to the ground some distance away. Lorna screamed and flung herself into Jeffrey's arms. Everyone was screaming, shouting or cheering.

'What was it?'

'The Jap emperor. He blew up.'

Lorna, not knowing whether to laugh or cry, clung to Jeffrey.

Then everyone started to dance round the bonfire, singing 'Roll out the Barrel'.

'I'll take you home,' said Jeffrey to Lorna.

'Yes, please. I think I've celebrated enough.'

He took her by the arm, and they walked through the village. The strains of singing faded behind them.

'I'm afraid it was all a bit of a frost,' said Jeffrey. 'That swine really did me over those fireworks.'

'Who was he?'

'No one you know. And he's no friend of mine after that. The only damn thing that had any life in it was the rocket.'

'I didn't see a rocket.'

'It was in the Jap emperor. It was supposed to make him go up. Instead he shot out sideways. And nearly killed you.'

'A miss is as good as a mile,' said Lorna.

'Oh dear,' said Jeffrey, 'what a way to end a war. Dud fireworks, and me nearly doing you in.' They stopped and stood still in the rain. He put his arms round her and began kissing her. Then, in a cautious voice as if making a tentative diagnosis upon a sick cow (thought Lorna), he said: 'D'you think we love one another?'

After a moment's consideration she replied with equal caution: 'Yes, I think we do.'

'I've been thinking so for quite a while, myself. But I suppose you haven't noticed it?'

'I'm always slow at noticing things, Jeffrey. As you know.'

'D'you think you notice it now?'

'I figure it may be kind of dawning upon me.'

'What d'you suppose we should do about it?'

'What do *you* suppose we should do about it, Jeffrey?'

'I think we should get married,' said Jeffrey. 'The world's obviously going to blow itself up sooner or later – probably sooner rather than later – and I think we'd be sensible to spend what time is left to us together, making one another happy. I'd've mentioned it before, only I was rather under the impression, as your father was, too, that you'd be going to the States maybe. But now you say you're not.' He stopped again. 'Well?' he said.

'I'll need to think about it. Ask me again tomorrow, when I've had time to go up to the Beacon and think.'

'Of course. Think about it all you want. But why go up to the Beacon? Are you Moses or something?'

'Just let me do it my way, Jeffrey. Give me time to think, where and how I want to. After all, it's very important, for both of us, to get it right.'

'Of course,' he replied. 'Consult the oracle by all means.'

'You better get back to those celebrations, as you're in charge.'

'I suppose I had. See you tomorrow, then.'

'Yes. See you tomorrow.'

He walked away, back to the village green. Lorna went indoors. She entered the kitchen, poured herself a glass of milk, sipping it leaning against the kitchen dresser. She wondered why she always left it so late, noticing things. She had so often wondered it before; now here she was wondering it again.

She should have asked herself, early on, why Jeffrey had so cheerfully turned out on the coldest of winter nights, after a long and hard day's work, to walk her home from the village canteen. And had she honestly believed that he dropped into The Warren, three evenings a week, month in month out, because he so enjoyed listening to the General bumbling on about how the war should be fought? And why, when she took her dogs for a walk, did she so often bump into Jeffrey walking his?

True, they were always arguing, and he seemed, more than any other man, to have the power to drive her mad, but why had she never paused to ask herself the reason for this? And, moreover, if his obtuseness really so jarred her, why did she always instinctively turn to him if anything went seriously wrong?

Why had she felt such an acute anxiety for him in that snow storm? Not to mention his obvious concern at the possibility she might be blown up while in London? With what foolish plausibility had she dismissed their desperate farewell kiss that night as no more than an overwrought reaction to a stressful situation!

If Megan had been able to detect their true feelings for one another, had even said, 'He's absolutely right for you', why had Lorna, after all these palpable straws in the wind, failed to see it?

To be sure, it had all developed slowly, over a considerable period of time; it hadn't been one of those headlong fallings in love.

And it had been cloaked by her out-of-this world starry-eyed affair with Herbie. He had been so right; without the war their loving could never have been. Whereas the war really had nothing to do with her and Jeffrey's growing attachment to each other. It would, she guessed, have happened anyway, war or no war.

Of course, with the wisdom of hindsight she could see it all clearly enough. But, she told herself, surely she should have cottoned on to it without having to wait until now?

She drained the last of her milk and put down the glass. Aloud she said: 'Lorna Washbourne, you certainly have been dumb!'

The sun was shining warmly next afternoon when she took the dogs and walked up to the Beacon. She slipped through the well-known gate and sat down close to the place where she and Herbie had made love and where she had gone to weep after writing him the letter breaking everything off.

She stared at the broad expanse of Fursey Down spread before her. She hadn't seen it since the bulldozers and demolition men had done their work, and she was amazed: all that remained as a token that the Forts had been there were the concrete runways. Nothing else of the bomber station and airfield remained. The ploughs had been over the ground; before long the grass would be growing again, cattle would be grazing.

She drew a deep sigh and stared up at the big open sky, cloudless and blue, empty of everything except sunshine and lark song. There was no other sound except a small murmuring wind.

She sat motionless on the grass, arms round her knees, dreaming and staring at Fursey Down where past, present and future met. She almost thought she could see those little farmsteads of a thousand years ago, the columns of black smoke where the Vikings had struck, pillaging and burning. Impossible as it now seemed, those farms had truly been there and the Vikings, too, in their turn; just as yesterday there had been hangars and hardstands and Forts, the Quonsets, the admin block and the aeroclub. One day, in the distant future, people would look at Fursey Down and say: 'Unbelievable, isn't it, that once upon a time the Americans were stationed here with their bombers?'

And now it seemed to Lorna that the wind brought voices, American voices; cries of excitement, of anger and alarm, anguish and the despair of young men. And laughter, and the ringing of bicycle bells and eager shouts, and music in the loud swinging Glenn Miller style; and, above all, the thunder of the Forts: the sounds ever to be associated with Herbie's celebrated Worst. And that one voice, closer to her than all the rest, murmuring: 'Fursey Down ... All those great young guys, and you lighting up my life ...'

The present never lasted. It was like snow on water: before you knew where you were it had become yesterday. That was why it was so important to make the most of it while you had it, like she and Herbie had made the most of their present. This was a vital lesson she had learned; and must take care never to forget.

For her there was full promise of more life to be lived, of more happiness to come. But for this moment she wanted to dream, reliving the past, the bad parts as well as the happy; all of it. Then she would leave it to become, truly, the past. So she sat motionless and intent, listening to the voices of memory speaking. Listening to the echoes of her yesterdays, she lived those past three years of her life over again. Until memory, having unwound, and then rewinding, returning like a kite brought in on its reel, fetched her closer and closer to the here and now, and the yesterday to whose echoes she was listening was no longer of three or two years, a year ago, but of recent weeks. 'If', Bunty was saying, 'you meet someone you love and you know you want to be with, then don't waste time not being with them.' 'I think' (Jeffrey's voice speaking the words he had spoken last night) 'we'd be sensible to spend what time is left to us together, making one another happy.'

How long she had been sitting there, listening and dreaming, Lorna had no idea. Her dogs had been stretched out asleep in the sun, but now the sun was setting and the dogs had begun to fidget. As for the voices, they had all faded, lost on the wind. But, miraculously, she could still hear the sound of the thunder of the Forts; so marvellously real that she turned her eyes to where they used to come, flying home at the end of the day.

But there were no Forts; their thunder had gone from the sky for ever. Instead a bank of heavy cloud flashed with summer lightning and rumbled ominously.

Time to go.

She began walking fast down from the Beacon, the dogs at her heels. Halfway down she spotted Jeffrey advancing up towards her. When he saw her he waved and shouted: 'You gone bonkers? You've been up there for hours. I was coming to see if you'd turned into stone.'

She began running towards him. When she reached him he caught hold of her and held her. 'Well,' he asked, 'what did the oracle say?'

'Like you said last night. Not to waste time, but get married and make one another happy.'

'Great,' said Jeffrey. 'Usually they speak in riddles, but that's good explicit English. Let's get cracking.'

BLITZ!

Molly Lefebure

A rich and sweeping novel of a courageous Britain
under fire, set against the early years of WWII.

War would change them forever ...

When World War II broke out, no one could predict the
impact it would have on their lives. As the conflict begins
to take its toll, the lives of four families become entwined.
The Duchamps, the Spurgeons, the Sowersbys and the
Tooleys are all faced with personal struggles while the
world around them is torn apart. Families become
fragmented, love is found and the young are forced
to grow up too quickly – but all are determined to
remain defiant and united against the upheaval.

An emotive and heartwarming novel, Blitz! *creates
a vivid portrait of a courageous Britain under fire –
strong, brave and in the end triumphantly alive.*